Welcome to the adventure

Where loyalty matters, magic runs deep, and nobody stands alone.

4

LISA CASSIDY

THE UNLEASHED STORM

THE INKWEAVER ARCHIVE

BOOK 4

TATE HOUSE

 A catalogue record for this
book is available from the
National Library of Australia

National Library of Australia Cataloguing-in-Publication entry

Creator: Cassidy, Lisa, 2025 - author.

Title: *The Unleashed Storm*

ISBN (paperback): 978-1-922533-18-0

Subjects: Epic fantasy fiction

Series: *The Inkweaver Archive*

First published in 2025 by Tate House

Cover artwork and design by J Caleb Designs

Map artwork by Chaim Holtjer

The Dock City Chronicle

·

Want to delve deeper into the Archive?
Buried in the depths of the Inkweaver Archive is a prequel novella: *The Stolen Throne: a hidden Record from the Archive.*
Set decades before *The Nameless Throne*, this story follows a dangerous escape involving the fearsome Nightstalker — and it's yours free when you sign up for my monthly newsletter, **The Dock City Chronicle**.

·

Each edition *of The Chronicle* is filled with:
Insider updates on my books
Fantasy world news and hot takes
Hilarious book memes
My book recommendations
Exclusive sneak peeks

·

Sign up for *the Chronicle* at my website: lisacassidyauthor.com
~

Contents

The Inkweaver Archive
ICELANDS
Cair is'Heim
Al'Eir's Village
Triannon
ANDA HAR
NAVARIA
The Hara
Storm Spire
Light Bringer's Tor
MARSHLANDS
Vespir
Draxclaw Deep
Ethereus Citadel
RAVENSTRINE
Heartbrook
Melgin
DUNIDAEN
FALCONCREST
Daxulan
HAWKES DALE
Sparrow Wing
Aren
Seelan
RIVERLANDS
Crow Talon
Gateport
EAGLESDAR
Anduil
To Restenar
THE STORM CHANNEL
Dreadwalkr Gate
Taskar
Cazaix Forge
A.G. DALE'A
KHADINI
Pirate Isles
N.

Chapter 1

D rip, drip, drip.

Drip, drip...

Silence.

Arya's eyes snapped open at the sudden cessation of a sound that had been her only companion for what felt like a very long time. The threadbare blanket over her knees slid off as she shifted, readying to stand. Maybe...

Drip.

Drip, drip, drip.

A sigh escaped her. She settled back against the wall, eyes sliding closed, senses attuned to any shift in the atmosphere that might indicate she was finally going to be released from the cell she'd been in since her arrival at Blackstone prison.

Four paces wide. Four paces long. Stone floor and walls. Damp, cold, air. A narrow bench with a single blanket and a bucket in the corner for waste. No exit apart from the thick wooden door. So dark she couldn't see her fingers in front of her face. The only light she ever saw was flickering lamplight when the slot in the bottom of her cell door was opened and a tray of food was shoved through, a hook then dragging out her bucket before replacing it with an empty one. The meals came irregularly, and she'd soon given up using those to keep track of the time.

She shifted, trying to get comfortable on the hard surface. It was hard to remember what feeling comfortable, warm, full, felt like. The cold ate into her bones, opening pathways for despair. Foolishly, Arya hadn't planned on being placed in solitary confinement. She'd assumed they would lock her up with the other prisoners. And as the long hours, and then days, passed, dread had slowly settled into her bones.

They could leave her in here for months. Years. Forever.

And none but the Nightstalker and his newly discovered heir knew where she was.

It had been a tactical error. But she'd known from the beginning that this plan was risky, relied on too many things that could go wrong, that were out of her control. It was why she hadn't wanted to use it unless she had literally no other choice. And now she was stuck. Possibly forever.

Arya tried to stay optimistic, to not let the despair win. She forced herself to be active, filling the impossibly long hours with stretching and strength exercises, keeping her body strong and limber. And as she pushed herself to exhaustion and beyond, she told herself it was because she *was* going to get out of this cell. And as soon as she did, she needed to be strong, so that she could do what she'd come to do and then escape.

The food was never more than slop that did nothing to satisfy her appetite, and she could *feel* the flesh melting from her bones, leaving only corded muscle and bone. When she wasn't exercising, she sat on the bench, huddled, shivering under the blanket, staring into nothing.

Waiting to get out.

A door slammed in the distance. Arya snapped out of her thoughts, body poised to move, but for a long moment, nothing happened. And then a high, breathless, scream. It was human. Terrified. And in pain. The scream came again. Another slamming door.

The silence settled back over her cell. Its damp and icy air fought a triumphant battle against the thin blanket wrapped around her shoulders. Her heart thudded as she huddled, shivering, wondering if they were coming for her next.

The more time that passed, nothing but formless darkness surrounding her, the harder the waiting got, but a spark of stubbornness, of fire, inside her refused to go out. She reminded herself *why* she was here. That she'd come with a purpose. The first step of her plan—to ally with the Dunidae warlords so that they would march at her back against the Nightstalker—had failed when the Nightstalker had allied with Khadini to invade Dunidaen itself. The Dunidae were now fighting for their lives and would be lucky if they had much of an army left, *if* they didn't lose entirely.

Or maybe they'd already lost. She'd been in this darkness so long. When she'd been captured, the Nightstalker's army had been marching on Gateport, allied with the fearsome Khadini Rangers. Her brother had been leading the Dunidae army. Was he all right?

Arya wished she were there with every breath she took. She was a soldier down to her bones, a war leader, a general. The battlefield was where she belonged. Instead, she'd chosen to abandon them for another path, a gamble, a chance at finding the knowledge she needed to face the Nightstalker and win. So that her son would be safe, and not hunted relentlessly like she'd been all her life. So that she could *be* with Kirin. So that the rest of her family would be safe too.

And so that she could sit the throne of Andahar as its queen.

But fear and worry continued to creep in at her darkest moments. What of her Sky Lords, her *cairdre*? The Nightstalker had made a deal with Darmanin to keep Arya alive, but she had no way of knowing if that deal extended to Essa, Leanir, or Chiarn. And what of Peemla and Anjurin, presumably trapped in the north at Heathrock while war raged in southern Dunidaen? Laskin and her old Icecliff shield? Her rebel Andahari army? Elendryl, her wyvern, a literal piece of her soul.

If anything had happened to them...

She'd already lost Taze, a grief that was a live animal in her chest, a constant companion. Every time the memory of him exploded like shards of glass in her chest, she sucked in a deep breath and pulled herself back from the precipice.

And she kept waiting. Kept fighting back hopelessness.

For Kirin. For Rorin. For her *cairdre*.

For Andahar.

Chapter 2

Arya's breath hissed in and out. Controlled and consistent. Two hundred press ups, two hundred and one, two hundred and two. Her arms and core burned. Sweat slicked her skin and dripped to the stone floor. But she kept going, a fast rhythm, her heart pounding. At three hundred, she dropped to the floor, rolled onto her back, and started crunches. One, two, three—

Bootsteps in the distance.

Arya rolled to her feet, making sure her bucket and her empty tray were near the slot at the bottom of the door before backing away. The cold air was already raising goosebumps on her sweat-slicked skin, so she pulled her filthy tunic back on, buttoning it up. The footsteps came to a halt outside, and lantern light flickered as the slot slid open. Her meal tray slid in—attached to some kind of utensil, which was then used to slide out her bucket and push in a new one. No opportunity for her to grab someone's hand or arm and force them to let her out.

"What's your name?" She tried, every now and then, to start a conversation.

Not once had anyone answered.

The bootsteps continued, stopping and starting—so far, she'd counted at least three other prisoners in isolation—before returning the way they'd come. It had started as four, but after the recent screams, the guard had only visited three cells to deliver food trays. Hungry as always, she scooped up every bite of the slop, uncaring of its bland taste. Almost as soon as she'd swallowed the final bite, an odd lassitude swept over her.

Before she registered that she'd been drugged, she was slumping to the damp floor, unconscious.

Rain pounded through her dreams, threaded with images of monsters in the dark and the Nightstalker's face smirking at her, silver eyes alight with delight in her terror. Then the memory of Taze, resolutely facing down a swarm of firedrakes to protect his warlord, too far away for Arya to get to in time.

Over and over, she tried to save her friend and failed.

Arya came awake with a sob, grief tearing through her so fiercely she curled into a fetal position, eyes scrunched closed. Every time she woke from those nightmares with the crushing realisation that she couldn't save Taze. She *hadn't* saved him. He was gone. Tears streaked her face, and she let them come.

There was no shame in grieving a man who'd been one of her closest and truest friends. Her family.

The losses were piling up, leaving scars on Arya's soul that tore open in her dreams. Thiara Ravenstrike and her husband. Being forced to abandon her son. Taze. Even Helden SparrowWing. Sometimes she wondered how many she could collect before she just wouldn't be able to function anymore. Or worse, how quickly the fear of experiencing another loss like that might leave her unable to make decisions at all. It had before.

Her breathing was just settling when a high-pitched squeal cut through the air. Arya reacted instinctively, rolling to her feet to face whatever threat came at her, teeth bared, fists ready. And then she winced, pain stabbing through her head as light flooded her eyes. Swearing, she slammed her eyes shut again. She'd been in the dark so long that any light was torturous.

Her head snapped up. She wasn't in the cell anymore.

Arya cracked one eye open, wincing as light stabbed through, and waited until the pain faded to bearable levels, then opened the other one. Soon she had both eyes half-open, but her vision blurred, and more tears streamed down her checks. Feeling incredibly vulnerable in a new location without being able to see properly, Arya concentrated on what she could hear.

Shuffling feet and murmured conversation.

Wherever she was, there were other people nearby. Her heart lifted with hope. Maybe she'd finally been released from isolation. But other people meant possible threats. Fear quickly killed the hope, and she swallowed down the spurt of panic that wanted to rise. Uselessly, she rubbed her sleeve over her eyes. She could *just* make out that she was in a different cell, this one with what looked like vertical bars instead of a wall at the front of it. And the squealing was from those bars sliding back enough to leave a doorway-sized opening.

A figure appeared in the opening. Arya instinctively reached for her sword and her magic but found neither. Panic surged more strongly, and she forced it back with an effort. Even so, her breathing came fast and sweat slicked her palms. She'd been in isolation so long that being back in the world felt overwhelming.

"You expecting a fight?"

The voice was male, young, with a lilting accent she hadn't heard before, and it sounded amused. She squinted at him through streaming eyes. The owner of the voice didn't *look* dangerous. He was maybe seventeen or eighteen years old, of average height, with tangled sandy hair, scruff on his cheeks, and a gangly build that was still trying to escape the awkwardness of youth. Freckles dotted his nose and cheeks, and his eyes were an unusual golden colour. He leaned against her open doorway, hands in the pockets of the tattered cloth hanging from his waist that seemed to pass for pants.

Arya eased out of her fighting stance, lowered her fists, but said nothing. He might not *look* threatening, but that didn't mean anything. This was hostile territory, a prison that Niallin had once told her held Andahar's most dangerous criminals. Every sense she had strained to pick up any potential danger.

His amusement deepened, mouth quirking in a condescending way that had her hackles rising. "You're new. I'd ask what you've been blubbering about in your sleep, keeping us all awake, but random screaming is normal for prisoners brought up from the hole."

"The hole?" Her voice was raspy from disuse. She coughed, tried to clear it.

He nodded. "It's used as extra punishment for the naughty prisoners. How long were you down there?" "I have no idea."

"That long, huh? You seem saner than I would have expected." He whistled, giving her a once over, like her sanity was an amusing trick a dog had just performed in front of him.

Irritated, she bared her teeth. "And what are you then, the welcoming party?"

"I'm merely bored, newbie." He glanced into the hallway behind him, pushed lazily off the doorframe. Arya's peripheral gaze had been tracking other prisoners shuffling past. Some glanced into the cell with interest, others kept vacant stares straight ahead. All studiously avoided looking at the man she was talking to. "You should come out before the guards come to roust you."

She swallowed, the fear creeping back. Going out didn't seem like the smartest plan, not until she got a better understanding of the lay of the land. "Where is everyone going?" "First breakfast, then the yard, then dinner, then back here." He looked her up and down again, this time as if assessing for intelligence that might be lacking. "It's not optional."

He wandered off before she could punch him in the face.

At least he'd given her useful information. Arya planned on following every prison rule to the letter. She would do nothing that might risk the guards putting her back in the hole. For her plan to work, she needed to be amongst the general prison population. *And survive it*, said a little voice in the back of her head. A shiver ran through her.

Before moving, she made sure the sleeve of her tunic was pulled all the way down, concealing her lightning scar. That was a piece of currency she planned to use *very* carefully. Depending on who saw it, the recognisable Stormrider mark could get her killed quicker than anything else in here.

Arya stepped cautiously into the corridor outside her cell, glancing in both directions. It was a long hall, filled with barred cells on both sides just like hers, although the cells were spaced apart so that no prisoner could see into the cell opposite. Was that to reinforce isolation, or for some other reason? The walls were constructed from dark stone, and despite the way her eyes had reacted to the light on first opening, it was dim inside. Small, barred windows set high at the back of each cell along her row were the only source of light. Arya made a note to investigate her window as an escape option as soon as she got back.

The young man had already joined the tail of the line of prisoners filing through a door at the end of the corridor to her left—there was no exit from the opposite end, only a stone wall—but he glanced over his shoulder when she joined the line. "You a recent arrival to Blackstone, or were you in one of the other cell wings before you did whatever it was that got you put in the hole?"

"I'm new," she said, still in that croaky voice. It felt good to talk again. And despite the danger, it felt good to *see* people again, even if they were condescending little shits. Arya had never done well alone.

As they passed through the door, she spotted a large winch sitting just outside that must be the guards' way of opening all the cell doors in the corridor. It reminded her of the gate-opening winch at Icecliff Fort, which brought a rush of bittersweet memories. What she wouldn't give to be back there again. Taze still alive, Arya only responsible for the safety of her shield of twenty Raiders. She'd certainly welcome their comforting presence watching her back in this place.

Two guards stood beside the winch, looking bored. They weren't Nightblades—or if they were, they wore a different uniform. Grey with silver accents and a sigil of crossed bars in black thread on their chests. Beyond the door, the line of shuffling prisoners turned right and walked a short distance before starting up a twisting stairwell narrow enough to force them to go single file. It was stifling in there, packed with unwashed bodies, and dark as night. Arya's terror of enclosed spaces rose, clamping her chest and quickening her breathing, the stench making her stomach turn. She gritted her teeth and managed to hold it at bay long enough to climb two levels and emerge into a much wider hallway.

More prisoners spilled into this hallway from other stairwells. It wasn't as packed as the stairwell, but her body stayed twitchy with discomfort at how closely they were pressed together. Her palms were curled tightly into fists, and she started violently when one man jostled into her. The look he gave her suggested he assumed she was mad.

She had to calm down. *Not* drawing attention was the best way to stay safe until she understood her surroundings better.

To distract herself, she studied her fellow prisoners. Their attire ranged from fully dressed in multiple layers, to those without jackets or shoes, or even a shirt, in one case. The better dressed ones looked stronger and healthier. She absently ran a hand over her filthy but warm tunic. The guards had taken her armour and weapons when she'd arrived but left her in her blue Etherean garb. She hadn't washed since before arriving, and her clothes stank, but they were warm and comfortable, if not a little itchy.

The wide corridor terminated in a long rectangular room that looked exactly like a mess hall. It had the same stone walls and floors as her cell. No windows, though, meaning it didn't face the outside world. It stunk of smoke from the torches along the walls mixed with body odour from the prisoners and the greasy smells of cooking. Arya followed everyone else as they filed in, went to the front of the room, took a tray of food from a line of waiting trays—the servers spooning slop onto trays were behind bars, presumably for their protection—then sat at one of the long benches.

Conversation and the clatter of wooden—and blunt—cutlery filled the space. Anxious with a mix of fear and nausea from the stifling smells, Arya sat alone at the end of one of the emptier tables. She had no desire to get the wrong kind of notice by accidentally sitting with the wrong group. Best to work out prisoner dynamics before making a move. Even so urgency tugged at her. Her leg jiggled up and down. The stinking space felt too small, too constricting.

As always when she grew anxious, dark thoughts tugged at her. What if the Nightstalker had *found* Kirin already? What if the Dunidae army had lost, and Rorin—

She cut off those thoughts with an effort and focused on her food. The slop was no different than what she'd been served in the hole, and she forced herself to swallow small bites until it was all gone, before draining the cup of water that came with it. She had just started discreetly studying the prisoners in the mess, looking for what she needed, when a bell rang. Immediately the prisoners rose and formed a line to file out of the same door they'd arrived through. Arya joined them, keeping her gaze downward.

They moved along the wide corridor until reaching its other end, where daylight flooded the space. Arya winced, shading her eyes with a hand. They'd reached the bottom of a wide set of steps leading upwards. Outside, if the light was anything to go by. The line dissolved here, and prisoners moved up the stairs at their own pace.

At the top, Arya sucked in a deep, relieved breath of fresh air, shoulders relaxing at being out in open space. Then, as she properly took in her surroundings, her eyes widened. She stopped dead, and someone bumped into her from behind, shooting her a dark look. She shifted out of the way but then went back to staring. The steps ended at one edge of a yard that looked like it stretched out from the prison walls into open space. The southern and eastern sides of the yard were open, the northern—where the steps were—and western sides were prison wall. The ground was mostly mud, with a few patches of grass. Keeping a wary eye on her surroundings, she headed for the waist-high wall along the eastern edge.

A thick mist shrouded the area, making it impossible to see very far, and giving the effect that the prison stood alone inside a soup of fog. Turning, Arya glanced up at the buildings towering over the western and northern sides of the yard.

Was *all* of this stone lined with cazaix?

Her terror, barely held at bay after her breakfast experience, surged again at the reminder she couldn't access her magic, couldn't reach out to see if Elendryl, her *cairdre*, were alive and well, or hurt somewhere. Or even worse—

She cut herself off, forcing a deep, steady breath, fingers curling against the rough stone, the painful scrape of her skin helping anchor her in the present. She was here for a purpose. There was no choice now but to have faith in those she loved. And hope that they would be well until she could return to them.

Movement in her peripheral vision had her shifting to face the prisoner who'd spoken to her earlier, hands in his pockets, whistling under his breath. She wasn't sure why he was approaching when none of the other prisoners had even attempted to talk to her, and it made her wary. Her heartbeat quickened. "Fog's too thick to see the causeway, I take it?" he asked, joining her by the wall.

She calculated the distance between them and shifted slightly to increase it, just in case he made a move. "It's always like this?"

He leaned over. "Yup. Some days it's thin enough we can *almost* see across to the other side." He gave a theatrical shiver. "Gives me the creeps, thinking about this place just hanging in the middle of a deep, dark, ravine. Somewhere down there is the causeway that joins the prison to the ravine edge. It's the only way in or out."

"Except for climbing down to the bottom."

He gave her a look, like she was a special sort of idiot. "Have a penchant for fighting off firedrakes, do you? You *do* know they nest in the ravine walls? And even if you did make it to the bottom, you'd only get eaten by one of the chasmfiends that make the darkness down there their home."

Her mouth thinned at his tone, temper slicing her wariness to ribbons. "Either I was misinformed about this place being full of dangerous criminals, or you have some kind of fighting skill that belies that scrawny frame," she said. "Or am I the only prisoner you talk to like I'm a particularly inferior piece of dung under your shoe?"

He flushed red. Anger, she thought, with an underlying hint of humiliation. His words were sharp. "I think the hole did something to your mind that you would dare talk to *me* like that. Don't worry, it might clear up in time. It often does. If you don't have to go back."

"And what's so special about you?"

Something shifted in his expression. Surprise, or annoyance that he'd slipped somehow. It was hard to tell. It was quickly replaced by that condescending expression. "I pity you, newbie."

"Why are you even talking to me? Nobody else is."

He shrugged. "Like I said. Bored. This is marginally better than doing endless laps of this yard until it's time to go in."

Arya glanced around the yard. The prisoners stood alone or in small groups, some talking, some not. None even looked in her direction. Rather than reassuring her, it made her uneasy. This young man might be intensely unlikeable, but he *was* the only one who'd tried to talk to her. To accomplish what she needed here, she would need allies. So, she held out her hand. "I'm Arya."

He cocked his head, amused condescension in his gaze. "Not much handshaking happens in this place."

"What can I say? I was raised with manners."

He gave her filthy hand a look and pointedly didn't take it. "Raised by who?"

Thiara Ravenstrike. The name echoed through Arya's heart, grief and love combined. But as much as the grief would always be there, Arya now found that when she thought of her warlord, there was also strength. And warmth. Thiara had believed in her. "An answer for an answer."

He shrugged. "My name is Miell. I was raised by the horselords. Your turn."

Arya had already thought about how to respond to this question. She knew so little about Andahar, she felt it was safer to tell the truth and name herself as a foreigner. "I was raised in Dunidaen, in a warlord's household."

His eyebrows shot up. "That's … not what I expected. How did a Dunidae end up in Blackstone?"

Before she could answer, a hubbub broke out in the centre of the yard. A large group of prisoners were gathering around two men. Loud, angry, shouts echoed. Arya frowned, gaze narrowing when she looked at Miell and saw the nerve pulsing in his jaw. His hands had curled into fists where they were jammed in his pockets. "What is it?"

When he replied, his voice was casual, diffident. "Looks like there's going to be a fight. Lucky you. First day here and you already get some entertainment."

She glanced up at where guards paced along the top of the western wall of the yard, armed with bows. "The guards let fights happen?"

"As far as the guards are concerned, there are only two rules in Blackstone prison. You do what they say, when they say. Outside that..." Miell yawned, but she got the distinct impression it was for show. "It's a free for all. You should be careful, Arya. As a Dunidae, you have no friends or allies in here, and that makes you incredibly vulnerable."

A shiver of trepidation ripped through her, and she did her best to hide it from him. She'd gotten herself where she wanted to be, but that didn't mean what came next wasn't going to be incredibly dangerous. "Who are *your* friends and allies? Maybe they could be mine too."

He gave her a contempt-filled once over, one that placed her firmly in the category of *inferior,* then wandered off. Although his pace was slow, he headed away from the fight, towards the top of the steps where guards stood.

So that was a no.

Arya watched the crowd of prisoners grow larger until almost all of those in the yard were gathered in a loose circle around two combatants. She couldn't see much through the huddle of bodies. At some kind of signal she missed, the fight started, the prisoners launching themselves at each other with a series of punches. The ground was still wet from rain the night before and the fighters turned the surface of the yard into a muddy mess as they punched and kicked and wrestled. Cries and cheers rose from the spectating prisoners every time a punch landed.

Her gaze shifted often to the guards above and at the steps. They looked alert, but not worried. Meaning this was a common enough event that they didn't feel under threat. Then one of the fighters pulled something from his pocket. Metal glinted as he lashed out, slashing at the other man's neck. Blood sprayed, and the injured man collapsed to the ground, clutching at his torn throat, panicked and desperate. Seconds later he lay dead in the mud in a pool of his own blood.

The crowd began to disperse into small groups, talking and gesturing as if nothing extraordinary had happened. The guards didn't move from their positions.

Arya let out a low whistle, a shudder running down her spine.

The entire fight, both combatants and the nature of the spectators' cheers, had been animalistic, brutal, raw. It deepened Arya's sense of vulnerability. Miell was right. She wouldn't survive long here as an outsider without power or friends.

She had to obtain one or the other. Quickly.

She turned and leaned over the wall, wondering if the mist had thinned enough to see the causeway below. She wanted to get a good look at it, to see if climbing down to it from the yard might be possible. No luck. If anything, the fog had thickened.

She pushed off the wall and began walking along the edge of the yard in the same idle way Miell had. She kept her gaze averted from other prisoners talking, playing games, or doing their own exercise, and moved with a slight slump to her shoulders, emphasising she was no threat to anyone. She figured they'd eventually get curious about her, but the longer she stayed out of their notice, the better.

And as she walked, she watched. She paid attention. And she memorised.

And wished her Inkweaver was there to map it all for her.

***

Miell slipped in beside Arya hours later as the horn sounded and the prisoners in the yard began heading towards the steps. "You've survived your first day in the yard."

"You sound surprised."

"The last newbie to arrive at Blackstone lasted three hours before getting killed in a fight over his shoes. That was last week."

Arya's gaze went to the body of the fallen fighter still lying in the mud. None of the guards had come to fetch it, and the prisoners had behaved all day as if it wasn't there. She glanced down at her filthy tunic and breeches and decided cleaning them *wasn't* such a good idea. The worse she looked, the less likely anyone would be to take anything from her.

Miell followed her gaze, an amused smile on his face. "Don't lose any sleep over a dead marshfolk. The guards like to shoot at those who don't make it out of the yard before the second bell sounds. It's target practice for them."

"How delightful," she said dryly, then glanced at him, pasting a puzzled expression on her face, wondering if provoking his temper was the best way to get information out of him.

"What?" he snapped.

She shrugged. "I heard Blackstone is for the worst of the worst. But you don't seem like you could catch a fly, let alone harm one. No offence."

His teeth bared. "Offence taken, newbie."

She continued, unafraid. "To me, the worst of the worst means rapists, torturers, murderers, and *you* don't—"

He snorted. "Political prisoners and marshfolk sit atop King Nightstalker's list of the worst criminals, newbie. Nothing else is a threat to him."

A spark of interest zapped through Arya. "Political prisoners, huh? Rebels, you mean?"

Miell let out a genuine peal of laughter that had prisoners in front of them glancing over their shoulders in surprise. "You mean the idiot riverfolk who call themselves rebels and seem to think there's still hope of removing the king and bringing back House Stormrider? I think that might be the funniest thing I've heard all year."

"Who *do* you mean then?" Arya fought to keep the edge from her voice. His disdain for Esdee, Niallin, and those in her little army had her temper flaring. She reminded herself she was trying to win him as an ally and couldn't push him too far.

He gave a sigh, as if growing bored with the conversation. "Mostly they're captured marshfolk warriors. There must have been some renewed fighting in the Marshlands recently, because we've had an influx over the last couple weeks."

She wanted to ask who, but held back. Best not to betray her interest just yet. "So, which of the categories do you fall into?"

He flashed her a grin. "I'm here because of a girl. Her father didn't approve."

"Oh yeah? And does messing with the wrong girl get you labelled as a political prisoner in Andahar? Or are you one of the not-so-terrible murderers or rapists?" By now, she knew for damn sure he wasn't the latter. There was nothing violent in the young man that walked beside her.

Those strange golden eyes flashed with temper, and Miell increased his pace, moving ahead of her in the line of prisoners moving towards the eating hall, ending their conversation. She'd hit a nerve. Interesting. Also interesting—several of the glances shot his way from other prisoners as he passed. They weren't afraid, but they weren't looking at him like potential prey, either. Yet as far as she could tell, he was alone as she was.

Back inside, the damp walls, press of bodies and stink weighed on her, threatening to bring back the panic. She kept her gaze down, senses straining, aware that a prisoner with something sharp could bury it in her chest or kidney without her knowing it was coming in quarters this close. She wouldn't even hear the approach amidst the shuffle of feet on stone and the low-level chatter.

She made it safely into the mess and sat down to eat in the same place as breakfast. The food proved to be bland and chewy, but she ate all of it despite her lack of appetite, wanting to keep her strength up. She'd only just finished when the bell rang and everyone stood up.

"Back to your cells and be quick about it." A guard ordered as if by rote, his voice flat and bored. "No dawdling."

Now *there* was something interesting to note. If all guards were so bored, they wouldn't be looking for trouble, or expecting it. Arya followed the prisoner ahead of her back to her cellblock. Not long after she'd entered, a high-pitched squealing started up and the opening to her cell slid closed with a loud clang that echoed down the hall as subsequent cells closed.

Standing at the bars, she could see a little distance down the hall in each direction, but the angle wasn't good enough to see into anyone else's cell, or the guards' post at the far end. Directly in front of her was stone wall. Turning away from the bars, she hopped up on the narrow shelf that functioned as a bed and looked out the window above it. It was open to the elements, and in lieu of a shutter three thin bars were set into the stone. The opening would be just wide enough for her to crawl through if the bars weren't there.

Arya gave the bars a good tug, unsurprised to find no give, then dropped back to the shelf and stretched out, arms over her head, pulling the single blanket over her. As darkness fell outside, the light in the cellblock vanished too, encasing them all in darkness.

In the dark, she gathered up all the snippets she'd learned that day; recent fighting in the Marshlands, Miell and his disdain for marshfolk, the relative freedom allowed by the guards within the basic rules, and the existence of only one viable exit from the prison.

And she started planning.

Chapter 3

S houts echoed.

Arya's attention snapped to the centre of the yard where prisoners were gathering.

Another fight, then.

Frustration surged. She'd been encouraged by how much she'd learned on her first day, but in the handful of days since then she'd had an opportunity to study every prisoner in her wing at mealtimes and come to the depressing knowledge that who she was looking for wasn't among them. It wasn't necessarily surprising that her target was somewhere else in the prison, but it made things harder. A lot harder. Especially since she hadn't made any progress on allies. She needed to keep herself safe until she found what she was looking for—and she didn't kid herself that the apparent lack of interest from other prisoners would last.

A movement in her peripheral vision made her turn, but it was only Miell, strolling at his usual unhurried pace, hands tucked into pockets. He didn't greet her, and his gaze was on the growing crowd as he said, "They used to keep us better segregated. There was less violence then."

Miell had taken to spending snatches of time with her. Initially, she hadn't been sure if it was just because he was bored, or whether he had another reason. She suspected part of it was that he just liked having someone he considered inferior around to toy with. He was rarely forthcoming with information, but something about the fights made him uneasy, frightened, even though he tried to hide it.

And that made her wonder, because none of the prisoners ever accosted Miell, yet she'd still seen no signs of him having friends or allies in the wing.

Arya knew from her rough upbringing amongst soldiers that scrawny, arrogant types like Miell were the first target of bullies.

Miell's voice startled her from her thoughts. "You with us today, newbie, or is that slow mind of yours struggling to understand me?"

She let the insults slide off. "Segregated how?"

In the centre of the yard, a loud roar went up as the fight started and one of the combatants wrestled his opponent to the ground.

"Keeping us, the riverfolk, and marshfolk in separate wings of the prison, with enough of a distribution of arwein amongst them to ensure everyone stays calm."

Huh? "Who's us?"

Indignant contempt filled his features, eyes snapping golden. "I'm a *horselord,* of course."

Of course. Arya's confusion deepened. "I don't understand. Why do you need to be separated? You're all Andahari, aren't you?" And what in raven's balls was an arwein?

He huffed an astonished breath, then shook his head, as if coming to a disappointing realisation. "Typical riverfolk comment. You *are* one of them, aren't you, despite all your claims of being foreign. I'd guessed from the blonde hair and blue eyes, but now I'm certain."

"I'm not..." Arya began, then stopped. She *was* riverfolk, technically, though her mind and heart still felt mostly Dunidae. Ravenstrike. "I *was* born in Dunidaen, Miell. If it's such a problem, why did they stop segregating everyone?"

"They ran out of room to do it, I suppose, or stopped caring." He shrugged. "I guess the fights are one way to keep the prison population at a manageable level."

Her gaze narrowed. Miell spoke with a careless indifference, like he was airing whatever superficial thought came to his mind first. But his answers to her questions—like just now—often displayed a canny understanding or analysis of the situation. It suggested he'd been educated. Well.

"That does make a ruthless kind of sense," she agreed. It made her think, though. Her one and only goal had been figuring out how to defeat the

Nightstalker and take the throne of Andahar. End the war and ensure those she loved were safe. But what would happen if she actually succeeded? Her ignorance about anything related to Andahar was staggering, yet she planned to become its queen? It was a sobering thought.

Some of her building impatience spilled over, prompting her to ask Miell a direct question. "Why hasn't anyone picked on me yet? I've got nice clothes, good boots. I don't look like I'd be hard to kill, and I have no allies or friends."

"Oh, they've been watching you." He smiled. "You're an oddity, and they're trying to place you, that's why nobody has moved. But once they realise you're Dunidae, you'll be a target. It won't be long now."

Arya glanced over at the fight, where the prisoner who'd gotten his opponent on the ground was beating the man's face to a pulp with his fists. She turned back to Miell, who'd turned slightly green. "That means you haven't *told* anyone I'm a foreigner." She held his gaze. "I'm thinking we're already allies, Miell."

"The minute they mark you, Dunidae, you won't see me again." Miell brushed off his tattered pants, then gave her that once over again. The one Arya had experienced many times in her life. The look that told her a lot about Miell without him even realising it. The look of a prideful noble to someone he considered a servant, beneath him, not worth the dirt on his shoes.

She watched him walk away, then turned to look at the now dead prisoner lying covered in blood in the mud. Her fingers curled into fists. Three days already felt too long, and staying out of notice wasn't achieving anything. Despite the danger, she was going to have to risk doing *something*. If her target was elsewhere, maybe coming to the notice of the prison population wasn't the worst thing.

Let them come.

***

The next day brought torrential rain, so the guards sent them back to their cellblocks after breakfast. Given the callous lack of care regarding prisoner welfare displayed so far, Arya was astonished they didn't just send everyone out in the rain. The cell doors were left open so prisoners could move around and talk to each other as long as they didn't try and leave the block, so Arya set about learning its layout. The sooner she had a plan for escape, the better.

Her exploration took a depressingly short amount of time.

There were twenty cells in total, ten on each side of the row. Miell was in the cell two down from hers, spread out on his shelf, eyes half closed. She leaned against the bars, arms crossed. "How many cellblocks and yards are there in the prison?" she asked.

His eyes slid open, gave a bored eyeroll, then slid closed again. "Don't know. Don't care. This big chunk of rock sticking out from the ravine wall is basically a rabbit warren."

"So, nobody knows how many prisoners are in Blackstone?"

Another shrug, followed by a theatrical yawn.

"And it's the same routine every day? Prisoners are marched out of their cells into the yard, then back through the food line, then into their cells until the following morning. Nothing changes?"

"It hasn't changed once during my entire time here," he confirmed.

"And how long is that?"

One eye opened. "You keep asking me questions, some other prisoner is going to overhear and tell the guards we're getting cosy. Then they'll be paying more attention to both of us. Go away."

"All right, then just tell me one thing. When do you get out?"

He laughed a dark, bitter, laugh. "There are no sentences in Blackstone. You get out when the powers that be decide you can. Usually it's never," Miell said, then turned towards the wall, presenting his back to her.

Arya couldn't imagine being trapped inside these stone walls for another month, let alone a year, and once again she had to fight back the panic that threatened to overwhelm her. Biting her lip, she pushed off the bars and wondered back to her cell, looking discreetly at the other prisoners from her block. Miell had implied some might report anything suspicious to the guards.

Something to keep in mind.

***

Arya went straight to her spot the following day, leaning over the precipitous drop to spot the causeway, but again the fog was too thick. She turned to study the buildings lining two sides of the yard. If she was going to escape, she'd need to make her way *through* the prison before even reaching the causeway, which meant she needed to understand its layout better. She moved into an idle walk, taking a closer look, circling the edges of the yard.

She peered over the southern edge, but only fog lay below. After ensuring no one was watching, she moved along the western edge, dark stone looming above. She had barely made it a quarter of the way when she heard scuffling, followed by a sharp cry of pain.

She continued more cautiously until she came to a break in the wall where steps led inside. They were narrower than the ones she traversed every morning. It was the only other exit from the yard she'd identified. No guards were stationed here today. From the shadows inside, she heard murmured voices, a thud, and another gasp of pain.

Arya leaned against the wall, affecting a casual pose, making sure nobody was paying any attention to her. She'd been wanting to explore this exit from the yard, and the absence of guards was the opportunity she'd been waiting for, but they were absent for a reason—likely something to do with whatever was going on inside.

But then another cry came. And she recognised Miell's voice.

That settled it. Running into other prisoners was a lesser risk than being caught by the guards and sent back to isolation. If she was going to achieve her goal, she needed to start taking more risks. After another sweep of the yard to make sure nobody was looking her way, Arya slipped around the corner and headed down the steps. She moved slowly, her eyes squinting, adjusting to the dim light.

A corridor at the bottom came into view, as dim as the stairwell. She was almost to the bottom when she could make out Miell pinned against the wall opposite the steps by a tall, broad-shouldered prisoner with hair shaved so short he was almost bald.

"What's going on?" she asked, pausing where she was. Best to give herself an escape route until she had a better read on the situation.

Both turned toward her, squinting in the gloom. The moment Miell recognised her, his expression darkened with fury. "Arya, leave us alone. This is nothing."

"It doesn't look like nothing to me."

A dangerous look rippled over the other man's face. He gestured with his free hand, and another prisoner appeared from the shadows. Arya swore, glad she'd kept some distance—she hadn't seen the second one. He was also tall and muscular, his face hard and made more intimidating by the thick scar slashing from his forehead across the edge of his left eye. He wore his hair shaved too, the intricate tattoo decorating his neck in midnight blue ink stark against his fair skin.

"Arya, leave!" Miell gasped, his face turning red. "Naster is one of the Spider's lieutenants. This is not your business."

Arya glimpsed the edges of an inky tattoo, exquisitely done, above his collar just enough to make out the legs of a spider.

Her gaze whipped to Miell, eyes narrowing. "The Spider? Who's that?"

"You don't want to know," Miell managed. His golden eyes flashed with anger even though he could barely breathe. He *hated* that she was seeing this. "Get out of here!"

Arya glanced over her shoulder up the steps, making sure the exit was still clear. She could walk away now, likely with no repercussions. But instinct had roused when Miell had mentioned the Spider … an instinct that learning more about whoever that was would lead her to what she needed. What she'd come to Blackstone for. "I do want to know, actually."

The second prisoner growled low in his throat. "The *finelin* is right. Unless you have a death wish, you won't speak, hear, or think of the Spider, little woman."

Triumph flared. *That* was even more interesting. Again, she considered leaving, taking this little snippet of knowledge and figuring out how to learn more about the Spider.

But she'd decided Miell would be her ally. And one didn't turn their backs on their allies, even if they were supercilious, indolent brats who didn't even want your help. Arya turned back to the men. Shrugged. And said, "I'll leave when Miell can leave with me."

Naster moved to the base of the steps. He had beady little eyes, his expression growing angry. The other man watched carefully, still holding Miell against the wall. "Leave us to our business, newbie, before I get interested in you. This is your last chance."

Arya had met bullies before, had quelled her share of them as Raider general, and this man didn't scare her any more than they had. "As I said, I'm more than happy to leave. With Miell."

"Arya." Miell grunted again, then cried out as the man holding him back-handed him across the face. He slumped, dazed, blood trickling from his lip.

Naster's teeth showed. An angry flush was rising to his cheeks. "Either you walk away now, or you and I sort this out in the yard."

Raven's balls.

Arya hesitated. The yard meant a fight to the death. She wasn't scared of fighting Naster, but a fight like that would bring a lot of attention on her. And she still had no allies to warn others off challenging her next. Naster caught the hesitation and smirked at what he assumed was fear. "That's what I thought. Get along, newbie. I'll be generous and forget this ever happened."

The amused condescension in his voice sparked Arya's pride *and* temper. She straightened her shoulders, crossed her arms over her chest. "How about *I* be generous and assume you're just hard of hearing. I told you—I'm not going anywhere without Miell."

Surprise flickered on Naster's meaty face, followed by bared teeth. "The yard it is." He turned to the man holding Miell. "Let the *finelin* down and spread the word through the yard. Tell them I'm going to teach another newbie a lesson."

He nodded and let Miell drop unceremoniously to the ground, dazed and choking, then moved up the stairs, glancing at Arya as he passed her, but saying nothing. Naster stepped closer to her. He was a massive physical presence, but she stood her ground. "Be in the yard in ten minutes, or we'll come hunting for you. The *finelin* stays with you until then. When you lose, we'll take him back."

"I'll be there," she promised. "And when I win, his business with you is done."

Naster didn't reply, merely started up the steps, making a point of shouldering past her as he did. She let him without retaliation, then headed to where Miell was staggering to his feet.

She went to help him, but he pushed her away, fury flashing again in his golden eyes. "What were you thinking? I *told* you to leave."

Annoyed by his tone, she stood back and let him help himself up. "I'm trying to help you. Who is this Spider, and how are those guys linked to him?" "The Spider rules the prisoners. Naster is his lieutenant—his pet killer. He's never lost a yard fight."

Again, the image of the tattoo she'd once glimpsed on Ranier's neck flashed through her mind, sparking her instincts. A smile curled at her mouth as she put that together with what Miell had just said. "I'm guessing this Spider is a person, not a large talking animal. Why didn't you tell me about him?"

Miell spat blood and didn't respond.

She tried again. "Why were they menacing you?" "I'm a horselord and Naster and his goons are marshfolk." His jaw was tight as he regarded her, superior and angry. "Like I said, *not* your business. Now you've made it so that we're both going to die."

Arya took a step closer. "I don't like bullies, Miell. I don't care what the rules are, I'll never back down to men like that."

He studied her, as if thinking she might be joking, but when he realised she was serious, he let out a contempt-filled laugh. "You *are* a fool riverfolk. There are no fancy ideals of honour and whatever garbage in Blackstone. There's only survival."

Arya couldn't help but grin. "Maybe so, but this fool riverfolk is now your ally, whether you like it or not. Now, we'd best hurry or we'll be late for our appointment with Naster."

He turned red. "I *told* you. This was my business. I don't want or need a riverfolk ally. I am—" He cut himself off.

"You're what, Miell? Better than the rest of us because you're a horselord?" She shrugged. "If that's the case, how about you go and fight Naster yourself?"

He glowered, jaw tight.

"That's what I thought." She started up the steps. "Come on. We've got a fight to go and win."

***

When Arya reached the top of the steps, most of the prisoners in the yard were already gathering in a circle in the centre. The guards atop the wall watched with interest. Two of them exchanged money.

It was late in the afternoon, almost dinner time, and dark clouds approached from the south, dimming any light that had made it through the thick fog. Rain started falling as Arya was halfway across the yard, Miell trailing behind her. She wondered if the guards would stop the fight at the dinner bell, or whether they'd be allowed to finish.

As she walked, she thought about the best way to play this. Try to win decisively enough to guarantee her safety until she found allies, or defeat Naster without fanfare and hope any interest she roused amongst prisoners or guards would die away quickly? The first was a gamble that would deliver the opposite of what she wanted if she failed.

Her boots sank into the muddy ground, her trained soldier's gaze taking everything in. The prisoners parted for her, allowing her into the circle where Naster waited. She could *feel* their excitement and bloodlust electrifying the damp air. A scan of faces revealed no humanity, only fierce anticipation. A shiver ran down the back of her neck.

She glanced back at Miell. At his youthful face and gangly frame. And wondered how he'd lasted a year in prison full of starving wolves. Maybe it had something to do with why this Spider's men were roughing him up. What had they called him? *Finelin.*

The circle of prisoners closed behind Arya. As they did, memories flooded her of that morning in the Heathrock drill yard, when she'd been barely seventeen years old and challenged by Arken, the man who thought she'd taken his place as General Desomer's apprentice. She'd won then, with nothing but pride and determination and a ruthless streak fed by her Stormrider temper.

Arya came to a stop opposite Naster. The rain was a curtain between them, soaking her hair and clothes, turning the ground to muddy pools. Naster stood bare-chested, cracking his knuckles. When she stopped, he raised his hand in the air and the spectators fell silent. His voice was loud and mocking when he spoke. "You should have known better than to mess with me. I don't know who you are, but I'm going to kill you today."

Savage gazes watched and waited for her response, all focused on *her*. A perfect stage.

In that moment, Arya's mind made one of those intuitive leaps it liked to make—reckless and brilliant and just as likely to fail as to succeed. If what she'd come here looking for wasn't in her cellblock or yard, where she could get to it, maybe she could make it come to *her*. Another smile tugged at Arya's mouth.

She slowly rolled back the left sleeve of her tunic, tucking it above her elbow. Muttering spread through the crowd at her deliberate movements. Naster shifted with impatience as she started on her right sleeve, rolling it up past her elbow and revealing the jagged lightning scar on her inner forearm.

Arya made sure Naster saw it before she spoke, using the parade ground bellow she'd perfected as general of Ravenstrike. "I am Arya Stormrider, Sky Lord and heir to the throne of Andahar. And you are *very* welcome to try and kill me, Naster."

The anticipation, the muttering, the shifting of feet … it all died.

For the briefest of moments, a weighty hush fell over that yard in Blackstone prison.

Even in the dim light and falling rain Arya caught the looks of shock and astonishment—even some fear—flashing on the faces of those in the crowd. And then the moment broke, and the hubbub roared back to life, stronger and louder than it had ever been. Naster's beady eyes narrowed. He raised a hand and silence fell.

"This is Blackstone prison," he spat in contempt of her claim. "Even if what you say is true, you have no Sky Lord magic here."

"No," she agreed, relaxing her shoulders and lowering her stance, allowing a challenging grin to spread over her face. "But I don't need magic to take you down."

Naster came at her swinging. The moment he moved, a roar erupted. A haunting mix of howls and screams from the watching prisoners eddied around them with the breeze. Arya's senses drank it in like a fine wine. Her teeth bared with fierce anticipation.

Arya ducked under the first blow, stepping aside so that Naster's momentum carried him past her. Judging the right moment, she lashed out with an elbow, slamming it into the side of his head. She quickly circled away, shaking the sting from her elbow. Naster swore, stumbling, but then blinked and shook off her hit as if it were nothing.

He came at her again, two quick blows, putting more strength behind his fists. Arya sidestepped both, shifted around as he passed, and drove her foot into the side of his left knee. It buckled under him, and he fell to the mud with a grunt of pain. As she'd expected, Naster relied almost entirely on the power and strength of his body in a fight. Which was a perfectly good approach, *if* he could land a hit.

The crowd roared again, but it was more muted. Two straight unanswered blows from the newbie were not what they'd expected. Arya took in a deep breath, tasting the rain on her tongue, allowing the crowd's animalistic energy to feed her temper and her razor focus on the man trying to kill her. He was back on his feet quickly, though with a noticeable limp. His pain threshold was impressive.

Arya circled him, waiting for the next attack. Rain soaked her hair and ran in rivulets down her face. It was her speed and agility that would win this. She wouldn't be baited into engaging in a way that gave him the advantage. Naster reached into his pocket and drew a metal blade. He was a fearsome sight, blood from her blow running in rivulets down his face, neck tattoo startling against his pale skin.

"Good to know that marshfolk don't fight fair," she commented.

"There is no such thing as fair in Blackstone," he snarled. "If you'd bothered to keep your head down, you would have learned that eventually."

Arya glanced at the knife, back to Naster's face. "Bring it on."

He came at her more slowly, adjusting to her fighting style, wary of her speed. Some of the prisoners shouted at him to make an end of her. Others were now pulling for her, cheering every time she dodged a blow. Others taunted Naster for not having put her down already. Arya loved every second of it. Every shout and cheer and whistle fuelled her.

She avoided the first few slashes of Naster's knife with relative ease, one hand lifting to push rain-soaked hair back from her eyes. He was a canny fighter, not about to underestimate her again. His limp slowed him, though, impacting his lateral movement.

Find the little things, Laskin had always taught her. And turn them to your advantage.

The next time Naster came at her, Arya let him get close enough to score a hit—a shallow slice down her arm. She let a wince cross her face and cradled the arm, as if the injury were worse than what it was. A flash of triumph speared through her as she saw him fall for it, the gleam of confidence returned to his eyes.

With his next move, he dropped caution and went for the killing blow. When it came, Arya moved as ruthlessly as Laskin had once taught her, every movement driven by utter clarity of purpose. Naster thrust the knife, arm almost fully extended as he aimed for her heart. But Arya was already moving, reading his attack perfectly. She stepped to his left side and grabbed his wrist. He tried to move sideways to adjust, but his left knee buckled and locked.

She brought his elbow down hard over her knee, snapping the bone with an audible *crack*. Ignoring his cry of agony, she caught the falling knife, shifted her stance, then drove it into his throat. His eyes widened in shock, and then he fell, breath gurgling. By the time his body hit the mud, he was already dead, his blood spilling freely into the mud.

The raucous crowd went completely, utterly, quiet.

Flushed with adrenaline and victory, Arya reached down to yank the blade from his neck, and then turned to the crowd, water and blood spraying as she spread her arms wide. "I am Arya Stormrider," she screamed. "Who else wants a piece of me? I will take every one of you down if I have to! COME AT ME!"

The silence lasted a moment longer, and then they were cheering, screaming, stamping in the mud. And then some of them began chanting her name, a steady beat that resounded through the yard. The wall of noise lifted into the night, billowed by a breeze sweeping in from the west.

She glanced up at the wall, saw the guards clustered together, watching carefully. A prickle of apprehension went through her, and she lowered her gaze, dropped her arms, tucked the knife into her boot. Her gaze searched out Miell in the crowd.

His expression was one of shocked realisation.

"I think you actually *do* want me as an ally," she told him, then passed him the bloody knife and pushed her way out of the crowd, leaving them still chanting her name behind her.

Chapter 4

Arya awoke with a start the next morning at the squealing of the cells opening. Despite her victory in the yard, her sleep had been tortured, filled with nightmares of the Nightstalker's face hovering over her as he beat her within an inch of her life, before segueing into the helpless horror of watching Taze die.

She rolled to a sitting position on the stone bench, breathing hard, sweat slicking her skin despite the cold air in her cell. When she opened her hands, she half-expected to see Taze's blood all over them. Instead, pain flared in her right hand; the knuckles were dark purple and swollen with bruising, and several cuts in the skin bled. Blood had dried around the wound on her forearm where Naster had scored her with his knife, a narrow line above her lightning scar.

"That looks painful."

Arya looked up, terror shivering through her body. Dreaming of the Nightstalker, what he'd done to her, had left her on edge, body bracing for more trauma. Four prisoners crowded the entry to her cell. All had shaved heads, and an intricate tattoo inked in midnight blue decorating the left side of their necks. Just like Naster. Arya had never seen anything like it before. Judging from the way they held themselves, they weren't here to attack … yet … but they definitely wanted something. She forced herself to take a steadying breath to control the panic so that she could speak calmly. "Who are you?"

"The Spider wants to see you." The same man spoke. His tattoo was more intricate, and larger, than Naster's had been, but was less visible against the dark brown of his skin.

Interest flickered, hope serving to help calm her further. She stayed where she was, kept her expression neutral. "About what?"

"It's not a request." He stepped into her cell, gaze flicking around its interior in a way that told her he was a man who'd always needed to look out for unexpected danger. "You won't do so well against the four of us as you did against Naster, I promise you that."

Arya came slowly to her feet, making sure to seem reluctant. She didn't want them knowing this approach was exactly what she'd been hoping for in defeating Naster so theatrically. "And if I go with you, what happens about breakfast? I don't care who you are or who the Spider is, I'm not incurring the wrath of the guards. Isolation wasn't fun."

"You let us worry about the guards. You won't get into trouble."

Her reluctance wasn't entirely feigned this time. Her plans would be in ruins if she got put back in isolation. "Lead on, then."

He gestured for the prisoners with him to begin walking. "Follow them."

She did, trying to keep a wary distance as she passed him to exit her cell. He came after, taking up a position behind her. She didn't like leaving her back vulnerable to such a man, but there wasn't much she could do about it. Arya walked lightly, her body ready to move in an instant if needed. And as she walked, she tried flexing the fingers of her right hand, hoping she'd be able to use it if there was another fight. It hurt like blazes, but she still had full range of movement, which was a good sign.

The other prisoners in her cellblock glanced at Arya in interest as she passed, but all looked away just as quickly when they saw the prisoners with her, clearly afraid. Once they reached the top of the narrow stairwell, Arya was led past the prisoners shuffling towards breakfast. The men in front of her turned into a stairwell leading off the main corridor and up to a higher level. Eventually they arrived at a cellblock identical to hers, except that there was a door at its opposite end rather than a blank wall.

A prisoner stood outside the door, holding a guard position, a knife sheathed at her waist. She opened it as soon as she saw them coming. Those ahead of Arya stayed outside, while the man behind followed her in. The door was closed firmly behind them. The instinct to reach for her magic was powerful, and she had to fight the fear that flooded her when it didn't come. Being in such a state of constant wariness, on hair-trigger to respond, was taking its toll on her. Focus was growing increasingly harder, but she fought for it anyway.

Arya's eyes took a few moments to adjust to the dimness of the room, a space much larger than any cell she'd seen so far. A fire flickering in a hearth was the only source of light—there were no windows. An impressive map covered almost the entirety of the wall to her right.

But her gaze went immediately to the man sitting on a comfortable chair by the fire. His grey hair was cropped short, his body lean, his dark eyes sharp. Lines around his mouth and under his eyes suggested he was in his early sixties, maybe older. It wasn't his appearance that first struck Arya though, it was the distinct air of command and control that surrounded him. Just like...

Triumph flared. Followed by shuddering relief.

She let herself take a deep breath, one that shook off the residue of fear. Her rapidly revised plan had worked after all. And even quicker than she'd imagined. No expression crossed that ice-cold face as the man spoke with a voice that sounded like he hadn't drunk water for days. "Roll up your right sleeve."

She did as he bade without comment. The Spider's gaze went straight to her lightning scar, eyes narrowing. "Well, well, if it isn't one of the Stormriders, risen from the ashes." His even tone didn't betray what he thought of this. "I didn't believe them when they told me, but looking at you now ... well, you're the spitting image of your father."

That rocked her unexpectedly. She'd never known her father, or her mother, but to hear that she *looked* like him ... Arya refocused. Remembered her goal.

And went for the throat.

"I wouldn't quite say you're the spitting image of your brother, but those eyes..." She whistled. "Not to mention the tattoos you're hiding under those long sleeves and that high collar. I'm very pleased to meet you, Remien Inkweaver."

A cold silence filled the room, broken only by the popping of the fire. Arya was surprised the flames didn't freeze over. The prisoner who'd brought her went still, as if readying to fight or flee. She shifted slightly, increasing the distance between them.

The Spider spoke. "How exactly did you come to be in Blackstone, Stormrider?"

"I came for *you*." Arya held his gaze. This was no time for beating around the bush. She had Remien at a momentary disadvantage, so she abandoned stealth and went for directness instead. She doubted she'd gain an advantage over this man easily again. "I need to know everything that House Inkweaver does if I'm going to kill Lucius Nightstalker and take my throne back."

The prisoner beside her huffed out an incredulous breath.

Remien blinked. His left hand, resting on the arm of the chair, lifted fractionally before resting again. After a long beat of silence, he spoke. "You have plenty of arrogance. That's to be expected from a Stormrider, I suppose." He shifted in his chair, crossing one long leg over the other. "Here's my problem. You killed my best lieutenant yesterday, and your very presence at Blackstone threatens the stability of this environment."

She smiled without warmth. "You mean I threaten your carefully cultivated power base?"

"You don't threaten me," he said. "Don't let your arrogance fool you otherwise."

Arya shrugged, letting that go for now. "I'm curious about something. You and Ranier are not marshfolk, not riverfolk either, from your appearance, yet you're running around Blackstone with marshfolk bodyguards and lieutenants. And I was starting to get the distinct impression that people from different tribes hate each other." "Let's just say that nobody likes the consequences of getting on my wrong side, no matter which Andahari tribe they're from."

"Knowing your brother as I do, that's believable."

Remien's gaze narrowed. "If you think you're going to get a reaction out of me by dangling my brother as bait, you're wrong. And if you think you've got a chance in hell of defeating the Nightstalker ... well, let me just say this ... you'd need to get out of here to do that. And nobody has ever escaped Blackstone." "With all due respect to you and your thugs, nobody was me," she said. "I *will* get out of here, after I get what I need from you. It's just a matter of time."

He smiled—an expression full of amused interest. She'd unsettled him for that one brief moment, but he was comfortable again. In control. Or so he thought. "And what is it exactly you need from me?"

"*I* think one of the biggest mistakes Lucius Nightstalker ever made was sticking you in here instead of killing you. I'm sure it suited his torture-loving nature to think of you rotting away in Blackstone for the rest of your life ... but the knowledge you hold. In your blood and bone, isn't it? And your skin. If there's a way to defeat him, you know it."

His eyes flashed, something dark and primal. She'd seen that look in Ranier's eyes too, the night he'd bellowed at her to tear the Nightstalker from her magic as she lay near death.

She had him.

Remien picked up his book, a signal that he was wrapping up the conversation. "I don't give things away for free, Stormrider, and you have no currency."

Arya affected a sigh. "You and your brother are so much alike. It's disappointing. Don't worry, Remien, I know exactly what you want, and I can give it to you."

He laughed under his breath, as if enjoying her audacity. "And what is that?"

She glanced around, back to him. She was ahead, she judged, still with a slight advantage. Best not to give up everything now, or she'd have no leverage going forward. This wasn't a man who was going to willingly spill all he knew on their first meeting. "How about I keep that to myself for now as leverage against you sending goons to kill me."

"*That* relies on me not becoming truly angry with you. Don't kill any more of my men, if you can help it."

"Tell them not to challenge me to any more fights, and I'll do my best."

He waved a hand, done with her, his gaze going to his book. "Arubon, take her back to her cell."

Arya paused by the map on her way out, impressed by its exquisite detail. "You drew this, I take it? The Inkweaver hand is familiar." The map showed the entire continent in rich colours; Dunidaen and Khadini in the south, Icelands in the northeast, and Andahar to the northwest, but it also showed a massive landmass to the north, and grouping of four large islands far to the east. They weren't as heavily notated, but one of the four islands had a sigil of crossed swords drawn in its centre. When she looked closer, she could see the sigil was made up of hundreds of tiny amber stars. "What's this?" Rorin's tutor had never taught anything about other kingdoms across the sea.

"Funnily enough, I don't do answers on demand." His gaze remained on the pages of his book.

She tried anyway. "Do you have a map of Blackstone this detailed?"

"Be nice and leave before I get impatient."

"Suit yourself." She turned away from the map and smiled at the Spider. "Chat soon, Remien."

Arubon took her back to her cell, but didn't say a word the entire way. Breakfast was over, but the pouring rain from the night before hadn't eased, so it was another inside day. Arya waited until he was gone before sitting down on the blanket she'd left bunched on the sleeping shelf as a cushion. When she sat, she heard a faint crackling sound. She pulled back the blanket. Lying underneath was a rolled piece of parchment. Leaving it there, she went to the doorway, making sure nobody was paying attention to her cell, then returned and unrolled it.

The parchment was bigger than it had looked, and drawn in black ink on its surface was a map. It was immediately clear the map wasn't Remien's—the skill of the illustrator was amateurish in comparison. She stared at the squiggling lines for a long time before figuring out that it was a floor plan of the prison. And if she was reading it correctly, a circled section depicted her cellblock and yard.

Footsteps sounded, and she quickly rolled the parchment, shoving it into a pocket in her tunic. Seconds later, Miell appeared, peering into her cell, as if he didn't know what he'd find. When he saw her, his voice expressed surprise. "You're still alive. How did you manage that after a visit with the Spider?"

"You really have to ask, after last night?"

Miell didn't immediately respond. His manner was different. More subdued. And he hadn't yet given her one of those looks of contempt he favoured. Perhaps after her revelation the previous day, she was no longer inferior to whatever he considered himself to be. "That was dangerous, announcing yourself as a Stormrider so openly."

"Dangerous because I have no allies in here?"

Resentment flared in his golden eyes. "You involved yourself in my business yesterday without asking. I owe you nothing."

"Even now, you would prefer I hadn't interfered?"

"Yes. It was none of your business." His mouth took on a petulant cast. "Why didn't you just leave it alone?"

"Naster and his thugs made me angry. You don't know me well yet, but you'll soon learn that I have a bit of a temper."

He scoffed. "It's as simple as that?"

"Answers for answers. Why are you truly in Blackstone prison, and what does the Spider want from you?"

He gave an impatient huff and an eyeroll, but he didn't leave, simply stood there, as if conflicted. The silence held, lengthened, until Arya shrugged. "Spit it out or move on."

Miell pushed off the doorframe, but then he wavered again. Eventually he started talking, spitting the words out as if he didn't really want to be speaking them, "A friend reached out to me a few days ago. He had a piece of information he thought might interest me. But now I know who you are, I suspect *you* might be very interested too." Miell looked over his shoulder as his voice dropped to a whisper. "There's someone claiming to be a Sky Lord in his cellblock."

The hope that leaped in her chest was so strong Arya was only *just* able to stop the emotion from reaching her face. Instead, she drawled. "Is that so? Who?"

He shrugged. "My friend didn't give a name. It's difficult to pass messages between cellblocks without the guards noticing. Not to mention it's almost impossible to get your hands on parchment and something to write with."

Raven help her, if he shrugged in that indolent manner one more time...

Arya swallowed her temper. "Can you get a message from me to whoever this person is claiming to be a Sky Lord?"

"No." He raised a hand to forestall her protests. "Even if I wanted to, my friend and I can only commit a few words to each message."

"All the message needs to do is let them know I'm here and that I'm going to figure out a way to talk to them." "How? There's no way to travel between cellblocks, and I'm not risking my neck passing messages on your behalf."

"You let me worry about that. Will you send the message?"

He hesitated *again*. Arya could see his hands were curled into fists even though they were buried deep in his pockets. "There are no other horselords in this wing."

"Is that an explanation for why you have no apparent allies or friends? Were you separated in this wing on purpose?"

His jaw tightened, all the answer she needed.

"And that's why Naster could get to you here. Nobody to protect you."

A simple nod.

Arya once again swallowed her impatience. For all his supercilious arrogance, Miell was young, and he was afraid, but his pride wouldn't let him admit it. "So, you brought news of the other Sky Lord to me as currency? You're not willing to ally with me in case it turns dangerous for you, but you *do* want my protection. And if I want you to reply to the message, I need to keep protecting you. Have I got that about right?"

A sharp nod, more resentment in his gaze. He *hated* asking a riverfolk for help.

"You have yourself a deal, Miell."

Miell pushed off the doorway in that lazy way he had, but paused, turning back. "My father used to tell me stories about the Sky Lords. He made them sound so magnificent. Then yesterday in the yard, your eyes were this blue like I've never seen, and the fury and power in your face ... some of the stories started to make sense."

As soon as he was gone, Arya pulled the map from her pocket with her uninjured hand, hope surging through her. Not only was one of her Sky Lords possibly in here, an ally to help getting out when she was ready, but someone had left her a map; someone who'd known she needed to be able to move around the prison.

But was whoever had left her the map a secret ally, or was it a trap?

Chapter 5

She waited a full day before making her next move. The night before, she'd dreamed of Kirin—a memory of seeing him at Taskari after her beating at the hands of the Nightstalker. Only in her dream, she'd stayed, and they'd been standing together at the top of the peninsula, his little hand in hers. Even now she was awake, the thought brought a sharp pang of bittersweet pain. She had barely spent more than a handful of days with her son, yet she missed him with a constant, gnawing ache. And then, as she stepped into the breakfast line, the prisoner ahead of her shifted, revealing the messy blonde curls of the man in front of him, just like Rorin's. It was too much. She needed to get out of here.

After breakfast, she followed the prisoners out into the yard, pausing at the top of the steps to scan the area, as was her habit. The bruising on her hand was bright purple, leaving a throbbing soreness, but the cut on her arm had scabbed up nicely.

Miell appeared beside her. "Looking for someone?"

Arya pointed. "Him."

"Arubon?" Fear flashed in Miell's eyes. "You *do* know that he replaced Naster as the Spider's lieutenant in this wing?" "Even better. I need to talk to him."

"No, you don't. If you want to survive in here, you stay *away* from the Spider's people."

"I think it's a bit late for that." She turned to Miell. "Why are *you* running scared of the Spider? Why were they hassling you?"

"It had nothing do with the Spider. They were marshfolk, and I'm alone in this wing." He waved a dismissive hand. "You don't just walk up to the Spider's lieutenant in the yard, Arya. *They* choose when to talk to you."

Arya watched him, unconvinced by his casual response. Whatever the truth was, he wasn't going to tell her. Not yet, anyway. "He's going to talk to me this morning."

"It's your funeral. Just don't forget that if I lose your protection, you lose your messaging ability." Miell shrugged and wandered off.

Arya crossed the muddy yard towards the man who'd escorted her to Remien the previous day, the one the Spider had called Arubon. The prisoners clustered around him openly watched her as she approached. When their warning glares didn't halt her progress, they shifted almost as one, surrounding him in a protective circle. Arubon carried on the conversation he was having, as if oblivious to it all. She'd bet gold he was aware.

"You'd best move along," a woman spoke as she stopped. Like male marshfolk, she had the tattoo on her neck as well, though hers were in a dark green ink, rather than midnight blue like Arubon and Naster.

Arya craned her head around her to address Arubon. "You afraid to come out and talk to me?"

His gaze finally turned to her. He pushed through his companions and stepped up to Arya, deliberately invading her personal space, and crossing his arms over his chest. He smelled of sweat and something else, sulphur? Up close, the tattoo on his neck was intricate, covering all the way from his collarbone to his jaw. It wasn't like the Inkweaver tattoos she'd seen, though, depictions of images. This design was symbolic, whirls and lines. "What?"

"I'd like to speak with the Spider."

"Why?" His tone was flat, emotionless. "That's my business," she said, refusing to back down despite his intimidating height and well-defined muscle. "Will you take me to him, or should I go by myself?"

"The Spider doesn't take unannounced visits. *He* decides who he sees and when."

"He'll take one from me." She smiled slightly. "I suspect he's already given you orders to that effect."

Arubon's jaw tightened. "Come."

The Spider's lieutenant clearly didn't fear her, despite her win in the yard, because he alone escorted her. The prison guards watching the main entry stairs took one look at Arubon and made no comment as he led Arya down the steps and into the prison complex. Interesting. She wondered how the Spider had cultivated enough influence that his people were allowed freedom of movement, then realised she was talking about an Inkweaver who'd had years to work on them. If he had anything like Essa's level of intelligence...

Arya reminded herself to be careful.

Once again, the older man sat by the fire reading a book, sipping from a steaming cup. Whatever it was smelled delicious, and reminded Arya of voseni. What she wouldn't give for a mugful of that hot, delicious drink.

"The Sky Lord wants to see you," Arubon said by way of greeting. "She was insistent. Shall I kill her?" "You can try." Arya gave him a flat stare.

Remien cocked his head, a bland smile on his face, steam from his cup rising into the air. "You can leave us, Arubon, but remain outside the door. We won't be long."

Arubon bowed his head and left.

"I wouldn't threaten Arubon lightly," Remien advised. "You wouldn't find him as easy to kill as Naster."

"Then why was Naster your lieutenant?"

"As competent as he is in the role, I find Arubon to be less ... malleable."

Interesting. "Arubon doesn't scare me any more than Naster did." Arya glanced around, gaze lingering on the map again, on those four islands far to the east, before returning to the Spider. This was a dangerous man, and she wanted to ease into the conversation, let him lead if necessary. "Don't you ever leave this room, spend a bit of time in one of the yards for fresh air and light? How many yards *are* there in Blackstone?"

Remien placed his book down, rose from the chair, and crossed the space towards her. He was taller, forcing her to look up into those dark eyes as he stopped, close enough to bury a knife in her if he had a mind to. "I'm not a man to be crossed, Arya Stormrider. I run this prison for a reason."

"You're so much like your brother," she murmured. "And therefore, I respect your strength and power in here, Remien, but I do not bow to it. There was a time when Ranier could drop me in the snow faster than a striking snow leopard. That time is long past. You won't find it any different."

"My brother is not me. I have thousands of prisoners at my command. A word from me and they'll come for your head. You won't be able to stop all of them." He spoke quietly, but with the same lethal simplicity Ranier often employed. "And you have no allies to call upon."

"That's why I'm here. I figured I'd start my alliance building by going straight to the top."

"I'm not allying with you, and you know better than to expect that." Impatience edged his tone. "What is it that you truly want? We had an agreement to leave each other alone."

She sensed she was on thin ice, so got to the point. "Fine. If you do rule all of Blackstone, then you must have a way of communicating with your lieutenants in the other cellblocks and yards. More, you must be able to keep oversight of them. I need to know how you move between the cellblocks."

His head cocked again, studying her. Was he parsing her words for hidden meaning or simply deciding whether it would be strategically sound to kill her. Arya tensed slightly, just in case.

Eventually though, he answered. "You are partially correct. I have prisoners like Arubon in each wing. They report to me, and I give them orders. There is no movement between blocks."

Arya said, "No lieutenant like Arubon would fear a faceless prisoner in another cellblock who has no way of getting to them to carry out their threats. Either you're lying about your influence over the whole prison, or you have a way of moving between cellblocks. Which is it?"

A cold smile crossed Remien's face. "I do hate to repeat myself, but there is no way to move between the cellblocks. Should you doubt the strength of my influence over this prison population, I'd be happy to organise a demonstration for you."

With that said, he returned to his chair and picked up his book.

Biting back her ire at his abrupt dismissal, she spoke. "One way or another, you're going to agree to ally with me."

The hand holding his book clenched slightly, then eased. When he looked up, he wore that killing expression his brother often used to good effect. "Curiosity prompts me to ask what makes you so certain of that?"

"Like I said, I have the one thing you want and can't get."

"And what would that be?"

Arya simply smiled. He hadn't been able to hide the brief flicker of interest in his eyes. "Let's chat again soon, Remien."

She passed by the map as she left, gave it a tap. "If you've got one of these of Blackstone, I'd be very interested."

No answer, of course.

Arubon waited on the other side of the door as she stepped through. He glanced inside, saw the Spider reading by the fire, and closed the door.

"Did you get what you wanted?" he asked as they started making their way back to the yard.

She smiled slightly. "You could say that."

Confirmation that there were multiple other cellblocks and a rough number of prisoners in Blackstone. Thousands. And ... she'd believed his claims of having firm control over all of them. The Spider wasn't a man who bragged. Which substantially improved her chances of escape. Almost guaranteed them, in fact. He hadn't *told* her anything, but he'd given enough away.

Arubon said nothing more for the rest of the walk, until they'd climbed the steps up into the yard. There, he paused. "If the Spider orders it, I will kill you."

"Arubon, are you *warning* me?" She narrowed her gaze. "Why would you do that?"

"If it comes to a fight between us, I want to make sure it's a fair one." Challenge and eagerness both glittered in his dark eyes. Then he turned and strode off across the mud.

He saw her as a worthy challenge. That was both comforting and terrifying.

***

As soon as she was back in her cell that night, Arya pulled out the map her mysterious benefactor—or betrayer—had left her, fingers tracing the now familiar lines. She'd not expected the Spider to give her access to whatever method he and his people used to move around the prison ... not yet anyway ... but during their conversation she'd planted the seed. Now she just had to let it grow. Until then, she needed to work on figuring out how to move between cellblocks herself.

No clarity came, and so she climbed onto the sleeping bench, uninjured hand exploring the window edges. If she could get rid of the bars, the gap was big enough for her to crawl through ... just. Climbing the outside of the sheer prison walls would be dangerous in the extreme, but manageable for someone who'd trained to run the Dreadwater Gate.

She dropped back to the shelf and picked up the map again, this time looking for where windows were marked. If she was going to climb, she needed to know where to climb *to*.

***

Over the next few days, Arya tried without luck to figure out how to acquire a tool that could file through the bars in her window. Still, coming up with a way to conceal her absence from the cell during the guards' nightly patrols proved easier. She stayed awake several nights in a row, studying the timing of the patrols, and learned that between the hours of midnight and dawn, there was only one cell check, and it was always at the same time. They were lazy checks too. The guards clearly didn't expect anyone to be out of their cell, and so didn't do more than glance inside and move on. Concealing her absence would be easy enough if she could acquire extra blankets to stuff under her normal blanket. Gaining those required another fight; one which left her with a shallow cut on her left arm and another dead prisoner.

Finally, she needed to learn where in the prison her Sky Lord was being held. To this end, she pushed Miell to communicate with his friend for more details.

He shook his head. "He hasn't been able to get a message to me. I would have told you if he had."

"Can you send him another message, tell him how important it is?"

"No," Miell said. "I'm not putting my life in danger for no good reason. What is your hurry, anyway? None of us are going anywhere."

"Just tell me as soon as you hear anything."

As more days passed, Arya grew increasingly anxious. She had no idea how long she'd been in the hole, and over half a month had passed since she'd been released into the general prison population. She had no idea what was happening on the outside. Had the Nightstalker defeated Dunidaen's army, or were they still fighting? If one of her Sky Lords was in here, then where were the others? She didn't even know if they were still alive.

And Kirin. It always came back to her fear for him. Even if he was still safe, the Nightstalker was never going to stop hunting him like he did her.

She stayed awake planning deep into every night, trying to work out the best method of escape. Her sleep was filled with restless dreams of violence and blood, and the memory of Taze's death, over and over. Then, one morning as the guards winched open the doors to the cells, Miell appeared. "I have something."She leaped off the bench. "What?"

"Just three words, that's all he could get to me," Miell said. "'Dreams' and 'five two'."

Frustration flashed through her. She'd waited so long for three words. "That was it?" He nodded. "Five two will be the location; your Sky Lord must be in cellblock two on the fifth level. Does the other word make any sense to you?"

"Yes." Arya nodded, sinking back onto the bench and letting out a heavy sigh. Relief and worry combined in an unsettling mix.

Leanir Mindbreaker was in Blackstone with her.

A man who hated her with a passion.

***

Arya ate breakfast, thoughts tumbling over themselves. Now she knew where Leanir was, she had to figure out how to get to him. *Should* she get to him? Could she trust him to help her, or would it be safer to do this on her own? A headache throbbed at her temples and despair threatened. What she had to do felt close to impossible, and one single mistake could bring it all crashing down around her. Trusting Leanir seemed reckless.

Yet there was no doubt Leanir's skills could be an asset. And surely, he'd want to get out of here as badly as she did, no matter his feelings toward her. Arya decided she would talk to him. She could decide after that.

Miell dropped onto the seat across from her. She looked at him warily. He'd never joined her at meals before.

"You didn't seem very happy about the message I passed you." He spooned up a mouthful of slop. "I thought you were desperate to get a response."

She didn't answer.

He heaved a sigh. "Fine, don't tell me. What are you going to do now?"

"Like you said, we're in here for life. There's nothing I *can* do."

Miell opened his mouth to say something, but it was cut off by the sound of horns blasting through the morning. "That's the gathering horn." He shot to his feet, all his usual languor gone. "We need to line up in the yard. Hurry!"

Puzzled and curious, Arya followed Miell and her fellow prisoners as they flooded out of the dining hall and straight down the main corridor to the steps leading up to the yard. Their movement was more chaotic than anything she'd experienced before—prisoners pushing and shoving, the hall clogging with bodies in a frantic rush. A palpable sense of panic filled the air, as if failing to move fast enough carried real consequences. By the time Arya reached the grass, lines of prisoners were already forming. She followed Miell to the third line and kneeled beside him in the muddy grass. The woman who knelt to her left pressed in close and Arya caught a waft of body odour as she tried to shift away, wary of potential threats. One row over, a scuffle broke out as two prisoners tried to kneel in the same spot in their hurry.

The armed guards weren't patrolling from above today. They were down in the yard, shouting for the prisoners to hurry up and dragging or kicking those not moving quickly enough into the lines.

"What's all this about?" Arya asked Miell.

"No idea." He looked around with an uneasy gaze. "It's only happened once since I've been here, and it was because the warden wanted to announce new rules after a riot broke out in one of the other cellblocks. One prisoner late to arrive was killed on the spot to set an example."

In short order, the roughly two hundred prisoners of their wing were lined up in neat rows, all kneeling, facing the southern edge of the yard that looked out over the ravine drop. The cold, damp air felt heavy. Prisoners spoke in muttered whispers.

All Arya could see was the usual thick mist. A man emerged from the top of the steps and walked briskly between the rows to stand in front of them. It was the warden from the night she'd arrived—Luri. Her lips curled in a snarl as remembered anger rose inside her. Coming to a stop, he shouted for quiet, and everyone fell silent.

"Whatever's happening, it's in our yard if the warden's here." Miell murmured, his expression tightening into fear. "Or we're the first for whatever this is."

The minute hairs on the back of Arya's neck prickled, and she was glad she and Miell were kneeling in the middle of the rows, not at the front. She'd be far too exposed up there. Luri's eyes scanned the prisoners, pausing a moment as they rested on her. She saw nothing in his expression that told her what was going on. Maybe—

A terrifying cry screamed through the morning.

All at once, every man and woman in the yard trembled, the sound pressing them into the ground, boneless with fear. Some sobbed. The sharp tang of urine edged the cool breeze.

Arya hissed. The wyvern's cry no longer affected her like it did most people. She knew what that sound meant, and it didn't bode well for her and her escape plans at all. In fact, Arya was in trouble. Her stomach sank.

Xaphistryl was coming.

Chapter 6

A shadow rippled through the fog.

Then, another cry roared out, closer this time. Louder. Steel rang as half the guards drew their swords, reacting purely on the instinct of fear. Some prisoners pressed against the ground, as if trying to hide. Sobs and moans of fear rippled through them.

The shadow grew darker, filling the mist beyond the wall. Arya caught glimpses of ink-black scales, leathery wings. And then, taloned feet flashed, reaching for the low wall, and Xaphistryl was there in all her magnificence, looming over them, wings outspread, serpentine neck flashing forward, teeth bared as she screamed her dominance to those gathered in the yard. The ground shook and stone crumbled from the wall as Xaphistryl's talons tore chunks from it. More screams scattered through the prisoners.

She was breathtakingly large. A magnificent creature.

Arya abruptly wished for Elendryl so badly it physically hurt. He was as much a part of her as her arm or leg. She'd been doing her best to supress the sense of loss as the length of their separation grew, but now, with Xaphistryl right there, she just wanted him with her.

The wyvern balanced on the wall, luminous eyes watching for any danger, tail swinging back and forth and tearing the mist to ribbons. Her rider, tiny against her size, gracefully dismounted, boots touching the top of the wall before jumping down into the mud of the yard.

Lucious Nightstalker.

Arya could *feel* his presence clear across the yard like a slap to the face. It took several deep breaths to contain her visceral reaction, a potent mix of fear and anger. Around her, the prisoners were utterly cowed, their terror so strong she could almost taste it. At her side, Miell had turned bone white, golden eyes wide.

"He's here for me, Miell, not you." She tried to reassure him.

"And I'm kneeling right fucking next to you," he hissed.

Lucius Nightstalker greeted Luri. The warden bowed deeply, and they had a brief conversation.

"He's brave," Arya murmured. "Coming in here with all this cazaix-lined stone around."

"He doesn't need magic when that bloody big wyvern is going to eat anyone that goes near him." Miell was trying to pretend calm, but his voice wobbled.

"Fair point," she said, tossing him a grin, but he didn't respond. His fear was too deep.

Even she was affected by the sight of her enemy's Valheran. She was easily four times the size of Elendryl, probably more, and her cry was powerful enough that Arya hadn't found it easy to ignore. As if she'd picked up on Arya's study, Xaphistryl's serpentine neck swung towards her, yellow eyes blinking, mouth opening lazily to reveal fangs as tall as Arya herself.

Arya stilled, but didn't look away.

Xaphistryl blinked once, slowly, then turned her head, swift as a striking snake, and closed her jaws around the woman next to Arya. Her scream was cut off as fangs ripped through the prisoner's body, hot blood spraying and splattering over Arya's left side. Everyone watched, horrified, as she chewed and swallowed.

"My apologies. Xaphistryl has flown a long distance this morning, and she's a little hungry." Lucius Nightstalker's voice carried across the yard. He ran his gaze over the rows of prisoners before it settled inexorably on Arya. She met his look unflinchingly, not allowing herself to be cowed by the power and violence flickering in his silver eyes. Inwardly, she quavered. Slowly, he raised his hand and pointed at her.

The warden gestured to the guards. They marched over to Arya, and she didn't put up a fight as two of them grabbed her arms and dragged her to her feet. She wanted nobody else coming to the Nightstalker's attention.

Neither of the guards were particularly gentle as they marched her out of the yard and through a tangled series of stairwells and corridors.

To stave off the fear of what she knew was coming, Arya paid close attention. It was the first time she'd had the opportunity to see that the guards moved between cellblocks and levels via a separate series of corridors and stairwells, and she quickly understood why nobody had ever succeeded in breaking out of Blackstone. The corridors were narrow and echoed with every footstep. It would be impossible to traverse them without being seen or heard.

Finally, she was taken up a short set of stone steps that ended in a wide landing. The door to what looked like an office—judging from its size and furnishings, probably the warden's office—stood open directly ahead of her, and a desk sat to her right, a uniformed guard sitting behind it. That guard came over at Arya's arrival, locking a pair of manacles around her wrists before waving her escort through into the office.

The guards left her standing before a large desk, then left. On the other side of the desk was a wall of glass that showed the causeway below—a stone bridge linking Blackstone to the ravine wall. It was the first time she'd gotten a glimpse of the only exit from the prison. Even though it was day, torches lined the causeway, and not a single section of it was hidden from the light of those torches. On the other side, two large watch houses—no doubt filled with Nightblades or guards—sat either side of the entrance. Beyond, a road wound into thickly forested hillside, quickly disappearing from sight in the mist.

Papers lay scattered across the warden's desk, and a warm fire crackled in the grate. Arya had just shifted her gaze to the cabinets lining the wall when the sound of shifting guards outside caught her attention. A warning. She turned just as the Nightstalker stepped into the room, closing the door behind him. A surge of remembered panic flooded her system, and Arya had to take several deep breaths to steady herself. He likely wasn't here to kill her—unless he was willing to break his word to Darmanin. But that didn't mean he couldn't hurt her. Her hands shook, and vertigo made her vision swim—her body's visceral memory of his beating.

It was all she could do to remain still and be watchful, as he placed something on the warden's desk, then leaned against the front of it, facing her. His raven hair was neatly slicked back, tunic and breeches expensive yet simple, and those silver eyes … something burned in there that made her nauseous. Despite herself, she glanced at what he'd placed on the table, then stilled. It was her cazaix blade, taken off her before she'd arrived at Blackstone.

"I wondered if you might like it back," he said. "It can kill me. But you already know that."

She forced herself to hold his gaze even though fear was slowly freezing over every cell in her body. Her blade *could* kill him. But she wasn't fool enough to think she could get to it before he stopped her. Placing it there was nothing more than a taunt. So she didn't look away. Didn't blink.

His gaze dropped to where her manacles were clinking from her shaking hands, and a little smile tugged at his mouth. "I admit, I'd hoped this place would have killed you by now. Those without allies usually don't last longer than a few days, if that."

She managed to speak evenly. "Is Darmanin aware of that line of reasoning? Or does your word mean nothing?"

"I promised not to kill you. If others do, that's not my fault. And as for Darmanin, well, let's just say he used to demand daily updates as to your still being alive, but now … well, it's far less often." Lucius smiled. "Eventually, sooner than you'd think, he'll forget all about you, and his loyalty will be to me and our House. There are substantial benefits to being by my side, and he's learning all about them."

Arya bared her teeth. "I don't *want* his loyalty. He is my enemy as much as you are. Your entire House can rot."

He leaned towards her, silver eyes alight like flame. "But you two were so close, even if you don't love him like he did you."

Arya didn't even have to lie. "I don't forgive betrayal, Lucius. Not ever."

"Spoken with genuine fury," he murmured. "I shouldn't be surprised. You Stormriders were always a rigidly honourable, unforgiving lot."

Arya said nothing, needing every bit of strength she had to hold his gaze, to keep her growing fear from showing. He was so close ... close enough to kill her with a single movement. Or inflict immeasurable pain. And holding herself back from flinching was one of the hardest things she'd ever done.

Lucius smiled, leaned back, glancing at her shaking hands again. She *hated* that she couldn't stop them. "You'll die in here, Stormrider. You know I'll make sure of that, and I'll do it in a way that doesn't break my word to Darmanin. And soon enough he won't care anyway."

Arya fought through her fear to take hold of that spark of temper always there inside her. And she used it to master her terror long enough to lean forward. "Keep sending people after me, *Lucius*, and I'll keep killing them."

His hand moved quicker than thought to close around her throat. His fingers dug into her skin as he yanked her face closer to his, so close she could feel his breath on her cheek. "You *will* die, Stormrider. You know, deep down, that you can't defeat me. It would be easier if you just gave in and joined me. We could make Andahar so powerful that none could ever threaten it. That's all I've ever wanted."

She didn't fight him, knowing that to struggle would only make him tighten his grip. "Never," she hissed as she held that silvery gaze until he snarled and backhanded her with his free hand. Pain exploded in her face. Blackness danced across her vision. She spat blood and turned back to him, taunting, "Are you going to kill me yourself?" she hissed. "Go on, do it. I dare you. Break your promise and lose Darmanin in the process."

He hit her again, and she saw stars, stumbling backwards, gasping for air. Dizziness swamped her, followed quickly by the panicked memory of the state he'd left her in last time they'd met. How weak and useless she'd been. She couldn't go back there again. If she did, she'd never get out of Blackstone. Her breath came in short, panting gasps. Her glance went to her cazaix blade, so close, yet so far.

Lucius caught the look, and twisted delight flashed in his eyes. "Darmanin fights at my side now, and your other Sky Lords ... well, let's just say that you have only yourself to rely on if you want me dead, Stormrider."

"Where are they?" she demanded, the question spilling out before she could stop it. She *did* manage to stop herself from asking why he'd also put Leanir in Blackstone, rather than killing him outright.

"I made no deal with Darmanin about keeping the rest of your *caidre* alive." He laughed, that hint of madness edging it. He stepped closer, smug enjoyment on his face. "Perhaps we could do a deal. You tell me where your child is, and I'll tell you what you want to know."

Arya bit so hard on her lip it drew blood, but the pain helped focus her, to keep any reaction from her face.

"You've been very clever in hiding the child. He or she is not in Dunidaen, I'm certain of that much," he crooned in her ear. "But that leaves fewer places you could have hidden them. My nazal are hunting, Stormrider, and a small child will be much easier to kill than you are. Tell me where, join me, and you can both live."

Terror swarmed Arya's insides, fear and grief and guilt all together. Kirin. Was he safe in Taskari? How long would it take for the nazal to find him there? But *joining* him, placing her son under his power? Never. Not while there was still breath in her body.

"No deal?" He leaned back, shrugged. "Disappointing. Well, I'll give you one piece of information for free. Your Mindbreaker is alive. For now. He hates you; I could see it all over him, and he's already agreed to work with me once before. He'd be a nice weapon to add to my already impressive collection. I don't *need* you to achieve my goals, Stormrider, remember that."

Arya shivered. Leanir would do anything for survival. Could she get to him before the Nightstalker turned him?

"One-by-one, I'm going to take away every weapon in your arsenal," he murmured. "Death by a thousand cuts, I think they call it. I only wish I could drag it out longer before your death, make it as miserable as possible."

"Why don't you?"

He chuckled. "Because I'm not a fool, and I won't be provoked into making tactical errors."

Arya almost snapped the reply that came to her, but at the last second, she managed to hold back. Because his words had made her realise something very interesting.

He smiled, as if reading every one of her thoughts, and then stood. "Enjoy the rest of your life in this hole, Stormrider. It won't be a long one." He glanced at her cazaix blade. "That will stay here, as a little reminder of how defeated you really are. I'll say hello to your child when I find them, make sure they know who is killing them and why. Or maybe I'll keep them for my own ... after all, he or she is still very young. Very malleable."

"No," she gasped.

But he was already gone.

***

The guards dragged Arya back to her cell, tossing her inside and leaving without a word. She slumped onto the shelf, reaching up to touch her swollen and bleeding lip and the cut just under her eye. They were going to hurt for a few days. She stayed huddled there, shivering, from shock. He'd bested her again. It was hard to feel as if she could ever be in a position of strength over him. And his threats against Kirin ... she had done well at compartmentalising the constant fear she felt for her son, but seeing how determined the Nightstalker was...

"That looks painful."

The barely subsiding panic surged back, and Arya stood fast, sending a stab of pain rocketing through her face. She swore, blurry gaze fixing on Arubon, who stood at the entrance to her cell. "What do you want?"

"What did the Nightstalker want with you?"

She huffed a breath, spat more blood, heart still racing. "None of your business."

Arubon's gaze looked her up and down, cataloguing her physical state. Did he look impressed to see her still standing? Or was he just bored. It was hard to tell. "And here I was thinking you were trying to make an ally of the Spider."

"Why does he want to know?"

"He wants to know about everything that happens in this prison." Arubon crossed his arms. "*Especially* when the Nightstalker has private chats with individual prisoners."

"You get me a file for those bars." She pointed. "And I'll tell you everything you want to know."

"You try and climb out of there..." He flicked a considering glance at the window. "... and you'll fall to your death. Others have tried before you. None survived. And climbing from here around to the causeway without being seen isn't possible either, even if you did have a small army to take out the Nightblades stationed at the watchtowers."

"You say that as if you've tried it."

No response. His impassive expression was genuinely impressive. She wondered what it hid. She let out a breath. "A file, and I tell you what the Nightstalker wanted."A smile full of bared teeth. "I'll be back soon."

Once he was gone, Arya reached for her map. No more waiting and planning. The Nightstalker had all but promised her death in Blackstone—and soon. She had to escape before that happened, or before his nazal found Kirin. As soon as she had the file, she needed to get through those bars and find a way to talk to Leanir.

And hope *he* didn't kill her.

Chapter 7

Arya returned from dinner that night to find a file lying under her blankets. Beside it, wrapped in cloth, was a small bundle containing a sticky substance that reeked of rat piss. Arubon had gone above and beyond—the Spider must *really* want to know about her encounter with the Nightstalker.

The moment the doors winched shut for the night she went to work, filing relentlessly, stopping only when a guard patrolled nearby. Eventually she curled up to get a couple hours sleep not long before dawn, fingers sore and blistered, her injured hand aching.

Mindful of keeping her word, she went straight to the yard after breakfast the following morning, blinking at the unexpected sunlight at the top of the steps. It was the first clear morning she'd experienced since arriving at Blackstone. Her gaze searched out Arubon, but her scanning paused when whispers began spreading through the yard like the rush of a summer breeze through the branches of the Wraith Forest.

"Stormrider."

She looked around sharply. The word sounded again, this time from a man reaching the top of the steps and passing to her right. Soon she could hear it coming from every fourth or fifth prisoner that passed her. Most had light-coloured hair. Arya moved further into the yard with caution. And as she walked, the chanting became more widespread.

"Stormrider. Stormrider. Stormrider."

She stopped, turned around in a slow circle. The prisoners were gathered in their usual huddles, or walking idly alone, but many—maybe a third—were watching her and chanting, and it was no longer a whisper.

Their voices raised in volume until the Stormrider name beat a regular rhythm into the still morning.

"Stormrider. Stormrider. Stormrider."

The chanting filled her with a surge of power—something she'd always craved, the power to make things right. But with that tantalising glimpse came guilt. She had done nothing to earn their loyalty except carry the right name.

"Miell!" Arya caught sight of the young man and waved him over. He wasn't one of the ones chanting. "What is this?"

He rolled his eyes. "You are the Stormrider." "They've known that since I won the fight with Arubon," she said.

"Yes, but now your precious riverfolk truly believe it." He huffed an impatient sigh at her puzzled look. "The Nightstalker came here for you, didn't he? Only a true Stormrider could draw his interest like that. At least, that's what they're telling themselves. None of the rest of us could give two shits."

Arya turned once again as the chants continued, all calling her name. The rhythm beat through her blood, quickening her heartbeat and flooding her with energy. Her gaze fell on Arubon, leaning against the yard wall, a couple of the Spider's men near him. His arms were crossed, and he was one of the many *not* chanting. A horn sounded, cutting across the chanting but not stopping it. Arya looked up and saw the soldiers gathering on the walls; some were knocking bows, all pointing down into the yard. The pride vanished in a flash, flooded by fear.

"Stop!" She raised her hand for silence, and the chanting stopped. Silence fell across the yard. "You will get yourselves killed. I don't want that. In here, I am nobody. That is safest for us all."

Several faces flickered with reluctance, but one by one, they glanced at the wall, then looked away, their shoulders sagging in disappointment. Whatever hope had been building in them died in an instant. Guilt twisted her stomach, but there was nothing she could do for them. Survival—and escape—had to be her priority.

Arya waited until she saw the guards lower their bows before making straight for Arubon. He waved his companions off, and without preamble,

Arya told him the conversation she'd had with the Nightstalker, leaving out the references to Kirin. He listened carefully, asked her a few questions, and then dismissed her with a gesture.

She ignored it. "I noticed you didn't join in the chanting just now. "

"Please, do go ahead and live up to all my assumptions about arrogant riverfolk," Arubon said dryly.

She probed carefully, wanting to understand more. "The marshfolk are at war with the Nightstalker, as I understand it. You don't hope for him to be unseated?"

"We will be the ones to unseat him, and then we will rule ourselves. We don't need a riverfolk Stormrider to do that for us." And with that, he pushed past her and left.

***

After that, the day passed at a crawl, miserably slow. Arya was desperate to get back to filing. She'd almost gotten through one bar the night before and hoped to have them all done in a few days' time. She spent the entire time in the yard eyeing anyone who drifted towards her, mindful of the Nightstalker's threats, but even Miell steered clear.

She forced down dinner, then paced her cell until the doors were winched shut and the guards retreated. Then she filed until her wrists and forearms ached, and her blisters broke open and bled. But she kept going. Dawn found her bleary with exhaustion, but she was through two of the bars. The pungent, sticky substance Arubon had given her now secured the bars in place, ensuring that even a strong wind wouldn't betray her handiwork to the guards.

Even so, the point of no return had passed. Discovery was inevitable; she just had to be out before it happened.

Two nights later she was through all three bars. It was near dawn by the time she finished, not enough time to go anywhere, so she let herself sleep instead. Another breakfast, another day in the yard, another dinner, then she would leave. Each minute dragged out, painfully slow. Arya was restless with worry that the bars would be disturbed, that a guard would notice them. That a prisoner would attack in a way she didn't see coming.

She was surprised it hadn't happened already and wondered if that had something to do with the Spider. She doubted the Nightstalker was unaware that Remien controlled the prison population—he likely allowed it within limits as a measure of control. It made the most sense for him to have delivered the kill order to the Spider.

But Remien wasn't hesitating out of altruism. More likely, he knew she wouldn't be easy to kill and was carefully planning a response, one she couldn't escape. And an Inkweaver wouldn't take long to devise one.

She got back to her cell after dinner to find the bars still in place, though one had shifted during the day, leaning slightly to the left. She fixed it with the last of the sticky substance, then sat on her bench, waiting for all the prisoners to return to their cells and the doors to slide closed.

Her thoughts inevitably turned to her confrontation with the Nightstalker, as they always did when she was alone.

His taunts about Kirin and her fellow Sky Lords made her ache with fear. Leanir seemed to be still alive, but the Nightstalker had intimated that Chiarn and Essa were ... Arya stopped that train of thought before it could continue. She could trust nothing the Nightstalker said. And Darmanin, well, she would deal with that situation once she was out of Blackstone.

The prisoners passing by her cell finally slowed and the cell doors winched shut. Arya's nerves pulsed. She listened to the surrounding prisoners settle in for the night.

As soon as it fell quiet, Arya arranged extra blankets on her shelf to make it look like she was sleeping on it. Then she reached up and quietly removed the bars on the window. She pulled herself through, scraping skin on the rough edges of stone, then, sitting with her legs still in her cell and her torso leaning out, she looked up at the wall above.

Leanir was on the fifth level, and she was on the third, which meant she had some climbing to do. Thanks to the map, she had a good idea where his cellblock was, but finding his cell was going to be the hard part. There was no guarantee it had a window, but tonight she planned to look for it. If she failed, then she'd have to figure out how to get into his cellblock some other way.

Below her, the drop was deep and dark, a thick mist hiding the bottom of the ravine. Feet balanced on the edge, one hand curled against the stone above, Arya placed the bars back in their spots, and then she started climbing.

It was a harder climb than the cliff below the Dreadwater Gate, but Ranier had taught them to make much more difficult climbs in their training for the run into Khadini, and Arya was not afraid of heights. Still, it made for slow progress as she sought a solid handhold on each move. Her blisters broke open against the rough stone.

She'd memorised the map and now used that mental image to move along the outside of the prison wall to where Leanir's cellblock should be. A cold, damp breeze tugged at her. One wrong move would see her plunge to her death. Her heartbeat quickened even further.

No wonder nobody had ever successfully escaped this way.

Crouching against the stone, looking along the wall where Leanir's cellblock should be, there were several cell windows, just like hers ... but she couldn't get to them

Shit.

A large gap where the wall turned inward separated her from the row of windows, too wide to bridge with a jump, even if she was willing to take that risk. Swearing, she rounded the corner into the gap, then carefully moved sideways along it to where an open-aired walkway bridged the gap between the two sections of the prison. It looked empty, unguarded at night.

Without a sound, Arya dropped to the walkway. She crouched, making sure nobody had heard her, giving her arms and legs a moment to recover from the climb, and the sting from her bloody hands to fade. Nothing moved, so she made for the door at the end. If her map was correct, beyond it was the wing that housed Leanir's cell.

This wasn't the greatest time to find out if whoever had left the map was intent on betraying her, but stymied from reaching Leanir along the outer wall, she had no choice.

A glance at the sky told her little about what time it was—the night was cloudy—but she figured she had at least another couple of hours before dawn. The door was barred from the outside, so Arya lifted the bar, placed it in the shadows so it wouldn't be easily spotted, then slipped into the dark hallway beyond.

Here Arya crouched, slowing her breathing. She couldn't access her magic inside these walls, but the bonds she shared with her *cairdre* were so fundamental, so much a part of her blood and bone, that...

She smiled in triumph. Leanir was close by; even though she couldn't reach out, or make him aware of her, she could *feel* him, just the faintest sense of his presence. She closed her eyes briefly, reorienting herself to the map she had in her head. At the end of the corridor was a guard station. Arya hoped they'd already done their nightly patrol.

Arya moved along the wall where the shadows were deepest, her eyes trained on the end of the corridor where the guards could appear at any moment. Eventually, she made it to the corner and ducked around. A long corridor of cells stretched out before her, but now Leanir's presence was as clear as day—in the cell at the end to her left. Just like her cellblock, however, gates were winched closed at the entry to the corridor. And the few windows around her were all barred.

Raven's balls.

Arya backtracked, returning to the walkway. This time she scrambled up the wall above the doorway onto the roof and then ran across it, coming to a stop right above the window where Leanir's cell should be.

And she started climbing down.

The Shadeweaver assassin had heard her coming and was awake, at a safe distance from the window, watching carefully as she crammed herself onto the ledge and stared inside. His dark eyes glimmered at her with a mixture of suspicion and surprise as he recognised her. He let out a filthy curse word, then, "How did you manage to get to my window?"

She huffed. "I'm surprised you didn't beat me to it."

"If I'd known where your cell was, I would have, if only to put a knife in your heart," he snarled. "I can't believe you'd risk this when the Nightstalker was just here."

"He left two days ago. Multiple prisoners in the yard saw him fly off on Xaphistryl." She'd made sure of that before venturing out of her cell.

"Yes." Leanir took a wary step closer. "But he brought Darmanin and Zaphirdryl with him, and nobody has seen *them* fly off yet."

Arya froze. "What?" Word of that had *not* reached her wing. Although it made sense that the Nightstalker wouldn't let Darmanin anywhere near her. Not until he could be sure he'd won his heir's loyalty.

"The Nightstalker visited your cellblock, but Darmanin visited others." Leanir glanced over his shoulder. "*And* spent a lot of time with the warden, I hear."

Arya glanced wildly to her left and right, as if Darmanin were suddenly going to appear on the wall beside her. How had she not known he was here? She took a deep breath, trying to calm her racing heart. "Why did the Nightstalker bring him? Has he spoken to you?"

"I gather the Nightstalker does regular inspections of this place—the guards seem curious about the visits, but are too scared to ask him why he comes so often." Leanir's mouth curled in disgust.

Her gaze narrowed. "But neither he nor Darmanin have spoken to you?"

"No."

Suspicion rippled through her. "The Nightstalker made sure to have a nice little chat with me before he left. Why would he single me out and not you?"

"Maybe he likes you better," Leanir snapped. "I can't dream-walk anyone in here to know their thoughts, remember?"

It was on the tip of her tongue to tell him the Nightstalker had claimed to want to turn Leanir into a weapon against her. And if that was true, why hadn't he spoken to Leanir during his visit? Or had he, and Leanir was lying, already turned? Arya swore under her breath. She couldn't trust either of them to tell her the truth.

"All right, forget about the Nightstalker and Dar. Are you okay?"

Rage kindled in his dark eyes. "You don't give two shits about my wellbeing, Raider. We can discuss what you *actually* want when the Nightstalker's heir isn't breathing down our necks. You've been here too long already."

She ignored him. "The prisoner who sent the message to Miell about you, you know who he is?"

"He says Miell is a friend, but there's a lot he isn't saying. He's something called a horselord though—there are a lot of them in this block."

"Help him as much as you can, it's the only way we have of communicating apart from me climbing over half the prison to get here." Arya hesitated. "Do you ... have you heard anything about the others?"

He was silent so long she wasn't sure he was going to answer. "I was captured almost immediately after you, but I saw Chiarn and Essa fleeing. They might have been caught too, but they were free when I last saw them."

She gripped the bars, trying to keep herself from thinking the worst. "Thank you, Leanir. I'll be back soon."

"I'd prefer if you weren't," he said.

She grinned, flipped him the file she'd carried in her tunic. "Get to work on these bars. You'll need to be able to get out this window."

"Why?"

"Why do you think, Leanir?"

***

Arya made it back to her cell without incident and scrambled inside as quietly as she could before replacing the bars and dropping to her shelf in exhaustion. Sweat slicked her skin, her arms trembled with fatigue, and her hands were covered with fresh scrapes and weeping blisters. She tried to sleep, but learning of Darmanin's unexpected appearance had left her unsettled and shaken; she'd not let herself think about him while she'd been in prison.

She eventually fell into a fitful sleep, only to be woken by the squeal of the cell doors being winched open. She stayed curled under her blankets until most of the prisoners had shuffled past her door, then reluctantly got up and joined them. Her stomach grumbled with hunger after the night's exertions, and she ate the too-small breakfast quickly.

At least the fact she'd successfully reached Leanir meant she'd made progress. The passage of time continued to weigh heavily, each hour that passed bringing the inevitable discovery or death. If she were killed before she could enact an escape plan...

She needed to buy herself some time.

Once in the yard for the day, Arya approached Arubon where he leaned nonchalantly against the wall. Today he was alone. He stared at her blistered fingers. "You have a death wish, Stormrider?"

"I assume you're referring to the fact that the Nightstalker has given the Spider orders to kill me, and that by coming right up to you, I'm making things easier for him?"

Arubon blinked. Showed no other reaction. "You seem to have a firm grasp of the situation."

"What's the timeframe?"

"The Spider does not share the inner workings of his plans with me. But he was left with the strong impression he should act ... quickly."

Arya looked up at Arubon's brown eyes; they were flat and uncompromising, but there was something about this man that told her there was more to him. As always, she trusted her instincts, and they told her Arubon was a wild card that could prove important. "I would appreciate it if you ignored any orders your boss gives you to kill me."

"That would result in my death instead of yours. So, no."

Arya considered. She hadn't expected Arubon to agree, so it was time to play her trump card she'd been holding in reserve for this moment. "Tell the Spider to give me three more days before enacting the bounty. In return, I'll give him the thing he wants most."

"Which is what, exactly?"

"That's between me and him. Three days. You keep me alive that long."

Arubon straightened from the wall, glancing around the yard as he brushed an invisible speck of lint from his shirt. When he turned to look back at her, that cold smile was on his face. "I'll discuss your proposal with the Spider, but I'm hoping he says no."

***

Arya returned to her usual place along the yard wall, but wasn't there long when Miell approached. He had his hands in his pockets, slouching, perfecting an air of lazy idleness. She said nothing as he settled next to her, gaze on the guards patrolling above the wall on the other side of the yard. "You know, there's a rumour this place wasn't originally intended to be a prison. That it was built to be a guard post, watching over whatever lurked down in that gorge."

She lifted an eyebrow. "A history lesson, Miell?"

He shrugged. "You've no doubt noticed by now that this wing of Blackstone is comprised primarily of marshfolk."

"Riverfolk are certainly in the minority, and you appear to be the only horselord," she said. "I'm guessing that was why I was placed in here. You too, even though you refuse to tell me *why*."

He ignored that. "No arwein, either."

Arya cursed. "What's an arwein?"

"It's what we call those who are tribeless." Miell shrugged. "Nobody has any fight with them."

She hadn't missed the edge of condescension in his tone. "Because they're considered inferior? What makes one a horselord or a marshfolk or a riverfolk versus an arwein anyway? I spotted a marshfolk yesterday with suspiciously light-coloured hair."

Miell's mouth thinned, golden eyes flashing. "Marshfolk are marked by their tribal tattoos, but for the rest of us it's in our blood. Our tribe tells people who we are, what we're about, where we're from. It's the most important thing about us. It is our identity."

"Yeah, and it seems to make for a real happy society," she muttered. "How did the arwein miss out on getting a special club to belong to?"

Miell spat, as if that were answer enough to her question. Then he cast her a sidelong glance. "Why did the Nightstalker leave you alive?"

Arya narrowed her gaze. "An answer for an answer, Miell. Why are you in here?"

His golden eyes, almost burning, watched her as he clearly teetered on the edge of saying *something* interesting. But at the last moment that lazy smile spread over his face. "Maybe one day I'll tell you."

"Then you can keep on wondering why the Nightstalker left me alive." He wasn't getting anything out of her if he refused to talk.

He crossed his arms over his chest, gaze going back to the guards. "There're more marshfolk than any other tribe in Blackstone, because of the ongoing war in the Marshlands. All captured warriors are imprisoned here. I'm not sure why he doesn't just execute them."

"And you're telling me this today because?"

"We're thinking about it." He pushed off the wall, started walking off.

She called after him. "Who is thinking about what?"

"The horselords. A formal alliance," he tossed over his shoulder.

His words should have pleased her, but all Arya felt was defeated, and not only because an alliance was no longer any use; she'd either be dead or free of this place in three days. She'd come to Blackstone to find Remien, to get him out so that she could access his knowledge, learn how to defeat the Nightstalker. But she'd learned more than she'd bargained for.

Andahar was riven by division, and it was nothing like the prideful but mostly superficial friction between States and warlords in Dunidae society. Until Mathas Crowtalon had come along, the warlords would have united without thought against a common foe.

It wasn't going to be as simple as killing Lucius Nightstalker. If that was all she did, she'd be inheriting his civil war with a large portion of the country, while the rest of it was busy thinking they were better than everyone else and acting accordingly.

Arya rubbed a hand over her tired eyes. She'd thought she'd won a victory, finding Remien. That her gamble had paid off. But she'd only learned how much more complicated her situation was.

It felt like taking several steps backward.

Chapter 8

When Arya returned to her cell after dinner, she found a package wrapped in paper lying underneath her blankets. It had been weighted down with a small piece of flint. She picked it up, curling her palm around its sharp edges, and feeling a smile tug at her mouth. She sat down and unwrapped the package. Inside was a small knife.

Her mysterious friend had left another gift. Remien? He was the only one with the resources inside Blackstone to help her, although his assistance would never be altruistic. And the map had arrived in her cell during their first meeting, before he'd known her, and before she'd promised him anything.

She quickly pulled up the right leg of her pants, and slid the knife into her boot, pulling the material back down to cover it. The weapon made her feel more secure. Now she could properly defend herself. Then she tucked the flint into her tunic pocket with the map. Exhausted from multiple nights of little sleep, she sank back on the shelf, refusing to close her eyes in case she fell asleep. Elendryl filled her thoughts; it was growing increasingly difficult being separated from him, like she was missing some of herself when she couldn't connect with him. She felt the same way about Kirin, and Rorin and Essa.

The screeching of the winch broke her from her thoughts, and she once again waited for her fellow prisoners to settle.

And then she was out the window again.

***

Leanir was waiting when she arrived at his cell window, so still and quiet that it took her a moment to see him through the bars. Exhaustion trembled in her muscles and her hands ached and stung, so she didn't waste time in preamble. "We're breaking out in two nights."

"Good luck with that."

"Nice try, Leanir, but I know how badly you hate being trapped. It's the one thing we have in common. You might hate me, you might distrust me, but you're smart enough to know I'm your way out of here."

His eyes glimmered but he said nothing.

"I'm offering a temporary alliance until we're safely away," she said. "My word on it. I've never broken my word to you before."

The silence lengthened, but eventually he gave a sharp nod. "Why so soon?"

"The Nightstalker left behind a parting gift," she said. "A bounty on my life, and likely yours too." That's if he hadn't already turned Leanir and the assassin was now playing her. "I've won us a three-day reprieve, but after that we can count the remainder of our lives in days, if not hours."

"He set the Spider on us?" Leanir asked, life flashing into his eyes. Maybe the Nightstalker *hadn't* yet tried to recruit him. But Leanir could just be hiding himself flawlessly.

"You've heard of him?"

Leanir snorted. "I'm a Shadeweaver assassin, Arya. You think I didn't immediately learn about the criminal running this prison. How did you manage to get a reprieve?"

"He's Ranier's elder brother."

A well of silence, and Arya waited. One breath. Two. Then:

"You got yourself in here on purpose." His voice was cold, deadly. "Didn't you?"

"The knowledge of House Inkweaver is critical if I want to defeat the Nightstalker. Ranier doesn't talk enough for my liking. I learned he had a brother, heir to the Inkweaver House, so I came looking."

"I don't give two shits for destroying the Nightstalker," Leanir seethed.

"And you can continue to go right on not caring about the Nightstalker as soon as we're out of here."

"Except that I'm only *in* here because of you. Because you forced me to face the Nightstalker as part of your plan to be deliberately captured, *after* you deliberately betrayed my existence to him."

"I got myself captured. You did *your* bit all on your own," she snapped, temper rising. "You could have escaped like Chiarn and Essa. I wasn't stopping you. But maybe you're not as good as you think you are."

Rage flashed in Leanir's eyes. "How do you plan on accomplishing an escape? The way I hear it, nobody has ever gotten out of Blackstone."

"I don't think anybody has ever tried to hold a Sky Lord in here before."

"Do I need to remind you that we're not Sky Lords with that blasted stone surrounding the place."

She raised an eyebrow. "You mean to tell me that these four walls can successfully hold one of the most dangerous assassins I've ever met?"

"Appealing to my pride isn't going to override my grip on reality," he said pointedly. "But fine. If I agree to this madness, what would I need to do?"

"You need to be out of your cell when I come for you. How's the filing going?"

"If you stop wasting my time with chatter, I can be through by tomorrow night."

"Good. Here's where you're going to meet me once you're out." She showed him the map and waited patiently while he memorised it. "Make sure your shelf looks like someone is sleeping on it, so the alarm isn't raised too early. I'll meet you at midnight."

He watched her for a moment with that flat look. "You'd have a much better chance of getting out if you didn't have to come for me as well."

His tone had been as flat as his look, but she sensed a test in there. So, she didn't hesitate, just answered honestly. "Debateable."

"From your perspective, you're far better off leaving me here to rot. I'm no threat to you that way."

Again, she went with honesty. "You're one of my Sky Lords."

"Rubbish," he hissed. "You were on the verge of killing me, back in Gateport, if I refused to join you. We both know you meant it."

"You mistake me, as you often do." Arya leaned closer. "I don't trust you; you're a cold-blooded killer who doesn't care about anything but himself and seems to experience no remorse for his actions." She paused. "But getting out of here will be challenging in the extreme, and when I weigh everything up, I judge I'll have a better chance of success if you're with me."

"Always so mercenary, Raider." He leaned back, a slight shift in his demeanour telling her he was satisfied with that response. "I'll see you at midnight in two nights."

***

Arubon appeared at Arya's cell soon after the doors opened the next morning. Without speaking, he led her out of the cellblock and through the twisting series of corridors and stairwells to the Spider's quarters.

Remien was sitting in his chair, reading a different book, as Arubon showed her in. She stopped him from leaving. "You get to stay for this bit, Arubon."

He glanced at the Spider and closed the door behind them. Arya readied herself to move at an instant. It was a calculated risk, allowing herself to be closed in a room with the Spider's pet killer. She was gambling the Spider's curiosity would stay his hand long enough for her to negotiate.

Remien tore his gaze from the book with a theatrical sigh. When he did, his gaze went straight to the bloodied blisters on her hands before lifting to meet hers. Interesting. Arubon had passed on that little detail. "You keep telling me you have something I want. Spit it out before I lose my patience and have Arubon carry out the Nightstalker's orders right here."

"How many years have you been in here, Remien? Forty-six, give or take a few months?"

He stared, expressionless.

She held his stare. "What you want most of all is your freedom. I can give it to you."

Remien remained very still, *too* still, one hand resting on the open book in his lap, the other on the arm of his chair. When he did speak, it was a lazy drawl. "Oh, I'm going to need a lot more detail than that."

"It's simple. In return for all the knowledge of House Inkweaver, delivered *whenever* I ask for it, I will break you out of here, restore your freedom, and keep you under my protection."

"And how exactly are you planning on accomplishing something no Blackstone prisoner ever has before?"

"You leave that to me." She crossed her arms. "I don't trust you—you're the one carrying out the bounty on my life, remember? But I give you my word. I will get you out of here."

"And if I were to agree to your proposal?"

"First, you'd have to tell me where we go once we're out of the prison. It's the first of several things I need to know, and why I got myself locked up in here. Where can we go that the Nightstalker and his nazal, or his spies, can't find or track me, my wyvern, or any of my Sky Lords?"

"Your question assumes there is such a place."

She merely smiled at him. It *was* an assumption. A big one. It had been the biggest gamble she'd ever made, getting herself placed in Blackstone.

"*If* there was such a place, it would be quite a distance from here. Yet even if you managed to get us out of these walls, the guards will be after us, on horseback, quick as a blink."

Her shoulders relaxed. There *was* somewhere. Thank everything. "Did I mention I have a wyvern?"

He cocked his head. "Where *is* my darling brother these days?"

Taken aback by the sharp segue, Arya shrugged, unwilling to let on that she had no idea where Ranier was, and feared he may be captured or dead. "A long way from here."

"Is he pulling your strings, Stormrider?"

Arya chuckled. "Would it matter if he was? Either way, you get out of here."

"If you don't think it matters, then you don't know my brother," Remien murmured.

She sighed. "Nobody pulls my strings, Remien. You'll soon learn that about me." She paused, sensing she didn't quite have him. "Look, here it is, plain and simple. You have the resources to get us to the prison exit and acquire what I need. But there you get unstuck. *I'm* the missing piece that can get you safely away—with my magic and my wyvern. We need each other, Remien."

Remien was silent for a long, long, time, watching her, testing her, presumably. She forced herself to stand and weather his gaze without moving a muscle or losing her veneer of confidence. Eventually, his gaze flicked to Arubon, then back to her. "What do I have to do?"

"Two things. First, I need you to acquire something sitting in the warden's office." She pulled the map out from her pocket, ignoring his look of surprise at the sight of it. Interesting, Remien *hadn't* been her mysterious benefactor. "Second, can both of you be there at midnight tomorrow night?" She pointed at a spot on the map.

At her side, Arubon started when she said 'both', and shot her a questioning look, but she ignored it, her gaze on the Spider.

"If you plan to wait until after midnight to move, we won't have long before they notice us missing and send a pursuit," Remien said. "Do you even know where your wyvern is and how quickly he can get here?"

"No and no." She smiled, all teeth. "But once we're far enough from these walls, I'll also have access to my magic." And Leanir would have his.

Another silence fell.

Arubon broke it, speaking pointedly to his boss. "You can't take something out of the warden's office without him noticing, and if this goes wrong, and that's likely, you'll be killed. All of us will."

Arya looked at the man. "Nobody is making you come. You can choose to stay."

"Why *is* he coming?" Remien asked mildly.

Arya snorted. "So much loyalty to your people, Remien. He's coming because I said he could."

"I'll be at that place at midnight. And I'll get what you asked for. We'll linger only a short time," Remien said, gaze returning to his book as if they were discussing his choice of shirt colour. "After that, I'll assume things have gone wrong and we'll return to our cells. And the bounty on you will be enacted the following morning."

She folded the map away. "Then I'll see you at midnight tomorrow."

***

"Why would you take me with you?" Arubon demanded in a low voice as soon as they left.

"Would you believe me if I said it's because Remien is an old man, and *I* don't want to be the one carrying him when he gets too tired?"

He gave her a look.

"I'm taking you in return for a favour you're going to do me."

"What favour?"

"It should actually be pretty simple for you." She explained what she needed of him.

"Very simple. But why would I help a—"

"Because you want to get out of here."

"You're not like any riverfolk I've ever known, despite what the marshfolk are saying about you," he murmured. She said nothing and after a moment he nodded, jaw still tight. "Deal."

"Good. Now, tell me, Arubon, how did you end up in Blackstone?"

"That's none of your business."

She came to a stop as they reached the steps up to the yard. "But you're marshfolk, right? You won't have far to travel to reach safety once we're out of here." The Marshlands started at the western edge of the Horn.

"Stop fishing for information," he snapped. "Now, if you're done wasting my time, we should not be seen together any longer."

Arya watched him leave. Something continued to niggle at her about Arubon. He appeared to be nothing more than the Spider's personal killer; he acted and behaved like one and seemed to have little remorse or softness within him. Yet, there was something else there she couldn't quite get a grasp on. In comparison, Miell was much easier to read.

After dinner, Arya returned to her cell, intent on getting a good night's sleep so that she'd be well-rested for the escape. But as she pulled back her bedding, she found another paper-wrapped package tucked beneath it. Inside was a thick coil of rope.

Arubon was going above and beyond—again. But why? She had been surprised he agreed to their escape at all, given how suspicious and calculating he was. The odds weren't exactly in their favour. Or maybe the rope wasn't from him. Another smile tugged at her mouth.

Running her fingers over the coarse fibers, Arya reached into her tunic pocket and pulled out the small piece of flint. Almost unconsciously, she tossed it in the air a few times before tucking it away and stretching out on the shelf, letting exhaustion settle over her.

Sleep eluded her, her mind endlessly cycling through the escape plan, searching for weaknesses, trying to account for every possibility. If everything went right, by tomorrow night, she'd be free.

Free to see Elendryl, to ride the winds with him. Free to find Rorin, Essa and Chiarn and hold them close. The thought sent a swell of emotion through her, and tears welled in her eyes. That hope—so bright, so fragile—felt almost too delicate to grasp.

She missed her family.

For the first time in a long while, Arya wished she was still Arya Ravenstrike. No grand destiny pressing down on her shoulders. No impossible adversaries to defeat. Just a general leading an army she loved, serving a warlord she loved, with her brother at her side and her family always within reach.

That thought—warm and bittersweet—finally carried her into sleep.

Chapter 9

The following day in the yard dragged. Arya spotted Arubon in the distance, but he ignored her. She tried to keep the impatience out of her bearing as she followed the prisoners into the dining hall for dinner, forcing herself to eat every bite of the food even through her stomach was in knots. When the bell rang for them to return to their cells, she deliberately came up alongside Miell and whispered. "Drop to the end of the line, immediately ahead of me, then go straight into my cell and crawl under the sleeping shelf, as close to the wall as you can get. Do it quickly but confidently. I'll cover you."

"What—"

"No talking," she hissed. "Stay calm and do as I say. Your life depends on it. I'll protect you tonight." Arya had thought about what to say to get Miell to do as she asked and had settled on a pretend threat to his life. It was what he feared most. She hadn't been willing to risk telling him her escape plans. She didn't trust him enough not to tell the guards.

Why was she even bringing him with her? It was a question she'd gone round and round on in her head, knowing it would be far less risky to leave him behind. But he'd given away a lot about himself without realising, enough that if Arya's suspicions about him were right, then he could be a key tool that she might need in the future.

His face turned sickly pale, but he kept his gaze ahead and said nothing further. His hands clenched and unclenched as they walked. When they reached the cellblock, her heartrate kicked up, but apart from a faint hesitation, Miell ducked quickly into her cell rather than his own.

At the same moment, Arya stretched out her arms in a yawn, hopefully concealing his movement from anyone watching. She slowed her own approach before turning into her cell. Once inside, she hovered near the entrance—if a guard decide to do a final check, she wanted his attention on her, not over near her sleeping bench. Although the light was dim enough, even she couldn't see Miell under there from where she stood.

But no guard came, and soon after the cellblock doors winched closed.

"They're going to see I'm not in my cell as soon as the first patrol happens before midnight," Miell hissed.

"No, they won't. I've arranged it so your shelf looks like someone is sleeping on it."

"Why? Who's coming after me? And how do *you* know about it?"

"Nobody is coming after you. I just told you that to get you in here. We're breaking out tonight, Miell."

"*What?*" A thump, followed by a curse, as if Miell had hit his head on the top of the shelf.

"Stay quiet while the prisoners settle," she murmured. "We don't want anyone raising the alarm."

The usual sounds of prisoners settling in for the night drifted through the corridor. Arya waited by the doors until everything was quiet. Then, she went to the shelf, reached under the blankets, and pulled out the rope, winding it around her middle. Next, she arranged her bedding, so it looked like she was sleeping in it. "You can come out now, but keep your voice down."

"What are you *doing?*" Miell whispered as he scrambled out from under the shelf.

"How good are you at climbing?"

He merely stared at her, golden eyes flashing with a combination of confusion and fear. "I'm not going to—"

"*Climbing*, Miell, can you?" she hissed.

His jaw tightened. "I can balance on two feet on a galloping horse, and I've climbed a tree or two in my time. What does that have to do with anything?"

It was about what she'd expected. "I'm going out the window, climbing up, and tying a rope for you to use to follow me. Clear?"

"Arya, what—" His eyebrows shot upwards as she pulled the bars out from her window.

"Shush!" she hissed

He started furiously, "I'm not—"

She slapped a hand over his mouth and an arm tight around his neck to keep him still, then spoke coldly into his ear. "I'm escaping tonight, and I'm taking you with me. But if you don't stop making enough noise to rouse the guards, I'll knock you out cold instead. Is that clear enough?"

Miell had gone completely still as she told him of her intentions, and now his golden eyes shone with a combination of hope and fear. "Why would you risk bringing me? You owe me nothing."

"Because I want to," she hissed. "Now stay quiet and don't move. As soon as you see the rope drop outside the window, you start climbing. Clear?"

He gave a shaky nod.

Arya went out the window and made the painstaking climb up to the roof, glad of the soupy mist filling the sky and concealing her from any watchers. Once there, she carefully tied the rope around a crenelation, tested it, then let it drop. Moments later, the rope wobbled. She waited, watching until Miell's tousled head appeared, slowly climbing towards her. He was panting and trembling by the time he reached her, but stayed quiet as he scrambled over the top.

She untied the rope, wrapped it around her waist, then helped Miell to his feet and set off across the roof. The route across rooftops to the walkway she'd found that first night was relatively simple and they were soon dropping down onto the walkway and heading for the barred door at the end. The bar lifted out of the bracket easily. When she opened the door, two figures immediately came through—Remien and Arubon. Arya lifted a hand for quiet, then closed the door behind them and replaced the bar. Without a word, Remien handed her a long sheathed blade, and Arya couldn't help the grin that crossed her face. He'd gotten her cazaix sword from the warden's office.

"We'd better be out of here by morning, when he's going to notice that's gone," Remien murmured.

Before she could reply, Leanir dropped silently from the roof above the door.

All four of her escape companions eyed each other warily, suspicious enough she guessed that only a fear of being overheard by guards was stopping them from demanding to know who each other was. Both Arubon and Leanir shifted so their backs weren't facing any of the others.

"Who's he?" both Arubon and Leanir demanded at once in a hissed whisper. Miell cowered from both.

She had to stifle another smile as she buckled her sword on. "Everyone here is breaking out with me, that's all I'm going to say. Introductions can come later." She pointed to the door on the opposite side of the walkway. "We're going straight from here to the causeway, across it, then we wait for my wyvern on the other side."

"Suicide." Remien drawled. His entire manner was of a gentleman going for a walk through the park on a fine evening. "Do you have any idea how many guards are posted in the entry cavern where the causeway terminates?"

"Leanir and I can take care of them, as long as we take them by surprise."

Arubon scowled. "Even if you're right, then what? The rest of the hundreds of guards posted here will mount up and chase us down in minutes, not to mention those stationed at the watchhouses on the *other* side of the causeway."

"As soon as we're across, we'll divert off the road and into the forest, which will slow the horses, *if* they can find our tracks in the dark."

"It would be safer to climb down to the ravine floor below and make our way out that way," Leanir murmured. "They couldn't get their horses down there after us."

"For you and I, yes, but not for our companions. Neither Remien nor Miell will make that long of a climb, even if we had the time using only one rope."

Remien snorted, "Even if I was a spry as a twenty year old, I wouldn't be going down to that ravine floor, my arrogant Stormrider."

She didn't bother asking why. "Can you get us to the causeway from here? I'm assuming you've had things in place for just an escape attempt like this to ease our way through?"

Arubon opened his mouth to protest further, but Remien made a cutting motion with his hand. "I can get you to the prison entry only. You will find the full complement of guards there. You'd damned well better be right about your ability to take them out."

Arya flicked a glance at Leanir. He merely smirked.

"Get us there and we'll take care of the rest."

Whatever he'd arranged to clear his movement out of his cellblock, Remien was able to take them through corridors and stairwells free of any guards. They reached the bottom of a narrow stairwell that looked out over the entry hall of the prison. There was no door, only the wide causeway leading out into the darkness. Twelve Nightblades stood guard either side of where the causeway ended, half of them facing inward, half outwards.

Stalls housing saddled horses ran along the wall directly opposite where they crouched—ten horses by Arya's count. Four more guards stood at a large, well-lit corridor leading away from the entry hall into the prison. Multiple torches lit the space, though their light couldn't penetrate far into the mist beyond the entry. A hissing rain fell outside, tapping on the stone surface of the causeway.

Arya's roving gaze moved from the entry hall upwards, to where another guard post sat a level above, directly across from where they crouched. She counted several more guards, though only one appeared to be paying attention to what was happening in the cavern below. She gestured for Leanir to move closer. "Best approach?"

"I can take down the four at the interior entry fast, but not without alerting the guards on the causeway—so you'll need to hit them at the same time."

She arched an eyebrow. "You want me to take on twelve guards while you take four?"

"You're the one with a sword." He gave her a disgusted look. "I can't believe you took it into battle against the Nightstalker knowing you were going to lose and he would take it from you."

"I had to sell it, Leanir." Still, she'd hated the thought of losing the blade she'd won from her run through the Dreadwater Gate. Arya pointed to Miell. "While all that's going on, you fetch four horses and bring them to the causeway entrance. Arubon, you cover him. Remien, you'll wait here until the guards are all down, then join us at the horses—you'll be riding double with the horselord here. Everyone clear?"

Miell's eyes flashed golden. "I'm not riding with—"

"You'll do as you're told, or you can stay behind," Leanir hissed.

Miell paled dramatically and even crawled back a few paces. "Understood," he managed.

"I appreciate not needing to risk my life in any way," Remien said. "But if any of you betray me at a critical moment, you will regret it. I hope that's clear."

"Threaten all you like, old man, but I'll be looking after myself alone," Leanir said.

"I'll be making sure everyone gets out," Arya jumped in before an argument could break out, or someone decided to bail at the last moment. "Let's go."

Arya and Leanir broke left and right at the same time, keeping to the shadows along the side wall, moving low and fast. Steps away from the causeway opening, she drew her gleaming blue blade. The nearest guard turned, picking up her movement in the heartbeat before she was on him. Stunned surprise flashed on his face as she thrust her sword through his neck. He crumpled, gurgling, and as he did, she withdrew her sword with a spray of hot blood and brought it up and ready to counter the blow from the next guard.

Shouts of alarm erupted through the cavern, mixed with clashing steel as Arya laid into the guards in earnest, using surprise and aggression to take them down before they realised what was going on. It felt good to have her sword in her hand again. She swung and slashed with ferocity. Blood and gore spattered her face and tunic, her breathing came fast, and the familiar burn in her muscles was sheer delight.

Even so, ten was too many. She found herself on the back foot as the soldiers gathered themselves. Then Leanir was there, hitting them from behind. For a few moments her entire world was clanging steel, grunts of pain, and the burn in her arms of swinging a blade.

Then she was face to face with Leanir, ten guards dead at their feet.

His snarling grin was vicious, victorious.

And so was hers.

He was hers, and she was his, and they were cairdre!

Cantering hooves snapped her back to the present. Miell raced towards them on horseback, three horses trailing on a lead rope he'd managed to fashion. More shouts echoed through the space and then an alarm bell sounded, deep and sonorous. The guard post above the entry was a hive of activity.

They'd be down on the floor with them in seconds.

"Mount!" Arya shouted.

Leanir was already doing that, swinging into the saddle, taking the reins from Miell. Arubon appeared, helping Remien scramble up behind Miell before mounting his own horse.

Arya kept shouting orders as she swung onto the final horse. "I'm going first—the guards at the other end will have limited visibility in the dark and rain but they're still going to fire at us. Ride low in the saddle and make yourself as small a target as possible."

With that, Arya spurred her mount out onto the causeway. The rain hit her in the face the moment she left the shelter of the entry. The mist was so thick she could barely see more than a handspan ahead and was forced to keep her horse to a slow canter to avoid the creature slipping and falling. But by the time they were halfway across, the flickering lights of the torches on the guard towers either side of the end of the causeway were visible, and the alarm bell was echoing loudly through the night.

Then the arrows started hissing towards them. She swore, hunkered as low as she could over the horse's neck. They were mostly going wide—the archers unable to see their targets properly in the weather. Presumably recognising this, the hail of arrows stopped, and Nightblades poured out of the watch houses, lining up across the causeway to block their exit. Arya lifted the sword she'd stolen, and drove her horse straight at them, hoping Leanir was at her back and Miell was keeping Remien safe.

They needed to break through before the wall of soldiers solidified.

A soldier came at her, his sword flashing. She avoided his thrust, but her horse slipped on the wet ground, and she fell from the saddle. Rolling to avoid the solder's thrusts, she stabbed at his leg and managed to slash her blade along his calf. He yelled out in pain and hopped backwards. Arya threw herself against him, tackling him to the ground. They wrestled for a few desperate moments, but eventually Arya managed to get into a position where she could drive her knife into his heart.

Scrambling to her feet, she reached for the reins. Voices sounded in the night, approaching quickly from both sides. Arrows started flying past her, making soft hissing sounds as they went by. One nicked her arm, but she got back into the saddle and urged the horse on. Leanir had killed three Nightblades, forcing a momentary gap, and Arubon and Miell spurred their horses after him through it. Arya followed. In moments they were off the causeway and onto the road leading away from Blackstone.

More Nightblades waited for them beyond the first line, spread out in a tight formation, preventing them breaking off the road into the trees.

Shit.

Arya reined in, sword lifted, breathing hard. "Leanir, cover our backs. I'll take front. Arubon, you keep the other two safe in the middle."

She could only hope they obeyed, because there was no more time for words. The Nightblades converged on them, seeking to overwhelm them with numbers. Arya and her companions were quickly encircled. Arya fought desperately, using her horse the way she once had as a Raider, as another weapon in battle.

It wasn't going to work. She knew that after only a few moments. If they didn't find a way to break through, they were doing to be cut down.

She looked around desperately, wondering how to get far enough from the blasted cazaix stone that she could summon magic. Or Elendryl.

"Arya!" Leanir shouted, calm, but pointed. He'd read the same thing she had.

"Yes, I know. What if we try—"

Arya did a double take as a blur of movement came from the area of forest she'd just scanned. It resolved into a flurry of arrows, each finding its mark in a Nightblade's throat or chest. And all aimed at one section of the circle.

Gambling that the archer was a helper and not a foe, Arya bellowed, "On me!" She redirected her attack to fight through the now-weakened area of the Nightblades encircling them. "Force a path through!"

And as the horse ploughed into the first Nightblade, the arrows stopped and a rider emerged from the trees, twin short swords in each hand, a maelstrom of flashing blades as they attacked the Nightblades from behind, quick and merciless.

Rain and blood splattered as Arya swung and thrust, lost in the focus of battle, teeth bared. And then she was through, and their unexpected helper sat his horse before her, swords dripping blood, eyes dark, jagged scar from eyebrow to mouth.

"Ranier!?" She couldn't believe her eyes.

For the briefest fraction of a second, Ranier swept his gaze over Arya and her companions. His mouth twisted, almost into a smile, then his attention was fully on Arya. "Into the trees," he snapped. "We need cover. I'll lead the way—stay close behind."

With that, he spurred his horse off the road and into the trees. Arya spun, waving Arubon and Miell and their horses after Ranier while Leanir, bringing up the rear as she'd asked, fought his way clear. Arubon hesitated. "They'll be after us on horseback. And they'll use dogs."

"Who was that?" Remien cut over him, gaze on the darkness between the trees where Ranier's horse had disappeared, arms wrapped tightly around Miell's wiry form as he fought not to fall.

"Just move, both of you, before we lose him. Go!"

As soon as their horses plunged into the dark and dripping trees, Leanir got clear and followed at a gallop, Arya falling in behind him. Up ahead, she could just make out Ranier hunched low over his own horse, leading the way upwards.

With each stride of her horse away from Blackstone, Arya began to feel sharper, more alert, a numbness over her senses she'd grown accustomed to in Blackstone fading away. Her magic came first as a spark of electricity, deep inside. She grabbed at it too late. But then it came back, flaring into an ember this time.

And then a conflagration.

Arya sucked in a shocked, gasping, breath, and then her magic roared back through her. She reached without thought for Elendryl, and the heady rush of relief and potent power she felt as their connection snapped back into place caused her to rein her horse just in time before she fell. Even then she slid halfway out of the saddle before she was able to stop herself. The horse whinnied in fright.

"What's wrong?" Miell reined his horse to an immediate stop with a ridiculous ease that almost sent Remien behind him flying, just as Leanir let out a similar gasping cry and slumped forward in his saddle, his reins going slack.

"Are we attacked?" Arubon bellowed.

"Their magic is restored now that we are beyond the walls," Remien replied, but his gaze was still ahead, squinting through darkness and rain at Ranier's hooded figure. "Give them a moment. They'll be fine."

"*Elendryl, come! Quickly!*"

"*I COME.*"

His promise trumpeted through Arya's mind, clearing it, leaving her fresh and strong. The returning magic within her surged to its peak and then began to level out. She settled back into the saddle and looked at Leanir. "Your wyvern?"

"She's coming," he said. She couldn't see his face properly in the dark, but the Sky Lord bond between them surged with profound joy—Leanir's.

She ignored it, knowing he wouldn't want her to feel that. "Good. Come on, we need to keep ahead of the pursuing guards until the wyverns arrive."

Ranier, who'd paused ahead, was already moving again. They pushed the reluctant horses onwards through the dark and dropping trees. Arya had no idea where they were going, but it didn't matter. Elendryl was on his way, and then he'd get her to safety. She held onto her link to him tightly, refusing to let go, sharing her love and relief and joy and feeling the same in return.

The rain had turned the ground into mud, and the water funnelled along the tree branches poured down on them, adding to the deluge. Arya continuously wiped water from her eyes, and the horses kept slipping, fighting the reins. Only Miell seemed able to keep his horse moving fast and easily. It wasn't long before they heard shouts and dogs barking behind them.

"We should head south, deeper into the Horn," Arubon called out. "The terrain will make it more difficult for their horses to follow us."

"How do I know you're not leading us into a marshfolk ambush?" Miell protested.

"Harder for their horses means harder for ours too," the Spider added.

Ranier stayed silent, a dark figure well ahead of them.

Again, Arya jumped in before a full argument could break out. "We just need to stay ahead of pursuit as long as possible, it doesn't matter in what direction. Our wyverns are on their way."

"Fall in behind me then," Miell said, sounding authoritative and confident, something Arya had never seen in the young man. His golden eyes glowed in the dark. "I'll find the best trail, all you need do is follow."

She didn't hesitate—the confidence in him convinced her. "Do as he says!" Arya ordered.

It worked well. In single file they followed the horselord ever southwards, deep into the Horn. They rode for hours, tired and soaked to the skin and shivering with cold. The horses slowed from a canter to an exhausted trot, and the sounds of pursuit grew increasingly louder, the barking taking on a new pitch as the dogs realised they were closing in on their quarry.

Then, Arya felt Elendryl's presence light up her mind. Ahead of her, Leanir stiffened in the saddle, scanning the skies above.

"*I come.*"

And then Elendryl's wyvern's cry ripped through the night.

It tore through the air, vicious and angry and powerful, and Arya didn't think she'd ever heard anything more beautiful in her entire life.

The horses reared in fright. Arubon and Miell hunkered over as if under attack, while Remien's eyes widened and then his gaze shot to Arya. Ranier watched silently; he'd moved to the back of the group when Miell had taken the lead. By the time they'd all gotten their horses under control, a gust of wind blew overhead as the dark shapes of two large wyverns swooped low, looking for a landing spot.

Ranier pushed his horse into a weary trot up the slope. "There looks to be a clearing up there," he said for Arya's ears only.

She frowned at his lowered voice, but as Elendryl swooped again, she forgot about his odd behaviour and urged her horse in the direction Ranier was going. Her wyvern was a bright golden light amidst the dark and rain as he touched down with another cry, this time of joy at seeing his rider.

Exhaustion forgotten, Arya swung down from the saddle and sprinted across the muddy clearing towards him, slipping and sliding and not caring at all. When she reached him, she threw herself at him, wrapping her arms around his neck, pressing her head against the scales of his jaw. His breath huffed in warm blasts over her hair. Tears of relief and joy flooded her eyes. "*You're here. You're here. You're here.*" She couldn't stop saying it.

"*Okay?*" he asked, panicked.

"*I'm all right. I told you I'd get out. They're close behind us, though.*"

Elendryl's snarl rippled through the clearing.

"Arya!"

At the note of panic in Miell's voice, Arya spun, and it took her a moment to register what she was seeing.

Ranier, dragging Remien from the saddle, then letting him drop into the mud. Even before the Spider hit the ground, Ranier's knife was out and flashing, no finesse, no showiness, just a blunt strike for his brother's chest.

Arubon watched from horseback, expressionless.

Arya reacted without thought. She burst into a run, at the same time drawing enough magic to send a concentrated burst flying at Ranier's knife. It hit the metal and sizzled, Ranier grunting in pain as it caught his fingers too. In the next second, she was on him, sending them both crashing into the mud. The Shadeweaver leader was a dangerous fighter who'd once repeatedly gotten the best of her.

But she'd promised him that one day those tables would turn.

Now she drove her knee into his stomach, sending the breath whooshing from his chest before flattening him and yanking his remaining knife from his belt to place at his throat.

He went still, staring up at her, a snarl curling the corner of his mouth. "Miell?" she shouted, not taking her gaze off Ranier.

"He's okay, he—"

"He can speak for himself." Remien levered himself to his feet, wincing, wiping mud from his hands and face. "It's been a long time, Ran. That wasn't the warmest of reunions, though."

Ranier let out a furious growl and tried to rise. Arya dug the knife in until it drew blood. "So, you *do* know he's your brother? Good, I was a little confused there for a moment."

"The dogs are almost here." This from Arubon, still sitting on his horse.

"I'm going to let you up," Arya told Ranier. She had a million questions, didn't know where to start, and knew now wasn't the time. It would wait until they were clear of Blackstone. "And you're not going to make a move without my permission, or I will disintegrate you. Clear?"

He gave a single nod.

Arya scrambled to her feet, keeping the knife. "Leanir?"

He was across the clearing, standing with a wyvern whose ivory scales shone in the darkness. Mistryl's tail swung in delight, her serpentine neck curled down towards her rider, and Leanir was glowing as he pressed his palms to her scales. "Yes, I know, soldiers coming."

"You're taking Remien and Arubon. I've got Miell and Ranier," she snapped, crossing back to Elendryl. She wasn't trusting Ranier as far as she could throw him, so he'd stay with her for now.

Leanir's jaw tightened at the order. "Where are we going?"

"Remien knows a safe place. He'll direct you, and we'll follow."

Leanir's gaze shifted between Arya and Remien, calculating. "He's been in prison for decades."

"Why do you think I wanted to break him out so badly?"

"Fine," he snapped, presumably realising there was no time for arguments. He waved Remien and Arubon over with a curt gesture.

Miell ran for Elendryl, while across the clearing Remien headed for Mistryl, shooting expressionless looks in Ranier's direction. For his part, the Shadeweaver leader ignored his brother as if he hadn't just tried to kill him and followed Miell towards Elendryl. Arya scrambled onto her wyvern's back, then reached down to help the other two up behind her.

The pinpricks of torchlight carried by their pursuers bobbed as they approached the clearing, dogs streaming before them, howling as they reached their quarry.

"Go, Elendryl." Arya roared.

He spread his wings, took two steps and lunged into the sky, the rain pouring into her face, the mist whipping through her hair. Arya closed her eyes and stretched out her arms.

She was free.

Taking a breath, she sank into her magic, reaching for the threads that bound her to her Sky Lords, and with an anxious ripple of hope she brought them to life. Fear surged in those first heartbeats until...

Essa. Then Chiarn.

The two threads pulsed with returning magic. Both far distant, and apart from each other, but alive and well. Arya sent joy and love and assurance through the bonds. And then she tried to convey 'soon' and 'wait'. Response shivered back through, matching joy along with relief.

Her Sky Lords lived.

Chapter 10

They flew through the remainder of the night and into the following day, the wyverns holding a steady altitude to help keep their extra riders from falling, wind whistling through Arya's hair, chilling her face and hands, a sensation she nonetheless delighted in. She was free and she was flying again. She checked over her shoulder regularly, but so far there were no signs of pursuit.

Miell slept in fits and starts, his arms around her waist, head lolling against her back, while behind him, Ranier held one of Elendryl's spines with a white-knuckled grip and stared into the distance. As the long hours passed, she wrestled with the anxiety that kept rising at knowledge that despite her triumphant escape from Blackstone, there were now greater challenges to conquer. Darmanin shivered into her mind, and she immediately shied away, refocusing on Ranier.

There was no way he could have known the timing of Arya's escape, even if he had somehow learned she was in Blackstone. Which meant he'd been encamped outside the prison for a while. Possibly since he'd left her that day in the Horn after helping her escape Darkclaw Deep, drawing off the nazal so Mervin and Fisk could get her to safety. She'd assumed him killed or captured. Apparently not. And trying to kill Remien ... was his *brother* the reason Ranier had been watching Blackstone?

Arya pressed her palms against Elendryl's scales, delighting at being so close to him again. Then she debated reaching out to Leanir through their bond to suggest looking for a resting spot—she *really* needed to relieve herself and doubted either her or Leanir's passengers had the strength to hold on to a wyvern for much longer, despite how smoothly they were flying.

Before she decided, however, Mistryl banked gently and circled lower over an isolated area along the south coast. Miell started awake as Elendryl followed, arms tightening around her waist at his movement. They landed in a grassy area near a swift-flowing stream that disappeared into thick woods nearby.

She scrambled down from Elendryl's back, helped a groggy Miell down, then looked at Ranier. "You don't step one foot away from Elendryl, or he eats you. Clear?"

Elendryl gave a rumbling snarl when Ranier didn't immediately reply. Eventually the Shadeweaver stiffly climbed down and stood silently by the wyvern, arms crossed over his chest. He refused to look at her. Shaking off her questions—time for those when they were safe—Arya headed over to the other group. "How far to go?" she asked the Spider.

The old man looked exhausted and frail in the morning light, but there was enough spark in his eyes and voice that Arya wasn't too worried. "We'll be there tomorrow morning if we fly through the night."

Arya glanced back at Elendryl. Her wyvern was weary, but he had plenty still in him. And it was best they stopped as few times as possible before they got wherever they were going. Each time they did, it gave the Nightstalker an opportunity to track them via his unrivalled spy network. She glanced up at the sky. It looked clear now, but she had no doubt that Xaphistryl and Zaphirdryl were in the air, searching for them. Not to mention the nazal and the bat creatures they flew.

"Couldn't we camp overnight before continuing?" Miell asked. He looked as bad as Remien. Flying on wyvern's back wasn't the most comfortable or easy mode of travel, especially when one had been subsisting on prison rations for months.

"Sure, if you want to wait a whole extra day to eat," Leanir observed. "Unless you escaped with snacks you plan to share with the rest of us?"

"I could hunt, bring down a rabbit," Arubon offered. He looked a little green around the gills.

"And then start a fire that Xaphistryl or the Nightstalker's spy network could see from miles off?" Ranier's voice snapped across the space between them.

"Zaphirdryl will be part of the search too," Leanir pointed out. "And she knows Arya's wyvern well."

To punctuate his point, a flock of birds burst into the sky from the forest nearby, as if disturbed. Fear flashed in Arya's chest. All it took was one hunter spotting two wyverns and mentioning it to one of the Nightstalker's spies. She glanced up at the sky again. "Stretch your legs. Drink from the stream. Relieve yourselves. Then we're straight back into the air."

They scattered, and Arya turned to Remien. "Why is your brother trying to kill you?"

"Giving you personal information was not part of the terms of our agreement."

"Fine." For now. "But let me tell you the same thing I just told him. You make a move on Ranier, or anyone in this group, and Elendryl will eat you."

Remien laughed as if genuinely amused. "Oh, I have no intention of harming my little brother, Stormrider. Don't worry on that score."

"Good." She turned to leave.

"Stormrider?"

"What?"

"He's not going to stop trying to kill me."

She glanced over her shoulder, where Ranier's dark gaze was focused unwaveringly on Remien. His hand sat on the hilt of the knife in his belt. A shudder ran through her at that look, and for the first time, she worried about whether she could, in fact, keep Remien safe.

✳✳✳

Dawn broke to find them still in the air, exhaustion settling deep into Arya's bones. They had planned to stop and rest halfway through the night, but a distant screeching to the east—too much like a nazal—had sent them pushing forward instead.

Miell sagged against her back, caught somewhere between exhaustion and nausea. She'd threatened to toss him off if he vomited on her, which probably hadn't helped. Ranier, stiff backed and silent, clung on, though he had to be just as drained after so many hours of flight.

As the sun rose golden over the ocean, the coastline finally came into view. Mistryl adjusted course, turning north along the cliffs. Arya straightened abruptly, nearly unseating Miell in the process. He yelped in alarm, scrambling for a better grip.

A smile spread over Arya's face. She knew where Remien was taking them.

Mistryl gradually flew lower and lower, until they were skimming the waves along the mighty clifftops of the coastline. And then Arya spotted the break in the cliffs, where twin waterfalls sent spray glittering into the sky. Her heartbeat quickened as Elendryl followed Mistryl through the waterfalls, along the narrow ravine, and then out into the turquoise bay framed by the palace of five towers.

It was exactly as she'd first seen it in her dreams close to a year ago at Taskari.

Mistryl circled the central tower before landing, and Elendryl came in behind her, though he landed a good distance away from the other wyvern, and the two watched each other warily. Arya helped a shaky Miell slide to the ground and then scrambled down herself. Ranier dismounted slowly, but then stopped and pointedly crossed his arms again.

Her legs felt rubbery, and she steadied herself against Elendryl. *"I'm so glad to have you back."*

A wash of love from him swamped her, and they communed silently for a long moment before Arya took a step back. *"Will you watch Ranier for me? It won't be long, then you can go to hunt and then rest."*

"Watch." He promised, then added hopefully. *"Eat?"*

She laughed. *"Only if he tries to move."*

"Where are we?" Miell asked, blinking in wonder as he stared around.

Arya lifted her eyebrows. "Perhaps one of the two members of House Inkweaver present could answer that."

"This is the Storm Spire," Remien said, then when Arya glared, added with a shrug. "We're safe here."

Ranier blinked, shook his head, then stared at his brother as if recalling something he'd once known but long forgotten. It was the first time she'd seen anything but his expressionless mask since leaving Blackstone.

Arya huffed a breath, but accepted Remien's assurance for the moment. After all, he wouldn't have brought them here if *he* didn't believe he'd be safe. "All right, let's head inside, get a fire going, figure out fresh water and food. Then we can get some rest."

"I'll take finding food," Arubon volunteered, then added: "You just broke me out of prison, Stormrider. The least I can do is help make sure we don't starve."

"I'll do a patrol, make sure nobody else is here," Leanir said.

"You won't find anyone," Remien said.

Ignoring him, Leanir disappeared down the staircase leading from the rooftop, Arubon close behind. Arya, Remien, and Miell followed at a slower pace. As they descended, Arya glanced over her shoulder and caught sight of Ranier. He had untucked his shirt and was tracing a tattoo across his left hipbone, an unreadable expression on his face.

Their boots echoed against the stone floor of the wide corridor at the base of the steps, the emptiness of the space pressing in around them. Yet when Arya idly placed her palm against the wall, she was startled to find it warm—almost welcoming.

At the end of the corridor, what appeared to be the central tower staircase wound downwards, so they started down it. Arya took a deep breath, the air filling her lungs and easing some of her bone-deep exhaustion.

She felt good here.

Nobody had energy for exploring—or traipsing all the way to the bottom—so after stopping at the landing three floors down, they settled on a room two doors along the corridor with a hearth that was large enough to hold them all. She didn't want anyone separating just yet.

Arya summoned the energy to shove the rotting sofa and two ornate chairs in the room over to the side—there was no dust, which she found astonishing, and the air was clean, not stale—while Miell sank down against the wall in exhaustion and Remien watched. She was peering out the arched window, which looked down over a massive square at the base of the tower, when Arubon appeared. He'd found a storeroom on the ground floor with stacked wood as well as dried food supplies and piles of linen, including wool blankets.

"Don't ask me how they're in such good condition, it's like they were freshly laundered this morning," he said, shaking his head. "There's a well near the storeroom exit too; it must have adjoined to the kitchens originally. I'll be back with fresh water soon."

Arya glanced at the rotting fabrics of the old chairs and sofa she'd pushed against the wall, then at the fresh woollen blankets, and wondered.

Soon they had a fire going and water boiling for tea. Rainfall began tapping on the window as they ate leathery strips of preserved *something* and sipped at hot tea.

Leanir appeared briefly to report that the tower was empty of threats, take a few sips of tea, then mutter something about extending his patrol. "There's something about this place … a presence. I'm sure of it. I want to check the entire grounds."

She'd felt it too. *Something* in the air. But it didn't feel malign to her. In fact, it felt like it was happy about their arrival, as strange as that sounded. Still, she wasn't going to protest his thoroughness. "If you're going out again, will you take some food and water up to Ranier first?"

"You're just going to leave him up there?"

"Do you care if I do?" she asked out of genuine curiosity.

He shrugged, said nothing.

"If you could find a secure room to hold him, or some chains or rope to keep him secured, while you're patrolling, that would help. Elendryl needs to hunt."

Leanir re-filled his mug with tea, grabbed a packet of the dried food Arubon had found, then left. Hopefully to take the food and water to Ranier, but who knew.

Despite her exhaustion, Arya couldn't bear her filthy state any longer. She left them and found the well Arubon had mentioned. The bucket was old and the mechanism unoiled, but she managed to draw up a good amount of fresh water. Uncaring of who might be looking, she shucked off her disgusting clothes and washed her filthy skin, immediately feeling better despite the iciness of the water. Two more buckets were enough to wash her tunic and breeches and underclothes. She wrung them out as best she could, wrapped the blanket she'd brought with her around herself, and headed back upstairs.

Miell watched as she spread her wet clothes by the fire, then put down his tea, and left, presumably to follow suit.

The crackle and pop of the fire filled the room after the door closed, and Arya felt herself drifting as she ate and sipped tea and listened to the rainfall outside.

Miell returned to lay his wet clothes by the fire. Arubon left. When he returned, towel wrapped around his waist, revealing an intimidatingly muscular chest and arms and a tattoo that extended from his neck and collarbone down over his heart, he laid out his wet clothes and then faced them. "We need to know how long we can stay here before the Nightstalker or his nazal find us. There's no way he's letting go the first prisoners to ever escape Blackstone. We'll have to keep moving to stay ahead of him and his spies."

Arya lifted her eyebrows in Remien's direction. She'd sacrificed a lot for his knowledge, and she'd trusted in his self-serving nature enough to come here on his instruction. But Arubon's question was the one she'd been planning to ask next.

"He won't come here, and he won't find us here," Remien said.

"Why?" Arubon asked, gaze narrowed. He clearly didn't trust the Spider any more than Arya. Miell sat away from them, sipping tea, looking like he wanted no part of any of this. His eyes were already drifting closed.

"It's a long story, and right now I'd like to rest," Remien said. Without further ado, Remien tucked a blanket around himself and curled up on the floor, eyes sliding closed.

"We don't stay here another second unless I can be sure it's safe." Arya kept her voice light, conversational. "So unless you'd like to go out in that rain, climb aboard my wyvern, and start flying again, you're going to convince me that it's safe to stay."

Leanir chose that moment to open the door and stick his head in, clothes wet, dark gaze darting around. "Ranier's getting a little cold up there, but I gave him an extra blanket. He's lived through worse in the Diamondfang. Mistryl came back to watch him so Elendryl can hunt. I'll look for a place that can hold him better on my search of the grounds."

"Thank you," she said, surprised. Was Leanir genuinely helping, or did he have an ulterior motive? She'd have to keep an eye on them both.

"Mistryl scouted before she came back. She says we're in an isolated part of the country, and the nearest town is miles away."

"Remien is about to tell us why it's safe for us to stay here, if you'd like to wait and hear it before you go," Arya said.

The old man's mouth tightened, but he sat up, voice terse. "So as long as we're not spotted by any of his spies, the Nightstalker won't know where we are. We made sure nobody saw us flying here. He'll be searching, but he has no idea where to start."

"Until his search reaches here," Arubon said with a hint of impatience. "He won't leave a corner of this country unturned in looking for us."

"He won't search here because he doesn't know the Storm Spire exists."

When Remien didn't elaborate and looked like he was about to return to his blankets, Arya lost her patience. "Why? I'm not convinced by anything you've said, and I'm two minutes away from dragging you up on Elendryl's back."

"Fine." Remien sat up properly. "Your grandfather had four Sky Lords; the Nightstalker, the WindDancer, the Daystormer, and the Lightbringer. Lucius Nightstalker murdered the Daystormer, then his lover, Marial Wind-Dancer. It wasn't until months later that he killed the Lightbringer, and finally, the king, Rian Stormrider."

"So?" Leanir snapped.

But Arya was already there. "Another potential came into their magic in those months, didn't they? A Sky Lord to replace the Daystormer."

"Yes. His wyvern was too young to fly or fight against the Nightstalker, but he was there when Lucius killed your grandfather—Rian had retreated to Darkclaw Deep's defensive walls in an effort to hold against the Nightstalker's forces. His newest Sky Lord was the last defence your grandfather had. He was born of House Mindbreaker." Remien shot a glance in Leanir's direction. "He died from the wounds Lucius dealt him in the days following the king's assassination, but not before tearing all knowledge of the Storm Spire from the Nightstalker's mind. And not only his mind, everyone else present in Darkclaw at the time. His plan was for the king to flee there to hide, but Rian never made it out of Darkclaw."

Arya frowned. "Hasn't someone just told the Nightstalker or his nazal or Nightblades about this place since?"

"Only a select few amongst the Valheran Houses knew its secrets, and only House Inkweaver knew the full extent. They were all at Darkclaw when Rian Stormrider fell. The Storm Spire is not on any common trading or travel routes, so few would have passed it since. Word of it has probably reached the Nightstalker in some form. But he doesn't have the knowledge in his mind to connect those reports to what this place is.

"In his quest for power, the Nightstalker has repeatedly and without remorse abused Sky Lord magic. Not only did he murder his fellow Sky Lords in cold blood, but he has also stolen the magic of potentials and twisted others into nazal," Remien said. "Put quite simply, Arya, the Nightstalker is not welcome at the Storm Spire."

"What does that mean exactly?"

"Generations of Stormriders and their Sky Lords have lived here. Every brick, every tile, every piece of marble is literally infused with their magic. That magic rejects the Nightstalker. To him, the palace is nothing more than an opaque fog. He can't see through it or inside it, and he certainly can't enter it—at least, not without a massive outpouring of power that would come close to destroying him."

"If that's true, why didn't my father come here when he fled with Ranier?"

Remien shrugged. "The Mindbreaker was desperate when he did what he did and he didn't have full control over his magic yet; he wiped the minds of everyone in Darkclaw, including Torin's."

"Then how did *you* retain the knowledge?" Arya asked.

Remien lifted his shirt, revealing the intricate tattoos inked all over his skin. "I was the heir to House Inkweaver, the oldest of my father's children. The knowledge of our House lives in my blood and bone. It cannot we wiped. And before you ask, I was a little too busy getting captured and thrown in Blackstone to have a chance to tell Torin to flee here."

"What of those who lived here at the time?" Miell spoke up unexpectedly. "I saw how big it was when we flew in, like a city. Hundreds, thousands, must have been here if it was the seat of the king."

"That I do not know," Remien said. "But I assume, without knowing their location had been wiped from the Nightstalker's mind, those that lived here fled when they learned of Rian's death, expecting the Nightstalker to come here next and raze it to the ground. They probably still think that's what happened."

"And what of the Nightstalker's heir?" Leanir asked. "Will he and his wyvern be able to come here?"

Arya looked away, staring into the flames.

"That I cannot answer," Remien said. "But it's possible, yes."

"And what are you going to do if he comes here?" Leanir challenged, turning his gaze to Arya.

She forced herself to look away from the fire and hold his gaze. "I will destroy any who threaten me and mine, Leanir."

The crackling of the fire filled the silence as they all processed what Remien had told them. Arya let out a long, relieved, breath. If only for his knowledge of the Storm Spire, breaking Remien from Blackstone was worth it. "Rest," she said eventually. "The wyverns will warn us if anything approaches."

Remien immediately curled up in his blankets, and Miell and Arubon followed suit, seemingly too weary for any further conversation. Leanir's dark gaze glimmered as he looked at Arya. "House Mindbreaker. That's me, isn't it?"

"I believe so."

His jaw tightened, but he said nothing. Turning on his heel, he left, the door clicking shut behind him.

Arya exhaled and leaned back against the wall, pulling a blanket over her legs. Her thoughts threatened to spiral—chief among them the overwhelming urge to leave, to go straight to Rorin, Chiarn, and Essa, or to find Kirin and make sure he was safe. The pull was almost unbearable.

But she forced herself to stay still. One step at a time.

First, she needed rest.

***

Arya woke from a light doze sometime later at the faint tugging of a thread deep in her magic. The fire burned low and Miell, Remien, and Arubon slept soundly. Leanir was nowhere to be seen, but she could sense he hadn't gone far and was roaming somewhere north of the tower. Nothing appeared out of order. Elendryl was sleeping with a full belly after a hunt, but he roused at her sudden alertness.

"*All's well,*" she soothed. "*Ranier?*"

He sent her an image of the Shadeweaver leader curled up under blankets near his wing, sleeping. Rising, Arya tugged on her clothes—mostly dry now—and slipped quietly out the door. Outside, she quickened her pace, taking the stairs down to the ground floor, following the single shimmering thread of her enlivened Sky Lord bond. Her boots echoed in the cavernous entry foyer, and she wondered what it had been like to live in the Storm Spire when it had been fully occupied. It must have been a bustling place, chaotic with noise and life. She could almost see it, hear it, the magic lying dormant in its bones wrapping round her like a familiar cloak. Arya got the distinct sense the Storm Spire was happy to have a Sky Lord within its walls again.

Leaving the massive, arched double doors closed and locked, Arya searched until she found a side exit. Outside, a light rain fell as she crossed the wide-open square before the central tower, then followed an avenue that connected the square to the western wall. Her footsteps echoed, reverberating through empty buildings, once homes and shops and places of work. Snatches of sound filled her senses. Children laughing, a smith's hammer banging on iron, the call of stallholders in a marketplace. All of it was interwoven with a thread of mournfulness. The Storm Spire wanted that life back.

The narrow iron gate set into the outer wall was chained and locked, but the lock had rusted in the salty sea air and a small burst of her magic melted the latch. The iron screeched as she pushed through, finding herself at the top of a set of narrow steps leading down the cliff face to the beach. At the bottom, the crushed pebbles that lined the shore of the bay crunched under her boots when she reached the bottom. The rain had lightened, and a faint moonlight shone above. The water was calm, lapping against the shore with a steady murmuring.

Darmanin stood a short distance off, in the shadow of the cliff looming above so that he'd be hidden from anyone looking down from the walls or towers. When she saw him, she stilled, relief filling her. Remien's guess had been right. Darmanin *was* able to be here. She pulled the piece of flint from her tunic pocket and walked towards him, holding it out. "It was you."

As she got closer, she could make out his face, his raven hair, those glimmering silver eyes. The stern mask he habitually wore faded with every step she took, until that little smile of his tugged at his mouth. "Of course it was me."

Arya's breath sobbed in her chest, and she launched herself at him. His arms wrapped around her, and she held on for dear life, breathing in his scent, his nearness, everything about him. They stood there for such a long time, the connection between them glowing with joy and relief and humming with magic.

Eventually Arya forced herself to let go, huffing a laugh of disbelief. "It worked, I can't believe it worked."

The tightness around his eyes relaxed at her words. "You got what you needed?"

"Remien Inkweaver is with me, and he's already given me vital information. It was worth it, Dar. All of it." She touched his cheek. "You've been incredible."

"You trusted me." His gaze held a hint of wonder.

"I *never* stopped believing in you, no matter what anyone else said," she whispered. "Not for a single second."

They'd all warned her. Elder Salyarin chief amongst them. Darmanin could not be trusted. He'd betray her in the end. But she'd never believed them. She never would. And now he finally knew it too.

Darmanin closed his eyes, eventually taking a steadying breath. "He's looking for you already. That's what Zaphirdryl and I are supposed to be doing. I expected to follow you straight back into Dunidaen."

The moment her magic had returned, Arya had reached for Darmanin, reigniting their Sky Lord bond and guiding him to their location. Now, with him finally here, she ached to ask him everything. But the rain was turning heavier again, so she reached for his hand. "We need to talk. Let's get inside where it's dry."

They climbed the cliff steps, Arya using her awareness of Leanir to make sure they stayed clear of him; he was a pulsing presence still on the northern side of the palace, but now an unmoving one. She wondered if he was unable to sleep with others close by.

Or maybe he was up to something.

She took Darmanin into one of the residences on the eastern side of the palace—the first in a row of narrow houses along a wide street—away from Leanir and where the others slept in the central tower. She left him to make a quick trip to the tower for blankets and firewood, then returned and got a fire going. She'd deliberately chosen an interior room with no windows so the light wouldn't betray their presence.

As soon as flames crackled, she wrapped a blanket around her damp clothes, and waved Darmanin to sit beside her before the warm fire. "I couldn't risk going back to Dunidaen, not until I was sure I could be clear of the Nightstalker." She cleared her throat, the fear she'd been holding at bay starting to creep back. "Dar, what's happening in Dunidaen? Is Rorin okay, the others?"

"Rorin and the warlords are besieged and gradually losing territory, but they're making the Nightstalker's army fight for every bit of ground it gains. The Nightblades are focusing on the southwest, sweeping through from Crowtalon with the aim of taking Gateport before moving north, so Heathrock is cut off but safe for the moment, and that's where Peemla and Anji remain." His jaw tightened. "The Nightstalker has kept me away from Dunidaen—I don't think he trusts me enough yet to fight for him there—so I don't know much more than that."

She searched his face, dreading his reply but having to ask. "Kirin?"

"Safe, as far as I know. The Nightstalker searches with increasing intensity, and he's grown certain Kirin isn't in Dunidaen. But now that you're out, he'll have to divert some of his efforts to finding you instead."

Relief shuddered through her, and he gave her a moment, one hand reaching out to run soothingly over her back. "And Essa? Chiarn? I can feel from the bonds that they're alive, but they're too far for me to know anything of their status."

"Chiarn and Essa both got away that day you faced us—Leanir was only captured because he stuck around to give Essa and her wyvern time to get clear. I assume they're in Dunidaen with Rorin, but I don't know for certain. I haven't heard any reports from the Nightstalker's army about wyverns being involved in the battles."

Arya let out a breath, feeling suddenly winded. She'd made such a massive gamble in getting herself locked away, leaving Rorin and the others to deal with the Nightstalker's invasion. Not to mention the danger she'd placed Darmanin in. Tears pricked at her eyes, and she fought them back.

It was okay. They were all okay. And now she could help them again. With the information she needed from Remien.

Then all his words processed. She sat up straight. "Leanir *helped* Essa escape?"

"That's what it looked like to me."

"Has the Nightstalker been hunting Chiarn and Ess?"

"He wasn't—it was part of the deal I made." Darmanin still looked worried. "But your escape changes things. He will still need to abide by his word to keep you alive, but he'll want you and Leanir recaptured and neutralised, the others too. And if he gets you in Blackstone again, you can be confident your avenue of escape no longer exists."

"I'll find them," she said, promising herself as much as him. "And I'll keep them safe. Rorin and Peemla and Anji too." And Kirin. Always, always, her son.

The weight of it—the number of those she held close to her heart and *needed* to keep safe—was growing ever more. She wondered how long she could hold it.

Darmanin nodded but said nothing, his gaze pensive as he stared at the flames. She reached out to touch his hand. "None of this can have been easy for you. Tell me how it all went down?"

"I left Gateport straight after you did and went to the Nightstalker, just as we'd planned. I told him his offer had been torturing me, that I couldn't bear the idea of losing you, and that I was willing to make a deal to keep you alive."

She searched his gaze but found nothing there. He was as closed off as he'd ever been. "And he believed you?"

"Not at first, but it didn't take a lot of convincing. I think he *wanted* to believe me. And I think you were right, that he doesn't truly want you dead. I can't get him to tell me why though."

His eyes were shadowed. Haunted. There was more he wasn't saying.

"Whatever it is, you can tell me," she whispered.

"I've had to prove myself to him, Arya, more than once. Prove that I'm on his side and holding to my end of the agreement." His voice was leeched of emotion, but his hands had curled into white-knuckled fists in his lap.

"You said he's kept you out of Dunidaen," she said carefully. "Where, then?"

"The Marshlands. I've fought and killed … two battles so far." He paused. "I tried to limit the damage without it being obvious, but…"

She reached out to frame his jaw with her palm, gently turn him towards her. "You did what you had to do, what I asked of you. At great risk to yourself. Whatever you did, you will find no judgement in me, Dar. Not ever. Only gratitude."

Slowly, finally, he lifted his eyes to meet hers. "I knew the Nightstalker would find a way around his promise to keep you alive. I knew your life was in danger every single moment you were in that place. But I also knew without a doubt that you would find a way to get out of Blackstone with what you needed."

"We're a pair, you and I," she murmured, holding his gaze. "One that could take on the world, if we wanted."

"I want," he said simply.

Her mouth curled in a smile. "So do I."

Darmanin moved first, his mouth pressing against hers as his arms came around her and pulled her close. She reached for the buttons of his tunic, working to undo them and then push the fabric off his shoulders, delighting in the bare skin and muscle she found beneath. His hands slid around her waist, pulling at the hem of her shirt, and she lifted her arms so that he could pull it off, laughing as it got caught in her long hair.

And then they were skin to skin, and she pushed him down to the blankets, the warmth of the fire on their bare skin, and for the first time in a long time, Arya forgot her fear and her guilt.

And she lived.

Chapter 11

Darmanin sat up and reached for his clothes. The fire had burned low, and the chill of the air pebbled Arya's bare skin. "Where are you going?" she complained.

"I can't be out of touch too long, or the Nightstalker will get suspicious."

"He can reach your mind?" she asked.

"Not like this." He tapped his bare chest, referring to the bond between them, "But he demands that I stay in regular contact through messages from local garrisons, or his three remaining nazal, if they're close enough. He won't realise I've travelled so far west, so I need to get back in contact before he realises. And you should keep moving too."

"Not necessary." Arya relayed everything Remien had told them the previous night.

Darmanin let out a whistle, grey eyes lightening. "Now I know what you mean by breaking him out being worth it. If what he said is true..."

"As long as Remien is with me, his life is at risk if the Nightstalker finds us, so it's in his interests to be honest."

He looked thoughtful. "You shouldn't tell me any more, including what you plan next."

He didn't have to say why. The danger he was in every moment he was at the Nightstalker's side, it was extreme. She took his hand. "Darmanin, you don't have to go back to him. Stay with me, with us."

"As much as I want that, if I stay with him, I can learn how to help you destroy him. Even better, I can feed him disinformation, identify his vulnerabilities," Darmanin said. "You know that's the right strategic move."

She searched his gaze, torn, trying to separate what she wanted from what was the right tactical approach. To have Darmanin on the inside for as long as possible, it could be critical to her plans. Yet the thought of losing him ... and she *knew* that losing him grew more likely the longer Darmanin stayed with the Nightstalker. He hadn't ruled so long and so completely without being a clever, canny, man. Darmanin wouldn't be able to fool him forever. "Then you go back to him as a member of my *cairdre*. Fully under its protection. If *anything* happens to make you concerned that he's discovered you, we ride to your aid."

He gave her his little smile. "I thought I'd just agreed to that earlier."

She searched his gaze. "What about being High Warlord of Dunidaen?"

He sat back down, shirt still in his hands, and ran a hand through his hair. "My father is dead, Arya, and there is no more revenge to be had." He turned to her, face lighting up. "I belong at your side. With our family. Taking on the world."

Arya stood, taking his hand and drawing him up to stand before her. "If you are formally joining my *cairdre*, you need a name. You might be able to shapeshift into a shadowhound, but you are not a Nightstalker, Darmanin. You never have been."

"What name would you give me?" he whispered.

She took his hands in hers, squeezed. "Darkslayer. It's what you do, you rise above the darkness; in yourself and everyone else. You defeat it, every time it tries to take you. You are the strongest person I know."

"The Darkslayer," he murmured. "It feels right."

"In that case." She lifted his hands and held them both over her heart. "As Arya Stormrider, your future queen, I welcome you into my Sky Lord *cairdre*, Darmanin Darkslayer."

Darmanin bowed his head, eyes gleaming. "Thank you, Arya."

He leaned forward to place a soft kiss on her forehead and then returned to dressing. Arya did the same, and they didn't speak again until he was buckling his sword on, ready to go. Then, he cupped her face. "I remember that cocky, full-of-life general that led the Raiders. I know Thiara's death shattered that for you, that your fear for Kirin and for your family only worsens it, but we need that woman if we want to win."

She raised her eyebrows. "You used to tell me off for being too arrogant, for acting like the world revolved around me."

He shrugged. "That's my job."

Joy speared through her. "We're going to fight a lot, aren't we?"

"Probably at least half the time."

"I can't wait."

He sighed, turning sober. "I don't know when I'll see you again."

"I fear for you," she whispered, stricken. "And I hate that I've asked you to do this. If anything happened to you, Dar..."

"Then you will survive. Because you are the strongest person that *I* know," he said steadily. "And no matter what comes, I will be here always." He rested his palm over her heart.

She reached up to lace their fingers together. "I'll miss you, Darmanin Darkslayer."

"And I you."

As his arms came around her, she buried herself in his embrace for a long moment, soaking up his warmth and strength. Eventually he sighed, let go.

"Right. Tell me what you want me to do next." That little smile curled at his mouth again. "And don't pretend you haven't already thought about it."

***

Dawn was breaking as Arya headed back to the tower. Almost as soon as Darmanin had left, harsh reality had descended upon her, not helped by how anxious she felt sending him back into such terrible danger. Restless impatience filled her now. She needed to be gone. The sooner she moved, the sooner Darmanin would be safe. And movement was a distraction from her fear.

When she reached the third-floor landing, she found Leanir leaning against the wall across from the closed door, watchful. She wondered if he simply didn't trust those inside, or whether he was ever able to fully relax.

His gaze flicked to her. "Ranier's gone."

"And Remien?" she asked sharply.

"Still alive and sleeping in there."

She let out a sigh. That wasn't entirely unexpected. "You let him go."

"He asked nicely."

"I bet he did," Arya said dryly, wondering how worried she should be. Wherever Remien was, she doubted Ranier would be far. Although he might have trouble keeping up once they left on the wyverns.

"Mistryl tells me Zaphirdryl was nearby last night."

Arya shrugged. She'd been prepared for this question. "Elendryl said the same. It seems she didn't come close enough to see this place though."

His eyes narrowed in suspicion. "Where have you been all night?"

"Same as you, Leanir, roaming about this place. I couldn't sleep. It's hard to feel safe after being in a prison surrounded by potential enemies for so long. I didn't find anything, though. You?"

"There's something here. I know it," he said. "The rain was heavy enough it would have obscured any tracks, but I can feel a presence."

"I think we're safe here."

His jaw set. "I know how ridiculously loyal you are to those you choose to love, Raider, but Darmanin is on the Nightstalker's side now."

Leanir was no fool, and he'd put two and two together easily enough. Arya kept her voice calm, even. "I'm aware of that. He didn't find us, did he? The Nightstalker and his hordes are not descending on us, and I assume Mistryl, like Elendryl, hid herself from Zaphirdryl?"

"Why was he searching so far west already, unless he tracked you here?"

Arya took a breath. "I can mute the threads that link us, as you know."

"But we can't do the same. It's unfair."

"I agree, but I didn't decide the Sky Lord magic rules." She threw her hands in the air. "And why do you care about who Darmanin is loyal to anyway? You don't give two figs for defeating the Nightstalker and freeing Andahar. You only care about keeping yourself safe."

"I will *never* be safe as long as the Nightstalker is alive," he said, the bitterness in his voice so deep it made her wince. "I will never be free of him, or of you. For me, there is no difference between the two of you."

"You insult me," she said. "I felt the same as you once. But I'm resigned to reality, Leanir. So quit griping about things that are out of your control as if they're my fault. They're not."

He surged forward, coming to stand toe to toe with her. "I *insult* you? You gave me up to him, Arya. You betrayed my name, knowing it would mean my death if he found me. You're as much of a monster as he is."

"And you would have done the same to me if he'd offered to exchange your life for it, no?"

His expression tightened, but instead of replying, he spun towards the door, hand dropping to his knife. A second later it opened to reveal Arubon and Remien. The old man seemed amused, but Arubon was holding a knife—where had he gotten that from?—low by his side.

"I believe we have a visitor," Remien said. "Loitering outside the main doors. Despite Arubon's rather aggressive reaction, she didn't look like a threat. Offered a friendly wave when I spotted her out the window, actually."

What?

Arya clattered down the main steps into the entry foyer, this time not bothering about being quiet. She summoned a burst of magic and sent it flying into the lock holding the chains on the great double doors together. The lock burst apart, the chains dropping to the floor. Arya closed her fingers over the handle on the right-side door and hauled it open.

Bright sunlight flooded in. The rain had cleared, and bright blue skies shone from above. The air was warm, too, and the slight breeze smelled of roses. And standing at the base of the shallow steps leading down from the doors was a tall, skinny, half-Etherean woman with a shock of curly white hair.

"Tiya!" Arya stared with wide eyes. "Raven's balls, you show up in the oddest of places."

"Arya!" Her smile was broad. "When I caught sight of the golden wyvern soaring overheard this morning, I guessed you must be here, so I emerged from my hiding spot to come say hello. I don't suppose you've got any voseni?"

"Fresh out, I'm afraid," Arya said. "What the hell are you doing here?"

She cocked her head. "Short answer. When Niallin and his rebels decamped for the Diamondfang and the Etherean citadel at your request, I couldn't go with them. I went my own way, but the Nightblades seemed to track me wherever I went if I stayed too long. So, I came here."

"You've been living here on your own for months?"

Arya chided herself. She'd brushed aside Leanir's certainty that someone was here, and she should have known better. Tiya came up the steps, dropped onto the top one, and gestured for Arya to sit beside her.

"Not a murderous assassin?" Remien's voice came from the open door behind them.

"No. An old friend," Arya said. "Tell Arubon to stand down. If you would all wait upstairs, I won't be long."

Remien settled a long, measuring look on Tiya, who bore it with a little smile, then turned and wandered off. Arya waited until his footsteps faded, then sat beside the other woman. "I've learned a lot about this place. It's hidden, wiped from everyone's minds decades ago. How did you know to come here?"

Tiya shrugged, opened her mouth to no doubt give a flippant reply, but Arya cut her off with a sharp gesture. "The truth, Tiya. I haven't hidden anything from you."

"The truth is that I *didn't* know any of that. I swear it. I was moving steadily west to keep ahead of the Nightblades tracking me, and figured I would keep going as the countryside grew more isolated. Imagine my surprise when I saw this place on the horizon? I keep a watch from those walls every day and I haven't seen a single person come near it."

"Then what *are* you hiding from me?" Arya scanned her face. "It has something to do with you being Etherean, doesn't it? Why didn't you go with Niallin and the rebels?"

Tiya looked away, jaw working, as if her next words were physically hard to say. "Because if I had gone with them, my father would have known I'd returned to the citadel. There'd have been no way to hide from being recognised. And I didn't want that."

"Your father?"

"Hmm, yes. Everyone else calls him Elder Salyarin."

The moment froze, filling with Arya's stunned shock. "*You're* Salyarin's lost heir?"

"Lost?" Tiya snorted in contempt. "No, I was not lost. I was cast aside because my wings never grew."

Arya stared, unsure what to say. Her thoughts tumbled over each other, too many to grab onto a single strand. *Tiya* was the heir to the Etherean ruler? She couldn't wrap her head around it.

Tiya seemed to take her lack of response as surprise about her wings. "It's rare. But it happens. Sometimes an Etherean child's wings simply don't grow." Tiya's shoulders turned rigid. "I couldn't bear the looks, the comments, so I left the citadel. Went to Heathrock. Started working with my 'stepfather' at The Ruined Arms—he agreed to call me his after he saw how I improved the profits of his business."

Arya stared for another moment longer, then, at the mention of the inn in Heathrock Tiya had once run, one of Arya's favourite drinking holes, she burst out into peals of laughter.

Tiya burst into a startled grin at Arya's response. "What?"

"Salyarin already doesn't like me much. I'm just imagining the look on his face if he knew I'd slept with his daughter."

Her smile vanished. "He wouldn't care."

"I suspect he does care. I've heard it in his voice, the rare times he's spoken of you." Arya touched her shoulder. "I won't pretend to understand what that was like for you, growing up without wings. But he misses you."

"He refused to name me as his heir, even though he has no other children. It isn't easy for Etherean to bear children, and—" Tiya cut herself off with a frustrated gesture. "If he cared, he wouldn't have disowned me."

"Then he's a fool," Arya said quietly, leaning in to press her shoulder against Tiya's. "An ignorant fool."

A comfortable silence fell, the sun spilling over the steps coming closer as the sun rose higher in the sky. Arya would have happily sat there with her old friend all day, processing the crazy knowledge that she was just like Arya, a nameless heir, and feeling a stronger kinship than she'd ever felt before.

But there was too much to do.

Arya rose. "I could take you with me when I go. It's been a long time since you've seen your father. Maybe—"

"No."

Arya accepted that. "Come with me anyway? I go to war, Tiya. We could use a healer with your skills. Dunidae attitudes to magic-wielders aren't what they once were." She didn't hide the note of vulnerability in her voice. "And the truth is, I could use another friend with me."

Tiya took a long, considering, breath. "I'd like that. Let me go and fetch my things."

"Come up to the rooftop. We'll be leaving from there."

***

Arya took two steps inside the tower doors to find Arbon standing there, a makeshift pack slung over his shoulder. "I'm leaving. The Nightstalker cares far more about your escape than mine, and the further I am from you, the less chance I have of being recaptured."

"I couldn't agree more," she said.

Arubon's gaze narrowed, as if he hadn't expected such an easy agreement. But Arya had no use for a marshfolk warrior she didn't know and couldn't trust, and the deal between them was complete. "It's not a trick, Arubon. We were of use to each other, but that's all it was. The best of luck to you."

Arubon shifted the pack on his shoulders, hesitated a moment, but then gave her a crisp nod. "Baenya, Arya Stormrider."

He walked past her and out the door.

"May the waters you travel always be calm, Arubon," she called after him. He stiffened as he caught the words of the traditional riverfolk farewell, glanced over his shoulder, then kept walking.

***

Arya went straight up the stairs to find Leanir outside their room again, presumably keeping a watch on Remien and Miell. Part of her was surprised he hadn't left like Arubon, only without bothering to say goodbye. Inside, Remien leaned by the window, seemingly enjoying the view. Miell was just waking, letting out a wide yawn. "I don't suppose this place comes with servants. I could really use a cup of fresh tagar right now."

Remien made a face. "I've never understood the horselord obsession with drinking what is essentially liquid grass."

Miell sniffed. "That's because you have the misfortune of not being one of us."

"We're leaving this morning," Arya announced before more bickering could ensue. Honestly, the way these people, all born of the same country, treated each other with disdain defied all logic. "Miell, where do we find your family, your home?" she asked.

His eyes widened with hope, and he scrambled to his feet, all affectations gone. "You mean—?"

"I'm going to take you there. Now get your ass moving and take Remien to pack some food and water for the journey. I'll meet you on the roof when you're done."

"Thank you, Arya." He scrambled for the door.

"I'm an old man. Stairs aren't good for my joints." Remien spoke from the window.

She smiled. "Then I hope you don't plan to eat or drink on the way to where we're going. Everyone here pulls their own weight."

"Rivers save me from high-minded Stormriders." The man heaved a sigh and trailed after Miell.

Once he was gone, Leanir appeared in the doorway. "What's next, Raider?"

She pushed past him, started up the stairs towards the roof with quick strides, enjoying the burn of her leg muscles. Where windows let in the morning sun, the marble walls glittered, and she couldn't help trailing her fingers along the wall as she walked. Little sparks lit under her fingertips. Every moment she spent in this place she felt more at home. Felt as if she were being *welcomed*. Wanted.

When Leanir started up the stairs after her, she glanced over her shoulder at him. "Why so much interest in what I'm doing? I thought you'd be gone by now."

"Will you stop asking me that!" he snarled. "You forced me into this, remember, by threatening to kill me if I didn't follow you."

Arya didn't reply until reaching the roof. The rose-scented breeze teased her hair. Elendryl was curled up on the eastern side of the platform, Mistryl on the other. The female wyvern glared daggers at Elendryl while he pretended not to notice, eyes half closed.

Arya faced Leanir, arms crossed over her chest. "How did you end up in Blackstone? That day we faced the Nightstalker, you were supposed to escape with the others."

"I wasn't fast enough."

Arya remained silent, waiting.

Leanir stared back.

She suppressed her irritation with him, kept her voice light, and asked, "Did you get caught because you helped Essa escape?"

"Once he had you unconscious, the Nightstalker went for your Inkweaver first—Xaphistryl was too big for Alletryl to get clear. I intercepted to give them time to get away, but I misjudged the timing, and he was able to grab me." He spoke quickly, like he hated each word he was saying. Like his admission that he'd helped someone was somehow a weakness.

"That's the second time you've literally risked your life for Essa. Why?"

"Just because you ask, it doesn't mean I have to tell you things. You're not my queen or my boss." Irritation threaded his voice, and he'd crossed his arms over his chest, mirroring her defensive posture.

In response, Arya deliberately uncrossed her arms and forced herself to relax her stance. "Fair enough. But perhaps you'll answer me this. Why didn't you tell me you'd saved her, back in Blackstone when you thought I was going to leave you behind? You know enough about me to know I'd feel obliged to help you in return."

He scoffed. "I don't want or need you doing me any favours, Raider. I could have gotten free of Blackstone all on my own."

Arya couldn't help it, she laughed. Probably thinking she was laughing *at* him, Leanir's face tightened with anger. It only made her grin wider. "Calm down, Leanir, I'm not insulting you. I know very well you could have gotten out of there on your own, and probably quicker than me. I'd have put money on it."

A hesitation, frown of puzzlement, then he dropped his arms too. "We got out faster doing it together."

"Indeed." She sighed. "I'm not letting you into my *cairdre,* Leanir, not when there is no trust between us."

He smiled then, a flash of white teeth. "The arrogance on you, thinking I want to be part of your *cairdre.* Staying out is fine with me, Raider."

"Well, it's *not* fine with me," she said. "I'm not convinced there can ever be trust between us, not after everything that's happened, but ... it definitely won't happen if we don't try. And the fact is, I need a full *cairdre* if I'm going to defeat the Nightstalker."

Wariness descended over the assassin like a cloud, and underneath his hard gaze, she thought she caught a flicker of fear. Guilt niggled at her. *She'd* put that fear there. "What does that mean?"

"It means I'm going to make the first move in building trust between us. You're free to go."

A long pause in which his assassins' gaze studied her like she was a rabid animal that could attack at any second. "What?"

"You're free, Leanir. I won't kill you if you leave, I won't try and track you down, and I won't compel you via our bond. Never again." She stepped forward, offered her hand. "My word on it."

He stared at her hand, his expression granite, so still it was unnerving.

"I'm not playing tricks and I'm not just giving you the illusion of choice." Arya spoke firmly. "I mean it, Leanir. Walk free. There's no trap."

After another long moment, he flicked that dark gaze up to meet hers, and crossed his arms over his chest again, leaving her hand hanging. "In that case, my choice is to stay."

Arya's eyebrows shot up. "What?"

"The Nightstalker kidnapped me and left me in prison to rot. If you hadn't gotten me out, he would have found a way to kill me in Blackstone. He's not going to stop hunting me." Leanir's gaze turned murderous. "I want the bastard dead, and you're my best chance of doing it."

Arya let out a breath, then started chuckling. Of course, there was a chance that this was a charade, that he was staying because he'd been turned by the Nightstalker. But something in Arya believed that Leanir was sincere; his anger and distrust were too real, too *him.* "This whole time you'd already decided to stick around, hadn't you? And still you made me go through that song and dance just now. Leanir, you are a piece of work."

"So are you, Arya Stormrider," he said.

"Touche." She caught and held his gaze. "You're sure?"

"I won't be your lackey, and I won't take orders from you, but I will help you bring him down." He paused. "I won't be in your *cairdre* and I'm not a member of your court. The first time you try to use our bond to compel me, I'll be gone so fast you won't even see me leave."

"Understood. An ally, then, until our mutual purpose is achieved?"

This time Leanir held out his hand. "My word on it."

Arya shook, the bond between them sparking briefly to life at their skin-to-skin contact. Both instinctively stifled it, which made Arya chuckle. "Well, as to your original question, we're going to deliver Miell safely home, and then I'll go to the Etherean to see what they know of the situation in Dunidaen. If Chiarn and Essa aren't with the Etherean, I'm going into Dunidaen to look for them, and Rorin."

Leanir's glance shifted to his wyvern, still watching Elendryl warily. After a moment, he turned back to Arya. "It suits me to stick close to you while the Nightstalker and his heir will be searching every inch of Andahar for us, so Mistryl and I will come with you."

Arya grinned. "That works out well. Because we're also taking someone else with us."

With perfect timing, footsteps sounded and Tiya emerged onto the roof, rucksack over her shoulders. Arya waved her over. "Leanir, this is Tiya. She's been hiding out here for months. It was her presence you were picking up."

"I knew it." Leanir scowled. "You're familiar. You used to work at The Ruined Arms in Heathrock."

"And you're a Shadeweaver assassin," Tiya said cheerfully. "What a pleasure."

Leanir's glare deepened, but his attention swivelled to the steps as Miell and Remien finally arrived. The young man lugged two packs made from blankets secured by rope while the older man carried nothing—if the sulking look on Miell's face was anything to go by, he wasn't very happy about it. Both came to a halt, eyes widening in appreciation, as Elendryl and Mistryl roused, wings spreading, and teeth snapping at each other.

"I never thought I'd see a Valheran again," Remien murmured, then looked at Arya. "They're small."

Elendryl let out a rip-roaring snarl, his serpentine head snaking towards Remien, teeth bared. "*Rude!*"

Mistryl merely stared at the old man, ice-cold aloofness in her stare, as if the opinions of a mere man meant no more to her than that of a fly.

Arya sighed, made no attempt to hold Elendryl back. "I think you've insulted my wyvern, Remien. Not the smartest course of action."

"I meant only that they're young, that in comparison to Xaphistryl, they—"

"Telling us things we already know is not part of the deal." Arya turned to Miell. "We're going to need directions to where your family are."

Miell dropped both packs, starting eagerly, "We—"

Remien let out an amused snort, cutting him off.

"What?" Leanir asked, glancing between the old man and Miell, who was scowling at being interrupted, as if nobody had dared to do that to him in his life before. Tiya stood off to the side, idly curling a strand of her silver hair, lively interest in her expression.

"Miell here never told you why he was in Blackstone, I suppose?" Remien asked.

No, but she had an idea. Arya looked at Miell, whose ire was fading, replaced by a flush in his cheeks. "Out with it."

"I was put in Blackstone as of way of keeping my father in line," he said.

"Who's your father?" When he hesitated, Arya gave a frustrated eyeroll. "I'm not quite as stupid as you seem to think I am, Miell. From the moment we met you treated me as if you were high lord of the castle and I a mere servant. I already know you're important somehow."

Remien started chuckling at the mix of surprise and annoyance on Miell's face.

Miell conceded. "My father is Rafel of House Lightbringer, prince of the horselords."

"You're a member of a Sky Lord House?" she asked, eyes widening.

Miell's golden eyes met hers. "Yes. I'm my father's heir, but neither of us are potentials. That's why we're still alive."

"What does that mean, prince of the horselords?" Leanir wanted to know.

"Horselords live in mostly independent tribes, but when needed, my father is the voice of our people. In old times, the prince represented us at the Stormrider monarch's court. Now, the position is no more than symbolic. Like everyone else in Andahar, we do what the Nightstalker says. And any born into our family with Sky Lord potential are hunted down and killed by his nazal. Or turned into nazal themselves."

Arya let out a long breath. She'd picked up on Miell being an important noble early on. It was the reason she'd taken him with her—knowing he could be a useful tool if he was from an influential family. But this was better than she'd even imagined. Still, she frowned. "If we return you to your family, won't the Nightstalker take you right back?"

"We horselords know how to hide, and none will talk of my return. My father can pretend I never came home after my escape," Miell said. "I'll have to stay in hiding, but I'll be safe."

"I've heard that the Nightstalker has spies everywhere," she said, not missing Remien's little nod of agreement.

"Not amongst the horselords," Miell said.

"All right then." The risk was his to take. "Let's get you home."

"I won't forget it, and neither will my father."

"Good," she murmured, resting a hand on his shoulder. "Because one day I'm going to call in that favour."

Chapter 12

They flew east from the Storm Spire. Miell cried out in excitement when they crossed the border into Navaria after half a day of flying. According to the prince, Navaria was the name given to horselord territory, and it spread across the entire northeastern corner of the Andahari landmass west of the Horn.

As far as Arya could tell, it was nothing but wide rolling plains covered in wavy yellow grass, interspersed by patches of thick woodland. There was the occasional lake or stream, but mostly they flew for hours over endless grass and trees. Every now and then she spotted large herds of grazing horses. Sometimes there were villages nearby, sometimes not. All the villages or towns she did see were located near the patches of woodland.

Despite the unwavering sameness of the lands below them, Miell seemed to know exactly where to go and directed Arya without hesitation. Leanir and Mistryl followed, but flew higher and stayed well back—Remien and Tiya riding with the Shadeweaver—so none looking up from below would see them. She was mindful of what Niallin had once told her about spies, how the Nightstalker had them everywhere. Miell said the horselords could be trusted, but she wasn't going to take that as fact. If her visit to the horselord prince was reported to the Nightstalker, she didn't want him to know that anyone else was with her.

Late in the day, as the sinking sun bathed the swaying grasses in a fiery orange glow, Miell stiffened with excitement and pointed ahead. Arya followed his gaze to the largest settlement she had seen yet—a sprawling town so vast that the smoke from hundreds of cookfires curled into the sky, visible for miles.

The rolling plains rose into a series of high hills, their backs pressed against thick woodland. At their base stood a handful of permanent structures, but beyond them, thousands of tents of varying shapes and sizes sprawled outward, stretching for miles. A wide avenue of untouched grass cut through the heart of the encampment, leading directly to a castle-like structure set into the hillside. From its elevated perch, whoever resided there—presumably the prince—held a commanding view over the makeshift city and the endless plains beyond.

"Lightbringer's Tor," Miell breathed in joy.

"House Lightbringer have always been horselords?" Arya asked.

He snorted, as if the question were ridiculous. "Always. Can you take me down, please? There's no danger."

"Maybe not, but I'm going to land on the high ground." She had no intention of bringing Elendryl down in the midst of thousands of people she didn't know, and who hadn't seen a wyvern other than Xaphistryl for decades, if ever.

Her wyvern touched down at the flat peak of the hilltop above the castle. As he did so, Mistryl veered out to the east, circling higher into the darkening skies to wait. Elendryl's descent from the sky—his golden scales blazing like fire against the setting sun—sent a ripple of controlled but urgent movement in the horselord city. Within minutes, a group of riders—roughly thirty strong—was charging up a narrow path towards them, their pace reckless even by the standards of seasoned horsemen.

Arya eyed them as they came. If all horselords could use a bow even half as well as they rode, they'd be an incredibly powerful weapon as a cavalry unit in an army. She gave Miell a considering look. He was watching them come with shining eyes.

She slid down from Elendryl's back then lifted a hand to help Miell after her. Miell slapped her hand away and scrambled down on his own, walking forward to meet the riders cresting the rise. They brought their racing horses to a standstill with ease, one by one lowering the bows they carried as they recognised Miell standing before them. Several let out cries of surprise and excitement.

The lead rider dismounted. She looked a year or two older than Miell, but had the same tawny hair and golden eyes. She threw herself at him with a shout of joy which he returned as he wrapped his arms around her. A sister, Arya guessed.

They clung to each other fiercely, much as Arya would have done if Rorin had appeared right now, and she was suddenly glad she'd broken Miell out of Blackstone if for no other reason than to bring him back to his family.

Arya walked forward, hands in the air to demonstrate she was no threat, wanting to keep some distance between Elendryl and the riders in case he got snappy. She was glad of it as her wyvern released a warning snarl when several riders moved in her direction. They halted, shooting the wyvern wary looks, and some of the horses backed away, snorting. None reared or responded with panic, which astonished Arya.

Miell grinned from ear to ear as he disentangled himself. "It's so good to see you, Rylea."

"He let you free?" she exclaimed, golden eyes bright, both hands still gripping Miell's shoulders. "But how, and why?"

"I escaped," Miell said, voice full of pride.

"Nobody escapes from Blackstone," one of the other riders called out.

Miell puffed his chest. "Nobody is me."

"Seriously?" Arya asked, lifting an eyebrow.

Miell turned towards her. "Everyone, allow me to introduce Arya Storm-rider, King Rian's lost heir. We escaped Blackstone together."

A hush fell over the group, eyes going wide. But there was wariness too, if not a hint of disbelief. Saying nothing, Arya rolled up her right sleeve and lifted her arm, showing them the lightning scar. The young woman's gaze narrowed, and she stared at Arya for a long moment, before returning her attention to Miell. "In that case, you can't stay long. We'll have to get you to one of our safe places before the Nightstalker comes looking for you here."

"I know, but I wanted to see you and Ma and Pere before I leave," Miell said. "Arya, this is my elder sister, Rylea Lightbringer. Those with her are her outriders, and mine. We all grew and trained together. It's the way of things for horselords."

"Pleased to meet you." Arya offered her hand. "You and your outriders responded with impressive speed and bravery to the appearance of a wyvern."

Rylea took it after a slight hesitation. "What do you want of us?"

"Nothing. For now. I just wanted to make sure Miell got home safely." Arya paused. "Why is *he* the heir if you're the older sibling?"

Miell snorted. "Women don't rule in Navaria."

"Why?" Arya asked.

"Yes, Miell, *why*? Do enlighten our Sky Lord guest." Rylea asked, lifting her eyebrows.

They'd had this argument before, many times. It was clear in the way they glared at each other. "It's the way things are. Men are better at leading."

Arya laughed, the sound erupting out of her and causing Miell's scowl to deepen. Rylea gave Arya a grudging nod.

"I think that's my cue." Arya turned to Miell. "Stay safe, Miell. You remember your promise?" Not to breathe a word of any of her companions to anyone, even those he trusted.

"I do, and I swear to keep it." He looked serious for once, and it reassured her. "Thank you, Arya, for your help."

"You are welcome to stay," Rylea said, and there was only a hint of reluctance in her voice. "Our father will want to meet the Sky Lord who helped Miell, and you have earned guest rights amongst us."

"I appreciate that, but I cannot stay, not this time, at least," Arya said. "But if I have my way, we will all see each other again." After all, she'd broken Miell out of prison for a reason. And if Rylea and her outriders were representative of horselord skill ... one way or another, she felt certain she'd be back.

"Farwell, Arya." Miell lifted his hand.

***

Arya and Leanir flew southeast through the following day—Remien with Leanir, Tiya with Arya—avoiding flying over the Horn and the Riverlands and instead crossing ocean until the magnificent peaks of the Diamondfang loomed on the horizon. Waves crashed against rocky cliffs far below as they left ocean behind and the wyverns weaved through snow-capped mountaintops towards the home of the Etherean.

As they flew, Arya reached for the bonds she shared with Chiarn and Essa, but it was clear they were much further away than the Etherean citadel—likely in Dunidaen, or possibly Khadini. Although ... as she got incrementally closer to them, it felt like Chiarn and Essa were in different places. Disappointment rippled through her. She was desperate to *see* her Sky Lords. Make sure they really were okay.

She fought the urge to reach for Darmanin and assure herself that he was okay too. Arya couldn't imagine the amount of focus it must take for him to maintain a flawless façade of loyalty in the presence of a Sky Lord as powerful as the Nightstalker. The last thing she wanted to do was distract him at a crucial moment, especially given what she'd asked him to do. Guilt and fear in equal measure continued to plague her, part of her sure she should have insisted Darmanin return and join their *cairdre* instead of risking his life so profoundly. But the rest of her trusted in him, in his strength and cleverness, that she knew it was the right decision.

The hazy outline of the Etherean citadel grew visible in the distance. Elendryl banked sharply, circling to land in a sheltered valley. Once he was down, Arya looked over her shoulder at her passenger. "Are you sure you don't want to come? We won't be staying long, so if things didn't go well with your father—"

"I am certain, Arya," Tiya cut her off gently.

Arya nodded and the woman scrambled down, showing no signs of cold despite the freezing wind whipping around them. She hefted her pack and looked up at Arya. "Please say nothing to him."

"If that's what you want." Arya let out a sigh. "I'll be back for you tomorrow morning. Try not to get eaten by a snow leopard in the meantime."

Tiya waved as Elendryl took off in a flurry of snow, swooping up to rejoin Mistryl circling above. The mid-afternoon sun gleamed off the marble city as the wyverns glided into the gaping entry cavern, startling a group of winged folk heading out to soar the peaks.

Arya dropped to the floor, lungs already struggling to suck in enough air. She'd kept her muscles strong during her imprisonment in Blackstone, but there'd been no opportunity to work on her stamina. At least Leanir was impacted too, she realised with some satisfaction, his breathing coming shallow and fast as he joined her. Remien trailed him even more slowly, wheezing with each step.

"Neither Essa nor Chiarn are here, so I won't be long. Do you want to wait here or come up?" Arya asked Leanir.

His watchful assassin's gaze stared around with interest. "I've never been here before."

Unexpected surprise flashed through her. Had Leanir ever looked interested in something? She didn't think she'd ever seen anything in him but anger, frustration, or that flat, killing stare. It was a sharp reminder that he was a person, not just a killer. "Then let's go."

Pride had her taking the main stairs from the entry cavern into the citadel proper with quick strides. That, and wanting to see whether she could get Leanir to ask for a break.

He did not.

Unfortunately, Remien was alarmingly red in the face by the time he struggled to the top, so she had to wait for him to recover, then continue at a slower pace. Leanir shot her a triumphant smirk, as if he knew exactly what she'd tried to do. She scowled.

Sun shone brightly through the arched windows in the reception area outside the elder's quarters, taking the edge off the icy mountain air. The two guards posted at the elder's door waved them through immediately—word had clearly gone ahead of their arrival—though their curious gazes lingered on Leanir and Remien as all three passed by. Leanir's look sent one of them stepping backwards a full pace, hand scrabbling for his sword.

"Admit it," Arya murmured. "You do that on purpose."

He shrugged. "I don't like to be crowded."

The reception area was empty, more sunlight spilling across the marble floors from the windows directly ahead. To Arya's immediate left a large door stood open. In all her previous visits it had been closed. What she'd always assumed was the entrance to the elder's bedroom was in fact a short hallway leading to another open door. Since the elder was nowhere in sight, she turned and headed along it.

The hallway opened onto the side of a wide stage at the bottom of a vast amphitheatre. The ceiling soared several stories above, where Arya could just make out a series of entry doors. A grand staircase descended from the central door to the stage, its steps worn smooth with use.

Only a few rows of seats lined the front—likely reserved for those too young, old, or injured to fly—while the rest of the floor remained open. Overhead, the domed roof, made entirely from glass, revealing an unbroken view of the sky.

It was spectacular.

The elder stood at the front of the stage, conferring with two other winged folk. At Arya's arrival, he gave one powerful beat of his sky-blue wings and crossed the space between them, landing gracefully. Astonishment and relief filled his voice. "Lord Stormrider. I must admit, I feared the worst after we learned of Darmanin's betrayal and your capture. It's incredibly good to see you."

Arya bowed her head, fighting the urge to study his features for any similarity to Tiya. "Elder Salyarin. It's good to see you. Thank you for seeing me so quickly—it seems like we've caught you in the middle of something."

He blinked, glanced over her shoulder. "It's nothing important. You've brought guests?"

Arya gestured to her companions. "The Nightstalker captured both Leanir and I and put us in Blackstone prison, but as you can see, we escaped and are well. Elder, this is—"

"Remien Inkweaver." The elder's gaze went wide with astonishment. "I thought you long dead."

Arya lifted an eyebrow. "You two know each other?"

"I visited a time or two before the Nightstalker's coup," Remien said. "Salyarin here was just a boy, then."

"How did you…" Salyarin's voice trailed off. "He put you in Blackstone. You've been there all these years?"

"When it was clear I wasn't a Sky Lord potential, yes. He put me in there and forgot all about me." Remien said. "Thought that was a nastier fate than killing me outright, I suppose."

Arya turned back to the elder. "I don't suppose *you* can tell me why Ranier wants his brother dead?"

"I…" Salyarin blinked again. "What do you mean?"

"A story for another time." Arya dismissed the question, impatience rising. "There are more important things to discuss. What can you tell me of events since my capture?"

Salyarin made a helpless motion. "We fled Gateport when you left to face the Nightstalker and haven't dared to leave the citadel since."

She frowned. "If you fled Gateport, how did you learn of Darmanin's betrayal?"

"Lord Flamewielder fled straight here after the Nightstalker captured you." Salyarin must have seen the concern on her face, because he hurried to add. "He was well. Exhausted from flying non-stop, terrified Xaphistryl was chasing him, but well. He stayed here a few days, but then left for the Icelands. He felt it best to keep moving. He expected the Nightstalker and his nazal to be hunting him and didn't want to place us in danger."

"What of Essa? Or Rorin and the Dunidae warlords—have you had *any* contact with them? News of how they fare against the Nightstalker's invasion force?"

"None, I'm afraid. We dare not fly messengers near the battle for fear of the firedrakes and the nazal. Let alone if Xaphistryl were to return."

"Then you've just been hiding up here hoping it all goes away?" Arya's frustration boiled over. Winged warriors would be a boon for the battle of Dunidaen, a way to counter the threat of firedrakes and the bat-like creatures the nazal flew, not to mention their healing magic. If he'd just though to *help* rather than—

At her side, Remien gave a little cough. Leanir had wandered off. Presumably making sure there were no threats in the area.

"We are not a violent people," Salyarin said. "Hiding is our best protection."

"I used to think the same thing, Elder. I was wrong. If Dunidaen falls, you will be in an even more vulnerable position than you are now."

A weighty silence fell. Salyarin eventually cleared his throat and changed the subject. "Why didn't the Nightstalker kill you and Leanir?"

"Chiarn was right, Darmanin betrayed us," Arya said. "He made a deal to join the Nightstalker in return for keeping me alive."

Arya gave Salyarin an immense amount of credit for not saying 'I told you so.' Instead, all he said was, "I have heard awful things about Blackstone. I am glad you won free, Lord Stormrider."

"Thank you." She let out a breath. "Our wyverns need to hunt and then rest. And we need fresh clothes and a bath. Can we stay here tonight before we travel onwards?"

The elder offered a warm, genuine smile. "You may stay as long as you wish, Lord Stormrider. Lord Mindbreaker, Arya can show you Lord Flamewielder's rooms, and Lord Inkweaver, you can—"

"Essa is Lord Inkweaver." Arya's voice cracked out. "You can just call Remien by his name, Elder."

Remien's mouth turned up in amusement. "The Stormrider, while arrogant as always, is right."

The elder bowed his head. "Rest as long as you need."

After seeing Leanir and Remien settled—although she assumed the Shadeweaver would leave as soon as she left him to go and *patrol*—Arya entered her old rooms and shed her clothing with relief. She ran herself a bath and sank into it, sighing with pleasure as the warm water soaked into tired muscles.

Reluctantly climbing out when the water went cold, Arya dressed in blissfully clean Etherean clothing, then left her room to return to the elder's tower. The guards didn't seem surprised to see her. "He asked us to show you straight in if you came back."

"Thanks, Rithil."

Salyarin sat on a plush couch near his stunning window view, quill poised over a piece of parchment. He looked up at her entrance, immediately putting the parchment and quill aside. "I was hoping you'd come back to talk."

Arya's stomach growled as she took a seat opposite him and spotted the plates of food set out on the table. "Do you mind?"

"It's for you." He chuckled. "I thought you'd probably been flying a long time and would be hungry."

Arya snagged a piece of toasted bread, put some cheese on it, and wandered over to the window as she chewed. The sun was lowering behind the peaks, and even her hundredth experience of the view over the citadel did not diminish its stunning beauty. "How was Chiarn when he was here?"

"He seemed very sad. And afraid. He was horrified that Darmanin had betrayed you. I think it broke his heart in a way."

Arya considered that. Chiarn and Darmanin had never been particularly close, neither much liking the other, but the Sky Lord bond was a powerful thing. She wondered how much that explained Leanir risking his life for Essa's. "But *you* weren't surprised." It wasn't a question.

"You know I've long held fears regarding Darmanin's ability to turn on you, and I've been open with you about them. The better question is how do *you* feel about his betrayal?" The elder looked genuinely curious.

She smiled, but it held no warmth. "I think you know me well enough by now to know the answer to that. I have no tolerance or temper for betrayal."

His gaze narrowed. "Can you really be so cavalier? You had feelings for him, he was one of your *cairdre*."

"Both were once true. Now, Darmanin is simply another obstacle on my path to defeating the Nightstalker."

Salyarin hesitated, eyes scanning her face. He wasn't sure whether to believe her. "There is no more protection for any of us, Arya, not after we publicly supported you at the State Council. We might feel we are hiding here, not stepping foot out of the citadel, but the truth is that safety is now an illusion. The fate of my people rests on you. I hope I have not chosen wrongly."

Annoyed by how his dramatic words touched on her doubts, Arya huffed a breath. "The fate of your people is on your shoulders as much as it is mine, Elder. Speaking of, don't you think this would be a good time to have your heir here, ready to take over if the worst should happen?"

Salyarin's expression closed over. "That is for the Etherean to decide if I die."

She pinned his gaze. "My understanding is that Etherean succession works the same as in Dunidaen, or Andahar. The title of elder is taken by a child of the previous elder."

He didn't look away, but he was uncomfortable. A sheen of sweat beaded his forehead. Eventually he said stiffly. "You are correct."

"Goodness me, Elder, this is like pulling teeth. You've told me before that you have an heir, though they are lost. I assume that means you *do* have a child?"

"My heir cannot rule, that is all you need to know as my ally. If I were to die, the Etherean would choose amongst themselves a leader to become elder."

"Why can't your heir rule?" she asked bluntly. "What of the dream-walking magic you've told me only you and your heir possess?" She saw his expression shutting down, but kept going. "I hope to everything you survive this, Elder, I consider you a friend as well as an ally. But if something were to happen, it would be in the middle of a war. Is that really the best time for your whole society to try and agree upon who succeeds you?"

He said nothing.

"I remind you that I have trusted you with the secret of *my* succession." Kirin, with Essa as regent until he came of age.

His jaw worked, then, "I have explained the process to you, which is all you need to know. As you have told me in the past, my country and my people are *my* business," he snapped.

He had her there. She'd thrown that argument at him more than once in a temper, so she reluctantly let it go. Arya returned to sit on the couch opposite him, leaning forward and holding his gaze. "Now that I'm back, you can't keep hiding here any longer. As formal allies, I expect your support when I ask for it."

"And you will have it, as before. Your demeanour, your new company, they tell me a lot." Salyarin sat back, relaxing, "You got yourself put in Blackstone deliberately, didn't you?"

"Ranier has only ever drip-fed me information, and only when it aligned with his interests. You don't know enough to help me. Remien was the heir to House Inkweaver, and has all the same knowledge as Ranier, if not more. I need that if I'm going to figure out a way to win against overwhelming odds."

"I would be careful with Remien if I were you," Salyarin warned.

"I don't trust him as far as I can throw him." Arya agreed. "Especially since Ranier showed up as we escaped Blackstone and tried to drive a knife through his heart." She told Salyarin everything about that night, and what had happened since. He seemed as bewildered by it as she did.

"I don't remember much about Remien that could help you." Salyarin said thoughtfully. "But it appears to me as if Ranier might have been watching Blackstone, perhaps even planning on trying to break in, to get at his brother."

"I agree. He disappeared eight months ago, leading the nazal away after he and Dar broke me out of Darkclaw. I question what happened in that time to make him hide out near Blackstone, looking to get at his brother, rather than returning to Dunidaen and his Shadeweavers, not to mention his own daughter?"

"I wish I could help you. Whatever it is, it can't be good. Both brothers could be incredibly dangerous to you."

"I'd initially planned on asking you to host Remien here safely while I venture into Dunidaen, but I worry that puts your people in danger if Ranier comes looking for him."

"The only way for Ranier to get here without a wyvern is to climb the peaks, and my scouts would see him coming. And he has no way of knowing his brother is here in the first place." Salyarin smiled. "We will host Remien here for you."

"Thank you, Elder. I won't be long in returning for him." With food in her stomach and the soft cushions under her, a sleepy lassitude was stealing over Arya. "I'd best get some sleep. Thank you for the food."

She paused at the door, a random question occurring. "Elder, I've never thought to ask this. I suppose I've never cared much, but what is the Storm-rider Sky Lord ability?"

Salyarin smiled slowly. "That is a question with an obvious answer, Arya. I suggest thinking on it a while."

Arya awoke from deep sleep suddenly in the middle of the night, eyes opening to the darkness of her room. A moment later she began chuckling to herself. The sound reverberated off the walls of the room, making it light despite the shadows.

An obvious answer indeed.

***

Arya woke early the following morning, opening her door to find Leanir waiting outside. Thick cloud draped the peaks, limiting visibility considerably. She hoped Tiya had been warm enough spending the night out in the mountains.

"Where to next, Raider?" he asked.

"Good morning to you too, Leanir." She tugged her woollen beanie down over her ears; the air was biting cold. "I'm going to find some food, and then Elendryl, Tiya, and I are headed to Chiarn in the Icelands. After that, Dunidaen. Remien will stay here for now."

He considered that for a moment, then pushed off the walkway's railing. "I've never been to the Icelands."

She smothered a smile. Who'd have thought it, a cold-blooded assassin interested in exploring new places? "Then you're in for a treat, Leanir. The Icelands are as cold as your temper."

***

They flew out an hour later, Elendryl leading the way as the two wyverns circled the peaks and then headed northeast towards the Icelands. Flying through such thick fog was an eerie experience; she had to rely entirely on Elendryl's flight instincts, trusting that he wouldn't fly them straight into a mountainside.

Unlike on the journey there, Tiya was quiet behind her, lost in her thoughts. Arya wondered if she was regretting not going to see her father. Or maybe she just missed her home. After a while, the quiet bothered Arya too. Left to her own thoughts, she couldn't stop the worries crowding her mind.

Kirin. Rorin. Essa. Darmanin. She'd won a small battle in retrieving Remien, but the Nightstalker would respond, she had no doubt of that.

She had so much to lose. And he was so powerful.

"*Afraid?*" Elendryl sent.

"*For those I love, yes.*"

He sent her a shiver of warm reassurance, and she pressed her palm against his scales, allowing her bond with her wyvern to soothe her doubts and fear.

Chapter 13

It was late afternoon when Elendryl led them over the village where Er'fin At'eir's tribe lived. As he landed in the snow, bright gold against stark white, Arya reached for the thread between her and Chiarn, and gave it a tug. Surprise and shock and delight shivered along their connection. He wasn't at the village, but he wasn't far, and already she could sense him moving towards her. One of the tangled knots of worry and fear in her chest loosened, and she let out a sigh.

Mistryl landed nearby, and the female wyvern watched Elendryl closely as Leanir dropped to the snow and slogged over to join Arya. Tiya seemed oblivious to the cold, despite her lack of cloak or layers. Her eyes were bright with interest as she studied their surroundings. Their arrival had been noticed and Icefolk streamed out of the village towards them. The first to reach them was At'near, At'eir's cousin.

"Arya!" She stopped in surprise, then leaped forward to wrap her in a bearhug, her long white dreadlocks whipping around to tap against Arya's back.

Laughing, Arya hugged her back. "It's good to see you too, At'near. Is the er'fin here?"

"He's out on a hunt, but we're expecting them back any moment." At'near stepped back, warrior's gaze raking over Arya's companions. "Who are they?"

Arya gestured. "This is Leanir Mindbreaker. And Tiya, an old friend."

"Another member of your *cairdre*!" At'near's gaze widened, impressed.

"No, I'm not," Leanir said.

"We're still working out some trust issues," Arya explained while Leanir glowered.

"Pleased to meet you, At'near." Tiya bowed her head. "You have an incredibly beautiful home."

At'near noticed Tiya's lack of layers, her comfort in the environs, and clearly saw a kindred spirit. Her smile broadened in welcome. But before she could say anything, a series of shouts whipped around them, carried on the breeze—patrolling guards challenging someone approaching the village. Elendryl's head came up, teeth bared, and Mistryl flared her wings with a snarl, ready to take flight. Arya turned to see a line of Icefolk warriors crest a rise in the distance and move towards them in their characteristic ground-eating jog.

One of the running figures had bright copper hair that shone bright against his stark surroundings. He ran as swiftly as the others, his gait loose, Icefolk twin swords sheathed at his back.

Her Flamewielder.

A little concerned about the mood she might find him in, Arya started towards them. Chiarn broke into a sprint as soon as he saw her, passing the line of warriors and sliding to a stop before her, blue eyes alight and flickering with his flame magic. The bond between them simmered to life, pulsing with energy and their combined pleasure at being reunited. "Arya! You're here."

Arya stared at him, shook her head and looked again. "Salyarin said you were..."

He grinned. "You thought I'd gone back to my old self. Hiding out and drinking my sorrows away?"

She winced. That was exactly what she'd worried about. Chiarn had never wanted to be a Sky Lord, or a warrior. He'd always run from danger, a self-proclaimed coward. "Not exactly."

"The er'fin and his warriors have been teaching me to fight," he said proudly, standing tall. "They still beat me within half a minute in every sparring match, but I can hold these blades properly now. *And* I can run."

"They look good on you," she said approvingly. "And if At'eir let you go on an ice bear hunt, then he thinks you're capable."

His face fell. "You still must think me a coward, running away like I did that day. Everything just happened so quickly, and I—"

"Chiarn, stop." She held up a hand. "I don't blame you for anything. I ordered you to run, remember? Darmanin's betrayal changed everything."

Chiarn's face clouded over. "I never thought he could do something like that."

"He's a traitor, it's as simple as that," Leanir spoke suddenly. He and Tiya had trailed after Arya without her noticing. She swore at letting her guard down like that. "You look as pretty as always, singer."

"Hello, Chiarn," Tiya said. "It's been a while."

Chiarn looked between Tiya and Leanir, eyebrows raised. "I'm not even going to ask why you're here, lovely Tiya." He jerked a thumb at Leanir. "But are we happy that the assassin is alive?"

"It's…" Arya cocked her head in thought. "Let's just call it useful."

Leanir glowered. "Your concern is touching."

"Where *were* you all this time?" Chiarn asked, darkness clouding his blue eyes. "Your connection to me snapped, gone, and I thought you must have…"

"The Nightstalker put both of us in Blackstone prison in Andahar. The walls are filled with cazaix to block a Sky Lord's magic," she said, then looked over his shoulder as At'eir arrived at the head of his warriors, towering over everyone. He'd deliberately slowed his pace to give them time to talk.

"Lord Stormrider. It is an absolute pleasure to see you."

More joy rippled through her at the sight of her old friend. "I feel the same, Er'fin." She reached out with her off hand, palm facing outwards. He did the same, pressing his palm against hers and they bowed their heads in the traditional Icefolk greeting and farewell. "This is Leanir Mindbreaker. And Tiya, an incredible healer and good friend."

At'eir acknowledged them with a nod. "We feared the worst after Chiarn brought news of your defeat at the hands of the Nightstalker."

"So did everyone, it would seem," Leanir said dryly. "Do you think we could talk further *inside*? It's freezing out here."

At'eir turned to his cousin. "At'near, gather the skinners. At'hur and At'kar will take them to the fallen bear. I will take our guests to my hut. You'll join us once you're done."

Built down into the snow as a form of insulation, At'eir's hut was nonetheless large, with room enough for a table covered with maps, a stove, and bedding in the back behind a screen. The Icefolk prince waved them to the table and sat a pot of water above the stove to boil for tea. Chiarn started a crackling fire with a single click of his fingers, earning a grateful nod from At'eir.

"What can you tell me of the situation in Dunidaen?" Arya asked as soon as the er'fin sat down. She'd explained to him about Blackstone on the walk to his hut. "I stopped at the citadel on the way here, but Elder Salyarin knew little."

"The most recent news I have is a message from the High Warlord over a month old, and it wasn't good," At'eir said without preamble. "At the time, his forces were holding the southeastern corner of Dunidaen, but they were under heavy and constant attack and losing ground every week."

"When you say High Warlord, you mean...?"

"Your brother, Rorin Ravenstrike," At'eir said, and Arya's shoulders relaxed in relief. Tiya gave her a little smile. "From what I understand, he was confirmed as High Warlord in an emergency Council right after you left Gateport."

Arya sifted through the parchment on the table until she found a map of Dunidaen, then pushed it towards At'eir. "Can you show me in more detail? Everything the message told you."

"The invading army holds most of Crowtalon State, but for now the Dunidae forces are holding them a few miles west of Gateport." At'eir pointed on the map. "Eaglesoar is free, as is most of Hawkesdale and all of Ravenstrike. But the invaders have pushed north into the lower half of SparrowWing, and they hold Seelan and the southwest corner of Hawkesdale. Rorin said the nazal general has concentrated its attack on breaking through the Dunidae lines to take Gateport and the entire south of Dunidaen—he believes the nazal wants to achieve that before pushing further north."

Arya nodded. "It's what I would do. Pushing north now would mean splitting its forces, a vulnerability the nazal doesn't need to risk if it's confident of eventually taking Gateport and the south. Did Rorin give you numbers?"

The kettle started whistling, and Chiarn rose to pour the water into four tin cups. The scent of cinnamon and vanilla filled the tent, and both Arya and Tiya sniffed appreciatively.

At'eir nodded thanks as Chiarn placed a cup before him, then answered Arya's question. "The High Warlord's scouts report roughly fifty thousand soldiers in the invasion force, all on foot, led by the nazal. They have shadowhounds too, but only use them sparingly. No wraiths or firedrakes so far. Your brother didn't detail the size of his remaining force—I assume he was worried the message might be intercepted."

"What about the Nightstalker? Has he engaged in the battle at all?"

"The High Warlord hasn't mentioned him."

Arya sat back, considering. It had been over a month since Rorin had written the message. The Dunidae army would likely have lost even more ground in that time. "And what of the Nightstalker's new ally, the Khadini emperor? Has he continued to supply the invading force with his Rangers?" She assumed Atan uq-Danresan's end goal was taking Crowtalon State; if he held that, then the Khadini controlled the Dreadwater Gate and Dunidaen's only land access to his country.

"Your brother indicated the Rangers still fight with the nazal's forces, but have not been supplemented with more warriors. He wrote to the emperor to request a truce, but had no response."

Chiarn leaned forward, "Arya, I know you're hungry for news of Dunidaen and your brother, but we are equally desperate. Will you tell us what happened to you?"

Arya glanced at Leanir, whose gaze was flicking around the tent, watching for threats as always. Tiya was studying one of the maps, a frown of concentration on her face as she absently sipped her tea.

"I've heard of Blackstone," At'eir added. "Nobody has ever escaped, at least, that's how I heard it."

"That's no longer true," Arya said, then detailed everything that had happened since the day they'd faced the Nightstalker.

"I'm so glad you're okay." Chiarn's gaze was downcast. "I came here to try and grow stronger, but if I'm honest, I was terrified. I didn't know what to do if you were truly gone."

"Dead is what you'd be," Leanir said bluntly. "You can swing those pretty blades around all you like, but without her protection, it would be a matter of weeks before the Nightstalker got to you."

"Enough, Leanir," Arya snapped.

He held his hands up. "I'm just stating the truth."

"The truth as *you* see it," she said. "That doesn't make it fact. The Flamewielder is far stronger and more capable than you think."

Chiarn's gaze shot upwards, surprise glimmering in his firelit blue eyes. "You mean that."

"I do." Arya sat back, turning her gaze to At'eir. "What is the situation here in the Icelands?"

At'eir called for the warriors on guard at the hut's entrance. A woman ducked her head inside, eyebrows raised. "Fetch our guest would you, Ish'aya?"

"Er'fin." She gave a crisp nod and disappeared.

As they waited, At'eir explained, "There have been no further leadership challenges since my mother put down the Ce'Garn months ago. Cair Is'heim is calm, but the queen has moved the Icefolk to war footing. She is not taking the Andahari invasion of Dunidaen, or the Khadini emperor's alliance with the Nightstalker, lightly. We both believe there is a good chance the Nightstalker will come for us next."

"What does being on war footing mean?" Tiya asked, finally looking up from the map she'd been studying.

"Regular joint tribal patrols along our border with Falconcrest State. Our navy sailing regular patrols of the western coastline. The walls of Cair Is'heim being reinforced to weather ground and naval attack."

Arya decided not to beat around the bush. "Will you send aid to Dunidaen, if I ask it?"

"I assumed you would ask." At'eir let out a breath "The short answer is yes, but we cannot afford to send the numbers you would need to make a difference against fifty thousand Nightblades."

"I will take whatever you can spare, Er'fin," Arya said. "I know you must keep enough in reserve to protect your own country. And if you *were* to come under attack, our alliance means that I would ride to your aid." She hoped it didn't come to that. It would split her forces in a way she doubted she could sustain and take her focus away from Andahar.

"The Icefolk will provide the aid you request, Lord Stormrider. It is something I have already discussed with the queen."

Before Arya could respond, the door flap rustled, and a hulking Icefolk man wearing a white wolf pelt entered. He looked about Arya's age, his long braids falling almost to his waist, twin swords strapped to his back. He bowed his head formally in At'eir's direction. "Er'fin."

"Lord Arya Stormrider, allow me to introduce you to Ja'hur Ce'Garn, chief of the Ce'Garn. The queen appointed Ja'hur to lead his tribe after the recent execution of his father."

Ja'hur again bowed in Arya's direction, his expression showing nothing of what he thought of At'eir's casual reference to his father's death. "Lord Stormrider." He spoke with a deep, resonating voice.

"Well met, Chief Ce'Garn," she replied just as politely.

"As he is young and untried, the queen thought it would be good for the Ce'Garn to spend some time with my tribe, learn how to be a good chief," At'eir explained.

"As you say, Er'fin." Ja'hur spoke without inflection. "I am honoured by the opportunity."

A canny move on the queen's part, Arya thought. Ce'Garn could not refuse without risking losing his tribe, and now he would be under At'eir's watchful eye so that the er'fin could be sure he wouldn't present any future problems for the queen.

At'eir rose to his feet; he was of a height with Ja'hur, but not as broad. Even so, his authority dominated the room. "Ja'hur, the Stormrider heir requests our aid in the battle for Dunidaen. I will send one thousand warriors to march at her back. You will lead your warriors into Dunidaen, making up the thousand with some of my warriors."

Surprise flickered on the young man's face, followed by fierce glee. "You send us to fight, Er'fin?"

"I send you to fight and win on behalf of our alliance with House Stormrider and Dunidaen. By doing that, the queen and I seek to keep the Icelands secure."

Arya had not thought it possible, but Ja'hur straightened even further. "I will not fail the Icefolk in this, Er'fin At'eir."

"Your generosity won't be forgotten." Arya rose too, voice full of gratitude. One thousand Icefolk warriors was more than she could have hoped for. "Chief Ce'Garn, I would ask that you march your warriors south along Falconcrest's east coast, then hold once you reach the southern border and wait for my word."

His gaze shifted to her. "And if we encounter enemy soldiers on the march?"

"Try to avoid being seen if you can. I'd like the advantage of surprise. But if it cannot be avoided, you take them out."

"Understood." Ja'hur glanced between Arya and At'eir. "Moving at full run, but being cautious to avoid discovery … I estimate that will take us three weeks to travel that distance."

"Then I will aim to meet you here." Arya stabbed at a spot on Falconcrest's southern border. "In three weeks."

Ja'hur studied the spot, memorising it, then his gaze snapped up. "If you need nothing else, Er'fin, I will go to prepare my warriors. I'd like to move out as soon as they can be gathered."

At'eir gave a short nod. "You may choose whomever you wish from my warriors to make up your thousand, but my cousin At'near will march with you as your second. Dismissed."

Arya whistled as the tent flap dropped behind Ja'hur. "Canny move, At'eir. Dispatch a possible threat and all his warriors in one fell swoop."

"It will at least get him out of my hair for a while. He's got a good tactical mind on him, Arya, and he's a fierce fighter. He will be a boon to you." At'eir gave her a sideways look. "He would be a good marriage prospect for you, too. Such a marriage would strengthen the bonds between Andahar and the Icelands, as well as assist my mother in keeping his tribe under control."

"I'm not exactly thinking about marriage alliances just yet, At'eir," she said, ignoring Tiya and Chiarn's twin amused snorts.

"You should be," he said seriously. "A strong one could bring you weapons, money, and soldiers. All things you will desperately need."

"I hear you," she said, then turned to Leanir. "Will you travel with the Ce'Garn, keep an eye on them, and scout the landscape at the same time? I'd like to get a sense of whether the nazal's army has spread much into the north. You can also let me know if there are any delays through our bond."

Leanir considered. "I'll do it."

"Where will you be going?" At'eir asked Arya curiously.

She gave him her wolfish smile. "I'm going to win a war, Er'fin At'eir."

***

"Where *are* we going exactly?" Chiarn asked as they left the hut, all three blinking as bright sun gleamed off the white snow.

"You'll see."

"Arya, wait." Chiarn stopped, forcing her to halt as well. "We faced down the Nightstalker and we *lost*. Darmanin is on his side now. He still has three nazal. Won't the Nightstalker be on us the moment we put our heads above the metaphorical parapet? And when he does, what is different now from when he soundly defeated us only a few months ago?"

She let out a breath. They were good questions, fair ones. And spoken out loud like that, they dug up all her festering doubts. She tried to beat them back down by infusing her words with confidence. "What has changed, as strange as it might sound, is Darmanin."

Even Tiya frowned at that. "What do you mean?"

"Neither of us have any reason to fear the nazal anymore, Chiarn. And while I'm sure the Nightstalker expects me to help Dunidaen, I can't worry about that. Darmanin's betrayal has made the Nightstalker overconfident. As long as he wants to keep Dar by his side, he can't kill me, or you. The best he can do is re-capture me, and that makes things easier for us."

"Because if he comes for you, you can withdraw, avoid, then return," Tiya mused. "And he can't track you through your magic anymore, so it won't be so easy for him to find you."

Chiarn turned that over. "You're assuming he keeps his word to Darmanin, or that Darmanin holds him to it. Dar betrayed us, Arya, how long will he continue to care about our fate?"

She couldn't tell them the truth. It would place Darmanin in far too much danger. She had to keep up the ruse. But she hated it. Hated every second that her friends thought Darmanin would ever betray them, betray her. But she held to the fact that keeping the secret meant keeping him safer. And she needed him to be safe more than anything. "Yes, both are assumptions, but for now, I do believe the Nightstalker will hold to the deal."

The minstrel's eyes narrowed. "So we're off to Dunidaen."

"Right where he expects you go," Tiya observed.

She flashed them both a grin as Elendryl and Asandryl landed nearby. "Sometimes it's fun to be predictable, don't you think?"

"What do you know that we don't?" Tiya asked suspiciously.

"A queen needs her secrets."

"You know who you remind me of right now?" Chiarn grumbled as they headed for their wyverns. "That insufferably confident Ravenstrike general who dragged me out of my nice comfortable life and made me a Sky Lord."

"I thought we'd agreed that wasn't my fault?"

"It's not, but I like to keep blaming you for it anyway."

She chuckled, but her smile, along with the façade of confidence she'd projected, faded as she scrambled onto Elendryl's back and helped Tiya up behind her.

What did she know that they didn't?

That right now, Darmanin would be diverting the Nightstalker's attention away from Dunidaen by informing him that he'd tracked Arya into the Marshlands, that spies had heard reports of her hiding out there. The Nightstalker would no doubt launch fresh attacks on the marshfolk in an effort to re-capture her. Marshfolk would die, as much as Darmanin would try to limit it. *Her* people, given she claimed to be their queen, sacrificed for what she believed was the greater good. It made her feel sick, but also despairing, because she knew more terrible choices like this lay before her if she wanted to win.

Did she have the stomach to keep making those choices? Arya wasn't sure, and that doubt ate away at her. So many were putting their hopes in her, and what if she failed them because she didn't have the strength to do what was necessary?

Sensing her distress, Elendryl sent her a shiver of love and reassurance. She let it fill her, let her wyvern help her climb out of the abyss. She'd resolved months ago not to wallow in the consequences of her decisions, had learned that unless she made them with confidence she would fail. But it was easier said than done, and there were times, like now, where it just wasn't possible.

Arya closed her eyes and pictured Rorin in her mind. She focused on the fact she was going to see him soon, that she was finally going to help him, and put aside the doubts, even if only for a moment.

It was time to go home.

Chapter 14

For three days, they followed the eastern coastline along the Storm Channel, the wyverns skimming low over the white-capped ocean as they travelled south into Dunidaen. When they finally crossed into Falconcrest, Arya guided them toward a secluded stretch of coastline, choosing a quiet cove where a natural harbour offered shelter. As the wyverns touched down, their talons sank into the soft, damp sand. The group dismounted, gathering on the beach, the salty breeze tugging at their clothing as they took in their surroundings.

Chiarn spoke first. "What are we doing here? It looks like the middle of nowhere."

"We're waiting." Arya replied.

"For what?"

"You'll see," she said. "But I'm going to need Asandryl's help, if he's amenable. Elendryl's off to find something for me, so I'd appreciate Asandryl keeping an eye on our surroundings, make sure nobody stumbles across us here."

"Don't ask." Tiya rolled her eyes as Chiarn opened his mouth. "She's not going to tell you what her wyvern is looking for. We'd be better off expending our energy looking for firewood and a sheltered place to camp."

He sighed and rolled his eyes. "In that case, I volunteer to get a fire going. Someone else can kill and skin poor defenceless things to eat."

***

They camped for two days, Arya ignoring Chiarn's repeated questions and Tiya's frequent querying looks while Asandryl kept watch over them. It didn't help that she *hated* waiting. Now that she was free of Blackstone, she was desperate to find her brother and Essa, set her eyes on them, make sure they were okay. And she *itched* to join the war for Dunidaen. At least when she was *doing* something her terror for Kirin faded to the back of her mind, even if only temporarily. Daily she had to fight with herself not to abandon her plans and run to him.

But this … if she was right. This could change everything.

And so she waited. She and Chiarn busied themselves sparring—her Flamewielder *had* learned a lot with the Icefolk, even though he couldn't beat her yet. While they did that, Tiya went foraging for herbs and plants that helped with treating wounds or could be made into medicines.

When Elendryl landed just after dusk on the second evening, he brought with him the news she wanted to hear. "We'll leave first thing," she told Chiarn and Tiya.

Arya didn't sleep at all that night, despite knowing she should get as much rest as she could. Dawn broke on the horizon as she paced along the beach, waiting for her companions to wake and gather their packs.

"It's never a good sign when you vibrate with excitement like this," Chiarn muttered when he joined her.

She turned to him, sober. "You're ready for this? War."

He looked out over the ocean. "It's not my favourite part of being a Sky Lord, I admit."

"We wipe out the invasion force, and that's a big hit to the Nightstalker's military strength, Chiarn. Re-taking Andahar, it's about more than just killing one man."

Arya spoke the words as much for herself as for him. She had thought long and hard about what she was about to do. It was necessary—she knew that. And over the past few days, brick by brick, she had built a wall in her mind, shutting out the thoughts of what it might cost her. She couldn't afford to dwell on the consequences, not now.

Dunidaen was her home, and she would do whatever it took to save it.

"I know." He reached up, tapping the hilt of the crossed blades on his back. "And I stand with you, as I promised."

"Thank you, my Flamewielder."

Spotting Tiya leaving their campsite, pack over her shoulder, Arya headed across the damp sand to where Elendryl waited, his tail waving with impatience, but stopped when Chiarn called her name.

"It's not just because I promised you anymore." He called out. "It's because I *want* to."

Standing there on the damp sand of an isolated beach, Arya gave her Flamewielder a half bow. "It is the same for me."

***

War was devastation.

Arya witnessed the devastation firsthand as Elendryl soared through the thick cloud cover above the battlefield in southern Dunidaen. Even from high above, she could see the red-streaked earth, the churned mud stained with blood. Between the two sprawling army encampments, the fallen lay scattered for miles—horses and warriors alike. Though distance obscured the details, her mind filled in the gaps with memories of past battles, painting a grim picture of torn bodies, lifeless and empty. Each one had been loved by someone.

Her chest tightened with fear for those she held dear—were they still alive? But she ruthlessly forced the terror aside. Now was not the time.

Behind her, Tiya gasped, fingers digging into Arya's waist with a painful grip. The Etherean healer was secured to Arya's back with a makeshift harness—without it, no non-Sky Lord could hope to stay mounted through the flight Elendryl was about to take. And when it was over, Tiya's healing magic would be needed more than ever.

"There has to be a way of preventing this." Tiya spoke right in Arya's ear, so that her words were audible over the wind streaming past them.

Arya—as much as she was a soldier down to her bones—fervently wished that were true. Instead, she said, "What comes next won't be easy. Are you ready?"

"Unleashing wyverns on a human battle. Arya, I don't need to tell you how much worse the destruction will be."

For a moment the walled part of Arya's mind trembled, threatening to collapse and wash away her resolve, but with a steadying breath she made it firm again. "If I don't join this fight, Dunidaen is lost. And there's nothing I wouldn't do to protect my family."

Tiya's response was slow in coming, but when it did, her voice was firm. "Do what you need to do, Arya."

Asandryl banked, circling Elendryl before coming to hover at his right wingtip, both wyverns riding an updraft. Chiarn looked over. "Should we delay?" he called over, pointing to the north, where dark clouds filled the horizon. "That approaching storm looks nasty."

"We'll be fine," Arya assured him. "But I want to get a good look at the situation before we make a move."

The wyverns held position, wings wide, keeping a light layer of cloud below to hide them from anyone below looking upwards, while Arya and Chiarn studied the battlefield. Tiya said nothing, but her arms stayed tight around Arya.

Eventually Chiarn let out a low whistle. "I'm no battlefield tactician, but that doesn't look good to me."

Arya nodded in agreement. It was abundantly clear how numerically superior the invading army was; their black tents covered the plains in almost all directions, encircling the smaller Dunidae army. From what she could tell, their progress towards Gateport had likely been hampered by a series of wide, fast-flowing rivers the Dunidae soldiers were using to bolster their defences. Arya could make out the colours of the Lances, Raiders, and Longbows. When she looked harder, she saw Firemen ensconced in a backup position. No Aggressors or Knights. Had Falconcrest and Eaglesoar abandoned Rorin, or were they somewhere else?

To the south lay Gateport, an easy two-day march for the invaders if they broke through the Dunidae defensive lines. And if they decided to turn around push north … disaster. The nazal general had to be considering that. Having seen the battlefield herself now, Arya would have done it already, despite the risks inherent in splitting forces. Victory here was guaranteed.

Suddenly Tiya shouted and pointed. "They're launching an attack. The Dunidae defensive line looks like it's about to buckle there, near the western riverbank."

Arya's gaze swung straight there, and she swore. She literally *ached* to get her hands on the army and position it herself. Whoever was leading the defenders was doing a solid, capable job, but she'd do better. "If they break through there, the invading force will be able to circle around and flank the centre of the Dunidae force. They should be reinforcing that section of the lines at all costs."

But they couldn't. The relief force of Lances riding in that direction were about to be intercepted by a swarming Nightblade unit bolstered by shadowhounds.

"Whatever we're going to do Arya, we'd better hurry," Chiarn shouted.

She looked at him and reached for her magic. She didn't need to be leading the Dunidaen army herself. She just needed her magic, her wyvern, and her Flamewielder. Arya pushed away any softness inside her, any empathy for the men and women on the battlefield below. The wall inside her was strong, impenetrable. She thought only of the fact that her brother was down there, and that he was in danger. Her voice crackled with Stormrider anger. "What are your thoughts on a brute display of Sky Lord power, Lord Flamewielder?"

Flame flared in her Sky Lord's bright eyes, anticipation leaping through the bond between them. "It's been such a long time since I got to start a *really* good fire."

"We need to remedy that." Arya smiled wolfishly. "Think you can use your fire to protect the position that's about to buckle?"

"Child's play." He didn't sound nervous, or anxious, and she didn't sense any lack of confidence through their bond either. He might realise it, but her Flamewielder *had* grown. "Where will you be directing your heretofore unknown magical ability?"

"At the rest of the Nightblade army." Arya cast one final glance over the battlefield. "Hold off until you get my signal before you attack. I want to soften them up first."

Asandryl banked sharply, sweeping out to the north, Chiarn riding his wyvern towards the weakening section of the Dunidae defensive lines, but staying high enough to remain out of sight.

Arya just needed to do one more thing.

Reaching for her Sky Lord bonds, Arya brought to life her link to Essa. And when she did, relief flooded her. The Inkweaver was here, somewhere below. Surprise and joy and relief came back along the thread between them, and Arya let it fade before sending back, as clearly as she could. *"Be ready."*

An assent, questioning, hope, it all came back, ending with a strong burst of *"be careful."*

Arya placed her palm against Elendryl's neck. *"How about we let everyone down there know that House Stormrider has joined this war?"*

A snarl ripped through her mind, his bloodlust igniting hers.

"Then let's go to it." She glanced over at her shoulder. "Hold on, Tiya, and if you can, stay quiet. I'm going to need to concentrate from here on out."

Arya closed her eyes and took a series of deep breaths, sinking down into her magic, then bringing it *up,* letting it flood through her, to join with Elendryl. She felt Chiarn's impatience through their bond, but she ignored it, waiting until her magic had built enough. It stormed inside her, electric and powerful, desperate to be unleashed on the world.

Then she caught hold of her bond to Chiarn. *"NOW!"*

Tiya gave a grunt of surprise as Elendryl dropped out of the sky in an almost vertical dive, his wyvern's cry roaring through the battlefield, sending trees bending, soldiers screaming, and igniting the magic already burning through Arya's bone and muscle.

As her wyvern plummeted towards the Nightblade army, then levelled out, teeth bared, wings spread, Arya raised both arms in the air and threw back her head.

"UNLEASH THE STORM," she screamed.

Thunder ripped across the sky and Arya's Stormrider magic exploded into the world.

The first thing the armies down below knew of the attack was a bright flash of indigo lightning that crackled through the sky and exploded into the ground in the middle of the invading army.

Then there was another.

And again, and again, and *again*, until tents were aflame, and the ground was smoking.

Elendryl banked, swooped high, letting out a bloodcurdling roar as across the battlefield Asandryl let loose his own wyvern's cry. The Nightblades pushing at the collapsing defensive lines were suddenly milling about in terror, half of them fleeing back the way they'd come.

Arya left that to Chiarn and turned back to the main Nightblade army, its tents and campfires, and all those soldiers, now in disarray. The deep rumble of thunder followed on the heels of the lightning, and those fighting on the ground looked up in amazement at the dark purple clouds racing along the horizon from the north. Thunder roared again, the ground shaking.

Arya took a single breath, and in that moment, her wall trembled, and she thought about the men who filled all those tents below. And then she wiped them from her mind.

And Arya and Elendryl rode the storm.

Orange flame flared in the dimness as Chiarn called up a wall of fire that surrounded the soldiers pushing against the buckling line of Dunidae defence. Arya closed her eyes and dived back into her magic, reaching out to the storm to draw even more power from it.

"*Can you help me control it?*" she asked Elendryl, gritting her teeth with the amount of raw energy roping through her.

Assent and a flood of power.

Arya raised her hands and let the storm's fury loose with a thunderous shout. A bolt of lightning—bigger, brighter, and more powerful than anything she had ever summoned—slammed into the enemy lines, detonating the ground beneath them and sending soldiers scattering in terror. The invaders crumbled, their formation shattered by the raw force of the storm.

As she channeled the destructive power, Arya felt Elendryl with her, steady and unyielding. He worked to shape and temper the storm's energy, keeping it from consuming her even as she drew more from the churning skies above.

Part of her saw the Nightblades turning to flee, hundreds cut down by the relentless lightning or hurled through the air by the howling wind and driving rain. She targeted the densest clusters of enemy soldiers, striking them down where they stood. At the same time, she could sense Chiarn in the chaos, wielding fire to obliterate entire swaths of the invading force.

Together, they unleashed devastation.

Twice Arya almost lost control of herself, her magic, as it exploded through her, fed by her anger and implacable determination to destroy those attacking her home. On both occasions Elendryl was there, steadying her, shaping the magic, keeping it contained until she was back in control.

They flew and fought as one. Chaos and destruction personified.

All of this raced through Arya's mind at once, and at the same time she sucked power from the storm, keeping her magic alive and intense. She kept going until she knew she was almost out of strength.

"*Chiarn, enough.*" She sent through the bond.

She felt his weary assent and then watched as the wall of fire slowed and then died, followed by the fading power of the storm, which began to drift away to the south. Arya lowered her hands and Elendryl levelled out, giving them both a breather.

Utter destruction ruled in the wake of the Sky Lord attack.

The entire front lines of the nazal's army had been wiped out, and the rest of their forces were fleeing west, away from the storm chasing them. Their previously ordered lines were in chaos. She estimated a third or more of their number had been killed, either by fire or lightning.

Arya and Chiarn looked at each other across the open sky, and then as one they threw their heads back and screamed their triumph to the world. Essa joined them, Arya having left the bond between them alive, and she shrouded their triumph with relief and joy.

Then the magic and adrenaline faded away and she slumped in exhaustion.

For the first time, Arya remembered Tiya behind her. The healer hadn't said a word, despite Elendryl's extreme flying. "Are you okay?" she called over her shoulder.

"I'm good." The words were quiet, but Tiya's arms tightened briefly in reassurance. "A little bruised from the harness, but fine."

Asandryl and Elendryl both banked, dropping out of the sky and heading for where their riders could sense the Inkweaver. They came in low over the Dunidae army, and the warriors below cheered, hands in the air. Elendryl arrived first, landing in a muddy space not far from what appeared to be a large command tent, Asandryl arriving only seconds later.

Raiders and Lancers encircled them immediately, shouting for them to halt, so both Arya and Chiarn dismounted and stayed where they were, making no threatening moves. Her gaze ignored the soldiers, instead sweeping their surroundings, knowing she was near...

"Stand down!" A commanding voice called, and the circle broke, Raiders moving their horses aside to let three hurrying figures through. "They're not the enemy. Stand down! That's an order."

The orders came from Essa Inkweaver, running, Rorin Ravenstrike several paces ahead with his long legs. Arya broke into a run for her brother.

"*Arya!*" Rorin stopped, hands shaking as he signed, staring at her in disbelief. "*Is it really you?*"

"It's me." She laughed as she crashed into him, throwing her arms around his neck. He lifted her off her feet and swung her around, squeezing her so tightly she could barely breathe. "I've been so worried about you both."

Tears shone in his blue eyes when he finally put her down. "*We thought you were dead.*"

"I'm fine," she promised him. "I'm better than fine. Truly."

"Arya!" Essa was there then, and Arya found herself enveloped in another hug that sent her staggering back several paces. Arya breathed in Essa's familiar sent, and held her tightly, the bond between them full of everything they would never say aloud.

When they parted, Rorin pointed to the skies. "*I suppose that was you?*"

"And Chiarn." She waved him forward. "It looked like you needed some help."

"High Warlord." Chiarn spoke politely, but did not bow.

"Tiya!" Essa's eyes went wide, and Rorin signed a similarly astonished greeting.

"I'm here to help. Can you point me to the healing tents?" The Etherean healer was all business.

Essa nodded, snapped at the nearest Raider. "Raster. Take Tiya to the healing tents immediately. The healers there are to do everything she says without question—those orders come direct from the High Warlord. You stay and make sure that happens. I don't want to hear any complaints about her using magic. Clear?"

"Aye, Lord Inkweaver." Raster saluted and waved for Tiya to follow him.

"Thank you," Tiya said, heartfelt, then ran after Raster.

"*Where have you been all this time?*" Rorin demanded as Essa spun back to Arya. "*After what happened with the Nightstalker, we thought he must have killed you. Essa said Leanir is missing too.*"

Arya hurried to reassure them. "The Nightstalker caught both me and Leanir. He put us in a prison in Andahar, one built from cazaix stone. It took me a while to get us out, but I'm here now. We're all okay."

"*Except Dar.*"

Essa's face fell. "Rorin, after what he did—"

"*I don't want to fight about this again.*" Rorin interrupted, his signing sharp with anger. "*Arya is back and alive. We should focus on that. But first I need to go and speak with our generals to work out the best way to press our advantage. If we've got the numbers to do so.*"

"I'd like to help with that, if you'll allow me?" Arya offered.

"*Does that mean you're staying?*"

She managed a smile for him. "Of course, I am. I won't be long, and I'll dive right in, I promise."

"*I'm so glad you're here.*" He squeezed her shoulder. "*Truly.*"

Arya watched as he walked away, not failing to notice the look of sadness on Essa's face. "What's wrong?"

"He doesn't believe Darmanin could have betrayed us. I told him what happened, what we saw, but he refuses to believe it. You know how stubborn Rorin can be." Essa reached out to squeeze Arya's hand. "I'm sorry, it must be difficult for you too."

She shook it off. "Rorin is right, there are far more important matters to discuss right now. Do you know where Laskin is? Did the Andahari stay with him? Are they okay?" The questions spilled out of her, worry returning now the thrill of battle was fading.

"They're all here. I don't think they knew what else to do after you disappeared," Essa said. "Rorin had them in a backup position, only using them when we really needed to."

Arya let out a breath of relief. "Will you take me to them?"

As they walked, the soldiers of the various States gathered around them, forming a growing crowd that followed in their wake. Some called out in gratitude, others waved, while a few stood uncertain—caught between triumph and lingering fear. Arya did her best to smile at them all, hoping to offer reassurance after the brutal devastation she'd just unleashed.

When they reached the Andahari section of camp, the rebels looked just as exhausted and bloodied as the Dunidae soldiers. Yet, despite the weariness, there was something else in their expressions—relief, maybe even hope. Laskin, Niallin, and Esdee came forward to meet them. Niallin's eyes shone with emotion, and Esdee's expression mirrored his, both filled with something that looked dangerously close to joy.

Laskin merely scratched his beard. "You finally decided to show up and lend a hand."

Arya shrugged. "Well, you know, I figured you had it covered, old man."

"Cutting it a bit fine, kid. I suppose you always did love a dramatic entrance," he said sourly.

"It's true, I do love the attention."

Niallin and Esdee were staring at Laskin in horror, but both Essa and Chiarn concealed smiles. Niallin spoke far more formally. "Welcome back, Lord Stormrider, Lord Flamewielder. Your return brings much joy and relief."

Esdee's voice was full of awe. "What you just did ... we'll be talking of today for many years."

"There is still a long journey ahead of us," Arya warned them. "Today was only a small battle in a much larger war."

"Of course. But..." Niallin hesitated, a slow smile creeping across his face. "I don't think you know what it means to us, that true Sky Lords have finally returned, to see them riding their wyverns to battle. To know that there is a chance the Nightstalker could be defeated. We have lived so long without hope."

As well as her internal wall had held, now it cracked at the reminder of how many hopes were riding on Arya's success. Abruptly she felt the exhausted weighing on her. "One step at a time. Now, I must get back. The Dunidae army needs to act quickly to take advantage of the rout today. Niallin, if you could show Chiarn a place to clean up and eat, then get some rest, I'd appreciate it."

"I don't need to be packed away like a fine piece of pottery," Chiarn protested.

"You just used a lot of magic, and I'm going to need that again and again, Lord Flamewielder." She laid a hand on his arm. "I am not packing you away. On the contrary, I'm asking you to rest and eat so that you can fight again, and soon."

"All right," he grumbled. "But I won't need long."

"Good." She smiled, "Laskin, you're with me."

Chiarn headed off with Niallin and Esdee, while Essa turned to lead them back through the camp. Laskin fell in beside Arya. She reached out, laid her hand on his shoulder. "It's so good to see you, old friend."

"I was worried there for a second." He lifted a hand to squeeze hers, dropped it. "Glad to have you back, kid."

Chapter 15

Arya, Essa, Laskin, Rorin, and Andrian Crowtalon congregated in Rorin's command tent. A pot of stew bubbled on a nearby cookfire. Everyone got themselves a bowl before sitting at the table. Rorin was the last to join them. He had dark shadows under his eyes and sat with his shoulders slumped.

"Here." Essa passed him a bowl and some bread, which he accepted.

Arya ate with gusto. "Even battlefield cooking tastes so much better than prison food."

There were a few half-smiles, but their weariness was a palpable, noticeable weight filling the tent. Arya sobered. They'd been fighting for months, suffering death and injuries, over and over. What she'd witnessed today, what she'd *done*, they'd been doing it far longer.

She should have come sooner.

"You can have the rest of mine if you want, lass." Laskin slid his bowl across to her, a scowl of distaste on his face.

She took the bowl, but hesitated before eating. "I'm sorry it took me so long to get here," she said.

Andrian looked over, a flash of his old spark on his handsome face. "No. You've singlehandedly turned the tide. What you and the Flamewielder did today…"

"*What are you going to do about Darmanin?*" Rorin asked Arya.

A tense silence enveloped the group. Arya put her spoon down and looked over at her brother. "What do you mean?"

"*Surely you don't believe that he actually betrayed you?*"

"I was there, Rorin. Essa and Chiarn told you the truth. Darmanin allied with the Nightstalker." Arya's chest clenched. She hadn't anticipated how difficult it would be to lie to her brother. How hard to bear the despair in his face.

"*I don't believe you,*" he said. "*This is Darmanin we're talking about. He would never betray you like that.*"

Her resolve rapidly fading—what she loved most about Rorin was his unshakeable love and loyalty for his chosen family—Arya tried to head him off. "Rorin, this isn't the place or the time to talk about Darmanin. There's still an army of Nightblades out there."

He nodded, dropping his spoon and pushing his bowl away, mutinous gaze directed at the tabletop. Arya felt dreadful, but she knew the Nightstalker must have spies in the camp. They had to believe she thought Darmanin had betrayed them.

"I feel much the same way," Andrian said. "He is my brother, and I love him."

Seeking to change the subject, Arya asked the question that had been in the back of her mind. "Chiarn and I heard that a nazal is leading the invasion. Is that true? There was no sign of it today."

"It's true. But it only joins the fighting when we get the upper hand in a battle," Laskin said. "We have no way to combat it. It can destroy entire shields with one blast of magic."

"If that's the case, why has it attacked so infrequently?" Arya was confused.

"*Because of Essa.*" Rorin signed. "*The first time it attacked, she almost killed it before it fled. Now it can only launch an attack briefly before she and Alletryl go after it, then it has to flee.*"

Arya met her Inkweaver's gaze across the table. She knew how Essa hated fighting, violence. "Thank you."

"Dunidaen is my home too, Arya."

"Lord Inkweaver's magic has also been critical in our ability to keep up with the healing supplies and weapons we need," Andrian added. "Whatever ill feeling soldiers in the army felt towards magic-wielders before, it exists no longer."

"No wonder you look so exhausted." Arya reached out to squeeze her hand. "All of you do. I'm so sorry I left you alone in this. But I'm here now."

The tent flap opened, and Gelfrey Hawkesdale entered, larger than life as always. He didn't look happy to see her. "Arya bloody Stormrider. What the hell was that today?"

"Warlord Hawkesdale." She rose with a warm look. "It looked like you needed some help, and Chiarn and I were in the neighbourhood."

"Damned terrifying, what you did," he barked. "Even though my entire army is mooning over you. This is why Sky Lords are a problem."

"It's why you want us on your side, Warlord," Arya said.

"Bah." He dismissed her with a wave. "Ravenstrike, I know you wanted a war council immediately, but I think it best we put it off until first thing tomorrow. We need to treat the wounded, and take stock of what's left of our forces, before we can mount a counterattack. And rested minds make for better battle plans. Our scouts can spend the night surveying the state of the enemy forces so that we are well informed when deciding what comes next."

"*Fine.*" Rorin rose. "*We meet here first thing tomorrow.*"

He left without another word, leaving Hawkesdale staring after him in stunned silence. After a brief hesitation, the warlord simply shrugged and followed, though not before casting one last, troubled glance in Arya's direction.

She considered going after Rorin but thought better of it. Magic had drained her, and she needed rest. Besides, she knew from experience that Rorin's tempers, though rare, were best left to burn themselves out on their own.

"I need to go too." Andrian apologised. "I'll see you in the morning."

"You look like you're about to fall over." Essa pushed her chair back. "How about I walk you to your tent and you can tell me everything that's happened since we parted?"

"That sounds perfect."

Despite their weariness, they walked for a long time, meandering along the paths between tent rows. Eventually Essa came to a stop near a larger tent that was clearly Rorin's, with the High Warlord sigil on the tent flap, and Raiders posted all around it. "So, I have an uncle."

"You do. And he's as shifty as your father."

Essa laughed, tired eyes lighting up. "You know, it always warms me, the knowledge that our fathers were best friends."

"Me too, Ess." Arya held her gaze.

"That one's for you." Essa looked away, pointed at a smaller tent nearby. "I had them prepare it. It's next to mine. And as you can see, Rorin is just there."

"Thank you."

Essa started to head off, but then stopped and turned. "Oh, I almost forgot. I made you a new set of mail and gauntlets while you were away. I'll ask Tiya tomorrow to infuse it with her healing magic, like your last set."

Warmth filled Arya's chest. "You knew I was coming back."

"I figured if you'd been captured, your mail would have been taken from you. I'm glad to see you got your sword back, though. Night, Arya."

Arya smiled, turned towards the tent. "Sleep well, my Inkweaver."

***

As dawn crested the horizon the next morning, Arya went searching for Rorin. He stood alone at the top of a small rise, his personal Defender shield arrayed protectively below. She nodded a greeting to them before walking up the slope to join her brother. The sun was just cresting the horizon, and the battlefield lay out below them, bathed in an orange glow. There was nothing romantic about it, despite the lovely morning. Mud tinged red from blood and bodies marred the landscape.

Rorin said. "*Scouts reported overnight that the Nightstalker's forces are in complete disarray. They're not going anywhere yet though.*"

"The nazal general will reorganise quickly. You need to press your advantage now."

He turned to her, mouth in a tight line. *"Do you plan on sticking around?"*

She winced. She'd hoped his temper would have died overnight, but it seemed not. Damn, she wasn't sure how long she could keep lying to him when it clearly hurt him so much. "If you have a problem, Rorin, just spit it out."

"You know what my problem is." He signed stiffly. *"Dar of all people. Arya, he loves you."*

"I'm aware of that."

"Then how could you believe him capable of betraying you to the Nightstalker?"

Arya rubbed her forehead where a headache was beginning to throb. Maybe she could share *some* of the truth. "Rorin, do you remember when we first talked about this? I told you it was complicated." She took a breath, then told him everything the elder had told her, about Lucius and Mariel, and how the Nightstalker had come to turn against his king and *cairdre*.

Once she'd finished, Rorin turned away to look out over the view. *"You're telling me that's what happened with Dar?"*

"I'm telling you that's why it is complicated. I'm giving you an explanation for what might have happened."

"I don't believe it."

"Oh, Rorin." She smiled. "Your loyalty does you credit."

He met her gaze. *"He's your family too, Arya. How can you just give up on him like this?"*

Rorin's expression pleaded with her, and Arya almost spilled everything. Only her deep fear for Darmanin allowed her to look away, shore up her resolve. "I haven't given up on anything, but I need to focus on what comes next. You have an army occupying a large portion of your country," she said firmly. "Rorin, you are the High Warlord. Your duty to Dunidaen comes first, before everything else."

He signed sharp and angry. *"I know that!"*

"You must be worried for Peemla and Anjurin. Have you had any news of them?" Arya suspected some of Rorin's anger was the result of constant fear that the invading army might turn north towards Heathrock. She knew that fear. Every moment, every breath, she wondered about Kirin. If he was safe. If the Nightstalker had found him.

"*None, but their last message indicated they were safe with Arken in Heathrock. None of our scouts have reported the Nightblade army trying to push north ... yet.*" He let out a heavy breath. "*Anjurin needs to survive this, or there will be nobody to lead Ravenstrike if I fall.*"

"You're going to survive, Rorin. You know I won't let you die." Privately, Arya hoped Rorin and Peemla had more children, because she thought it unlikely Anjurin would ever be warlord of Ravenstrike. He was going to be a Sky Lord to Kirin, if both survived to manhood. Another pang shot through her at the thought of her son.

"*I do love you. You know that, right?*" Rorin leaned into her side.

She wrapped an arm around his shoulders. "Of course I know that. Now, is there any chance I can get some breakfast before we meet with your warlords and their generals? Wrangling with them always requires fortification."

***

It was a weary and sombre group that met in Rorin's command tent. Niallin and Laskin were there, along with all the Dunidae warlords except Falconcrest, their generals, Arya, Chiarn, and Essa. Amius SparrowWing seemed pleased to see Arya, if a little awed after her display the previous day, but Eaglesoar wouldn't meet her gaze.

Essa took a seat beside Arya instead of Rorin, and she raised her eyebrows at her friend. "Aren't you Rorin's chief advisor?"

"Maybe I just want to sit next to the friend I haven't seen for months and feared was dead," Essa said indignantly, then added with a touch of sheepishness. "He's still pretty mad at me."

"I tried talking to him. I hope it helps."

Essa winced. "Thanks, but your kind of talking usually involves bludgeoning people over the head with what you think."

Arya shot her an offended look. "I know how to be sensitive."

Essa burst out into peals of laughter before subsiding and looking at Arya knowingly. "Stop trying to make me feel better."

"I'm not doing anything of the kind."

Essa turned serious. "The Dunidae scouts reported seeing the nazal flying north on its bat creature last night. It hasn't come back." Essa hesitated. "A large unit of Nightblades and shadowhounds headed in the same direction."

Arya swore under her breath. She didn't like that at all. No wonder Rorin was so anxious. What if the creature had flown north looking for new prey? Like his family in Heathrock. Arya shifted in her seat, suddenly uneasy. She felt an echo of it through her bond with Essa.

Rorin signed, signalling the start of the meeting, and nodded to man wearing violet and black and sitting beside Andrian. Laskin translated for Rorin, although Arya noticed that Hawkesdale, Andrian, and Amius seemed to mostly follow his signing. "*A summary of the situation, please, General Avignar.*"

"High Warlord." The older man stood and leaned over the map unrolled on the rickety table. "Gateport and Crowtalon are currently lost to us, as are the southern halves of SparrowWing and Hawkesdale. We have approximately thirteen thousand able-bodied warriors left; most of those are Lances, Raiders, and Longbows."

Arya raised a hand. "What about the Knights and Aggressors?"

The general's mouth tightened, clearly unhappy that she was addressing him. She stifled a sigh, and tried to keep a pleasant look on her face. Eventually Avignar looked toward Warlord Eaglesoar.

"I had only a battalion of Knights with me in Gateport for the State Council. The rest remain in my State, cut off by the Nightblade lines," Rian Eaglesoar said stiffly. Matte's older brother had aged since Arya had last seen him. There was far more grey in his blonde hair and he looked tired and overwhelmed.

Hawkesdale added, "Due to their previous warlord's intransigence, there was no time to muster the Aggressors before the invading force hit us either."

"They're all just sitting up there in the north?" Arya asked.

Laskin scratched at his beard. "Reports on what is happening beyond our lines are scant. We've sent messages to Falconcrest, but they haven't replied. The messages may not even have reached them."

Arya nodded. "And what of the Khadini Rangers? Has the emperor been supplying reinforcements? I didn't see any on the battlefield yesterday."

"What is this, an interrogation?" Eaglesoar demanded. "What right have you to demand answers about our sensitive military information."

"Lord Stormrider saved us yesterday, Warlord," Andrian spoke at the same time as Rorin began signing. "I think she's entitled to a little sensitive information."

"*He's right, answer her questions,*" Rorin added.

At a look from his warlord, General Avignar continued, "Last we knew, the Rangers are holding the Crowtalon borders in a fall-back position for the Nightblades in case they need to retreat. Our best guess is the Night-stalker offered Emperor uq-Danresan Crowtalon State if he wins—which as you know encompasses the Dreadwater Gate and would effectively end all illegal entry into Khadini."

"But he's not sending extra troops? So it's a limited alliance." Arya thought about that. It would be worth talking to Kulan, trying to under-stand his brother's thinking better.

And if she did, she'd be able to see Kirin.

Arya tucked that hope away before it could take root. It was too danger-ous for Kirin.

Rorin signed. "*We need to push forward against the Nightblade army before they rally themselves and dig in for a counterattack. Right now, they encircle us, but if we can break through, we can go on the attack.*"

"I agree," Hawkesdale grumbled. "We throw everything we have at them now, and quickly."

Mutters of agreement followed his words, but Arya sat forward, project-ing her voice so that it caught the attention of the room. "I disagree. Their forces are still numerically superior to yours. If you throw everything you have at them now, you risk being unable to overwhelm them and losing significant numbers in the process. Then you'll be back to where you were."

"High Warlord, I must protest." Eaglesoar said angrily. "Now we're letting her dictate our military strategy?"

Amius SparrowWing cleared his throat. "Nobody is letting anyone dictate anything, but I—and I suspect, our generals—would appreciate knowing if Lord Stormrider and Lord Flamewielder could send more storms and fire at the enemy?"

Arya sent him a grateful nod. "We can use flame, yes, but I can't actually conjure a storm. I won't be able to do what I did yesterday unless another convenient storm happens to come along. If we wait for that, we give their commanders too much time to rally."

"*I would appreciate your advice, Arya. What do you suggest?*" Rorin asked.

"Raven's balls, Eaglesoar had a point, Ravenstrike. We're not seriously letting *her* plan things again?" Hawkesdale barked.

Eaglesoar nodded vigorous agreement. Everyone else turned to stare at both of them, and after a long moment Hawkesdale raised his hands in surrender, then settled back in his chair with a grunt of discontent. Eaglesoar turned red with stifled frustration.

Arya stood, gaze roving over the map, conscious of all the gazes on her. "I would first use the Raiders to harry them, now, before they settle and entrench themselves into a new defensive position. Don't give them an opportunity to reach ground that gives them an advantage. Keep them on the move and off balance without fully engaging in battle. Rorin, do you have enough Raiders to do that successfully?"

He gave a thoughtful nod. "*I think so, yes.*"

"While the Raiders do that, I'd send the Lances and Longbows combined in targeted attacks against multiple points along their eastern flank, splintering the edges of their main force into smaller groups that can be overwhelmed. It could also serve to create a gap for your Knights to attack from the east, Warlord Eaglesoar. Do as much damage as possible, and then withdraw before their numbers overwhelm you."

"And once they're in smaller groups, we can start taking them out one by one," Amius said.

"Exactly. You'd effectively be wearing them down from the inside out, while the bulk of the force is prevented from entrenching to stand its ground." Arya sat down, shrugged. "At least, that's how I'd do it."

"It's a risky gamble." Rian Eaglesoar spoke with a ponderous condescension that made Arya itch. "With their greater numbers, we'd risk getting caught with our force even more dispersed, allowing *them* to pick *us* off. It's tactically unsound."

Arya glanced at him, keeping her irritation hidden. "Yes, you'd be taking a risk. You'll have to move slowly and be disciplined and well-coordinated."

"Even then, the numbers aren't in our favour." Hawkesdale said bluntly. "We can't afford the type of gambles you like to take. We have our entire country on the line here."

"I don't like to say it, but I think they're right." Andrian said unhappily.

"Actually, the numbers *will* be in your favour after your reinforcements have arrived." She looked around the table, trying to hold herself back from looking *too* triumphant. "A thousand Icefolk warriors."

A beat of silence, then...

"The Icefolk are marching to our aid?" Hawkesdale barked, sitting forward abruptly.

"A *thousand* of them?" Amius SparrowWing spoke over him, barely audible.

Eaglesoar's mouth opened, and stayed open. Rorin stared at Arya, blue eyes shining with hope.

"Yes, and *yes*, Warlords." Arya sat back. "You're going to win this war. I'm going to make sure of it."

"Right, well, where are those damned scouting reports?" Hawkesdale demanded. All his grumpy bluster had vanished as if it had never been.

"Here." Andrian passed them, pointing at a spot. "What if we moved here and here first? Your Longbows softening them up for my Lances, then—"

Suddenly everyone was sitting straight in their chairs, leaning over the maps, conversation breaking out as they began discussing and refining

Arya's proposed plan. She heard the hope in their voices and was glad of it. She leaned over to ask Laskin, "Are there shadowhounds and wraiths with the invading force?"

"Just shadowhounds, but not many. They're used for targeted attacks, mainly to try and instil panic, which mostly works, as accustomed as our soldiers are to them now."

"Yet no wraiths?" Arya frowned in though. "I wonder if he has less of them at his disposal now, or just has less control over them? The firedrake attack over Gateport might have cost more of his power than we thought."

"So that's your conclusion? That the Nightstalker has magical control over the creatures."

"Or one of his nazal do." She shrugged. "How else do you imagine he got thousands of wild, vicious creatures over the Diamondfang? Or that he's always had a nazal in command of his invading forces, despite the fact I'm sure he's got capable generals who likely have better tactical and strategy training than those monsters."

If true, *that* was the nazal she needed to kill as a priority. She made a note to herself to ask Remien about a Sky Lord House with the ability to control creatures.

Rorin gestured for everyone's attention. "*Warlords, Generals, I want to move quickly. Commander Derrin, get our Raiders mobilised and riding within the hour. Andrian, Gelfrey, your Lances and Longbows will need to be ready to march out soon after. Make sure they're ready to go.*"

"High Warlord." Andrian leaped up with alacrity, crossing straight to Hawkesdale. The two left the tent together, heads bent close in conversation.

Eaglesoar stood up, cleared his throat. "With your permission, High Warlord, I'll take a shield of your fastest Raiders, sneak around the enemy lines, and ride into Eaglesoar to bring my stranded Knight battalions to attack from the east."

"*Permission granted, Uncle!*" Rorin beamed.

"Yes, well, just make damned sure you've weakened the eastern lines by the time we arrive. I don't want to march my Knights into a massacre."

Arya rose too. "Chiarn, you and I will provide cover for the Raiders. We won't have much power to use until we've recovered from yesterday, but we should be able to help some."

Chiarn nodded. "I'll call for Asandryl."

Arya went to follow him out, but turned as Rorin took hold of her arm. His light blue eyes were alight with purpose. "*You're really back, aren't you?*"

"Oh yes, Rorin," she told him with a wolfish smile. "I'm back."

Impulsively, he leaned forward and hugged her tightly, before turning and going back to planning with his commanders.

"Lord Stormrider?" Niallin followed her out of the tent. "Where do you want us? You weren't specific in there."

"That's because I have a different plan for you, and I didn't want to talk about it in front of everyone. I'm sure the Nightstalker has spies in this camp."

He frowned in acknowledgement of that. "What are our instructions?"

"Laskin will stay with me, but you and Esdee will take the rest of our army back into Andahar via ship from Gateport to the Riverlands." She smiled as his eyes widened. "I want you to use your rebel contacts to start gathering an army that is strong enough to face the Nightstalker's."

His eyes glowed. "We're truly going to begin the fight in Andahar?"

"You've done a lot for me here, Niallin, and I appreciate it more than I can say. But yes, it's time to begin the real fight." She gave him a warning look. "Going back to the Riverlands will be incredibly dangerous. If the Nightstalker learns what you are doing—"

"I've lived with that threat my whole life, Lord Stormrider, as has every man and woman in your army." He hesitated. "We've always needed multiple safehouses though, which limits our ability to gather, let alone train, in any serious numbers."

"There *is* a safe place for us to gather. It's an isolated area, so those travelling will need supplies and the ability to provide shelter for themselves for a march of several weeks. You will be in charge of that, and Esdee will be in charge of your security and protection." She gave him a location within a day's hike of the Storm Spire. "Someone will meet you there. You don't tell anyone in advance where you're taking them, is that clear?"

"Very much so, Lord Stormrider. We'll pack up today and leave first thing tomorrow." He hesitated. "Are you sure you don't want to send someone more senior and experienced to manage our protection?"

Arya's gaze narrowed. "Have there been any problems with Esdee?"

"No, not exactly. She's proven a capable warrior and keeps a clear head during battle. The warriors respond to her leadership."

"They all sound like good things to me."

"She's strong-willed and stubborn and she questions me often."

"Has she ever disobeyed a direct order from Laskin?"

"No."

"Then I'm not sure why you're questioning her, Niallin." A thread of impatience entered Arya's voice.

"As you say, Lord Stormrider." He bowed and strode away. Arya watched him go. She wasn't sure about Niallin leading her army back to Andahar, but desperately needed his local contacts and knowledge. Laskin wouldn't be able to gather the rebels himself.

Esdee chose that moment to appear, carrying a message for Laskin, who remained inside with the warlords, and Arya called her over. "Captain?"

"Lord Stormrider." She stopped and saluted sharply.

"I've just given Niallin some instructions." Arya relayed everything she'd just told Niallin.

She frowned. "Who will protect you until we meet you in Andahar, my Lord?"

"Elendryl and my *cairdre* will take care of that just fine," she said. "Your task is far more dangerous. You can expect the Nightstalker's attention to be firmly on the rebels in Andahar now that the war here is over. And, as ever, he will focus his attention on the Riverlands."

"Understood, Lord Stormrider," Esdee saluted. "We'll make sure Niallin and the rebels are safe until they reach the west."

"Good. Dismissed."

Although Arya immediately felt better that Esdee and those she trusted implicitly would be with Niallin in Andahar, unease rippled through her.

It had been too easy so far. Escape, return, winning a decisive battlefield victory. The nazal general hadn't even tried to challenge her. It was more than plausible to argue that it knew it couldn't defeat three Sky Lords together, but even so...

Arya shook off her doubts.

For now, she had to focus on getting Dunidaen back on the front foot in this war.

Chapter 16

Arya walked through the camp, restless and unable to sleep, despite having spent the day in the saddle fighting. Just over two weeks had passed since her arrival. In that time, the fighting had been constant and bitter. Employing Arya's strategy, the Dunidae hadn't lost any more ground. Their grit was impressive, but on several occasions already, they'd only been saved from disaster by Chiarn's flame or her blunt lightning magic.

Her boots sank into mud, while around her soldiers talked around crackling fires. It was normally a sound she loved, but tonight, tired and down, she only feared what might happen to them all come morning. Arya wasn't sure how long they could keep it up before the tide turned against them again.

Or the Nightstalker came for her. If Xaphistryl showed up now...

She found herself at the healing tents, large canopies sheltering long rows of cots. Healers and their helpers moved amongst them, administering food, water, and treatment. The moans of those in pain were an eerie counterpart to the murmur of conversation from nearby campfires. When a breeze kicked up, it carried with it the scent of illness and blood.

"Arya!" Tiya appeared from the darkness. She had shadows under her eyes, and dried blood splattered her tunic, but she looked otherwise well. "I was just taking a break. You look like you could use one too."

"As long as you don't mind my state. I haven't washed yet." She was covered with dried blood and gore and mud, smearing her otherwise lovely mail.

Tiya gave her a bright smile. "I've smelled worse."

They sat on a log that had been fashioned into a bench nearby, sharing a flagon of ale between them along with some bread and dried meat Tiya had rustled up.

"Thank you for coming to help." Arya couldn't tear her gaze from the long rows of injured. "It was brave of you." She couldn't imagine how many more dead there would be if Tiya hadn't been with them. Anger flared at Salyarin and his cowardice. The difference his healers could make would be enormous.

"I have to admit, it's taken me some time to stop hesitating before using magic in front of the Dunidae. But apart from a few strange looks, I've had very little reaction. In fact, the Raiders that come in have started asking for me straight away, no matter how serious their injury."

"Rorin has done a lot of work to improve things for magic-wielders in his home State," Arya said. "And so he should." She shuddered at how she'd once been, as bad as everyone else in Dunidaen. Wary of those who wielded magic. And just because she'd been told her whole life they were bad, or dangerous. It had taken her far too long to question *why* they were supposedly bad.

Tiya gave her a sideways look. "What's on your mind? You're focusing very intently on your piece of bread."

So many things were on her mind. She picked the most immediate one. Her internal wall was weaker than it had ever been as she sat here confronted with so many injured warriors in pain. What she and Elendryl had done ... she doubted the Nightblades had an Etherean healer helping them. Nausea curdled in her gut. "Is it worth it? War? Worth all this pain and loss?"

"Never." Tiya's response was swift and decisive. "But sometimes it cannot be avoided."

Arya said nothing. She would have to bring a larger war to Andahar if she wanted to win. More blood spilled. More lives lost. To save her family. To keep Kirin safe. For the larger goal of peace. She wasn't sure it *was* worth it. Or that she should be the one to decide whether it was the right way forward. And yet, she knew she would make that decision. Because she had that ruthlessness inside her when it came to protecting her own.

"I remember you well enough to know you become introspective when you're uneasy about something." Tiya's soft voice interrupted her musings. "What is it?"

Arya let out a weary chuckle, but her amusement didn't last long. "I feel like I'm missing something, Tiya. Some plan of the Nightstalker's I'm not seeing. I wonder why he hasn't come here yet."

"I wish I could help with an answer."

Arya turned to her. "Would you want to rule the Etherean, if your wings had grown as they should?"

Startled surprised flashed over her face at the segue. "I ... honestly, I don't know. I've never really thought about it. Mostly my life has been about trying to survive."

"You're a lot like Salyarin. I remember how you used to chide me about violence, about our intolerant attitudes towards magic-wielders. He told me once that only the elder and his or her heir can dream-walk. Can you do it?"

"No." The word came out low and bitter. "I am the most powerful healer born to the Etherean in generations, but I do not possess wings *or* my father's dream magic, and so I am not good enough."

Arya reached out to touch Tiya's hand. "You'd make a great leader. Better than him, in my opinion. Something to think about."

"It's impossible."

Arya stood, stretched her cramped muscles. Dawn was lighting up the horizon, which meant she should get some proper food before the day's fighting began. "Is it? I'll see you later, Tiya."

She was halfway back to the mess tent when a wyvern's cry sounded in the distance.

Mistryl.

Arya reached for her bond with Leanir, bringing it to life, letting him know where she was. Moments later, Mistryl swept over the camp and landed in a cleared space on its eastern perimeter.

Leanir carried a passenger with him; the hulking figure of Chief Ce'Garn. She waited for them to dismount and walk over, not wanting to get too close to Mistryl. Leanir's wyvern was already eyeing the Longbows guarding the camp perimeter like they'd be a good snack.

"Bitter fighting," Leanir spoke while the Icefolk chief gave Arya a nod of acknowledgement. "But it doesn't look like you're losing. Yet."

She chuckled. "That's an apt assessment. I hope you're not bringing me any extra problems?"

"As much as I'd love to make life more difficult for you, Raider, I have good news. Chief Ce'Garn's warriors have arrived at the rendezvous point. They encountered no issues on the way, and I'm confident the Nightblade army doesn't yet know they're in Dunidaen."

"I am glad to hear it. Welcome to Dunidaen, Chief Ce'Garn."

"Lord Stormrider." His gaze, which had been scouring the war camp around them, alive with interest, returned to her. "The lack of obstacles on our journey so far has made my warriors restless and eager for action."

"There will be action soon enough, I promise you." The Ce'Garn certainly seemed more bloodthirsty than At'eir's Is'heim tribe—who revelled in the hunt and the fight with an ice bear, but didn't seem to hunger for battle against other humans. "Though as you can see, you will have no ice or snow to aid you."

"We don't need our magic to be victorious in battle." He showed teeth. "I thought it would be useful for me to accompany Lord Mindbreaker and speak with the Dunidae war commanders myself, so that we could coordinate our forces more effectively."

"An excellent idea." Arya smiled. "Come with me, and I'll introduce to you High Warlord Ravenstrike."

The Icefolk chief fell in behind Arya and Leanir, towering over them. She studied Leanir's face, expressionless as always, eyes dark and flat. "You didn't fly here just to bring the Ce'Garn, did you?"

"There's a nazal in the north. I found it while dream-walking two nights ago. It didn't notice me, and I've been keeping an eye on it ever since." Hatred rippled in Leanir's voice. It was easy to forget that the nazal had been hunting him as much as they had her these past years. And at least she had the benefit of having faced and killed two.

Arya frowned. It must be the nazal general that had disappeared from the battle front after her arrival. Unease wriggled through her. "In the north where?"

"Not Heathrock, as far as I can tell," he said, guessing at the reason for her concern. "Much further east."

"Why would it be scouting up there?" She wondered. "Its army is in disarray right now—it seems strange to plan for a push north when they haven't stabilised their position here."

Leanir said nothing. She liked that about him. If he had nothing to say, he simply didn't speak.

"If you learn any more from dream-walking, I would appreciate if you let me know."

He flashed her a quick look. Surprised she was asking rather than telling? Annoyed she was asking at all? It was impossible to tell. And before he could reply, Chiarn appeared, walking toward them from the direction of his tent.

"Chief Ce'Garn, well met."

"Lord Flamewielder," Ce'Garn said politely.

The Flamewielder made a face as his gaze shifted to his fellow Sky Lord. "Leanir. How delightful to see you again. You're not here to try and assassinate more warlords, are you?"

"What would you know about assassination," Leanir said in a bored tone. "Don't you play the fiddle for a living?"

"I could play a song for you now, if you like?" Chiarn offered. "I've been composing a new one about an assassin that falls over his own knife and cuts off his—"

"Enough," Arya snapped.

Chiarn subsided, Leanir remained bored-looking, and the Ce'Garn continued to hungrily study every detail of the war encampment like he was going to go back and write it all down. She decided not to think about why he might want to do that.

Instead, she worried over the nazal in the north. The Nightstalker had tried to use Rorin's family against them once before. It hadn't worked, but that didn't mean he wouldn't try again. The Nightstalker knew Arya's family was her weak point, and given he still hadn't found Kirin, even more was at stake for him now. If he lost this war, he'd be forced back into Andahar, bloodied and bruised, with a significant loss of manpower and a civil war still to fight in the Marshlands.

Why hadn't he come himself to finish Dunidaen off? Her thoughts circled back to that question. Even worse was the relief she felt that he hadn't. Her encounter with him in Blackstone had only reinforced her instinctive terror of the man. He'd dominated her so easily each time they'd faced each other … shame filled her at the knowledge that she never wanted to face him ever again.

It was a relief to arrive at Rorin's tent and have a distraction from her thoughts. He was inside, with Essa and two Raider captains. Arya made the introductions, and Essa translated as Rorin signed in response. *"Chief Ce'Garn, welcome to Dunidaen. Your help is deeply appreciated. Allow me to thank you on behalf of all the warlords."*

"I was pleased that Er'fin At'eir asked my warriors to answer the Stormrider's request for aid, High Warlord." Ce'Garn said with that same polite formality. "I bring a thousand of our fighters, and we are impatient to join you."

"If you come with me, Er'fin, I will introduce you to my generals and the other warlords," Rorin said. *"Together, we can plan the best way to combine our forces."*

Ce'Garn bowed his head. "I would be honoured."

Arya lingered when Rorin and Ce'Garn left the tent, followed by Essa and the Raider captains, leaving her with Chiarn and Leanir. Her unease about the nazal continued to grow. She couldn't ignore it any longer.

"What do you want from me after I take the Ce'Garn back?" Leanir asked.

"That is up to you, as per our agreement," Arya said. "But I would like to suggest that you and I drop Chief Ce'Garn back with his people, then go on a little hunting trip?"

Leanir's eyes glinted with interest. "The nazal?"

"I want to find out what it's up to and kill it. It's a loose end we can't risk leaving hanging," Arya said. "Chiarn, you and Essa will stay here to protect the army. If there are any unexpected problems, you'll be able to contact me quickly through the bond."

She didn't like leaving so soon, but with Chiarn's powerful flame magic and Essa's powerful brain *and* magic, she was leaving Rorin and his warlords in good hands, especially now the Icefolk were close. She judged the risk was acceptable.

"You're going to go off alone with a cold-blooded assassin to hunt a nazal?" Chiarn's eyebrows shot skyward.

"Oh, Leanir couldn't kill me if he tried," Arya said cheerfully. "And after all, he does have some catching up to do. You and I have both killed a nazal each, and he's killed none."

Chiarn sent a smug grin Leanir's way.

Leanir turned his cold gaze on Arya. "I'll wait with Mistryl until the Ce'Garn is ready to leave."

He stalked off, and Arya turned to Chiarn. "Best keep a discreet eye on him. Let me know if he tries to murder any warlords before we leave."

"Will do, my queen." Chiarn bowed with a flourish and headed off in the direction Leanir had gone.

From there, Arya went in search of food in the mess tent—it would be a long flight north—and served herself a bowl of the same stew she was now beginning to get heartily sick of. Despite that, it was hot and filling. Rorin found her there a short time later.

"*I missed breakfast this morning, and Ce'Garn's chat with the warlords and generals is going to go on a while longer yet,*" he explained. "*It's interesting that At'eir sent the troublesome Ce'Garn though.*"

"Yes. The Icefolk queen's clever application of the 'keep your enemies closer' rule."

"*Have you ever met her?*" he asked curiously.

"A couple of times. She's quite old. I think she had At'eir rather late in life. For all that, she's a formidable woman." Arya paused. "At'eir thinks I should marry the Ce'Garn."

Rorin blinked at her, astonished.

"He makes the very good point that a strong marriage alliance could address a lot of critical needs I have in terms of financial and logistical backing."

He chuckled. "*Well, yes, but I know what your views on marriage are.*"

She said nothing to that, merely stirring the remnants of her stew idly around the bottom of her bowl and thinking back to her conversation with Tiya the previous night. Was it worth it? The path she was on seemed set, but maybe...

"*Are you actually thinking about it?*" Surprise made his signing more exaggerated.

"I don't know," she said. "To rule Andahar, I will need more than just the right name and a rag-tag rebel army."

Rorin smiled. "*Now you sound like my mother.*"

"It just seems so *big* sometimes, Rorin, what I have to do." Arya pushed her bowl away, sighing as melancholy took over. Sometimes she wished desperately that Thiara Ravenstrike was still there to seek advice from. Her presence would make things so much easier to bear.

"*If anyone can do it, you can.*" Rorin reached over to touch her hand. "*You've always got me, Arya, always. Never forget it.*"

She stood and rested her hand on his shoulder. "I'm going after the nazal that fled the battlefield. I want to make sure it doesn't go after our family at Heathrock. It could be a while before I'm back."

Relief flashed over his face. "*Thank you, Arya. I've been so worried for them. Just knowing you'll be there ... it takes a weight off my shoulders.*"

"I'll keep them safe," she promised.

Chapter 17

A dreary drizzle fell as Arya and Leanir guided their wyverns down near one of the bigger towns in the east of Ravenstrike State—Frost Hollow. Leanir's magic couldn't pinpoint the exact location of the nazal, but the assassin could gauge its proximity based on how easy it was to reach it when dream-walking. For two days they had flown north from the Ce'Garn's camp, searching without success.

"I thought you could read minds with your ability," Arya grumbled, mood sour from the weather and frustration of not finding the nazal yet. "Why can't you see where it is?"

"I can enter dreams and create them. And I can create illusions in a waking mind. I can't *read* minds. How many times would you like me to explain it before it sinks into your tiny Raider brain."

"And the nazal hasn't had any useful dreams about its location?"

Leanir's mouth tightened. "The monster's mind doesn't work like ours. It's a rotting, treacherous place to be. If there was something useful in the dreams I've seen, I would have told you. Why are we here? The wyverns don't need rest yet."

She hadn't even thought of how awful it must be to be inside a nazal's head. A shiver ran through her. "Frost Hollow has a good inn, so we'll stay there tonight and continue the hunt in the morning. Hopefully your dream-walking won't be quite as horrible from a warm bed."

"Fine." He snapped, but notably didn't complain about a night at an inn.

For a town of its size, Frost Hollow's main street was eerily empty. Dusk crept over the surrounding hills, swallowing the last of the light. The snow from the previous day, now churned to a muddy brown, lined the street in uneven patches, adding to the town's bleak feel.

"Someone cleared that snow off the road," Leanir murmured. His hand hovered where his cloak concealed a knife, and he walked with the air of a trained killer expecting to be attacked at any moment.

"You're sure the nazal's not here *in* the town?" She had visions of finding the torn and broken bodies of the residents, and her stomach lurched.

"It's not here," he said decidedly.

Arya pointed down a side street. Light spilled out from the windows of a large building. It had been years since she'd been here, on a patrol with her Raider shield, but the inn looked exactly the same. A few horses were tied up outside, nosing at the water trough. "Maybe they're all inside warming themselves with a drink. Which sounds like a mighty fine idea to me."

They stamped their boots free of snow and mud before going inside. A brief silence fell as the patrons registered the arrival of strangers, but Arya and Leanir had left their mail and weapons with the wyverns so as to appear as normal as possible. Even so, a few gazes stuck warily on Leanir, who couldn't look harmless if he tried. But after a moment, the hubbub of conversation resumed.

"Will you find us a table? I'll get food and drinks," Arya said, figuring preventing Leanir from interacting with anyone was the safest bet.

The bar was packed, but Arya's presence as a stranger caught the bartender's attention. Curious, he made his way over to serve her. "We haven't seen strangers through here for several weeks," he commented. "Folk are steering clear of travelling right now."

"My cousin and I are travelling to Aren for his sister's wedding," Arya said. "I warned him it would be dangerous, but he loves his sister and refused to miss it."

"Fair enough. Have you encountered any troubles on the road?"

"None yet. We've heard a lot of rumours though. Apparently, the High Warlord's army has the upper hand against the invaders."

"I hope that's true," a farmer nearby spoke suddenly. "The war hasn't touched us yet here in the north, but it will if we don't win soon. Prices for my cattle are already dropping and that's likely to worsen the longer war drags on."

"It'll worsen to zero, Trava," another man remarked. "Invading armies don't pay for their food."

The barman turned his attention back to Arya. "What can I get you?"

"Just two mugs of ale, and your dinner special for my companion and me. Thank you."

"I'll have our boy bring it right over."

Leanir had chosen a table in the far corner, with his back to the wall, facing the rest of the room and the entrance. Always the trained assassin. It made her curious about something. "Did many Shadeweavers survive the Nightstalker's invasion through the Diamondfang last year?"

He didn't reply for a long moment, but eventually said, "We got most out. Moved them to Gateport and other towns where we have a presence. It was harder with Ranier gone. He had no successor in place."

"Which is why you launched a coup against his leadership with the assassins?" She lifted an eyebrow, but let it go when he scowled. "I have an interesting story to tell you about Ranier." She relayed how he'd come to Andahar when she'd been captured by the Nightstalker, then stayed, apparently in an attempt to locate his brother and kill him.

A boy arrived with their food and ale, but Leanir didn't immediately sit forward to eat. "That's a lot of information to give me freely, Raider."

"I told you I was serious about building trust."

His mouth tightened. "I see through you. You think I'm a murderer without any redeeming qualities. You only want to gain my trust because you think you need me to win. It's a manipulation."

"You're not just a murderer. You're also fearless, and the most skilled assassin I've ever known. You don't back down, not ever. I also think you're not quite as calculating as you like to make people think. You didn't have to risk your life, twice, to save Essa, but you did it anyway."

"You're a fool if you think there's anything soft about me."

"Maybe," she said. "I'm not trying to be your best friend, but I am your leader, and you should know by now that I am fiercely protective of my people."

There was a moment of silence. He reached out, pulled his bowl of food closer, picked up his spoon, then put it down again. He looked at her, then he spoke with devastating simplicity. "I don't have friends, and I don't give my loyalty to anyone. That won't ever change."

"You gave it to Ranier."

"I submitted myself to his command in order to survive as a magic-wielding child with no money, home, or protection. That's different."

"Fair enough." Arya sat back. "In that case, how about we aim for respected comrades? We might not ever like each other, but I think we can learn to work together, at least for the length of time it takes to defeat the Nightstalker."

He said nothing to that, and they both dug into their food. More villagers trickled through the front door and soon the place was packed full. Arya shrugged off her cloak as the air grew warm from the press of bodies. The door opened again, and scattered cheers went through the crowd at the sight of three musicians. Arya ordered a second mug of ale and settled back to enjoy the music, but Leanir took his leave.

"I'll organise rooms for us and get them to bring you over your key," he said as he rose.

"You don't want to stay and have another drink? The music isn't that bad."

"This amount of people gathered in one room isn't a comfortable place for an assassin," he said. "I'll see you at dawn, or earlier, if I learn anything useful from my dream-walking."

Arya waved him off and lifted her mug, savouring the rich, nutty ale as she took a slow sip. With Leanir gone, she took the opportunity to stretch her legs beneath the table. It felt good to be dressed so simply, without the weight of heavy mail or weapons, just the small knife tucked in her boot. The music swelled, growing livelier, and some of the inn's patrons took to dancing, their movements turning the atmosphere rowdy. Arya soaked it in, buoyed by the infectious energy of the crowd.

Then, without warning, her bond with Darmanin rippled with awareness. She straightened, startled. Now that the nazal could no longer track them, she kept all her cairdre bonds open, but she hadn't expected—

A hooded man slid into the chair across from her.

Arya's pulse quickened as he reached up, pushing back his hood to reveal sharp, light grey eyes. Stubble shadowed his jaw, and his raven-black hair fell loosely around his face.

"Is this seat taken?" he asked.

Desire and delight leaped in her in equal measure, but she kept her voice casual. "Hello, stranger. What brings you to these parts?"

"I heard the ale was good. The music leaves a little to be desired though."

"Their enthusiasm counts for something," she said, then discreetly glanced around, making sure nobody was paying undue attention to them. Worry pulsed in her chest. "Why risk coming here? Is something wrong?"

"Maybe." He glanced around. "The Nightstalker ordered me to bring a sealed message to his nazal here, and then return directly to the Marshlands." His jaw tightened. "I didn't dare break the seal to read the message, so I don't know what it was, but I got the distinct impression the Nightstalker wanted me well away from Dunidaen after I delivered it. When I realised you were nearby, I had to come and warn you."

"Leanir and I are tracking the nazal," she told him. "I don't like that it's anywhere near Heathrock. Your news makes me even more worried about its purpose. Is the Nightstalker suspicious of you?"

A slight shake of his head. "I did as we discussed. I suggested the diversion in the Marshlands, and then waited a week after you arrived at the battlefield before telling the Nightstalker that I'd found out you were in Dunidaen with Rorin and his army. It worked well—he was pleased with me. I played my part, reiterated that he'd promised me not to kill you. He agreed to hold to his word." Darmanin paused. "He's trusted me a little more since, though he won't let me go anywhere near the Dunidae battlefield."

"So we can assume the message he asked you was important, not a test." Arya swore. That didn't bode well.

Something flashed over Darmanin's face.

She narrowed her gaze at him. "What is it?"

"Speaking of tests…" Darmanin hesitated again. "The Nightstalker has sent a nazal after Kirin, and that nazal is not in Dunidaen right now."

Fear, hot and sharp, flooded Arya. "Where is it?"

"He didn't say." Anguish curled at Darmanin's mouth, and his voice was low, pained. "Arya, I couldn't ask. The way he told me … it was clear he was doing it deliberately. He wanted to see if I would push, maybe even if I would leak the information to you."

Arya's gaze dropped to the tabletop as emotion churned away inside, so powerfully that she couldn't catch her breath for a moment. The urge to run to Kirin was overpowering, yet the fact remained that he was safest where he was. The nazal still didn't know anything and the chances of it finding Taskari were surely small. But what if it found someone who knew about Arya and Kulan?

Under the table, Darmanin's hand reached for hers, squeezing tightly. Through the bond, she could feel he was as worried as she was. "Arya, sometimes I fear so much. Of stepping a foot wrong. He's so confident, despite the little wins you've had, despite how much stronger you're growing. It doesn't make sense. There's something about his confidence … like he knows something we don't."

"He probably does. There's so much we don't know." Arya expelled a breath, fighting to regain control of herself, focusing on the feel of Darmanin's hands in hers, allowing it to steady her. "And I haven't had a chance to speak properly with Remien yet." She needed to prioritise that, but she had to make sure Dunidaen was safe first. The warring priorities tore at her. Kirin … what if the nazal found him?

Darmanin was silent, his grip on her hands just as fierce. "He'll have eyes on you, Arya. If you suddenly leave to go and check on Kirin … you can't risk it. It will blow both my cover and Kirin's."

"I know," she said, anguished. "But what if the nazal finds him? I wouldn't know, I wouldn't be able to protect him."

"Trust Kulan, he's a good man and a smart one. And his mother shouldn't be underestimated either."

"You're right." The only thing she could do to protect her son was end the Nightstalker. Stick to her path. But did she have long enough? Seeking steadier ground, Arya asked a question that had been at the back of her mind for a while. "Speaking of the Marshlands, how is it that the marshfolk have been able to hold out against him and Xaphistryl all these years?" she asked.

He accepted her segue without comment. "The low-level sulfuric gases prevalent through the Marshlands smother Sky Lord magic."

Arya's eyebrows shot upwards. "That explains a lot."

"It won't stop him from eventual victory though," Darmanin said. "In fact, I believe the Nightblades will win out there within a year, two at the most."

An interesting nugget she filed away for later consideration. Darmanin had been trained as well as she had on battlefield strategy, and she trusted his assessment. "What about his Nightblade forces still in Dunidaen?"

Darmanin smiled bitterly. "He wishes them the best in taking out as much of the Dunidae army as they can before being overwhelmed and destroyed."

Arya shuddered. She shouldn't be surprised by such a callous disregard of lives. A cold-hearted monster indeed. She couldn't ever imagine abandoning her own soldiers like that. Not ever. "Why isn't he coming here himself? It would force me off the battlefield and Xaphistryl could win the day."

"I'm not entirely sure, he doesn't trust me with all his thinking yet. What *does* seem clear to me is that Dunidaen is not his primary focus. It's almost as if he wanted to give it a go, but now that it's not working out, he's willing to cut his losses and move on." His gaze dropped. "But I could be wrong, he could be pretending. I worry so much, Arya, for Peemla and Anji, for *all* of you."

"Keep having faith in me, Dar. Whatever it is, I'll deal with it," she said softly.

He caught her gaze. "I miss you."

"Yeah, me too," she admitted.

"Really?" A smile curled at his mouth.

"Yes, really. That's all you're going to get," she warned him. "I don't do sappy."

"I should go." He glanced around. "You need to be careful, Arya."

"You know I will." She tossed at the words at him with a teasing smirk.

Amusement flickered in his eyes as he released her hand, preparing to push back his chair and stand. Impulsively, Arya reached out and grabbed his wrist, tugging him towards her so she could press her mouth fiercely against his. The kiss only lasted a moment, but felt like everything.

When she pulled away, he was smiling—that little crooked smile she loved so much. He said nothing, just rose and slipped into the crowd. Arya exhaled, settling back in her chair. She picked up her mug of ale, took a sip, and let a matching smile spread across her face.

***

Leanir knocked on her room door in the pre-dawn darkness.

"Something wrong?" she asked, rubbing at bleary eyes.

"It's further away than it was last night, *much* further, which means it's suddenly moving quickly. And it's further to the west, towards the Diamondfang." Leanir said, his breath steaming in the cold air. Autumn had only just started, but in the north of Dunidaen, that was as good as winter.

"Raven's balls," she swore. "You think it's realised we're coming and is fleeing us?"

More likely it was responding to whatever orders had been in Darmanin's message for it from the Nightstalker, but she couldn't tell Leanir that.

He gave her a considering look, but she kept her expression bland. "I have ensured it has not sensed me dream-walking it. How would it know we're following it? No, this sudden shift means something. Its dreaming mind was different last night, more agitated. I..." He seemed to be searching for the words, then his expression cleared. "Like a hound that's caught a scent. Something's off, Raider."

Leanir's misgivings were almost an exact echo of Darmanin's, and whatever his faults, the assassin had keen instincts. Arya turned away from the door, sat to pull on her boots. "What if it *was* up here scouting, looking for the best route to march its army northward. Or maybe it's planning to go after Rorin's family, use them as leverage." Except that Darmanin had told her that the Nightstalker had given up on Dunidaen.

What had been in that damned message?

Leanir shrugged, tucking his gloved hands under his armpits in a vain attempt to keep warm. "If it *is* heading for the underground road, I doubt we'll beat it there."

Arya stood, grabbed her cloak, slid her knife into her boot. "Then we fly in the direction its gone, and if we don't find it, we try and catch up with it in the tunnels underneath the Diamondfang. Can you get us to the tunnel entrance your Shadeweavers used to use?"

A crisp nod was all she got in return.

"Let's go. The wyverns are on their way."

***

Arya fought the urge to veer west toward Heathrock, desperate for even a glimpse of Peemla and Anjurin to be sure they were safe. But there was no time to spare. Her instincts screamed to find the nazal and kill it before it could carry out whatever orders the Nightstalker had given. Yet, despite the wyverns speed, they saw no sign of the creature—no tracks, no lingering traces of its presence. The chase carried them far east of Heathrock, deep into the Wraith Forrest, before they finally angled westward into the foothills of the Diamondfang. At the base of the steep incline, Leanir guided them down into a clearing. Arya and Leanir dismounted, but when they turned to leave, the wyverns voiced their protest with low growls.

"You won't fit in the tunnels," Arya explained patiently to Elendryl for what felt like the tenth time. She stood close to him, forehead pressed against his scales. "You know that already."

Firm displeasure.

"I'll be careful." She rubbed his nose affectionately. "And I'll be back before you know it."

Mistryl growled again as Leanir and Arya began walking off, and when Arya glanced over her shoulder, she swore she caught the two wyverns exchanging an almost friendly look of shared disgruntlement.

"What do you think happens if our wyverns become friends?" she asked. "Do you think it impacts our bond?"

He gave her an unamused look.

Arya followed the assassin up the incline, being careful with her footing. "I don't understand why it's suddenly fleeing," she said.

He gave her a quick look. "Me either."

Excellent. He was as suspicious as she was. That boded well.

Silence reigned for the rest of the walk, until Leanir brought them to the cavern entrance that the Shadeweavers had once used as a storage depot. They scrambled inside, both pausing once through to allow their eyes to adjust to the darkness. Memories flashed for Arya. Huddling, frozen and exhausted around a fire in the middle of their training for the Dreadwater Gate. Her heart twinged. At least they'd all been together then.

She banished the memories. "Can you control your magic well enough to create just a glimmer of light?" Arya asked.

"I don't need to. I can see in the dark."

Huh. "I thought only Darmanin could do that."

"It's got nothing to do with my Sky Lord magic." Leanir brushed past. "It's a skill I picked up when I was young."

Arya allowed a trickle of magic to emit a blue glow around her right hand before following. "How did that happen?"

"None of your business."

"Fair enough," she murmured. "We should speed up if we want to catch this thing. How long can you maintain a swift jog?"

"Longer than you can."

She grinned and set off at a ground-eating Icefolk run, trying not to think about how dark and narrow the tunnel was. The stone echoed under their boots, despite their attempts to move quietly. The haunting sound only put her more on edge. Her hope was that the nazal would be travelling along the main underground road, and by using the side tunnel, they could get ahead of it. Then she could force it to tell them what it was up to before she killed it. Or let Leanir kill it.

By the time they emerged onto the main road near the amphitheatre, Arya guessed they'd been running for several hours. Both came to a halt, taking a moment to catch their breath and stretch their burning legs. Relief trickled through her at the openness of the space after so long confined in the tunnels. Nearby, water dripped steadily down a stone wall. She drew in more magic, letting it feed her light until it glowed brighter, pushing back the surrounding darkness.

Arya couldn't help but smile as Leanir took a couple of steps and then stopped dead in his tracks, staring around with amazement. Even though she'd seen it before, she'd forgotten exactly how impressive the underground road was. "Quite a sight, isn't it?"

He said nothing.

"I'm surprised you Shadeweavers never explored these tunnels further. They would have made an excellent hiding place."

"Tunnels are too constricting," he said. "Most of us preferred the freedom of the forests. The idea of being trapped here, in the dark..." A barely noticeable shudder rippled through him.

Arya took a breath, hesitating. Revealing one of her deepest vulnerabilities to an assassin who wasn't even on her side ... it was incredibly difficult. It was probably also stupid. But she'd promised to try and build trust. "I'm terrified of enclosed spaces," she said. "I can't control it. I can't do anything but panic and get out as quick as I can."

He turned to her, eyes glimmering.

"It's the truth. I've never told anyone." Arya cleared her throat, uncomfortable, and stepped over to one of the images on the wall, the smear marks still there from where she and Darmanin had wiped away the dust almost a year earlier. "Back when this road was in use, it would have been lit by Sky Lord magic. It would have been beautiful," she murmured.

Again, nothing.

She sighed. "We should keep moving; this road opens up into an amphitheatre ahead, what was once a waypoint. If we've managed to get ahead of the nazal, we'll be able to set up a good ambush position there."

They reached the amphitheatre soon after, Arya stifling a smile at the look of unconscious wonderment on Leanir's face. It was still daylight outside, and a watery light shone over the floor and the gemstones in the walls, setting them glittering. The STORMRIDER letters shone in the centre of the space. The roof was so high above the space felt endless.

"I would have liked to have seen this, back when it was all alive," he admitted quietly.

"So would I," she said. "Leanir, we can make it that way again."

He scoffed. "A man like me? A cold-blooded murderer, making something beautiful? I don't think so. The beauty is long gone, and none of us are bringing it back."

He walked off before she could respond, eyes trained on the floor. He stopped a short distance away, bending down to touch something on the marble surface. "Fresh horse droppings. Either a random traveller has come riding through here in the last day, or we're too late."

Arya swore bitterly, even as her soldier's gaze snapped up to study the space more carefully for threats. "If it's mounted, we won't catch up. We'll have to let it go."

He gave her a long look. "The droppings are fresh. Would you like to at least check our quarry hasn't decided to rest its mount here before continuing on? Unless that blasted light of yours has warned it we're here, of course."

Swearing inwardly at herself, she immediately extinguished the light and dropped her voice to a murmur. "See, you're a details man, Leanir. This is why I have you along. Let's indeed do that."

"Fuck's sake, Raider, you're a pain in the ass," he hissed back.

At the idea a nazal could be close, the dim, cavernous space took on a more eerie air, Arya jumping each time one of them made the slightest noise. They crossed the massive amphitheatre floor, Arya sparing a glance for her name written out on the floor as they passed it. Leanir ignored it.

They reached the other side without seeing any more signs of a horse or rider passing through, and a short foray further along the road didn't reveal any either. Either it was long gone or resting amongst the buildings along the amphitheatre wall. In silent accord, Leanir and Arya climbed to the first tier and split up to search, steadily working their way through what had once been homes and shops.

Arya heard a faint scratching sound and spun, her heart pounding, eyes straining through the darkness. But nothing moved, and she continued on. Up where the streets were narrow and spaces more confined, Arya's heartbeat quickened. She ducked into an empty shopfront, the dim light from the amphitheatre illuminating neatly placed pairs of mouldering shoes on shelves at the back of the room. This place had once been a cobbler's. Arya wondered idly where the shop's owner was now, whether he was still alive, or if his children had carried on the family—

Something rippled through the darkness. A shoe scuffing. A stifled cough.

Then, the low snarl of a shadowhound.

"Leanir!" she shouted, spinning out of the shop and drawing her sword with a loud ringing sound. At the same moment she sent her ball of light flying high into the air, feeding it more magic so that it lit up her surroundings.

Leanir was further along the row of shops, already reaching for his bow, knocking an arrow. And below them...

...Nightblades poured into the amphitheatre floor from the narrow side entrance she and Darmanin had once used. Already they were moving towards the amphitheatre wall, shadowhounds streaking ahead of them.

She and Leanir were trapped halfway up amongst the tiers of buildings with a small army coming at them.

Only now did Arya realise what the nazal's instructions had been. Her weakness was her family. The Nightstalker knew that. He knew if he hung his nazal out as bait, loitering in the north, she'd worry about Heathrock. That she'd be driven to come after it.

So it could lure her into an ambush.

Chapter 18

"An ambush," Arya shouted, running to meet Leanir. "Dammit, the nazal *led* us in here."

"Stupid of us both." He spat the words, clearly furious. Around them, howls started echoing through the cavern, shadowhounds who'd found their quarry.

"*Danger?*" Elendryl roused in her mind.

"*Yes, but let me concentrate.*"

A low growl in her mind, but he subsided.

"Do we move up higher and hope there's an exit at the top, or try and fight our way through to the amphitheatre floor?" She lifted her voice above the incessant howling.

"Neither option is going to work." Leanir pointed, his eyes having already pierced the darkness at the top of the amphitheatre wall to see the Nightblades boiling out of the buildings they'd been quietly hiding in.

Arya swore under her breath. "We're neatly flanked. Excellent." She glanced between the approaching forces. "Then we fight our way through to the amphitheatre floor where there are multiple exits. Do you know how to use your magic apart from dream-walking?"

"No."

There was no more time for talking. The Nightblades were almost on them.

"Take left, I'll take right," Leanir said, his bow already up and drawing to fire.

Arya spun to face the Nightblade who ran along the street towards her. Their boots echoed on stone, their breathing heavy. The street was narrow, sandwiched between shopfronts on one side and a low wall on the other, which meant only one soldier could come at her at a time.

Surprisingly, though, the first Nightblade halted rather than attacking. "Agree to put down your weapons and come with us, and we'll let you live. Those are our orders. You'll be bound, but not harmed."

"Leanir?" Arya asked.

"That's a hard pass from me."

"Me too." She couldn't allow herself to be captured again. There would be no second escape from Blackstone. "What happens if we don't give ourselves up?"

The soldier hesitated. She thought she saw reluctance in his face. Was he afraid of taking them on, or was he here only because he had no choice? "You have our word. Give yourself up and you won't be harmed."

"I'm sorry," she said, meaning it. "We can't. But you have a choice too. Let us go, and we won't touch you."

The Nightblade's reply was to come at her, sword swinging. *Damn.*

Grunts echoed off stone as she quickly dispatched the first two, then ducked desperately as a snarling grey shape leaped from the shop's roof above. Regaining her feet, she managed to slash her sword along the creature's ribs before spinning back around to face the next Nightblade attack. It yowled in pain as it hit the ground. "Leanir, watch for shadowhounds coming from above!" she shouted a warning.

More Nightblades came at her, and as soon as she had a moment of breathing space, Arya used a burst of magic to send the nearest soldiers flying backwards into those crowding in behind them. Then turned and did the same to those attacking Leanir. "Quick, over the wall. We need to move before they bottle us up here."

The two of them swung over the wall and dropped down onto the tier immediately below. Shadowhounds came streaming after them, large, ominous shapes in the dim light. Leanir lifted his bow and fired in rapid succession, killing most. "Neat trick with the magic," he said as they ran. "Think you could do it again, take out most of the force?"

"If I used that much magic in here, I'd risk bringing down the roof and killing us both. That's why they ambushed us in here rather than outside, dammit." Arya swore, wincing as another shadowhound snarled nearby. "I can only risk smaller bursts, and no, I don't have enough to take out this many soldiers and shadowhounds that way." Even if she had the stomach for it.

They burst into an open square—only to find Nightblades closing in from both streets feeding into it. Cursing, Arya veered toward a low wall, scrambling over it and dropping into a deserted alleyway tucked behind a row of buildings. The passage was narrow, the walls pressing in on either side, and the weight of the earth above them only made it worse. They were underground, trapped—

"Wait!"

Leanir's shout stopped Arya mid-stride. She spun to see him duck behind a section of wall jutting into the alley. He didn't move, didn't rush—just waited, patient and still, until their pursuers came into view. Then, with deadly precision, he raised his bow and loosed his arrows, each one striking true. Not a single one missed its mark. "Okay, go." He turned and sprinted towards her.

"Nice shooting."

"I've only got a few arrows left."

Shadowhounds were faster and more agile than the Nightblades, and cut them off at the next cross-street. They fought bitterly to avoid being overwhelmed. Arya tried to work out what to do. They couldn't stay in this rabbit warren—there were too many adversaries and eventually they'd be completely holed up. They had to find a way to escape, get *out* of the tunnels, where her powerful magic could wipe out their attackers.

"*Where?*" Elendryl ploughed into her thoughts again, growing increasingly worried for her, and angry, too, that she was under attack, and he wasn't here.

"*You can't get to me,*" she tried to be calm, and not let on how bad a situation she was in. "*I'm coming. Please, Elendryl, just let me concentrate.*"

Her eyes roved their surroundings, trying to come up with a plan. She needed an overview of the area, a map to plot a route out to the amphitheatre floor. But her panic of close spaces was slowing her thinking, making her tired and hesitant.

Nightblades caught up to the shadowhounds, flooding into the intersection. They couldn't stay here.

"Up there!" she called, veering to leap up onto a low wall that ran under the eaves of an empty building on the tier above. From there she was able to swing herself up onto a first story balcony, and from there to the roof. Leanir followed her, as quick and agile as she was.

Once at the top, they crouched, panting, trying to get an idea of what they were dealing with and plot a route through. It was a good vantage point, and Arya's heart sank as she saw shadowhounds and soldiers pouring through the streets on almost every tier.

"They're coming from every direction. Too many to take by ourselves." Leanir spoke the obvious.

"I can use my magic in controlled bursts to win a path through," she said, gaze roving the area. "Once we hit the amphitheatre floor, we'll have more room to move and plenty of exits. That's the goal."

"Agreed. What about that square?" He pointed down and to their right. "There's only one entry into it, so they can only come at us from one direction. We bait as many as possible into following us into it, then you use your magic to kill them? It might clear us a temporary path."

Arya nodded, and they clambered down the other side of the building. Soldiers and shadowhounds were still on their tail as they ran for the square, surrounded on three sides by buildings. Once there, Arya and Leanir pretended to look for a way out, backing up and letting more and more Nightblades and shadowhounds enter, filling the space. Arya waited as long as she dared while shadowhounds raced across the stone towards her, snarling. When they were close enough to leap for her throat, she drew deeply on her magic and let loose with a controlled electric blast which enveloped and destroyed everything in the square.

Gore rained down. Blood was everywhere. Arya glanced upwards, but the explosion hadn't gone too high. Another wave of Nightblades poured into the square, and Arya let loose another blast.

Silence ushered in. Nothing else emerged into the square.

"Go!" Leanir snapped.

They ran, turning right out of the square along a road that would lead them to steps down to the next tier. The ambush party moved quickly to cut them off, but another two bursts of magic won them a path through. By then, Arya's reserves of magic were running low, and she slowed, drawing her sword.

"You all right?" Leanir asked, noting her heavy breathing.

"Fine. In the absence of a storm to draw power from, that's about it for my magic." A thought occurred to her. "The rest we'll have to manage between the two of us. Can you shift their perception? Make them think we're somewhere else?"

"Not on so many at once when they're spread out like they are."

She glanced around. "Okay. Only three more levels to get down and we're clear."

"No, we're not." Leanir pointed.

More Nightblades entered the amphitheatre, making their way up into the tiers of buildings, arrowing towards Leanir and Arya at shouts from their commanders. Arya swore. The freedom from pursuit they'd won was momentary. How many had the Nightstalker committed to this ambush?"

"You can still give yourselves up." A loud voice shouted over the clomping of running boots and snarling of the shadowhounds, coming from somewhere above. "Put your swords down and live. You have to know you can't fight off so many of us. Our king doesn't want you dead."

"The answer is still no." Arya bellowed back.

Despite their hopes, the Nightblades were closing around them again before they could reach the amphitheatre floor. Arya found herself temporarily separated from Leanir as her world narrowed to dodging the sharp teeth and claws of the shadowhounds and the swords of the Nightstalker's soldiers. Sweat poured down her face and loosened her grip on her sword.

Her hands and arms stung from a myriad of tiny cuts, though Essa's mail kept her from serious injury.

Time after time, she and Leanir tried to fight their way through to move down another level, but each time they were forced back and in a different direction, utterly stymied. They scrambled up a roof and along to another narrow street, once again hoping to cut through to the way out.

But instead, they ran straight into a waiting cohort of Nightblades. Taken by surprise, Arya barely managed to counter a heavy blow and run her opponent through. Her legs were shaky with fatigue, and it was an effort to keep standing as she looked around for Leanir. He battled two Nightblades, doing well enough, but as she watched, she spotted a shadowhound creeping towards him, belly low to the ground, clearly waiting for an opening to attack.

Arya moved to intercept, but was stopped by another Nightblade. She pushed him back and swiped at his head unsuccessfully. He lunged at her; she stepped aside and slashed at his ribs, breaking through his tunic and eliciting a cry of pain. Spinning around, she searched out Leanir—the shadowhound was shifting to attack the assassin.

"Leanir, ware!" Arya ran. He was pinned down, unable to move fast enough to defend himself, despite her warning.

She reached the shadowhound after it had started its leap towards Leanir's throat, so she had no time to do anything but collide with it in mid-air. It snarled and twisted as they hit the ground, its sharp claws raking down her arm, teeth snapping at her neck. Swearing in pain, Arya turned aside barely in time to avoid it ripping out her throat, but the creature was heavier and stronger, and she was too weary to summon the strength to push it off. She squirmed desperately as fangs snapped at her throat. It growled deep in its chest, claws raking viciously over her mail, burying deeper into the flesh of her upper arm where it wasn't protected by the gauntlet. Somewhere in the back of her mind Elendryl raged, desperate to fight his way to her.

Then hot ichor splattered against her face and the body of the shadowhound slumped lifelessly on her. A moment later its weight lifted and Leanir was there. "Arya?" he asked tensely. "How bad is it?"

"Just my arm." She swore in pain as she sat up. "Bastard got me good."

"Your neck?"

"The creature's blood, not mine." She scrabbled upwards, inspiration hitting her as pain sharpened her thinking and pushed away fear and exhaustion. "Leanir, we're twice fools today. *My* magic might bring down the roof, but what if I used it to augment yours, make you *stronger*? When the Nightblades get here, you make them see us heading east along the street, while we move down towards the amphitheatre. Then you can make more of them see us fleeing along the road towards Andahar. They'll all head that way, and we head in the opposite direction back to Dunidaen."

"No." His mouth tightened stubbornly. They'd never used the bond between them like that before.

"I won't use our connection to compel you, I swear it. My word holds." Arya swore as running footsteps grew closer. Pain throbbed in her arm. "Leanir, we can't fight our way through. It's our only way out of here."

His face tightened further, but then he glanced at the dead shadowhound beside them, the one Arya had jumped in front of to save him. He let out a low angry growl. "Fine."

She took a breath and brought to life the bond between her and Leanir. It was the weakest of her Sky Lord bonds, and so it took a moment before she could steadily send what was left of her magical strength along it.

Leanir's eyes flashed with magic, and he sucked in a deep breath. "Wow."

"Wow, indeed," she murmured. "Now make them see us running away before my strength runs out."

Cries of alarm and surprise came from the Nightblades, and as a man, they turned along a narrow street heading away from where they were, shouting and pointing.

The bond between Arya and Leanir grew bright and strong.

"We don't need to sneak," Leanir said in wonder. "I can make them all see what I want now."

"What about …" She gritted her teeth against the pain, "the shadowhounds?"

"Them too," he said in glee.

He was strong, her Sky Lord. Not raw power like Chiarn or measured skill like Essa, but shifty, canny, and filled with cold purpose. Around them Nightblades and shadowhounds raced down the levels towards the amphitheatre, turning to follow the underground highway towards Andahar.

And then Arya's strength ran out with a pop. The bond faded. Leanir sagged and leaned against the nearest wall.

"That went well." Arya managed. "Thanks, by the way, for saving my life."

"You saved mine first." He kneeled and looked at her arm. Her tunic was in shreds and blood soaked through the cloth and dripped to the ground. "This doesn't look good."

She sucked in a breath. Now that the adrenaline of battle was fading, agony was a live creature in her arm. "It doesn't feel good either. Come on, we have to move before they realise they've been duped."

"We're not getting anywhere if you bleed out, so let me take care of this first."

Leanir efficiently pulled away the torn pieces of Arya's tunic and shirt sleeve, revealing multiple ragged gashes. One was deep enough that bone glinted through blood and muscle. Black ichor mixed with her own blood. Her stomach heaved at the sight, and she quickly looked away.

Leanir tugged his water bottle from his pack and poured it over the wounds, trying to rinse out the poisonous ichor. Sharp pain stabbed through Arya's arm, and she groaned, biting through her lip and tasting fresh blood on her tongue.

"We need to stop the bleeding, but I don't have anything to stitch you up with, and no time to start a fire to cauterise the wounds. Where's the damned musician when you need him?" he muttered.

"Just do your best so we can move. We don't have much time before they come back," she groaned.

He scrambled over to the nearest body and tore two long strips from the Nightblade's thick tunic. Returning to Arya, he rinsed the wounds again, before binding the strips of shirt tightly around the wounds.

"Dammit, Leanir," she snapped as white-hot pain engulfed her arm.

"Deal with it," he snapped back. "If the bleeding doesn't stop, you'll die. Of course, I'm wrapping poison in there with the wound, so infection is going to set in, but the blood loss will kill you faster, so that's what we're treating first."

She said nothing more as he finished wrapping the makeshift bandage around her arm before tying it off. Arya took deep breaths to control the pain, but it took a long few moments before the agony began to subside to a bearable ache. As soon as she felt able, she struggled to her feet. "Let's get moving before I pass out."

"Elendryl, I'm coming. I'm going to need you to get me to help."

"Ready." He promised, clearly agitated. *"Come fast."*

Leanir spoke. "It's a long walk back through the tunnels."

"You want to tell me anything else I already know?" Irritation threaded her voice. Arya wasn't ignorant to the seriousness of her situation; shadowhound bites and scratches became infected quickly if they weren't treated properly. Hers were deep, and it was an hours' long walk out of the tunnels where their wyverns waited. Still, there wasn't anything she could do but keep moving as long as she could.

He bent down and picked up his pack. "Let's go."

***

Too soon, weariness, compounded by blood loss, seeped through Arya. The steady throbbing in her wounds morphed into spikes of sharp, hot pain all the way down her arm. It felt as if burning tendrils were spreading from the wounds, throbbing with each beat of her heart.

Leanir pushed the pace hard, leading the way since her magic light had sputtered out, forcing them both to keep drinking water at regular intervals. Arya's pace lagged when light-headedness made it hard to keep her balance. Leanir stopped when she stumbled sideways into him as they rounded a corner in the tunnel.

"Raider? You still with us?"

"I'm fine." She blinked, trying to clear her vision. It didn't matter; everything was dark. "Why did you stop?"

"Because you look like you're about to keel over."

"If I stop walking I probably will, so let's keep going."

He looked dubious, but did as she asked, nonetheless. As the hours passed, her arm grew hot and inflamed, and the pain became steadily worse. Agony spiked with each movement of her body, no matter how small, until she had to grit her teeth to stop herself from crying out in pain.

"Raider!"

She blinked, squinting, not quite able to see Leanir standing right in front of her. "What?"

"You're swaying on your feet," he said flatly. "Let's rest a minute."

She didn't have the strength to fight him as he guided her into a sitting position against the wall of the tunnel. The cessation of movement lessened some of the throbbing in her arm, and Arya let her head fall back against the cold stone, eyes closing in relief.

Leanir's hand pressed against her sweaty forehead. "You've got a fever. Infection is setting in."

She nodded faintly.

"Maybe I could try cleaning out the wounds again? Re-bandage them?"

"Too late, it won't help. Just keep walking. Once we're out, Elendryl can..." she blinked, trying to remember what she'd been about to say.

"*Hurt?*" Elendryl asked quietly. His agitation had faded to quiet panic.

"*Coming,*" she promised him.

"Mistryl says your wyvern is upset. She thinks you must be dying," Leanir said.

"Not yet," she managed. "Sorry."

She hissed as he gently took hold of her arm. Despite the complete darkness, she could feel that blood had soaked through the bandages and was seeping down over her fingers before dripping to the ground.

Leanir cursed. "No wonder you're swaying on your feet. You're losing too much blood."

She chuckled, a little delirious. "You should sound more cheerful, Leanir. You may have finally gotten me."

She heard a ripping sound, fabric tearing. Then he was back, and she cried aloud as he bound another strip of cloth around her arm. He ignored her cries, grimly tightening the binding. By the time he was done she was sobbing with pain, curled up against the wall.

Leanir's voice in the darkness drew her from the pain. "When I was a small boy, my father used to beat me and then lock me in a chest when I misbehaved. He'd leave me in there for hours sometimes, days even, and it was so dark in there I couldn't even see my fingers right in front of my face. Sometimes it got hard to breathe. It happened so often ... I suppose my eyes just learned to see through the darkness."

There was a moment's silence.

"I ran away when I was eight. Taught myself how to pick the lock on the chest from the inside. Caught my father sleeping and slit his throat with a kitchen knife on my way out. I was half-starved and almost dead from the cold when Ranier found me in the forest outside my town."

"Leanir—"

"If there's one thing we share, Raider, it's sheer bloody-minded stubbornness. If I could survive that dark chest as a boy, you can walk the rest of the way out of this damned tunnel."

Right.

Arya pushed herself to her feet, swaying a little before steadying.

"Drink this." He pressed his water bottle against her mouth. She managed a few mouthfuls before choking and gasping. "All right, let's go. Keep your arm high, like that, yes, it will slow the bleeding."

His hand curled around her uninjured arm, helping to offset some of her weight. More pain flooded through her, but she did her best to ignore it and follow Leanir as he started moving again. "Keep walking, Raider. You owe me a new shirt, and I intend to collect on the debt."

A while later she stumbled, crying out as pain shot through her arm. Leanir helped her steady herself. "How you doing?" he asked.

"Feeling pretty bad right now," she gasped. "Can't stay upright ... so dizzy."

"I'll help you. Come on."

She felt his arm come around her waist and then they were walking again. With her weight leaning on Leanir, she was able to remain upright and keep moving, although every step was an exercise in debilitating pain.

By the time they emerged from the tunnels, Leanir was practically dragging Arya's entire weight. Her skin was slick with sweat, her fever spiking. Her arm felt huge, like it was double its normal size. The pain was horrific. Part of her knew she was in trouble; even with Elendryl, it would take too long to get her to the help she needed.

Leanir's voice sounded distant and exhausted. "Just a little bit further."

She couldn't do it. Gasping for breath, she stumbled, falling hard onto the soft ground.

"Arya, come on, stay awake." He slapped her hard, bringing her back to some sort of awareness.

"*Arya!*" Elendryl. He felt so close.

"Arya!" Leanir's voice echoed his. "The wyverns are almost here. You need to hold on and—"

Her eyes slid closed again.

"Raven's balls." She heard him mutter to himself, followed by a lot of cursing, a long silence, then, "All right, Raider, let's build some damned trust."

Ayra felt him wrap his fingers around her arm just below the rotting wounds. The most incredible sensation of warmth and energy emanated from that skin-to-skin touch, and she sagged at the temporary relief from the pain. "Open up the bond and let me in, Stormrider," he ordered.

Too out of it to argue, she did what he asked, and the bond—stronger now they'd joined their magic in battle—flared to life between them.

A moment later magic seared through it. Arya's eyes snapped open, and she looked straight into the assassin's dark gaze. They stared at each other for an endless moment as Leanir used his magic to strengthen her life force and tether it to his own. New vitality flooded her, and she gasped. His eyes widened and she felt shock and wonder both from him, his magic pouring into her heedlessly as he forgot to concentrate, to think—

"Leanir, careful!" she warned. "Stop now, stop!"

He did as she asked, breaking off the connection abruptly. Her eyes slipped closed, the grogginess and pain flooding back once Leanir's magic was gone, but she knew he'd bought her crucial time.

"*Arya!*" Elendryl's voice broke into her mind, and she closed her eyes again, embracing her wyvern's love and support. A moment later she felt herself being picked up. And then all was blackness.

Chapter 19

Golden sunlight streamed in through the arched window and woke Arya laying in the bed. Mountain peaks were visible through the window to her left. She was in the Etherean citadel. A dull ache had replaced the fiery agony in her arm, and the remnants of exhaustion and magic depletion made her body feel heavier than usual.

She turned her head. Salyarin sat by her bed, his wings folded neatly behind him. It was impossible to tell what he was thinking, but he smiled when she turned towards him. "I'm glad to see you awake."

"Thank you." Arya felt well enough to shift upwards on the pillows, although she did so carefully to avoid putting weight on her arm. "I assume I'm going to live?"

"Your arm was badly mauled, and your blood was poisoned from the shadowhound ichor, but our healers did a good job. You'll have scars, but you'll keep full use of your arm."

"More scars." She sighed. "Did Leanir tell you what happened?"

"It sounds like you and he fought quite a battle, one you were lucky to escape. It was a well-planned and cunning ambush, relying on the Night-stalker's knowledge of your weaknesses."

So Leanir had figured it out too and explained to Salyarin.

"And there's the disapproving elder I know." She smiled faintly, and for once, he returned it.

"I think we've sufficiently exhausted that argument between us, and as you have reminded me many times, we are equals."

"Even though..." She hesitated. "After I brought Darmanin back from death, you chided me about accessing old Sky Lord magic. I didn't know what you meant at the time, and you didn't really give me to opportunity to ask, but I'm pretty sure Leanir used the same thing to save me."

The elder's eyebrows shot skywards, and he seemed both deeply troubled and utterly taken aback. "*Leanir* did?"

"I need to know what you're keeping from me." Her gaze narrowed. There was something important here.

His jaw tightened. "I wasn't in the mood to share it with you then, Arya. I didn't trust you with the knowledge, if I'm honest. But…" He let out a long breath. "The knowledge is yours by right."

"Then tell me, please." She tried to keep the impatience from her voice.

"When you tried to heal Darmanin, you gave him access to your magical life force to keep him from dying. It was a terribly dangerous thing to do, especially because you had no idea what you were doing. It could easily have resulted in both your deaths. If Darmanin had drained too much from you, with you unable to stop him … the same could have happened to Leanir."

Arya sank down against the cushions, remembering how she'd given Darmanin almost everything she had in her desperation to keep him from dying. Salyarin had been right to fear. What they'd done was dangerous. "You should have told me this long ago, at least I would have been warned." She tried to keep her voice free of annoyance. "Is that the limit of our linking ability? Being able to lend magical strength to each other?"

"No, but we've reached a point where the Etherean knowledge of Sky Lord magic ends."

This time her irritation flared, and she snapped. "What is it, Elder? I can tell there's more."

"I'm not sure how, but my mother suspected the *cairdre's* linking ability was key to how the Nightstalker managed to defeat your grandfather."

"Your mother was right."

Both Arya and Salyarin turned as Remien appeared in the doorway. He'd already put weight on his gaunt frame during his short time in the citadel, and there was new colour in his cheeks. But her gaze went right to the glorious tattoos visible on his forearms where he'd rolled up his sleeves. "Right, how?" she demanded. Was she *finally* going to get some answers?

"I don't know why Ranier hasn't told you this." He frowned. "The ancient magic of Sky Lords goes both ways. It can give. *And* it can take. When the Nightstalker killed each of his *cairdre*, he stole their magic as they died. By the time he faced the Stormrider, your grandfather had no hope of besting him."

A beat of shocked silence filled the room, and then...

An icy shiver ripped through Arya's magic, as if in echo of her grandfather's horror and fear. She stared at Remien, hoping desperately she'd heard wrong, or understood wrong, or *something*. "Are you saying the Nightstalker has the power of at least five different Sky Lords *combined*?"

"In addition to the magic of any Sky Lord potentials he's killed in the decades since."

The shock that filled the room was so heavy Arya could almost feel it. Salyarin had turned bone white, quite the feat given how pale the Etherean naturally were. She looked away from both of them, realising she'd wrung her hands so tightly that her nails had gouged into her palms. "No wonder he's so confident he'll defeat us." She breathed. "What chance do we have to triumph over such a superior force?"

"The answer is simple," Remien said. "You do as he did. You kill *your* Sky Lords to gain their power before facing him."

Arya huffed. "Raven's balls, Remien, a serious answer for once would be much appreciated."

He simply stared at her, those dark eyes glittering just like Ranier's. The silence in the room crystallised into sharp glass. Horror speared through her so profoundly that she felt physically sick. "No." It was all she could get out.

"I cannot fathom why Ranier hasn't already communicated this to you." Remien paused, realisation flashing over his face. "Oh, Ran's daughter is one of your *cairdre*. Well, that explains it."

"You told him about Essa?" Arya turned on Salyarin.

"He's under your protection. I assumed there was no issue in telling him about your Sky Lords."

"I ..." Arya blinked, forcing herself to separate her wringing hands before she could do anymore damage. Spots of blood dripped onto the bedcovers. Nausea continued to roil in her gut. "Remien, I am *not* killing my Sky Lords."

"You broke me out of Blackstone for one reason, and one reason only, to give you the key to defeating your enemy. The information held by the Inkweaver archives." He held his arms out towards her, the tattoos rippling in the sunlight. "This is it, Stormrider. Don't blame me if you don't like the answers you're getting."

She stared at him, unbelieving. Part of her wished he'd take it all back. Even the *thought* of ... no! Arya swallowed down bile.

"Your denial is written all over your face," he said. "But let me be clear, Stormrider. There *is* no other way. The sooner you accept that, the better."

"Remien, enough." Salyarin stood, finally mastering his own shock. "You've said your piece."

"Elder, Lord Stormrider." Remien bowed his head, amused, and left without another word.

Ayra didn't like the mix of despair and hopelessness on Salyarin's face as he watched Remien leave. "Tell me you don't agree with him."

He turned towards her, mastering his expression, but his wings continued to rustle in agitation. "I hope with everything I am there is another way."

No, she wasn't going to entertain this. It simply wasn't ... Arya took a deep breath as her stomach roiled again, then pushed off the covers and swung her legs over the side of the bed. She had to focus on something else, something practical, or she was going to get lost in the implications of what she'd just heard. "It's time for me to go."

"Rest here for the night at least. Your need more time to heal."

"I need to get back to Dunidaen." She stood, reaching for her chainmail. As she pulled it on, she pushed Remien's revelations behind the wall she'd built in her mind. And as she did, her shoulders relaxed, her breathing came easier, and her stomach settled. Yes, she had things to do. "You need to be wary, Elder. The war in Dunidaen is almost over, and any Nightblades or shadowhounds that escape the Dunidae army will be fleeing under or over the Diamondfang. Is there a path up to the citadel from the tunnels or the underground road?"

She watched as Salyarin hesitated, almost said something, then his shoulders straightened. "Possibly, but it would be a long and extremely difficult climb. You know how high we are. Even if they did make it up here, they would struggle with the thin air."

"Even so, I think you should place guards at any ground level entrances to the citadel."

"Arya—"

"I hope I'm wrong and the Nightstalker continues to ignore you," she interrupted. "But you are the one always telling me to be careful. Surely a few extra guards won't hurt?"

He nodded. "I will speak to Cirilla about it today."

"Good. I'll see you, Elder."

She slammed the door behind her.

***

Leanir waited in the entry cavern when Arya arrived, her left arm strapped in a sling against her chest. She stopped dead. After Remien's explosive revelation, she hadn't even thought to ask about the assassin. Their bond pulsed quietly, stronger than it had ever been. Astonishingly, just the sense of it eased the tendrils of horror and despair still leaking through the cracks in the wall she'd shoved her knew knowledge behind. The two wyverns waited a short distance off.

"Nothing has changed," he warned, arms crossed over his chest.

"Oh, something *has* changed." Arya headed towards Elendryl, pausing as she passed Leanir to hold his gaze. "I trust you, Leanir. And I call you friend. Do with that what you will."

She kept walking, smiling as Elendryl's head snaked down to greet her with an affectionate bump. *"Thanks for getting me here."*

Love and worry and reassurance came back. She pressed her hand to his scales, then shifted away to scramble onto his back. As she settled in her usual spot, he sent her a query—he'd sensed her emotional turmoil. "*Later*," she murmured to him.

"Where are we going next?" Leanir was halfway to Mistryl.

Arya straightened, bolstered by Elendryl's touch and the presence of her Sky Lord. One step at a time. "Back to Dunidaen. We're going to finish the war so that we can get started on the real one."

***

Rorin's army had made significant gains in the time Arya and Leanir had been away, presumably due to the arrival of the Icefolk warriors. The Dunidae army was camped on the border dividing SparrowWing and Hawkesdale, only a few days march southeast of Melbin and southwest of Darulan, the seat of Hawkesdale. Elendryl circled out of the sky, Mistryl following them down to a landing spot east of the encampment.

Lances guarding the perimeter offered an enthusiastic greeting as Arya and Leanir entered the camp, all their fear of magic-wielders and wyverns vanished. They hadn't gotten far when Laskin appeared, making straight for them, Chiarn not far behind.

"What happened to you?" Laskin demanded the moment he caught sight of Arya. "Chiarn and Essa said you were hurt, but couldn't tell how badly. Apparently, you were hiding from them."

Arya shot her Sky Lord a glare. "I wasn't *hiding*. I just didn't want them to worry. I'm fine."

"She wasn't. The nazal led us into an ambush," Leanir said. "A shadowhound almost killed her."

Chiarn's mouth hung open. "The two of you were *ambushed*?"

Leanir scowled, started walking off. "Don't come and find me until I've had several hours' sleep, Stormrider."

Laskin scratched his beard. "You found the nazal, then. Is it dead, at least?"

"No, it escaped after leading us into the ambush."

"It drew you in?" Chiarn frowned, still looking puzzled. "But why didn't you think of..."

The Flamewielder's voice trailed off as Arya settled a glare on him. "Laskin, can you take me to Rorin and Essa?"

Laskin crossed his arms over his chest.

Chiarn chuckled. "I'll take you."

Laskin glared at her one final time before stalking off.

"Things seem to be going well," Arya said as they walked.

"The Ce'Garn and his warriors proved the difference." Chiarn's tone was a mixture of awe and respect. "Once they joined the fight, our harrying attacks on the dispersed Nightblade units became far more effective. We have the upper hand now, and without reinforcements, the Nightblades will lose. The generals think a few more days will do it, and then it will just be a matter of cleaning up."

Arya stopped, delight filling her voice. After so many knocks in a row, she hadn't been prepared for *good* news. "That *is* good to hear."

Chiarn came to a stop outside Rorin's tent, eyes shining. "It is. You should find the High Warlord inside. Come and find me for a drink when you're done." He waggled his eyebrows. "I want to hear all about how the famous Arya Stormrider allowed herself to be ambushed."

The Defenders guarding the entrance recognised Arya and stepped aside to let her pass. She pushed through the tent flap into delicious warmth. Rorin sat by a flickering brazier, staring into the flames, looking tired and drawn. Essa sat on a chair nearby, drawing idly on a scrap of parchment.

Rorin shot to his feet, concern flicking across his face. "*What happened to you?*"

"A shadowhound," she said. "It's all right, I'm fine now. The Etherean healers looked after me."

"*Your arm is in a sling!*"

"You mustn't have been all right, if you needed Etherean treatment." Essa sided firmly with Rorin. "Come and sit down, Arya, you look exhausted."

She allowed Essa to shepherd her over to a chair by the brazier. "I'm okay, I promise."

"*What happened?*" Rorin asked.

Sinking onto the soft surface, Arya relayed a short version of the story, leaving out her conversation with Remien. Even the thought of it made her stomach start to churn again. "Chiarn gave me an account of your status," Arya said, keen to change the subject. She still smarted over the fact she'd walked so blithely into an ambush. "You've done well."

"*The remainder of the Nightblade army has coalesced to the north and dug themselves in—a last ditch defensive effort. We're in the midst of planning a final assault on their position. Once we take it, it's just going to be a matter of cleaning up as we head further north,*" Rorin agreed, weariness in his signing and bearing. "*Unless the Nightstalker himself comes.*"

"He won't," she said distantly. "And the Sky Lords and I will help with that final assault. We'll ensure your victory, Rorin."

"Arya, what is it?" Essa asked.

She settled further into the chair, stretching her feet towards the warmth of the fire. "What do you mean?"

Across the flames, Essa's green eyes met hers, far too knowing. She wouldn't push in front of others if Arya didn't want her to, but she knew Arya had left something out. "I just feel the fool for walking straight into an ambush," she said.

Thankfully, Essa accepted that with a nod. "You and Leanir were fortunate to make it out."

"Actually." Arya pondered that. "I agree that we were fools not seeing the trap, but I did learn something from the experience."

"*Oh dear.*" Rorin signed with a smile. "*The Nightstalker better watch out.*"

"Nothing quite so useful." Arya shook her head. "But it gave me a little piece of an idea I might be able to use."

They were snippets of a plan that she still couldn't quite put together. There were more pieces to be found. Arya let them go for now. Rorin asked about Leanir, then, and the conversation moved away. She hoped Essa let her earlier questions go. She had no idea how she was going to tell her Sky

Lords what she'd learned. The wall inside her shuddered and she fought to hold it upright.

She would never hurt them. She *couldn't*.

But what if it would save Kirin?

Chapter 20

Arya came awake with a cry, her breath choking in the back of her throat at the horror of her dream. She shoved away the blankets covering her and rolled off the cot, her gasping breaths gulping in the cold pre-dawn air. She dressed quickly, escaping the confines of her small tent and the lingering darkness brought on by her nightmare.

She *should* have been sleeping well. The Dunidae army, with the support of the Icefolk warriors and Arya's *cairdre,* had routed the remaining force of Nightblades the previous day. Some had fled north, but the invasion was officially failed.

Dunidaen had won the war.

Yet her sleep last night had been even worse than the previous nights. She might be able to bury what she'd learned from Remien behind her makeshift wall during the day, but the knowledge was like a rot, sinking deeper and deeper into her, and spilling out when she slept.

Outside her tent, she took a deep breath, hoping the open space and the biting cold would steady her. But it was all too quiet, leaving space for her thoughts and fears to keep spiralling. Arya tipped her head back, staring up at the stars above.

She had to do something. There was too much building up inside her—too much to fear, too much doubt. And Kirin, her *always* overriding concern. A nazal hunted him. And yet she had to stay away, which was growing harder and harder to do. Surely it would be better if she just *went* to him, and...

"Arya?"

Essa's voice snapped her from her thoughts. She realised that her heart was still racing, sweat slicking her palms despite the cold air.

She tried for a smile as Essa came over to stand beside her. "I didn't think anything short of an emergency could get you out of bed while it's still dark."

Essa made a face. "Normally that's true, but every now and then I have a night where I just can't sleep. It was the message we got last night from Falconcrest that did it. I'm trying to figure out what to advise Rorin to do."

Arya nodded, grateful for a small tactical detail to focus on. With the Dunidae army in control of the war for the first time, they'd been able to get a message through to Falconcrest and receive one back. Rudderless without a confirmed warlord, the remaining Falconcrest household had hunkered down and prepared defences in case the war moved north. The good news was that the entire Aggressor force was unharmed. The bad was nobody knew what the Falconcrest mindset was, or if they'd gotten the news about Arya's murder of their warlord.

"If you want my two copper pieces, I'd avoid ordering Dahlia here and risk the household disobeying until we have a better sense of their loyalty to Rorin. We don't need their Aggressors anymore."

"That's what I was leaning towards. Rorin can go there once things are over, formally appoint Dahlia as warlord and ensure her loyalty in person." Essa gave her a sidelong glance. "Something has been weighing on your mind since you got back from the citadel."

Arya forced what she hoped was a genuine smile. "I'm just trying to focus on ending the war."

"Arya." Essa's voice was quiet, knowing.

"I can't..." she whispered. "Please, Ess, I can't. Not yet."

"All right." Essa's hand slid into hers. "Then let's just stand here and breathe for a while."

So they did.

When Rorin emerged from his tent sometime later, as the sun crested the horizon in an orange line, Arya was steady again, the wall inside her solid, her thoughts clear. And she'd decided what to do. Her recent run of tortured nights made one thing clear. The fewer secrets she had to keep from those she loved, she more focused she'd be able to be. She couldn't keep carrying everything inside.

"*Arya, Essa!*" Rorin signed enthusiastically.

Arya let go of Essa's hand and stepped towards him. "Good. You're finally awake. Come with me, both of you."

They fell into step happily enough, Rorin sharing a curious glance with his chief advisor. "*What's going on?*"

"You'll see."

As they walked, Arya reached for Leanir and Chiarn, sending a pulsing request through the bonds. The first was wide awake and sent back a reluctant assent. The other was firmly asleep and displeased about leaving his warm blankets.

They reached the southern edge of the encampment at roughly the same time, Chiarn still rubbing sleep from his eyes and yawning dramatically. Arya kept walking, heading for where the wyverns rested, all a wary distance apart. "Leanir, can you make sure anyone looking this way doesn't see us gathering? Rorin especially."

He opened his mouth, as if to protest from habit, but instead, after a moment's hesitation, simply said, "I can. It will help if we stand in the shadows so that we're not visible to anyone looking this way."

"Thank you."

"*Can you ask the wyverns to behave as if we're not here?*" Arya came to a stop near Elendryl, who cracked open an eye and sent her a warm burst of regard in greeting, but did nothing more. Asandryl grumbled low in his throat but made no more protest, and Mistryl and Alletryl shifted so they were slightly further apart but closer to their riders. Arya almost had to laugh. She pitied any assassin or adversary trying to get at any of them in this moment.

"What is going on?" Chiarn asked. His hands were tucked into his armpits, and he looked miserable. "Asandryl is annoyed about the cloak and dagger and us interrupting his sleep."

"Do they all have to do what Elendryl tells them?" Essa asked curiously, presumably after communicating with her wyvern.

"I've never tested it, but I suspect so," Arya said.

"Mistryl says she does as she pleases," Leanir said tightly. "But it's hard for her to ignore a command from Elendryl."

"I'm with Chiarn." Rorin shivered, his gaze jumping warily between the fearsome creatures sprawled so close. *"I feel my chances of being eaten rise with every moment I stand here, so if you could get started, Arya, I'd appreciate it."*

"Several months ago, while we were at Icecliff Fort defending against the Nightstalker's first invasion, Darmanin and I came up with a plan," she said, breath frosting in the cool air.

"This is about *Darmanin*?" Chiarn hissed.

"Quiet!" Essa ordered him, commanding, and the singer's mouth closed with a wide-eyed snap.

"Yes, it's about Darmanin," Arya said. They were silent as she relayed the full story, explaining that he'd never betrayed them, that he was working as a spy to keep the Nightstalker from killing them for as long as he could. "It was a last ditch plan, a stalling tactic, to keep him from coming for us while I built the strength and knowledge I needed. When the Nightstalker allied with Emperor uq-Danresan and marched on Gateport, I had no choice but to use it."

Pure relief sheeted over Rorin's face well before she'd finished, shoulders relaxing, that sweet smile crossing his face. *"I knew it."*

Chiarn was less happy. Fire flared in his angry gaze. "Why didn't you *tell* us?"

"If the Nightstalker suspected what we're doing, even for a second, then Darmanin's life is forfeit. You all had to believe he was a traitor; it had to be convincing." She looked them all in the eye. "Once we walk away from here, you must go back to believing it. We don't speak of it again, not aloud, not ever, no matter how safe you think you are. Darmanin's life depends on it."

"If it's so dangerous, why are you telling us now?" Essa asked, worry furrowing her brow as she glanced sidelong at Leanir.

"Because you are my *cairdre*, and I trust you." She managed a smile. "And because Rorin refused to believe it anyway. He's kinda ruining the whole thing."

Rorin crossed his arms over his chest, unrepentant.

"Stormrider, that's a fine and cunning plan, but if Darmanin made an agreement to join the Nightstalker in return for not killing you, then why did he ambush us in the Diamondfang?" Leanir asked. "I know they agreed not to kill us if we gave ourselves up, but the Nightstalker had to know you'd never agree to be captured."

"It's a good question." And one that had been weighing on her mind along with everything else. "Perhaps the nazal acted on its own. Perhaps the Nightstalker never had any real intention to hold to his word and thinks Darmanin has been won sufficiently to his side that he doesn't need to worry about it anymore. I don't have a good answer."

"*Dar should leave now, while he still can,*" Rorin said. "*The longer he stays, the more dangerous it gets.*"

"I've told him that, but he believes he can learn more if he stays. He says he can do it." Arya hesitated. "And if we lost that protection now ... I'm not ready to face him, Rorin. Every day Dar buys us is incredibly important."

A silence fell, each of them thinking it over. Doubts over her decision to tell them stirred but she didn't allow them to take root. She trusted her *cairdre*. She had to risk them knowing or else she didn't think she'd be able to keep going forward alone.

"It's brave, what he's doing, incredibly brave." Tears sheened Essa's eyes. "I can't believe I ever doubted him. I don't think I'll ever be able to forgive myself."

"There's nothing to forgive," Arya said softly.

"I must admit, it's a weight off my shoulders, knowing he didn't truly betray us," Chiarn said.

Eventually, Rorin started signing. "*We shouldn't be out here any longer or people might start wondering where I am. Arya, Ess, we're due for a meeting with the warlords shortly.*"

"Agreed. You should all make your way back separately," Arya said. "Leanir, I'd like to speak to you before you go."

He made a face, but waited as the others dispersed.

She waited until they were out of earshot. "I have an idea, one that suits your particular skills." She outlined one of the little plans that had been percolating in the back of her mind.

He was silent for a long moment. Arya got the distinct sense he was parsing her words for a trap, an ulterior motive. He still hadn't learned to trust *her* yet. That was all right.

Eventually he said, "You've just told me an incredibly dangerous secret, and now you want to set me loose, out of your control?"

His voice made clear he thought she was a prize fool for doing either, and he was right. Doubt stirred again. She wouldn't let it. Darmanin had told her to trust her gut, her instincts, and in this they were strong. "I promised you that you were free."

Something unnameable flickered over his face. "You've got limited time until either Darmanin is caught and has to flee, or until the Nightstalker decides to come for you anyway. What you're asking of me couldn't be in place quickly enough to help you."

"I'm aware."

He folded his arms across his chest. "Then why?"

"I'm not exactly sure yet," she said, then sighed when his scowl deepened. "I *will* have a use for it, I just haven't quite nailed down the details."

"For someone who is supposedly a strategic and tactical genius, I've seen little signs of rational decision making from you, Stormrider. It makes me wary of doing as you ask."

"I *will* earn your faith if you stick with me a little longer. And you can walk away at any time."

He still hesitated. "If I did this, I still wouldn't be taking orders from you. *I* would decide how to run it."

"Understood. And agreed." Arya hid the shudder that went down her spine at the thought of what she was risking, giving something like this into

Leanir's control. It was another mad idea. Something she'd *never* have even countenanced a few weeks ago.

But then the ambush under the Diamondfang had happened.

His mouth curled in a smile, as if he could read her thoughts. "Count me in."

"Then you and Mistryl should leave this morning." Arya said. "The sooner you get started, the better."

Arya left as Mistryl roused, wings stretching wide, dawn's light glittering like silver on her ivory scales. As she walked, she hoped she hadn't just made a massive error.

"I hope you've got good news for me, Ravenstrike," Hawkesdale barked just as Arya entered the command tent. Rorin and Essa were already there, the other warlords and generals too. "I'm sick of sitting on my hands while a third of my State is yet to be cleared."

"*You have my leave to go, Gelfrey,*" Rorin signed, Essa translating. "*Our scouts and the wyverns have confirmed the battle yesterday was decisive. Only small, fleeing units of Nightblades remain. Shadowhounds too, though they've scattered into the countryside and will be much harder to track. You can take your Longbows, and the remainder of the Defender force. That should be enough to clear the rest of your State.*"

"Right, very good. Thank you, High Warlord." He sat back in his chair. "I'll be off today, then."

"I plan to leave today too," Andrian said. His hair was rumpled, handsome face haggard with weariness, stubble coating his jaw. "The invading force made a mess of Crowtalon as they marched through, and I have a lot of rebuilding to do. Not to mention rebuilding our coastal defences against any further attacks from Khadini."

Roan Eaglesoar shifted in his chair, and grumbled. "I'll send two battalions of Knights with you to help with the coastal defences. That will leave me sufficient to secure my State."

Rorin's head came up, eyes alight. "*Warlord Eaglesoar, thank you.*"

Hawkesdale gave them a considering glance, then added. "Illia can handle Hawkesdale. If it will help, I'll ride on north to Falconcrest to make sure all is in order and that Daliah has any support she needs establishing her rule." *And make sure she's loyal* was the subtext. "Hawkesdale and Falconcrest have always gotten along, and I have friends there."

Arya couldn't help the smile creeping across her face. Seeing the warlords of Dunidaen starting to work *together* ... she hadn't been sure she'd ever see it after what Mathas Crowtalon had done to them.

"I would like to help too," Amius said. "I will send Firemen with both of you to bolster your forces, but mainly to display my State's solidarity."

"*This is good to see,*" Rorin said formally. "*I give you all a full month. At that time, I expect you to ride for Gateport for a State Council. I won't hold you there long, but there are decisions that will need to be made that require all our input—not the least of which is what we do about Khadini.*"

"Understood. What are your immediate plans, High Warlord?" Rian asked.

"*I return to Heathrock to ensure my family and State are secure and prepare my wife for taking over as warlord. We will then both ride for Gateport to meet you and have Peemla officially confirmed at Council along with Daliah Falconcrest.*"

A series of nods, no objections, to this news. Arya stifled another grin.

Rorin paused, gave them all a warm smile. "*I thank you, warlords of Dunidaen, for helping me save our country. You should all be proud of your efforts, as I am proud to be your High Warlord.*"

He'd won them, heart and soul. Arya could see it in the way gruff old Hawkesdale gave him a firm nod, in Eaglesoar's grudging smile, Andrian's grin, and Amius's half bow of respect.

Rorin Ravenstrike had always been the best choice for High Warlord of Dunidaen.

***

The warlords and their armies left later that day, moving at a slow march to rest their battle-weary soldiers. That left Rorin's Raiders, his personal Defender shield, Arya, Laskin, and her *cairdre*, and the Ce'Garn and his Icefolk. Tiya, too, chose to remain with them. She would help watch over the remaining wounded as they were transported back to Heathrock to recover.

Soon after Rorin's meeting with his warlords, he summoned the Ce'Garn. The big Icefolk warrior was unharmed from his weeks of fighting, and he vibrated with the contented energy of one who'd been allowed to unleash his ferocity and come out victorious.

"High Warlord. Congratulations on yesterday's victory."

"*We couldn't have done it without you and your warriors, Chief Ce'Garn. You and your queen have Dunidaen's deepest thanks.*"

"We marched at the request of Lord Stormrider, our ally," Ja'hur corrected politely. "It is to her you owe your thanks. But it has been an honour to fight alongside you and your warriors, High Warlord. Their discipline and courage are to be commended."

"*As are the ferocity and skill of yours, Chief.*" Rorin smiled slightly. "*I would like to tell you that you are free to depart and return to the Icelands.*"

"I would offer to take a slower route home, and follow the pockets of fleeing Nightblades," Ja'hur said. "The blades of my warriors' hunger for more blood, but I will not trespass on your territory without your permission."

Rorin glanced at Arya, she gave him a little nod. She believed Ja'hur could be trusted, and his Icefolk warriors would effectively deal with the remnants of the Nightblade army, saving the weary Dunidae soldiers the effort.

"*You have my approval, and my thanks. You may tell your queen that I will remember your help when next we negotiate fishing rights in the Winter Sea.*"

Ja'hur gave a wolfish smile. "My queen will be most pleased to hear it."

Rorin reached out with his off hand, palm facing outwards. Looking surprised but pleased, Ja'hur did the same, pressing his palm against Rorin's as they bowed their heads; the traditional Icefolk farewell. "It has been an honour, High Warlord."

Rorin's army packed up their tents and began moving out, long rows of mounted Raiders keeping their weary horses to a walk. Chiarn and Essa took to the skies on their wyverns, but Arya remained with the Raiders. She'd always loved riding with the mounted army she'd once led, and nothing had changed that despite Elendryl's strident objections. Spotting Rorin riding a short distance to the side of the column of Raiders, Arya urged her horse over to join him. They hadn't had a chance to talk privately since her dawn revelation. "How angry are you at me right now?"

He gave her a sidelong glance, then sighed. "*I understand why you did it.*"

"I'm so sorry, Rorin," she said.

"*Apology accepted.*" He smiled. "*I'm glad we're going home together.*"

Arya took a breath. She felt the same. Ravenstrike was her home. Heathrock. Her family. But Arya had chosen to make Andahar hers, and even though she'd done that as a way of protecting her son, her *cairdre*, that didn't make it any less real.

She'd helped save the home of her heart, to keep it safe for her family who lived there. She would return to that home one last time, see her family settled. Then it would be time to turn her attention to the future. To her crown and the country she'd claimed.

It was time to leave Dunidaen behind.

Chapter 21

Riding at the head of the long column with Rorin, Arya drank in the sight as Heathrock came into view ahead. It looked exactly as she remembered; the lake already frozen over, great stone walls a forbidding sight, framed by the looming peaks of the Diamondfang. Startled cries broke out as Rorin abruptly spurred his horse into a gallop. With a whoop, Arya sent her horse flying after him.

They'd sent messages ahead, so the gates were already opening as Rorin and Arya raced through and reined to an abrupt halt in the entry courtyard. Seconds later the front doors swung open and Peemla and Anjurin came running out, the little boy clinging to his mother's hand.

Rorin leaped from his horse's back and ran to his family, throwing his arms around them and holding them tight, tears streaking down their faces. Arya dismounted, but waited quietly by her horse, waving for the army to hold back. Essa came to join her, sliding a hand into hers and squeezing. The bond between them shivered in mutual joy—*home, family.* Eventually, Rorin loosened his hold on his wife and son, his hand framing Peemla's face and drawing her in for a long kiss before they grinned at each other and stepped apart.

Arya let go of Essa's hand then, striding forward to hug Peemla fiercely, before turning to pick up Anjurin and swing him around, his delighted giggles music to her ears. Essa and Peemla were still hugging when she put him down, grinning into his blue eyes.

Kirin's eyes. Her heart skipped a beat, and Anjurin noticed her smile fading. His little hand reached up to touch her cheek. "Aunt Ayah, don't be sad."

"I'm not sad to see you, Anji." Her grin returned and she bopped him on the nose, earning a delighted giggle, before standing.

"*We're home.*" Rorin signed, face glowing.

Arya hesitated.

"*I know.*" He read her expression, sadness replacing the joy. "*But we have a day or so before you need to leave, right?*"

She managed a smile. "A day or so, yes."

***

After exchanging warm greetings with Arken and having a drink in the mess with her personal shield and their old Raider comrades, Arya headed up to her room. It was late by the time she pushed open the heavy wooden door, but of course Peemla's staff had a roaring fire crackling to greet her, as well as a warm bath steaming in the corner, and...

A visitor.

"Ranier." Her gaze went to the open closet door, where her old Raider uniforms still hung, and where she supposed the passageway entrance at the back was open. "I hope you're not here to try and off me like you did your brother."

He took a step forward, moving out of the shadows. It had been a long time since the Shadeweaver leader had posed her any kind of threat, but she watched him carefully anyway. As usual, his tattoos were concealed by long sleeves and a high collar, but his hands were empty of weapons. "Greetings, Stormrider."

"Was it Essa or Dar who told you about the passageways behind the walls when you sent them here all those years ago?"

"Actually, it was Thiara Ravenstrike." At her scoff, he shrugged. "In her younger days, she had a lover. He was a friend of mine. The passageways were useful to them."

"Right." Arya let the word draw out, unsure whether he was making an attempt at humour. Proper, honourable, clever Thiara Ravenstrike and a lover? It didn't seem likely. "What brings you here?"

"I've been waiting for you to return. We need to talk about Remien."

She hid her surprise over the fact he seemed willing to actually *give* her information and pierced him with a look. "About why you tried to kill him?"

Ranier always shimmered with an air of violence, of darkness, but now that darkness grew deeper, almost sucking the light from the room. "Remien betrayed his king, our House, his family. He helped Lucius isolate and kill his fellow *cairdre* and then the king and his heir. It was *his* plan that allowed Lucius to succeed."

Shock flared through Arya at that revelation. But… "And for that the Nightstalker locked him away in Blackstone to rot for the rest of his life?"

"Lucius Nightstalker has no more honour than my brother."

Arya watched him, wondering what his motives were in telling her this. Because she was certain he had one. "You mentioned the king's heir. You meant Torin, my father."

His mouth tightened.

She pushed. "That's why you've helped me in the past. Because Torin was your closest friend."

A brief flicker of *something* in those dark eyes. "You've been speaking with Salyarin."

"At least he and Remien are willing to tell me what they know." She crossed her arms over her chest. "Why didn't you tell me about…" She faltered, still unable to say the words aloud. Nausea rose and she had to swallow hard.

His expression told her he knew exactly what she'd meant. "Because telling you would only have done what I see Remien telling you has done. Made you sick with regret and despair that defeating the Nightstalker is impossible."

Was he right? Maybe. But that still didn't explain all the other knowledge he'd refused to pass on. Suddenly exhausted, she dropped her arms. "Why are you here, Ranier?"

"To warn you. Remien cannot be trusted. He thinks like a snake, with layers you couldn't even imagine. You should have let me kill him."

"Then I'll lock him up and *you* join me instead." She took a step towards him. "I need the Inkweaver archives if I am to win this, Ranier."

"No." The word was final. Absolute. So much so she knew there was no point arguing.

She asked, a little helplessly, "Why?"

To her surprise, he answered. "I cannot lose again. I've lost a man I considered a brother, my entire family, my world, all of it crumbled to dust before me. And my daughter, born to walk a deadly path I cannot change or stop, and I will not..." He took a deep, heaving, breath. "No more war. No more loss."

"But you could help me, help Essa, avoid that loss."

He looked her in the eye. "I do not believe that is possible, with or without the Inkweaver knowledge."

"Ranier—" The bleakness in his voice sucked the breath from her. He truly had no shred of hope that she could emerge victorious. The wall inside her trembled, threatening to give out.

"I have helped you where I can because you are Torin's daughter, and because I love my own daughter, little as I have shown it. But I will not let myself risk everything again and then watch it destroyed in front of me. I refuse."

Arya understood far too well what he was afraid of. She felt it herself, that lack of confidence, the terror of more loss. She didn't know what to say to change his mind. Silence expanded. If he truly believed she would lose ... then what hope did she have?

The sound of bootsteps from her closet had Ranier spinning, drawing a knife in the same instant, but it was only Rorin, eyes widening in surprise at the sight of Ranier in Arya's room.

"*You didn't tell me you were having guests over.*" Rorin signed as he came to stand next to Arya, keeping a wary distance from Ranier as he moved.

"This one was uninvited." Arya swallowed, still struggling with the weight of Ranier's despair.

Rorin settled a hand on her shoulder. "*Are you okay?*"

Ranier's glance flicked between them, and then he turned to leave. But something made him hesitate. She thought she heard him whisper something like, "One more thing I can gift to Torin."

He turned back, pointing between them. "Have you ever noticed that when you stand together like that, you look like two halves of the same coin? Impossible not to tell you are siblings."

Rorin rolled his eyes and signed, Arya translating. "*You know Arya's adopted, Ranier.*"

Dry amusement curled his mouth. "Yes, a very clever move by Thiara to do that, wasn't it? She couldn't have raised Arya as her own, but she found a way around that anyway."

What?

Arya frowned. "What are you talking about?"

Ranier chuckled. "Have you two ever stood beside each other and looked in a mirror? That should give you all the answer you need."

They stared at him.

"Thiara Ravenstrike was your mother, Arya Stormrider."

For the second time in a month, Arya felt as if the floor had dropped out beneath her, and she clutched at Rorin's arm, needing his solid presence at her side as an anchor to stay on her feet. His hand closed tightly over hers, white-knuckled, as if needing the same thing. "Explain, now!" she snapped.

"Your father and I hid with the Etherean after fleeing Andahar, but we eventually left because Torin knew his presence put them in danger. We came into Dunidaen, hiding out in the Diamondfang, where I built the Shadeweaver organisation as a way of protecting my best friend. Your father met Thiara one day by sheer happenstance. They fell in love. At the time, Thiara was not the heir to Ravenstrike and had more freedom than her brother. She fell pregnant, but soon after Torin was found and killed by a nazal." Ranier's expression twisted. "I wasn't there when it happened ... I came upon his body after ... Thiara's parents took you away after you were born, Arya, and almost immediately afterwards they arranged her marriage to Matte Eaglesoar."

A silence fell over the room, broken only by the crackle and pop of the fire in the grate. The first thing to spear through her was hurt—why hadn't Thiara ever told her, told Rorin? And she'd *known*, about Torin, who Arya was. It explained so much. Why Thiara had sheltered them in her home, kept her secret, all of it.

And then came a wave of bitter regret. Because she'd missed so much, having Thiara in her life as she struggled with all of this. Yet on the heels of all of that came quiet joy and pride. If Arya could have chosen anyone in the world to be her mother, it would have been the woman she'd loved, respected, and admired more than anyone else. Tears stung her eyes. Thiara was her mother.

Arya struggled to speak over the lump in her throat. "When she came to Icecliff after ... did she know who I was?"

Ranier lifted an eyebrow. "How soon after she became Warlord Raven-strike did she invite you to be fostered into her home?"

"*Barely two months,*" Rorin answered when Arya couldn't, signing so fast she could only just keep up. He was looking at her, uncaring of whether Ranier could understand his signing. "*And nobody could understand why she apprenticed a Nameless to her general. She wouldn't hear a word against it, though, not from anyone.*"

"She knew?" Arya whispered, turning to Rorin. "Why didn't she tell me?"

"*She probably thought she was protecting you,*" he said. "*But think about it Arya; all those years she treated you like her own daughter. She loved you and protected you as much as she did me.*"

She looked at him. "You really are my brother."

His signing was shaky. "*Do you remember when she introduced you to me? I was playing in my room, I was so lonely, and then you came in, and you knelt down to greet me, and—*"

"I knew," Arya whispered. "The way you smiled at me, even then, I knew."

Tears streamed down his face. "*Me too. I was never lonely again, because I had you.*"

"Heed my warning on Remien, Arya. This will be the last time we speak." Ranier's sharp words broke the bubble of emotion between them.

She turned towards him, one hand still clinging to Rorin, swiping the tears from her cheeks. "And Essa? Will you see her before you go?"

But he was already gone, disappearing into the closet and out into the passageways.

Arya barely cared. She turned back to Rorin. "She knew I was a Sky Lord; she knew the whole time. I could never figure out how much she knew or why, but my father must have told her everything and I…" Arya trailed off, realising she was babbling.

But Rorin was simply grinning at her, eyes brighter than she'd ever seen, so much delight on his face it made her heart ache. "*I love you, sister-mine.*"

Chapter 22

Heathrock buzzed with activity the following day. Tiya had been working tirelessly since her arrival to establish a makeshift healing centre in the castle's great hall. Up early after a restless night, Arya found her already busy, settling the injured and organising their treatment with help from Peemla's staff and the Raiders Arken had assigned to assist. Though too occupied to stop and talk, Tiya caught Arya's eye and offered a friendly wave across the room.

Outside, the barracks were alive with the sound of morning drill, the atmosphere noticeably lighter. For the returning Raiders, the familiar routine was a welcome reprieve after months of bloodshed and chaos. Those who had remained at Heathrock throughout the war were just as relieved to see the household settling back into the rhythms of normal life.

Arya wasn't sure whether she wanted to walk on air with the joy of Ranier's revelation about her mother, or disappear into a deep hole to escape the crushing weight of Remien's revelation and Ranier's unwavering certainty that she would fail. The mixed emotions left her restless, anxious, and suffocated by the presence of the others, who remained blissfully unaware of the truth she held. Elendryl was her refuge. So they flew, just the two of them, soaring high in the endless sky, where only the icy wind and the vast world below could touch them.

Late in the evening, after dinner, Arya slipped away, seeking solitude atop the walls. The cold air bit at her skin, and the stark beauty of the frozen lake stretched out before her, its quiet stillness soothing the storm of emotions churning inside her.

Then, her bond to Darmanin stirred to life. A slow smile spread across her face as she turned away, descending the steps and slipping through a side gate in the walls. She made her way toward the little boathouse on the shore, the same place she had found Darmanin skating on the eve of Winterfest the year before.

And there he was, waiting for her now, seated on a bench, gazing out over the frozen expanse.

She took a seat beside him. "Is something wrong?" Panic spiked. "Is Kirin—"

"He's safe, as far as I know." Darmanin said immediately. He wrapped an arm around her shoulders and drew her close. "But I heard the news of Dunidaen's victory, and I wanted to flyover with Zaphirdryl, make sure Peemla and Anjurin were safe. When I felt you were near through the bond, I couldn't leave without seeing you."

"Is that safe?" she asked in concern.

"Actually, he wants me to turn my efforts to finding you now that he's given up on Dunidaen. He expects you'll come for him in some way and wants to be prepared."

"Then he does trust you more after you told him where I was in Dunidaen." She smiled into his shoulder and closed her eyes, soaking in his solid presence. "We'll have to think up something good for you to tell him."

They were quiet for a long moment, but despite her joy in Darmanin's presence, she couldn't relax fully, and he sensed it through the bond. "What's bothering you?" he asked.

"I'm afraid."

"Of?"

Her initial instinct was to say nothing, to wave it off like she had when Essa and Rorin had asked. Then she remembered what Rorin had said once, about what Darmanin could be to her, if she allowed it. Even so, it took enormous strength to willingly bring down the wall and let the fear and horror come rushing out. Her voice was a whisper when she forced the words out, "I found out why the Nightstalker is so confident of defeating me."

"Tell me," he commanded softly.

Eyes closed, squeezing Darmanin's hand so tightly it had to hurt, she relayed everything Remien had said, and what the Spider's solution was. "I'm not going to kill my Sky Lords, Dar." She bit her lip so hard it almost drew blood. "But he tells me there is no other way. Ranier believes the same. I don't know what to do."

He settled back on the bench, arm still around her, staring out at the lake with a narrowed gaze. "Well, I for one am glad to know this."

She looked at him in surprise. "How can you be *glad*?"

"Because now we know. I was uneasy before because I knew there was something behind his confidence and we didn't know what it was. Now all the cards are on the table. No more secrets. As difficult as it might seem, at least now we know exactly what we're up against."

She scowled. As hard as telling him had been, now that he knew, she felt inexplicably lighter, the nausea fading away. "I thought you were supposed to be the pessimistic one?"

"I'm finding it a little more difficult to be pessimistic these days."

He kissed her, and for a moment they lost themselves in each other and the warmth flaring between them. Arya closed her eyes as she pulled away and rested against him, curling one of her hands around his.

"Arya, if there's anyone who can think of a way to win, it's you," he said. "I know it with every fibre of my being. Ranier is wrong about your chances."

"And if I can't?"

"Then I will love you anyway. And so will our family."

"All right," she whispered. "I can live with that."

He tangled their fingers, squeezing gently. "Whenever you feel scared, I'm here for you. Stop thinking you need to go through everything alone. All right?"

"Agreed," she conceded. "And the same goes for you."

The smile lit up his face. "That's what saved me, Arya Stormrider."

Arya abruptly stood, straightening her shoulders and facing Darmanin as he sat on the bench before her. "I'm going to have to marry, Darmanin Darkslayer, because I'll keep getting offers from those who want to align themselves with the queen of Andahar until I do. I've been putting off At'eir's offer of the Ce'Garn for weeks."

His eyes widened in surprise. "Are you proposing to me right now?"

"What do you think?"

"The right marriage could bring you the strength you need to win a war and establish a secure rule in Andahar, Arya. I bring you nothing."

She held his gaze. "I love you, and while marriage isn't something I particular care for one way or the other, I want you with me when I do what comes next. And I want you standing at my side, not in my chain of command. I *need* that."

Darmanin stilled. "You're actually serious about this?"

"Completely and utterly."

"Arya, I can't..." He shook his head. "You can't marry me. You know you can't. You need what an alliance can bring you; it's literally the only tool you have to build your strength and power."

It was all true. It was exactly what her mother would have told her. Yet ... "A marriage to you would bring me something just as important as money or weapons or armies, Dar," she said. "The emotional safety and strength I need to be capable of beating him."

"*I* give you that?" he asked.

"You do. That and more."

"Then my answer is yes." He surged off the bench and pulled her into his arms and a warm, slow kiss.

Boots scuffed on stone, and they pulled apart to find Rorin standing on the lake path, grinning at both of them. "*Darmanin, nice of you to join us.*"

Arya cleared her throat, gently untangling from Darmanin's embrace and shifting away from him.

"He doesn't look very surprised to see me," Darmanin observed.

"That's because he refused to play along, and I was forced to tell him and our *cairdre*." She sent a pointed glance in her brother's direction. He smiled in response.

Darmanin's stern expression softened and he moved to shake Rorin's hand. "It's good to see you, Rorin."

Rorin spurned the hand and pulled him into a tight hug before letting go. "*Come on over to the boathouse. Your family wants to see you. Only those that can be trusted are gathered.*"

Darmanin's smile lit up the night.

***

Essa, Chiarn, Peemla, and Laskin were sitting in the old boathouse, a makeshift fire crackling in the centre of the space thanks to the Flamewielder. All smiled in delight at the sight of Darmanin. Wind whistled through the gaps time had carved into the wooden walls and roof, but the atmosphere remained warm and inviting. A fire crackled in the hearth, casting flickering light across the room, and a large flagon of wine sat nearby, with everyone nursing a cup.

Darmanin and Rorin joined the gathering, and after only a brief hesitation, Arya settled beside Darmanin. She reached for the flagon, poured herself a cup, then leaned back, instinctively shifting into his solid frame. Without a word, Darmanin wrapped an arm around her shoulders, pulling her closer, holding her as if it were the most natural thing in the world.

"*I can't believe we're home again, together.*" Rorin signed, eyes sheened with tears. "*Sometimes it felt like this would never happen.*"

"Sometimes I thought *that* would never happen." Laskin waved his cup between Darmanin and Arya.

"What are you...?" Essa frowned in puzzlement, then her eyes widened when she looked properly at the two of them. "Oh, I see."

Rorin laughed silently and drained his mug. Arya's gaze met Essa's across the circle. She gave Arya a little smile but then looked away, unable to hold her gaze.

"*Do you remember that Winterfest when we spiked the punch?*" Rorin asked.

"That was our first year here, wasn't it?" Arya asked. "My very first happy memory. I hadn't known before that what it was like to have a family, to feel like I *belonged*, like I was loved."

"Me either," Darmanin agreed softly.

"Or me." Essa smiled into the flames.

Peemla sat forward. "When you all came ... it was the first time someone saw me. Not the chamberlain. *Me*. And you all thought I was wonderful. I've never told you how much of an impact that made on me. How it changed my life."

The fire crackled into a suddenly emotional silence. Arya sniffed, scrubbed at her eyes before they could betray her. Rorin's arm settled around his wife, drew her close.

"You were all brats," Laskin said. "It was a nightmare trying to look after you all."

Laughter rippled through the boat house, breaking the heaviness.

"I was *not* a brat," Arya said. "I was General Desomer's apprentice."

"You were a stubborn, cocky brat who thought she knew it all," he corrected her. "And you, *all* of you, made this place alive."

"*And we will again,*" Rorin promised. "*It won't be long before Anji is spiking the punch at Winterfest.*"

"And Kirin too," Darmanin murmured in her ear. Arya swallowed and squeezed his hand tightly in gratitude.

"We must find a young Raider who will help Anji in his pranks, just like Taze," Essa said.

"And maybe some young Shadeweavers to be his friends, too," Darmanin said, sharing a small smile with Essa.

"I think that will be more important than you all realise." Arya said. "Peemla, your father was the master of stables here, wasn't he?"

"That's right. Rorin's mother took him in as a groom, but he was so good with the horses that he was put in charge within a year, and he managed the stables until his death."

"And your mother?"

Peemla's gaze dropped. "She died not long after I was born."

"What are you getting at, Arya?" Chiarn asked.

"Anjurin carries the blood of a Sky Lord House, and since we know that doesn't come from Rorin, it must be you, Peemla," Arya said. "And after what you've just told me, I suspect your father was a horselord, likely a descendent of House Lightbringer."

Eyes went wide and a shocked silence fell on the room.

Rorin sat up straight, signing furiously. "*And you just decided to tell us this now!*"

"In my defence, I only learned of Anji's Sky Lord potential after the nazal kidnapped him, and things have been a little hectic since then."

Peemla looked at her husband, worry and pride both in her eyes. Rorin smiled at her, kissed her on the forehead, and held her close.

"Whether he becomes a Sky Lord or not, you know I will protect Anji with my life," Arya promised.

"We all will," Darmanin added, Chiarn and Essa nodding too.

"So Thiara Ravenstrike basically turned this place into a safe house for hidden Sky Lords?" Laskin noted wryly. "Does anyone have *any* idea why she'd do that?"

"Because she loved my father, and me," Arya said softly.

Now all eyes turned to her, but she was looking at Rorin, sharing the silly grin on his face.

"I knew it!" Darmanin slapped his leg. "I mean, I didn't *know,* but I knew. You and Rorin look so much alike. I can't believe nobody ever put it together."

Essa let out a delighted laugh and then fell backwards dramatically, arms spread wide. "Everything suddenly makes SO much sense."

"Someone's enjoying the wine." Chiarn beamed. "And *I'm* not convinced they're siblings. Rorin is way too calm to be our hot-tempered Sky Lord's brother."

"Oh no." Laskin was shaking his head. "Where else could Arya have gotten that incredible tactical brain of hers."

Arya drank the last of her wine. Finally, some of her anxiety faded. It felt good to be home again.

"Once the Nightstalker is gone and Arya is ruling Andahar, we will have to share our Winterfests," Peemla said. "One year here, one year there."

"That sounds nice." Essa smiled.

"I hope ... well, perhaps I could sing for you, at your Winterfest once in a while," Chiarn spoke into the silence. "It would be nice to have somewhere to go."

"You are welcome any time, Chiarn," Arya promised. "And I hope you travel to play for us in Andahar far often than once a year."

"*My sentiments exactly.*" Rorin reached over to clap the Sky Lord on the back. "*You are always welcome in my home.*"

He beamed, cheeks pinking in the firelight.

"*Arya, what comes next for you?*" Rorin asked over the crackle and pop of the fire. "*I know you can't stay.*"

"I'll have to go back to the Nightstalker within a day or two, or he'll start wondering why I haven't made contact," Darmanin said regretfully.

"And lingering here for me is only putting off the inevitable," Arya said. "First though, there's a favour I'd like to ask you, Rorin."

"*You know I'd do anything for you.*"

"Then you'll marry Dar and me?" she said.

Rorin stared between them, his eyes shining. "*Truly?*"

"Truly. If you're willing."

"*Willing?*" Rorin shot to his feet. "*Peemla, can we prepare a wedding in a day?*"

Peemla opened her mouth, closed it. "I can do what needs doing, and ensure nobody else knows of it," she promised.

"*The day after tomorrow it is.*"

✳✳✳

There was some debate over which wedding rites should be applied. Arya and Darmanin had been raised in Dunidaen, but both were Andahari Sky Lords. Arya ended the debate with a simple solution. "Unless Dar objects, I want to be married as a member of House Ravenstrike." It would be her final chance to be part of her mother's House before she left it behind.

Darmanin's slow smile warmed her from head to toe. "The son of Warlord Crowtalon marrying the daughter of Warlord Ravenstrike. My father will be rolling in his grave."

"It's a match I think even our mother would have agreed to." Rorin chuckled.

They held the wedding in the boat house, hidden from sight of anyone at Heathrock, but with the doors opened to give a view over the frozen lake and the mountains looming to the south. Peemla put it about that she and the warlord wanted some private time for themselves and their family after being apart for so long, and that they weren't to be interrupted.

Tiya—busy with the healing centre—didn't seem to think this was odd. Arken protested until Rorin informed him that Arya would be there, Elendryl nearby, and if attacked, she'd be able to defend him perfectly well until Raiders could arrive from the castle.

The day dawned bright and sunny, despite the autumn cool. Rorin looked resplendent in the black and bloodred of Ravenstrike as he stood near the lake's edge. Peemla was at his side, Anjurin holding her hand and looking grown up with his fine clothing and neatly brushed curls. Chiarn and Essa watched from the side, wearing their Sky Lord cloaks and polished mail. Elendryl was nearby, sharing in his rider's quiet joy. Darmanin wore the Crowtalon black and violet, his hand resting loosely on the hilt of his sword.

Arya had asked Laskin to stand with her. The veteran had teared up at the question, for the first time ever unable to mutter a word. Now, as Arya came to stand opposite Darmanin, Rorin passed Laskin a long strip of silken cloth. Arya and Darmanin joined hands, and Laskin proceeded to wind the cloth around their wrists and hands, binding them together. Arya couldn't tear her gaze away. The Sky Lord bond between her and Darmanin was more powerful than simple cloth, but watching them physically bound together, it felt more solid than anything she'd ever felt. With this, them, together, she felt like she could conquer the world. Slowly, she let the wall down.

When she finally tore her gaze away to look up at Darmanin, she could tell he felt the same way. Rorin checked that the knot was secure before giving his brother a firm pat on the back.

A hush fell then.

"*Welcome, Darmanin Crowtalon-Darkslayer, to the seat of Ravenstrike,*" Rorin began formally. Anjurin proudly translated his father's words, back straight and toothy grin in place. "*You are here to marry my sister, Arya Ravenstrike-Stormrider?*"

"I am." Darmanin didn't take his eyes from hers.

"*Arya,*" Rorin turned to her. "*Do you accept Darmanin's wish to marry you?*"

"I do." A smile tugged at her mouth. Those were words she never thought she'd say. For all the fear and doubt she felt, this choice was the one certainty she could hold onto.

Outside, a bird squawked loudly as it flew over the lake, breaking the silence and causing a ripple of laughter to go through the room.

Rorin didn't even try to hide the glee he was feeling. "*Then I ask you both to speak the words of the Dunidae marriage oath. Darmanin, Lord Darkslayer and son of House Crowtalon. Do you promise to take Arya as your wife? To always raise your sword in her defence. To always bring your House to her aid?*"

"I do." His hands squeezed hers. Through the bond, she felt his strength bolster hers, uncompromising, unconditional.

"*Do you swear to shelter her at your fire? To support her with your body and your love, and to be true to her always?*"

"I do."

"*Arya, Lord Stormrider and daughter of House Ravenstrike. Do you promise to take Darmanin as your husband? To always raise your sword in his defence? To always bring your House to his aid?*"

"I do." Now it was her turn, to share with him her love, her faith in his strength, her certainty in her choice. His eyes turned damp.

"*Do you swear to shelter him at your fire. To support him with your body and your love, and to be true to him always?*"

"I do."

Darmanin squeezed her hands again, the only thing betraying the joy shining in his eyes. Part of Arya felt the eyes on them keenly, but the rest of her stared straight into Darmanin's gaze and knew with every part of herself that this choice was a blow against the Nightstalker he would not easily recover from.

"*Laskin, Peemla.*" Rorin signed.

Laskin came forward, drawing his knife and cutting the silk ribbon binding their hands. Peemla then placed a simple silver ring on Darmanin's upturned palm. Darmanin took Arya's left hand, sliding the ring onto her finger and speaking the traditional words. "I pledge my House and body to you always."

Grinning through his beard, eyes suspiciously damp, Laskin placed a similar ring on Arya's palm. She slid it onto Darmanin's finger. "I pledge my House and body to you always."

"*You have spoken your oaths to each other before a sworn warlord of Dunidaen,*" Rorin signed enthusiastically. "*Darmanin Crowtalon-Darkslayer. Arya Ravenstrike-Stormrider. You are now wed.*"

Arya thought Chiarn was the first one to whoop, his melodious voice carrying clear across the space, but then the others were cheering and clapping and Anjurin was jumping up and down in excitement.

Darmanin kissed her, and she smiled into the kiss before they were drawn apart by Rorin thumping Darmanin on the back, all decorum forgotten. Arya found herself set upon by an excited Anji, and she swung him up into the air with a laugh. Peemla was just behind and leaned over to hug Arya. "Congratulations."

"Thank you, Peemla."

"*Well, it finally happened.*" Rorin signed, then heaved a sigh. "*Save us all from an Arya Ravenstrike and Darmanin Crowtalon pairing.*"

And Arya laughed.

Chapter 23

Darmanin left at dawn the following day, he and Arya making their private farewells before he hiked into the forest under the cover of darkness, Zaphirdryl waiting not far off.

She watched him go, reluctant beyond measure to be parted from him so soon, and filled with fear for what he had to do next. "Dar!" she called without thinking.

He turned, eyebrow lifted in question, that little smile on his face that she loved.

"Be careful."

The little smile widened into a big one. "I will. After all, I have you waiting for me."

"You do. Always."

She waited until he was gone from sight, then left the boathouse and headed back to the castle. Melancholy tugged at her, but she fought it off. She'd see him soon enough. The fear was harder to quell—the longer he stayed with the Nightstalker, the more dangerous it grew, despite all the careful planning they'd done.

Laskin was out drilling with the Raiders barracked at Heathrock when Arya arrived at the yard. He came straight over when he spotted her, and as he approached, she tried to smile, but failed.

"No," he said, crossing his arms over his chest.

"I ask you to stay here, to lead Rorin's personal shield, to keep him and my family safe." She forced the words out, hating every one of them. But she needed to do this. Because she was leaving her heart behind, and she needed to know they would be okay. "Please, Laskin, do this for me."

His scowl deepened. "Who will lead your army?"

"I have something in mind. This is not about your capability. I trust you like I trust few others in this world, Laskin. You've always, *always*, had my back. Now I ask you to protect what I love most so that I can do what I must."

He scratched his jaw. "When it's over, I can rejoin you?"

"I wouldn't want anything else."

He saluted. "Then I will do as you ask, Lord Stormrider."

***

By the time Arya returned to the castle proper, the joy of Ranier's revelation and her wedding were already fading. In its place came the familiar tendrils of despair over how she was going to do what came next. There was no more time left. No more steps to take. Nothing in the way.

Rorin, Peemla, and Essa were eating breakfast with Chiarn in the kitchens, and the mood was subdued when Arya entered. Peemla sat with a fidgety Anjurin on her lap, the boy not understanding why all the adults were so glum.

Eventually Essa glanced over at Arya. "It's time."

She nodded. Rounding the table, she stepped into Rorin's warm hug.

"*You keep safe, big sister.*"

"I will," she promised. "You too."

"What about breakfast?" Peemla protested. "You have to eat something before you go."

"I couldn't eat anything right now," Arya admitted as she kissed Anjurin on the cheek and wrapped Peemla in a tight embrace. Then Arya left, leaving Chiarn and Essa to their goodbyes. Arya couldn't linger any longer, or she might never leave.

The wyverns circled in the sky above, ready. Essa and Chiarn appeared soon after. Essa's shoulders were straight and face clear, but Arya could tell how hard this departure was for her in her shuttered expression.

"You two will be swinging by the Etherean citadel to pick up Remien, while I undertake another task. We'll converge on the western foothills of the Diamondfang where it hits the coast, after which we'll head northwest across the ocean and into Navaria, staying well clear of the Horn," Arya said, forcing briskness into her voice.

"Another mysterious task, huh?" Chiarn tried for his usual cheerfulness. "Sounds intriguing."

Essa's gaze was clear. "I'm ready."

"Arya!"

She turned as Tiya's voice sounded from the top of the steps. The Etherean woman had her rucksack slung over her shoulders. "Tiya! I looked for you to say goodbye but couldn't find you."

"I want to come with you." She came down the steps. "If that's okay."

"Are you sure? You could make a home here, a safe one, now the war is over. And Peemla could use a powerful healer. In Heathrock city you could build a healing centre to train other healers."

"I would like that, very much. But *you* will need a powerful healer, too." Tiya looked troubled, but she'd clearly thought this through. "I don't think I'll be able to settle down anywhere until I know the wars are done. I'd like to help you make that happen."

"I'd be more than glad to have you with me." Arya told her warmly.

"Excellent." Tiya shouldered her rucksack and headed for Elendryl.

Arya reached for her bond with Leanir—currently faded with distance—and gave it a gentle tug. Then she looked at Essa and Chiarn, gave them what she hoped was a confident smile. "Let's go and take our country back."

***

A short time later, Elendryl circled slowly out of the sky, eventually landing on a patch of open grass. Nearby sat a picturesque farmhouse, which looked over the distant roofs of the port of Aren, where the outline of the Diamondfang peaks loomed and ocean glittered. Near the farmhouse, a gurgling stream wound its way towards sunlit woods. Daffodils bloomed amongst the grass. Arya slid down from Elendryl's back, then helped Tiya down so she could stretch her legs, and the Valheran settled down to nap in the sunlight.

"Where are we?" Tiya asked.

"You'll soon see. Do you mind waiting here?"

Tiya nodded, closing her eyes and leaning her head back to soak up the sun's rays, and Arya walked a short distance towards the house before stopping to wait. It was a beautiful day, and she was in no rush. Besides, the person she'd come to see had always done things on his own terms.

Sure enough, a good while later, the door to the farmhouse opened and an older man emerged, pushing himself easily in a wheeled chair. He paused in the doorway before slowly wheeling his way down a ramp to the ground and then across the grass towards her.

Arya couldn't help the wide smile that stretched across her face at the sight of him. "General Desomer. It's been a long time."

"I haven't been a general in years, girl," he barked.

"Rubbish."

A silence fell as he looked her up and down. "You're older. Harder, too. There's a lot of experience and suffering behind those eyes."

"You heard about what happened after I took over from you? At the State Council vote?"

"I'm old, not senile," he snapped. "Of course I heard about Thiara Ravenstrike's death."

"You didn't want to return to Heathrock after it happened?" she asked.

"My time was over. Thiara Ravenstrike managed to leave behind a capable heir, and you, despite your idiotic actions that night, left behind a capable general." He scowled. "Why are you here?"

"I'll get right to it," she said. "I need a war general to build me an army."

He barked out a laugh, then sobered as he realised she was serious. "An Andahari army? As part of your bid to knock off the Nightstalker and be queen of Andahar?"

Arya smiled. "You *are* well informed."

"I still live in the world, don't I? Need to keep up with what's happening in it."

"The answer to your question is yes. I'm going to Andahar to take the fight to the Nightstalker, but to do that I'm going to need to address some rather unique problems. I need more than a capable general. I need one who can build a fundamentally sound, disciplined army that works seamlessly together."

"Not asking for much, are you." He looked at her a long moment, then sighed. "I'm an old man now, Arya. My back aches constantly, and I'd be hard-pressed to raise a sword."

"I need your mind, not your sword. You taught me everything I know."

"What makes you think your Andahari are going to accept an old Dunidae ex-general leading them?"

"They're not," she said bluntly. "Some of them aren't even going to accept *me*. It's one of the challenges we'll have to face together. Imagine an army full of Arkens."

"I'm not up to it, not anymore."

"That is absolute rot," she scoffed. "Rorin has made me realise some things about how we make assumptions about people based on how they appear. He's a mute, *and* a highly capable High Warlord. You can't walk, but you're a highly capable general. I don't believe for a second that's changed. I need you, General Desomer. Please."

Even then, he hesitated, eyes on the distant port.

"What is it?" she asked quietly.

His gaze came back to hold hers. "Do you think *you* can do it? You had many strengths as a leader, Arya, but there were some glaring flaws too, ones that led to some pretty nasty consequences."

She respected him enough not to rush to an answer, or to lie to him. "I'm not certain that I can do it," she said. "But I *am* certain that I'm *never* going to give up trying. And I'm just as certain that to succeed, I will need help, because I can't do it alone."

He sat back in his chair, regarded her, then glanced over his shoulder at his home. "It was getting a little boring here, pretty as it is."

She let out a startled breath. "Does that mean you're in?"

"On one condition. You let me bring my cigars."

Arya laughed. "Deal. *Thank* you, General." She glanced at Elendryl. "How do you feel about flying? And don't worry, we can take the chair too."

***

Tiya's eyes shone with something unnameable as Arya marched over, Desomer returning to his house to pack some things. Of course, he'd refused her offer of help.

"What?" Arya asked, taken aback.

"Nothing." Tiya shook her head. "I just remember a conversation we had after he was hurt. Where you assumed that because of the severity of his injury, his life was done."

"I was *incredibly* wrong, Tiya. I'm not that person anymore."

"I can see that. And suddenly ... suddenly I have hope, Arya."

"For something in particular?"

Tiya shrugged, heading towards the house. "We'll see. I'm going to help him pack his things. No doubt he'll want to bring those cigars of his, no matter how many times I told him they're bad for his health."

Almost a week after leaving Heathrock, Arya led her Sky Lords through the twin waterfalls and into the Storm Spire. Elendryl made a brief stop to let Tiya, Desomer, and his chair down in the square outside the central tower, then all three wyverns landed on the open roof above, where they dismounted and took in the view.

Essa—the only one to have never seen it before—exclaimed in astonishment at the beauty laid out around her. "It's so strange. I can *feel* this place like a presence in my very bones. It *likes* that I'm here."

Arya chuckled agreement. Of course, Essa had found a way to perfectly encapsulate what she'd struggled to.

"I can't believe nobody ever moved in," Chiarn agreed. "All this empty space, shelter from the weather, and not even any squatters."

Essa looked at Remien. Arya had filled her friend in on what Ranier had told her about his brother, and so far Essa seemed undecided about having an unexpected uncle appear in her life. Arya made a note to talk to her about it later. "Is it a specific kind of magic that protects the place, or a build-up of centuries of Sky Lords living here and leaking magic into the very foundations?"

"A good question," Remien said. "I'd say it's a mixture of both."

Arya sighed. It was hard to read his reaction to meeting his niece, too. Bloody Inkweavers and their aversion to displaying emotions. "I wonder if the Nightstalker would choose to come here, even if he could remember it?"

Remien raised an eyebrow. "You think it would make him feel guilty?"

"I don't know. People are rarely one thing entirely. He might be evil now, and slightly mad too, I think, but I doubt he started that way."

Chiarn made a face, as if he didn't believe that for a second, then changed the subject. "What next, fearless leader?"

Arya glanced up, warned by the tug on her bond with Leanir of the Mindbreaker's arrival. Mistryl let out a challenging cry as she landed, wings spread wide, snapping at Alletryl when she snaked her neck out towards her. The assassin's wary gaze raked over the ragged group before settling on Arya. "Who's that down below?"

"Tiya and General Desomer."

Something flickered in Leanir's gaze at the mention of Desomer, but she couldn't place it. "I was making progress, Raider, and don't appreciate the sudden summons."

"I'll make it worth your while, I promise." Arya took a deep breath. "But for the remainder of today ... well, you are my court, and this is going to be our home, hopefully for a very long time. Given there are five towers, I'm guessing each of them is supposed to belong to a Sky Lord, with the wyvern nest on the roof." Remien nodded agreement with that theory. "But we can spend time choosing personal quarters later. First, this place is as big as a city. I'd like to choose the communal spaces we'll be sharing."

"Why is that a requirement?" Leanir asked flatly.

Arya sighed. Somehow, she had to forge this disparate group of highly skilled people together into an efficient team. She knew from experience that started with a sense of home, of collaboration, and then, a shared enemy. She already had the latter. "Because I said so. Now let's get to it."

***

The wyverns went out ranging, hunting and ensuring no threats were nearby. After telling Arya to let him know when his army arrived, Desomer sat in the sun smoking a cigar and enjoying the warmth on his face. Neither Remien or Leanir cared two figs which rooms they picked for communal spaces, and maintained an air of amused and disgusted impatience respectively as the others wandered around.

They agreed that their shared spaces should be in the central tower for convenience. From there it fell apart into heated disagreement. Essa and Chiarn were far too elaborate with decorating ideas and Tiya was ruthlessly practical. Leanir glared at anyone who asked his opinion. Remian made little noises in the back of his throat every time Chiarn suggested something.

And Arya had to bite down the urge to simply make the decision and tell them what to do. This needed to be their space as much as hers, or they'd never feel at home in it. But she couldn't help the feeling that the inability for them to agree on something so simple boded ill for what she had to do next.

In the end, with Essa quietly taking the lead, they settled on a kitchen on the ground floor, a large sitting room tucked away far from the main entrance, and an empty room with good light directly opposite the sitting room for planning—all of which would be accessible for Desomer.

There was only a small amount of old chopped wood left in the storeroom Arubon had discovered from their previous visit, so Leanir and Chiarn carried that into the sitting room and kitchen. While they did that Essa, Tiya, and Arya worked to drag random pieces of furniture left scattered through the ground level of the tower into the sitting room and planning room. Throughout all of this, Remien sat by the fire in the new sitting room, sipping on a mug of tea and reading a book he'd pilfered from somewhere.

After hearing two loud cracking sounds, Arya was horrified to find Leanir in one hallway having kicked two simple wooden doors off their hinges, leaving gaping openings to those rooms. "What are you *doing*?"

He didn't look at her as he dragged the two doors together, so they lined up, then reached for a hammer and a rusted box of nails he'd scrounged somewhere. "The general's going to need a ramp to get up those steps at the front entrance."

Arya's mouth fell open. "Do you want some help?"

"Nope."

She left him to it.

By the time this was done, everyone was tired and crabby as they gathered in their new sitting room, Desomer too, thanks to Leanir's makeshift ramp. Sensing their patience beginning to thin beyond her ability to control it, Arya dismissed them all to find their own personal quarters. "Go wherever you like. This is your home, and I want you to feel comfortable here. The rest of the day is yours."

Desomer immediately wheeled off, barking something about finding the barracks. Tiya too, bright with excitement, went off in search of a nearby building she could turn into a healing centre. Essa, Leanir, and Chiarn had a brief and surprisingly amiable conversation about who wanted which tower—at which point they all set off to investigate their new homes.

"Your grandfather's rooms were on the top floor." Remian spoke when Arya lingered in the sitting room, unsure where to go. "Close to the roof and his wyvern."

She looked at him. His head was in his book—where had he gotten a book from already? "Thank you."

He shrugged and didn't look up.

Arya headed back towards the main entrance. The massive double doors were open, letting in afternoon sun, which glittered on the marble of the incredible staircase leading upward. At the fourth-floor landing, the stairs narrowed, winding ever upwards until she reached the top floor. At the end of a long hall were the stairs that led up to the roof, with ornate doors set into the walls halfway along the corridor, facing each other.

The door to her right opened into a spacious room that had a beautiful view out over the twin waterfalls, the ocean beyond, and the high cliffs that ringed the bay. While the curtains and bedding had begun to moulder and rot away, the furniture was just as it had been decades ago when her grandfather had ruled.

She paused at the window. The orange glow of the setting sun lit up the waves crashing against the cliffs, making them fiery and beautiful. The presence of Storm Spire settled around her, welcoming, happy she was here.

For the first time, Arya began to feel the first tendrils of *home* unfold inside her.

***

Remien claimed a residence from one of the myriad palace buildings, close to the central tower. Tiya and Desomer settled in rooms near each other on the ground floor of Arya's tower. Essa's incredible abilities meant that with a series of beautiful drawings, they all had warm blankets and new down-filled mattresses on the bedframes that had been left behind. The Inkweaver had already started talking about drawing them bowls and cups and utensils for the kitchen, her eyes alight.

Not long after dawn the next morning, their small party gathered in the open square outside the central tower, everyone having dragged chairs outside. The golden light of the rising sun lit the palace with a soft glow and warmed the air. That little sense of warmth and home sparked again, and Arya smiled as she sipped from a steaming mug of tea, while the others shared bread and cheese they'd brought with them.

Desomer sat straight in his chair, colour in his cheeks, gaze swinging often to Remien and Leanir. Remien watched him, and Tiya, with sharp curiosity, but Arya ignored it. She wasn't letting him in on anything he didn't need to know. Hovering in the back of her mind was Ranier's warning about Remien. At least here he was effectively trapped, unable to go anywhere or talk to anyone.

Chiarn hummed a beautiful melody, and she looked at him. "Sunrise over Andahar?"

He nodded. "The ballad is coming along. I've got the first verse and a chorus."

"If we're staying here for a time, we'll need a source of food, firewood, and fresh water." Desomer spoke. "Someone should go hunting today."

"We have water." Leanir spoke. "There are wells spaced across the city. They all seem to be functional. Firewood will be harder; it's a good walk to the nearest forested area."

Arya stifled a smile. So, his patrolling had been useful after all.

"We also need healing supplies. Ointments, medicines, bandages," Tiya said. "I could travel to the nearest town to organise that."

Arya sighed, putting aside the peace of the early morning. "I agree, but before we do any of that, we need to talk."

"Finally," Leanir muttered. "I was beginning to think you'd brought us here in an effort to learn how to be maids."

Chiarn yawned and stretched. "Yes. I'm assuming there's more to killing a despot and taking his throne than moving furniture around."

"I hope this conversation includes telling me where this army I'm supposed to be training is," Desomer grunted.

"Before all this starts." Arya waved a hand to encompass the empty city within which they sat. "There's something you all need to know."

"Oh dear." Tiya sighed. "I know that tone of voice."

Arya took a breath, catching Remien straighten in his chair out of the corner of her eye. "It's not good news, so I'll just spit it out. According to Remien here, Sky Lords can transfer their magic to each another. It's not easy to do, but apparently the Nightstalker is a master at it."

"You're saying...?" Chiarn's words faded, his face turning white, as the implications of what she was saying sunk in.

"The Nightstalker has stolen the powers of all the Sky Lords he killed? Yes. It's why he's displayed so many different magics in front of us, when Sky Lords are only supposed to have one."

Leanir's jaw clenched. "That makes him four times more powerful than any of us individually."

"Is that actually true?" Essa looked at Remien. "I mean, he obviously has four extra magical abilities, but does taking another Sky Lord's magic actually increase your own *strength*? Or just diversify your abilities?"

"Another excellent question." Did Remien look a little proud of his niece? "The transfer includes not only the specific magical ability, but also the depth of magical power held by that Sky Lord."

"And that's not counting other potential Sky Lords he's killed in the past decades," Arya pointed out.

Remien lifted his hands in the air. "Sky Lord potentials don't break out with their magic unless an existing Sky Lord dies, creating a vacancy, so to speak. But the power is presumably always there inside them. The question is whether that dormant power is accessible."

"Either way, this information changes things considerably," Essa said. Her green eyes were dark with worry.

"It does more than change things," Chiarn sat up straight, expression decided. "It makes what we're trying to do impossible. There's no way for us to defeat that kind of power."

"There are still five of us," Arya reminded him. "That's five different skills, five sources of power. Those odds are not unreasonable."

Remien's gaze narrowed. "Five?"

She ignored him, and Leanir started talking. "We are five separate individuals who barely like each other against one who can flawlessly integrate all his abilities," he said. "We'll never achieve that. Essa can barely stand to kill a bug, and the musician isn't exactly unwavering when facing down a dangerous threat. And I will never submit my will to a group."

Astonishingly, Chiarn added his agreement. "Not to mention the Nightstalker has had years to hone his skills, while we don't even understand fully how Sky Lord power works yet."

Arya tried not to sink into her chair under the weight of the truth of their words. "What other choice do we have?"

Desomer barked a laugh. "I taught you better than that."

"You always ask that question when you're about to do something foolhardy and reckless!" Chiarn scowled. "It's not a solution. We *do* have a choice. We can choose to walk away."

"And be hunted by the Nightstalker and his nazal for the rest of our lives until we're all dead?" Arya snapped. "We'll have much better odds if we face him together."

"Either we die when we face him directly, or we run now and die when he eventually tracks us down. At least with the latter option we get to live longer," Leanir said.

"There is *always* a third option. Just because he's more powerful doesn't guarantee he can beat us. He is one man alone, and we are a team." Arya tried to sound like she believed this, even though she'd been saying the same words to herself for months, and they'd sounded hollow each time.

"How can you expect us to think we can win when it's clear you're not certain we can?" Chiarn accused.

"We're no team," Leanir said coldly. "The musician's right. You know that already."

"That's why we're here, Leanir." Arya's temper was dangerously close to boiling over, but she fought hard to keep her voice calm.

"What?" he snapped.

"We're here to learn to trust each other." Essa looked at Arya, and she gave her a grateful nod. "We're here to learn to fight together, to become a proper team."

"And how are we going to do that?" Chiarn asked. "Darmanin isn't even here."

As if on cue, a wyvern's cry cut through the morning. Tiya, Desomer, and Remien started, peering towards the sky in fear. But Arya and her *cairdre* remained relaxed, watching as Zaphirdryl circled before landing nearby. Soon, Darmanin's tall form strode towards them.

"Sorry I'm late," he said as he arrived.

"Well, well, well." Remien chuckled. "By the lack of swords and knives being drawn, I'm guessing Darmanin being a traitor is all for show."

"General Desomer!" Darmanin ignored him, eyes lighting up as he saw the general. "A genuine pleasure to see you, sir."

Desomer smiled. "Young Crowtalon. You've turned out well."

"Your general, I assume?" Darmanin turned to Arya. "Genius, wife of mine."

"I thought so," she said. "Tiya has joined us too. Her healing abilities will be sorely needed."

"Welcome," Darmanin gave her his small smile. She waved.

"How long have you got, Dar?"

"He's got me patrolling the west looking for rebels, so as long as I check in every few days, I'll have a couple of weeks before he'll expect me back at Darkclaw."

"Good." She looked at Chiarn, then Leanir, then Essa. "We're going to take it one day at a time. That's all I'm asking of you right now."

Chiarn held her gaze, but there was no conviction in it. He looked defeated. Silently she urged him to step up.

"I'm in, Arya," Essa said firmly, breaking the silence.

"Not exactly sure what you're talking about, but I'm in too," Darmanin said.

Chiarn hesitated then sighed. "I have to admit, I'm not convinced. As much as I respect and admire you Arya, I truly don't see how we can win this."

"Will you at least stay for now?" Arya asked. "When it comes to the point where we face the Nightstalker, you can make your choice then."

"All right," Chiarn said reluctantly.

Leanir rose smoothly to his feet. "I'm going hunting. The general was right about food."

So, he was staying. She tried not to smile. "I'd like us to do something else first."

"What's that?"

"Step one of learning to defeat the Nightstalker." Arya grinned. "We're going to learn to fight together. That's what we're going to do this morning. This afternoon we can hunt."

Chiarn gave Leanir a dubious glance. "Sounds wonderful."

Arya stood and drank down the remnants of her tea. "Remien, you're up. You've got two weeks and then Dar and Leanir must go."

"Absurd." Remien huffed. "You need months, years, not two weeks."

"You've got two weeks." She pierced him with a look. "Make it work."

Chapter 24

The following days were ... challenging.

None of them but Essa, not unsurprisingly, were patient students. Arya was frequently forced to mediate disputes, drag either Leanir or Chiarn back to the roof after one or both had walked out, or keep Darmanin from eating Remien after shapeshifting in frustration. She'd even had to eject Remien from the training session on day two after his constant 'minor' suggestions had come close to driving *her* to murder.

"You could try having some patience with them," Arya snapped at her husband early on the sixth afternoon after a particularly trying day. She'd returned to their room after an hour spent wrangling with Leanir trying to convince him not to leave. She'd only just barely managed it, and right at that moment she was sick of all of them.

They had just over a week left for this, and they were making no progress at all.

"Maybe Remien could try actually teaching something," he snapped back. "He's smug and far too amused by all of this and it gets under everyone's skin."

Arya tried very, very hard to keep a lid on her patience. "I'm aware, but he has the knowledge we need. Perhaps *everyone* could learn to hold their temper."

"Leanir isn't even trying. He smirks the entire time Chiarn or I talk, and spends the remainder of the time glowering in contempt over our attempts to implement what Remien is teaching, which is very little, by the way."

"That's because we haven't actually succeeded in his first lesson yet." Which was joining and sharing their magic as a full *cairdre*. They could do it for brief moments, but always someone lost trust or focus and the connection dropped. Usually that was Leanir. "And Leanir is part of our *cairdre*, Dar. We have to learn to work with him."

"No, we don't," Darmanin snapped. "You insist on it because he's a Sky Lord, but he's also a murderer without any redeeming qualities than I can tell. Have you forgotten how many of your Raiders he killed? Or the time he tried to kill Rorin and me? Or what he did to your general?"

"How dare you suggest I don't?" Arya's tenuous hold on her temper snapped. "If General Desomer is mature enough to deal with Leanir, then we damn well can be too. What do *you* think we should do about Leanir, exactly? Kill him? Imprison him?"

"I don't know, but keeping him around as a Sky Lord isn't the answer."

"It *is* the answer, and you'd know that if you calmed down enough to think about it properly," Arya said. "You are not the leader here, *I* am, and that requires me to do unpleasant things, like work with a man who once tried to kill the two of the people in the world I love most."

His mouth tightened. "I'm your husband, not your subordinate, remember?"

And here they'd reached the crux of the issue. Darmanin was capable of far more patience than he'd shown so far—he'd always been reserved, willing to wait for the right moment, able to master his emotions. But he'd come from being a warlord running his own State to this ... harried by Remien and subordinate to his wife. She understood how he must feel, but ... "You are my Sky Lord, Darmanin Darkslayer, whether you like that or not," she said firmly. "The Nightstalker is the enemy we must focus on, not Leanir, and not Remien. You're letting your anger and frustration get the best of you."

"You're one to talk!" he snapped. "You never *stop* letting your anger get the best of you."

"I'm trying to—"

"No, you're not. You and that fierce temper of yours ... you lord it over everyone. You insist that we all listen to him day after day, hour after hour, even when it clearly isn't working."

"I'm insisting upon it because I'm trying to save us all." She barely stopped from yelling. "If I don't win, we all lose, can't you see that? It's all on *me,* and I'm doing the best I can here, Dar."

That only made him angrier. "The world does not revolve around you, Arya Stormrider!"

Darmanin turned and stalked out of the room, slamming the door shut behind him. Arya kicked out at the nearest thing, which happened to be a chair, then swore when it went careening across the room to smash into a wall and break into pieces. Her toes throbbed painfully.

A knock sounded at the door a few moments later, catching her in the middle of ruefully picking up the pieces. When she opened it, Essa raised her eyebrows at the sight of Arya holding two bits of splintered wood. "I don't think it's going to make it," Arya sighed.

"The chair?" Essa peered around her at the remnants on the floor. "No, I don't think so."

"Have you come to try and get us back to the tower? I think training is pretty much done for the day, Ess. If we try and force Leanir, Remien, and Darmanin back into the same room, I fear there will be actual bloodshed."

"I came because Alletryl is out hunting, and she warned me there is a large group of people approaching the palace from the east."

Arya straightened, all ire forgotten. "Nightblades?"

"No, Alletryl swooped as low as she dared for a look and apparently many of them are wearing your blue uniform."

"It must be Niallin's rebels!" She brightened. "We'd best go down and meet them."

It was a misty and cool day. While they assumed it was autumn in Andahar as it was back in Dunidaen, so far it seemed the weather didn't get anywhere near as cold here. They'd yet to see any snow, although most mornings they woke to find the palace wreathed in a thick fog that usually thinned and then disappeared altogether as the day progressed. A few evenings earlier, when Chiarn had idly mused on the topic, Remien's sharp remark about a bard's level of education had nearly earned him a ban from both the sitting room and their training sessions. Arya had barely resisted the urge.

Essa and Arya's boots echoed eerily in the empty square as they exited the tower and walked along a wide avenue that led directly to the so-far-unused palace main gates, which faced east. They had been built of thick steel, although some magic in them caused them to shine a silver colour, rather than the usual dark grey.

"I don't like him," Essa said.

"Your uncle? I don't think I do either. He's so smug and superior."

"It's not that." Essa's mouth had thinned. "It's the way he's treating us, and why. Haven't you noticed? He needles and taunts and condescends because he thinks *we're* superior and elite and look down on everyone else. He hates what we represent."

"We do *not* behave like that!" Arya said indignantly.

"No, but I bet they used to. The previous Sky Lords, I mean. And their Houses."

"Even if that's true, we're going to be different."

"Yes. And that's why I don't like him. Because he refuses to get his own head out of his ass to see that."

Arya let out a surprised burst of laughter. Essa *never* cursed.

"What? We're getting nowhere, Arya, and it's largely because of him."

"I hear you." She sighed. "But the truth is, even if the training was working, we're never going to have the time and space to practice enough to be what we need to be."

"Then why even try?"

"That's a very good question, my Inkweaver," Arya said, troubled.

A comfortable silence fell between them, then,

"Who killed the chair, by the way, you or Dar?" Essa tossed her a little smile.

"Me." Arya sighed again. "He struggles with the fact I'm in charge. He's always been his own man, so fiercely independent, and until recently he was a warlord, in supreme command of his own State."

"Well, loving someone doesn't make everything easy, Arya."

Arya gave her a sharp look, but they'd reached the main gates, and Essa was looking through the gaps in the intricately designed metal, where shapes had become visible coming towards them through the mist. She began looking for the mechanism to open the gates.

"You can see here and here where bars could be placed to barricade them shut," Essa pointed. "But it doesn't look like they're locked right now, just closed over."

Agreeing, Arya put her shoulder to one of them and pushed. It held for a moment, then gave way and began swinging outwards. "We'll have to see about those bars," she muttered as Essa pushed open the other gate with equal ease.

Gates opened, the two of them stood and waited. A wide stone road led out into the flat grassland beyond, maybe half a mile long. Some in the approaching group were mounted, their horses' shod hooves clattering loudly against the road as the riders moved forward. The two lead riders quickened their pace the moment they spotted Arya.

"Nice place you've got here," Charlin reined in. "Bit out of the way though."

"It's good to see you both." Having some of her personal shield arrive had Arya's knotted shoulders relaxing.

Etan grinned. "You too, Arya."

The rest of the group were approaching so Charlin and Etan moved their horses aside to make room. One man broke free of the pack, a smile spreading across his face at the sight of Arya.

"Rengalin!" Arya said with genuine pleasure. "Welcome to the Storm Spire. I'm glad to see you safe. How many are with you?"

"Thirty-seven. About a third of whom would insist they're warriors." He gestured to where the new arrivals were staring up at the towers peeking over the walls and Alletryl soaring in the sky above. "But none of them have been trained to fight in an army."

The last rider reached them, then, a broad-shouldered man with shaven head and warm brown eyes. Arya smiled warmly. "Antonn!"

"Lord Stormrider." He bowed from the saddle. "Niallin asked that I bring Rengalin and some of his people with me. I hope you don't mind—I left Kait and Allicen to help escort other groups of rebels here in case they ran into trouble."

"Excellent work. Have you heard any news of Esdee?"

"No." A flicker of concern crossed his face. "She hasn't arrived yet?"

"No, but that's not unsurprising. You're earlier than I thought you'd be."

He nodded, glancing around. "With your permission, I'd like to organise a roster for guard duty. At first glance, this place looks too big to maintain a full perimeter with the numbers we have now, but I'd like to start by manning the walls facing the ground approaches."

She stifled a smile at his earnestness. "I'm sure your new general will have some ideas on that. You'll find him at the barracks." She gave directions. "Take Charlin and Etan there, along with any of Rengalin's people who wish to fight."

"At once, Lord Stormrider." Antonn urged his horse over to address the gathered folk still staring up at the sky in wonder.

Arya turned back to Rengalin and Essa. "Essa, would you mind taking those of Rengalin's people who are not fighters through to one of the residential areas near my tower? Then join us in our rooms. Rengalin, you're with me."

***

A short time later found Rengalin seated in their sitting room, a warm fire flickering in the grate. Chiarn and Leanir were still off in a snit—a quick check of the bonds revealed them on the grounds but sulking—and Arya didn't want any of the new arrivals seeing Darmanin, and so they were all absent as she poured cups of steaming tea. Remien sat in his usual chair by the fire, and at a warning glance from Arya, had been perfectly polite in introducing himself to Rengalin.

"It seems odd, the future queen of Andahar brewing tea for me," Rengalin commented.

"Unfortunately, there are no servants to be had," Remien said dryly. "As convenient as they might be."

Essa came through, accepted a cup of tea from Arya. "They're all settling in. Tiya's helping to show them where to get firewood. We'll need to start thinking about food supplies soon, though."

Arya nodded. "Rengalin, will you give us an update on what you know?"

The river trader sat forward. "Niallin divided your army up to spread through the Riverlands and carry word of your rebellion, asking for volunteers to join you. As you requested, we are moving in small groups and staggering our travel so that it's not obvious that so many people are coming this way. Some of us are also travelling by boat, and so you might want to start keeping a lookout to the ocean. As with my group, not all that are coming are warriors. There are some that have been helping the rebels in other ways, like me, and family members of the fighters."

"Good, there's plenty of room for them here, and they are no longer safe in the Riverlands," Arya said.

Rengalin let out a long breath. "An air of excitement has infected all of us. It is almost impossible to believe that a Stormrider heir has finally returned to Andahar to challenge the Nightstalker."

"That excitement is appreciated, but I hope you all understand that we have a long and wearying road ahead of us," Arya said.

"Of course, Lord Stormrider."

Arya rose. "I know you've had a long journey, so I'll let you go to join your people and settle in."

Essa gave Rengalin instructions on how to find them, and the man left with a smile of mixed gratitude and hope. Once he'd gone, Arya shared a look with Essa.

"I hope we're not leading them all into ruin," Arya murmured.

"It's a bit late to worry about that now," Remien remarked.

Essa shot him a scowl.

***

Later that night, Arya sat by the fireplace in her top floor room, staring into the flames, her thoughts full of Rengalin and his people. She'd gone to see Desomer after her chat with Rengalin and found him expressing despair at the sight of the men and women lined up before him. But he'd had life in his voice and renewed vigour as he'd wheeled his chair around them, snapping orders to stand up straight and stop leaning and straighten their tunics properly.

Sadly, she'd left him to it. Leading an army, *building* one, that was her comfort zone, what was familiar. It was what she loved most of all. But that wasn't her job anymore. She'd given it to Desomer. Because she wasn't a general. She was a queen.

Her husband came in quietly, and she stayed silent, watching him as he crossed to the window. Outside, a full moon had risen, and its silvery glow lit the areas of the room that weren't reached by the firelight.

"I'm sorry," he said.

"I'm sorry too, Dar. I understand how you must feel. I just don't know how to fix it."

He shook his head. "It's not your problem to fix."

"Of course it is. Or am I the only one of us who's supposed to share her problems?"

"Stop being so damn rational."

She smiled, rising from the chair to cross to him. "I'm worried."

"About what?"

"I'm worried that for me, marrying you was the best decision I ever made, but for you—"

He cut her of mid-sentence. "Do you mean that?"

"Of course, I mean that." She smiled. "I feel happy, settled, more than I ever have before."

His hands settled on her hips, and he drew her closer. "Really?"

"Really." She kissed him.

When they broke apart, he was studying her. "Something is weighing on you. More than just me."

She nodded. "I'm trying to figure out how I'm going to solve my second impossible problem."

His grey eyes glimmered as he looked at her, his thumb drawing soothing circles on her hip. "There's another impossible problem apart from the Nightstalker?"

There were many. "Yes. How I'm going to run this country if I do manage to somehow defeat him."

He frowned. "You don't think Andahar will welcome you with open arms if you kill their oppressor?"

"No, I don't. I get the distinct sense the Nightstalker has held the country together with a mix of fear and violence. Without those things, without *him*..." She let out a breath. "Dar, I'm not sure it *will* hold together."

Darmanin looked thoughtful. "Kingdoms don't fall apart for a single reason. Extra abilities or no, the Nightstalker could not have found it easy to kill his *cairdre* and his king. I imagine he took advantage of existing problems to help him succeed."

She was glad he understood what she was driving at. "I learned in Blackstone that there are deep divisions between the various folk of Andahar. Has the Nightstalker ever mentioned anything to you about that?"

"Not really. He's mainly focused on putting down rebellion and discontent, no matter where it comes from. He doesn't care about differences as long as they all fear and follow him." He cocked his head. "There's something else, though. His insistence on taking the Marshlands, it feels like more than just pride or a need to win. I get the distinct impression he feels it's necessary that all of Andahar is united under him. I think it's why he tried for Dunidaen too."

"Necessary for what?"

"I don't know. He fears something."

She was troubled. "Well, the Nightstalker's paranoid fears aside, I'm not sure if you've noticed, but our entire rebel army is made up of riverfolk."

"They're from east of the Horn, yes? The Riverlands."

"Right. Then you have the horselords in Navaria west of the Horn and marshfolk tribes living in the Marshlands to the southwest, engaged in a bitter civil war against the Nightstalker. Added to that are the regular folk all over the country that don't claim to be part of any of those three. They're called arwein."

"If all the rebels are riverfolk, do the other tribes support the Nightstalker?"

"I don't get the impression they care for Sky Lords at all."

"Sounds like something to ask Remien. You'll need to bring more than just the riverfolk under your banner. It's why you rescued him, no?"

"It is, but first I need to speak to him about his training. It isn't working, and you were right, he's a big part of the problem." She gave him a look. "But not all of it."

Darmanin scowled. "You were right too. I'll try and be more patient."

"You're not particularly convincing," she said dryly.

"I have to fly out tonight to go and check in, which is probably best given all the new arrivals. Unless the Nightstalker has new plans for me, I should be back in a week. Maybe without me here the training might progress more smoothly."

She leaned up to kiss him, arching her body into his. "Do you have to leave right away?"

"Mmm." He smiled into the kiss. "I could spare a few minutes, I suppose."

She laughed, tugged him towards the bed. "You're going to need a bit longer than that."

***

Arya didn't sleep. Instead, she paced the roof while Elendryl watched.

And she planned.

All the little bits and pieces she'd learned. Her knowledge of the Nightstalker's overwhelming power. The sight of the battlefield in Dunidaen.

Their training wasn't working. And even if it was, Arya doubted they'd ever reach a place where they could challenge the Nightstalker on magical power alone. And Desomer was training her an army, an army to wage a war she would have to win. A war that would devastate Andahar.

Unbidden, memories of Heathrock flooded back to her. Of arriving there from Icecliff, being raised up as Desomer's apprentice.

How she'd succeeded there.

Arya stopped pacing. Turned on her heel and looked at her wyvern. He cracked open an eye. *"What?"*

"Your rider has an idea. Another piece of her jigsaw puzzle of a plan."

"Good." He closed his eye. *"Sleep."*

"No sleep for me. I'm nowhere near the complete picture yet."

And Arya started pacing again.

Chapter 25

Early the next morning, Arya was pleased to find Leanir in the kitchen doing his best to prod a fire into existence. She felt exhausted after a night of pacing and thinking, but energised about putting her nascent plans into action. She busied herself gathering ingredients for tea and putting on a pot of water to boil. Leanir sliced stale bread and hard cheese, enough for both of them.

"Ready for another fun-filled day of training?" he asked.

"I am," she said. "But you're not."

He eyed her. "What does that mean?"

"This last week hasn't been productive, and what you *were* doing is. I want you to go back to it." She'd set him the task with only a vague idea that it could become useful. But now she knew *exactly* how she was going to use it.

He put down his mug of tea. "You're getting rid of me."

"Damn right I am. You're not even trying to cooperate, so you might as well leave and be of some use." Arya chewed and swallowed, watching him think on it.

"How do you know I won't just disappear, never come back?"

He might. He wasn't hers, probably never would be. And that mercenary nature of his would always see him putting his own survival first. But she was banking on him *liking* the task she'd set him—it was why she'd suggested it in the first place. "I told you you're free to make your own choices. I hope you start believing that soon."

Leanir picked up a piece of bread and cheese and took a bite, chewing slowly. Arya sipped at her tea. Eventually, he finished eating and rose, crossing to drop his plate and cup in the sink. "I'll leave this morning."

"Be careful," she said, unable to help herself.

He gave her a cold look and left.

Moments later, one of Antonn's unit stuck their head in to tell her that another party of travellers approached the main gates of Storm Spire. Arya drained her tea and headed out. Storm Spire seemed as alive as usual this morning, its presence dancing around her, unobtrusive but happy. It was starting to look less desolate now, with riverfolk moving around, but what was most stark to Arya was the lack of anything that could bring in food. It was all residential buildings and shops. No parkland, no trees, no soil. Plenty of shelter, but not much else.

How they were going to support a growing community weighed on Arya's thoughts as she strode down the wide avenue to the open front gates, but at the sight of the two blond figures leading a group of travel-stained and weary-looking riverfolk, a smile tugged at her mouth, busy thoughts falling away.

"Esdee." She smiled a greeting. "Niallin, you made it."

"Lord Stormrider." The young woman saluted. "Sorry it took me so long."

"Antonn beat you by a day."

Esdee's smiled died. Arya chuckled.

"Lord Stormrider." Despite his travel-worn state Niallin looked excited, even though whenever he glanced at Esdee, it was with faint disapproval. "We are thrilled to be here. I'd never heard of this place, but as soon as I saw it in the distance, I just *knew* of it somehow. Magic, I'm guessing?"

"Magic indeed." Arya nodded. "Come in and be welcome. Esdee, a watch plan is in place, which you'll no doubt want to review with your new general. Tell your warriors to eat, wash and get some well-earned rest."

Esdee hesitated. "New general?"

"General Desomer. The man that taught me everything I know. He's expecting you, and he knows you're his second." Arya smothered a smile at the thought of how that meeting was going to go and gave Esdee directions to the barracks.

"I look forward to meeting him, thank you Lord Stormrider." Esdee saluted again and left with the warriors.

Arya was surprised at the level of relief she felt at seeing the woman arrive safe and well. Turning back to Niallin, she said, "Bring those that aren't fighters with me; I'll show you to those who've already arrived, and they can help you settle in." She hesitated, then, because he deserved it. "You've done well in getting so many here safely. It can't have been easy."

"On the contrary, our network has survived underground for decades. It wasn't difficult to wake them." He looked up, taking in a deep breath as he gazed in wonder at the towers. "All we ever needed was somewhere to go."

***

On returning to the tower after leaving Niallin and his people, Arya cancelled the day's training session, then summoned Desomer to their map room.

"She's just like you, dammit." The man wheeled in with angry vigour. "I didn't agree to an apprentice, and I *certainly* didn't agree to teach another you."

"And here I was this whole time thinking you liked me, even if begrudgingly."

He was not disarmed. "I won't do it. You already want me to achieve the impossible, and now you saddle me with a—"

"That's quite enough, General," Arya said with quiet command. She'd been waiting for this moment, and did not intend to shy away from it. "I am no longer your apprentice. I'm your queen, and I've given you an order."

He stiffened, anger flashing over his face, but after a moment, he gave her a curt nod. "You are right." Was that grudging respect in his gaze?

"Thank you," she said. "And it's not as bad as you think. You'll take Esdee on with the same terms my mother gave you about me. If she's not up to it, you can let her go."

His mouth opened, closed, and his ire was entirely derailed, as Arya had intended. "Your *what* now?"

"I'm Thiara's bastard daughter." Arya grinned. "That surprised you, didn't it?"

"It explains a lot, actually," he said.

"I think you'll find Esdee surprises you. All I ask is that you give her a chance." Arya pulled out a chair and sat down, waving him over to join her at the table. "Now, I asked you here for a status update."

He wheeled his chair over to the spot at her right hand. She stifled a smile. "There remain some areas of this place we won't be able to maintain a watch on, not until more warriors arrive. And I have zero faith they could fight off a scarecrow, let alone Nightblades, but only time and training will fix that."

Arya nodded. "Don't be too concerned about the gaps. The wyverns will warn us if anything dangerous approaches."

He grumbled acceptance of that. "Darmanin's reports on the Nightblade army; its numbers and deployment, I've been studying them."

"And?"

"It makes me wonder what you're planning." He pierced her with a look. "Because we aren't winning a war anytime soon, and since I *know* I taught you the basics of tactical strategy, you already know this too."

Arya chuckled. "It's such a shame there are no coloured stones here, or I could show you my plans."

"Why did you truly bring me here?"

"General, I meant it when I told you I needed you to build me an army. It's going to take time for you to do that, I'm aware, but I need to think beyond—"

They both looked up as the door opened to admit the other members of Arya's court. She'd asked them to join her. Niallin filed in with them.

"We need to discuss supplies," she said as they took seats around the table.

Essa looked at Niallin, "Were you able to bring much with you?"

"Only a few weeks' worth if we ration. We didn't have a lot to begin with, Lord Inkweaver, and most of that was used on the long journey here."

"We've got shelter and water aplenty, but we need a way to keep everyone fed, especially with more coming. Thoughts?" Arya asked.

"We need more than that. If you want me to train an army, I need weapons," Desomer said bluntly. "And proper footwear and some kind of armour, even if it's only thick leather."

Essa spoke up. "The last thing we want is to draw attention to our presence here by suddenly buying up large quantities of food, weapons, and other supplies from the nearest towns, even if we had the funds for that, which we don't," she said. "The best solution is for us to become self-sufficient."

Arya eyed her fondly, even as Remien gave his niece a look before addressing the table. "I thought you were fighting a war to destroy the Nightstalker, not rebuilding a city."

"Damned straight," Desomer barked.

"Actually, we're going to do both." Arya sat forward. "Here's my plan." Well, *part* of it at least.

When she outlined the details, she didn't quite get the reaction she'd expected. Chiarn snorted, then choked on his mouthful of tea, while Essa hid a smile behind her hand. Remien looked skyward and heaved a long-suffering sigh. Niallin gaped at her as if she'd sprouted horns and a tail. Desomer looked the way he always had in meetings with Thiara and Magen when the topic was anything but Ravenstrike's army—impatient.

"What?" she demanded, looking around the table. "Essa was right. We must be self-sufficient."

"Farming?" Chiarn asked. "You're going to *farm*?"

"Well, *I'm* not," she said. "But we have to get food from somewhere. Essa can help a little with her magic, but she can't feed an entire population."

"And who are you going to get to do this farming?" Remien asked, eyebrows cocked in an infuriatingly condescending way. "With your palace full of nobles and riverfolk?"

Arya frowned. "I saw farms when I sailed through the Riverlands last year."

"I'd bet you a large bag of gold pieces none of the farms you saw were run by riverfolk. They run the shipping trade, Arya. They transport the goods, not grow them."

"The old man is right." Niallin gave him a heavy look of suspicion; clearly Rengalin had told him who Remien was. "We're water people, Lord Storm-rider, not labourers."

"I'm sure we can all learn." Tiya spoke for the first time. "We could grow medicinal supplies as well as crops. And I could start teaching healing to some of those who've come here who aren't fighters."

"We going to grow our own weapons and armour, too?" Desomer demanded.

Arya shook her head. "No, that we're going to have to give some more thought to. In the meantime, I'd like you to speak with your people, Niallin. Perhaps some of them have relatives who are farmers or know something of it themselves."

"Lord Stormrider, I realise we are all in this together, however—" Niallin began.

"Are we?" Arya cocked her head. "Because as far as I can see, we're all riverfolk. Not a horselord, marshfolk, or arwein to be seen."

Niallin opened his mouth, closed it.

Remien chuckled, leaning back further into his chair. "I was wondering when you'd begin to figure it out."

"Figure what out?" Chiarn glanced between them.

"I began to figure it out quite a while ago, actually," Arya said evenly. "I just haven't been in a position to do much about it while I was trying to escape Blackstone and then free Dunidaen."

Essa looked at Remien. "Andahar wasn't united under Arya's grandfa-ther, was it?"

Her uncle sat back in his chair. "Technically, it was. All the folk of Andahar swore loyalty to the king and his Sky Lords, and they had enough power to ensure that loyalty was maintained."

"And practically?" Arya asked.

"The riverfolk, marshfolk, and horselords are all very distinctive peoples, with different attitudes and cultures. Conflict between them often broke out, and the arwein would get caught in the middle, not that anyone cared much about them," Remien said. "Let's just say the Sky Lord *cairdres* were kept busy. If not here, then there were the not infrequent disputes between some combination of Dunidaen, the Icelands, and Khadini. And, of course, the occasional threat from the lands across the ocean to the north."

"Lands to the north?" Tiya asked in surprise.

"To the east as well, though nobody has heard from them in a very long time, not since long before even your grandfather's day, Arya. They have a winged race too, and magic that is similar to—"

"We're getting off topic." Arya jumped in, uninterested in tales about far distant lands. "The Nightstalker exploited these divisions in his coup, yes?"

"King Rian was able to raise a riverfolk army and some half-hearted horselord assistance in his defence, but the marshfolk refused to march for him, and when war broke out, the arwein cowered. He'd allowed the fractures in his society to grow so deep he couldn't unify his people against the threat the Nightstalker posed. And for his part, the Nightstalker was able to win an army of marshfolk with what he offered them."

So he didn't win just because he was more powerful Arya thought to herself, tucking that thought away.

"What did he offer them?" Essa asked.

"King Rian believed in his peoples' right to make their own decisions. He would interfere if violence spread, but otherwise he allowed them to live as they chose. He and the Nightstalker fought about it constantly. Lucius wanted to create peace amongst the tribes—he foresaw future threats that would require a truly unified country. When his lover, Mariel, was hurt mediating a conflict between marshfolk and horselords, it was the final straw. Lucius decided the only way to achieve true unification and peace was to get rid of the king and his family."

"I guess you want us to believe the Nightstalker is a good guy?" Chiarn raised his eyebrows.

"I am telling you that the Sky Lords weren't perfect, nor was King Rian, and that there's no such thing as purely good or purely bad."

Chiarn snorted. "You're quite the philosopher, old man."

"He's right, though," Arya said. "And if I want to rule Andahar, then I have to work out a middle path between those taken by the Nightstalker and my grandfather, because clearly neither worked."

"I suppose you're right, but surely all our focus needs to be on defeating the Nightstalker first. We can worry about ruling Andahar once he's gone." Chiarn said.

"We?" Arya said. "You're gone once we win this, Chiarn, you and Essa both. It will be left to *me* to rule the country. Dar is the only Sky Lord I will have at my side."

He said nothing to that, merely looked down at the floor. An awkward silence filled the room. Arya stood. "I want a plan for how we're going to feed and clothe everyone here; a scalable plan that allows us to grow as more rebels arrive. Essa, you'll take point on that. Tiya, you'll help her from the perspective of ensuring we have enough medicinal tools and supplies."

"What about you?" Niallin asked.

"I have other problems to address. Remien, please stay. I need a word. Everyone else can go."

Ranier's brother lifted an eyebrow as the others filed out, the door clicking closed behind them. "How may I—"

"What did he offer you?"

The air froze to glass-like stillness, that sense of incredible violence swirling through the room. Arya felt a spike of satisfaction at having broken through Remien's smug façade to the true man underneath. "You've spoken to my brother."

"I have." Arya leaned over the table, placing her palms flat on its wooden surface. "Shall I guess? It wasn't just the marshfolk the Nightstalker promised peace to, was it?"

Remien's mouth thinned, his eyes flinty with a hardness she'd only ever seen in his brother.

"But not just peace, not for you. Power, too, am I right?" She smiled without warmth. "It was Essa that helped me figure you out."

"She is a true Inkweaver," he murmured. "There was a time I cared about peace. When I thought it was necessary, when I felt our country needed to be unified if we were going to survive..." Remien blinked, cut himself off.

"Survive what?" she asked. She felt like she was on the verge of understanding something, of getting the piece of the puzzle she needed. Arya held his gaze, inwardly urging him to tell her.

"There are threats beyond our shores, Arya Stormrider. I hope you don't foolishly imagine the Inkweaver archive contains only knowledge of Andahar and its Sky Lord Houses."

"What?" She shook her head, frustrated. This wasn't what she needed.

"Never fear, I had all my fanciful illusions shattered long ago. Thirty years in a ruthless prison will strip away any caring for something as useless as peace."

"So now it's just power you hunger for." Arya leaned back, regarded him. "The question is, what *kind* of power?"

"Our deal includes me telling you what I know from the Inkweaver archives written into my skin to help you defeat the Nightstalker." Remien stretched and cocked his head, that air of violence gone in a blink, the smug old man back. "And I've done that. You already know what the key is to defeating him."

"I am *not* killing my Sky Lords, Remien." She held his gaze, made sure he understood her.

"Then he will take them from you, one by one, and *he* will gain their magic instead. And whatever infinitesimal chance you have to defeat him will vanish entirely."

A shiver went through her, his words holding the ring of foretelling. She shook the sudden chill off. "Even so. I won't do it."

"Then we all lose." He shrugged, stood. "I believe we're done here, Lord Stormrider."

Arya waited until he was at the door before she said, "It still makes me curious, that you had marshfolk lieutenants at Blackstone. If I were to guess that you also had horselord and riverfolk lieutenants in other wings, would I be right?"

All she got in response was the clicking of the door closing behind him. Damnit. She'd been close to something. Arya leaned back in her chair, thinking.

What was Remien's game?

Chapter 26

Over the following week, training went smoothly with Darmanin and Leanir gone. Arya, Essa, and Chiarn joined and shared their magic with relative ease, and increased the length of time they could hold the connection. Their improvement was rapid enough that Remien even gave them a half-serious compliment one afternoon.

Each day, more groups of riverfolk arrived, Niallin welcoming them and sending those who wanted to be fighters to the barracks to join General Desomer. When not training, Arya paced the walls, or her tower rooftop, working away at the puzzle of pieces in her mind, trying to fit them together into a tenable plan. At the same time, she tried to figure out the best way to get weapons and equipment for the army, but was coming up blank. They may have to resort to risking buying them from a large town—perhaps in multiple smaller lots so it wasn't as noticeable. But where would they get the money for it?

Arya returned to her room that night to find Darmanin standing by the window. His stance told her all was not well.

"What is it?" she asked, sliding her hand into his and leaning into his side.

"The nazal he sent after Kirin hasn't returned yet. I don't know where he is, Arya, I'm sorry."

Her heart clenched with fear. There was only two places the nazal could be if not in Andahar or Dunidaen. Khadini or the Icelands. She tried to reassure herself with the fact that the nazal had no ability to magically track Kirin. It didn't even know if he was a boy or girl.

"I can't bear this not knowing," she whispered. "Maybe I should bring him here."

"If you do that, everyone here will know of his existence. Word will reach the Nightstalker then. Kirin's location and you staying away is the one thing keeping him safe."

She nodded, even though staying away was growing harder and harder every day. She couldn't bear the thought that the nazal mind find her son and she wouldn't be there to protect him. She squeezed his hand. "What else?"

"There was a message waiting for me at Darkclaw. He's scented blood after recent victories and knows it's only a matter of time until the Marshlands fall. He wants me there to help him break them completely."

She let out a breath. "Once the Marshlands fall, he can turn his full attention—and army—to finding me, and Kirin."

"That's why I have to stay with him." He squeezed her hand. "If I'm there, I can find small ways to delay his victory, buy you as much time as I can. And if the nazal does find Kirin, I might be able to warn you."

"That's incredibly dangerous, Dar. If he noticed what you were doing—"

"We have to take risks if we're going to win this."

She let out a breath, tugging him so that he was facing her, and she could press her head against his chest. "General Desomer will want to talk to you in the morning. He's been pouring over your reports on the Nightblade army composition and deployment. He has questions."

"Of course he does." Darmanin chuckled, chest grumbling under her ear.

They stood there in silence for a long moment, Darmanin's hand stroking through her hair, Arya relaying all the small events of life in the Storm Spire he'd missed while he was gone. Eventually she stepped back so she could look up at him. "What's he like, Lucius, when it's just you and him?"

"I don't see him that much." Darmanin frowned. "Even when he's at Darkclaw, he's busy, occupied in the library. Something holds his attention, and it's not just you or the civil war. I sense a purpose in what he's doing, one that isn't about ultimate power. Or at least, the reason he wants ultimate power is because he thinks he needs it for some purpose."

Arya parsed through those words, puzzled. "That echoes something Remien said to me the other day, something about a threat from beyond our shores. I can't quite put it together."

"If there *was* some kind of threat, why hasn't it manifested? It may just be that all those magics inside him, the things he's done, that it's a form of madness," Darmanin said quietly. "We've both seen it in him."

"True." Arya shook away thoughts of the Nightstalker's madness. "So, Lucius wants to finally end things in the Marshlands. We can't change that, so we need to find a way to take advantage of it."

His little grin lit up the room. "I recognise that look. You've come up with a plan, haven't you?"

She leaned up to kiss him. "It might be time to contact the marshfolk. What can you tell me about his attack plans?"

His eyes flashed silver. "I can delay my arrival to join the Nightstalker so that you get there first. He'll hold off on a fresh offensive until I'm there."

She smiled her wolfish smile. "Exactly what I was thinking."

***

Arya rose the next morning as the pink glow of dawn lit up her room. Darmanin slept at her side. She pressed a soft kiss to his cheek before rising, pulling on a robe and crossing to her door. Kait and Allicen were on guard outside; two of her personal shield always with her since their arrival at the Storm Spire.

"Off to the barracks with you," she told them. "Find Captain Aurelian and the rest of your shield. We're riding out today."

Both straightened, pleased. "Aye, Lord Stormrider."

A knock at the door came just as Arya finished dressing, donning her mail and gauntlets and shining Stormrider cloak. After a lengthy farewell with Darmanin—something in her reluctant to let time with him go—it was closing on mid-morning. He'd already left to go and speak with Desomer.

Chiarn's eyes widened as she opened the door. "You look … impressive."

"Good morning to you too. Something wrong?" Before he could reply, Arya felt a ripple of frustration and anger spark through her bond with Essa. "What's Essa doing?"

He scowled. "Arya, I'm sure you've been doing something important this past week while endlessly pacing the walls and the tower roof, but Essa has been trying to work with your court to do as you instructed, and I really think—"

"Where are they?"

He stepped away from the door with a sigh. "I'll take you."

She waved him ahead of her, wondering if her shield were ready yet. They started down the steps, and Chiarn explained, "Essa chose a building across the square to use as a formal meeting place for your court, keeping the communal areas in this tower just for us. We've been meeting there after breakfast each morning."

They left through the main tower doors and crossed the square. It was bustling, people moving around on various errands. All bowed politely as she and Chiarn passed. Arya could feel the Storm Spire's delight at having people within its walls—its marble walls literally glittered this morning. The Flamewielder led her inside a rectangular building directly across the square and up a wide set of steps to its first floor where a large room took up the entire western half of the floor. Niallin and Essa's voices floated out the open doors, both sounding frustrated.

"You have to find others to do it, Lord Inkweaver," Niallin said, a note of stubbornness in his voice.

"Niallin, we *all* have to contribute to—"

Arya walked in, cutting Essa off. The Inkweaver sat at one end of a long table, shoulders tense. Niallin sat directly across from her, arms crossed over his chest. Desomer and Tiya were next to each other further down the table; Tiya's blue gaze snapping with anger, Desomer a mixture of impatient and bored. Remien hadn't even shown up. Windows on the western side of the room weren't high enough to see over the outer wall, but had a nice view of an avenue down below and empty shopfronts across the street.

"Arya, you're here!" Relief filled Essa's voice, then she took in Arya's appearance. "Are you going some—"

"Yes, I'm here." She remained standing. "What are you debating?"

"The Inkweaver is insisting that my people help with the planting of the new fields and care of the sheep and cattle if we get them," Niallin said. "I've tried explaining to her that riverfolk don't farm. We're traders. Once the crops are grown, of course we can then help ship them to be sold."

"Essa and I have been trying to explain that we all need to work together if we're going to succeed," Tiya said.

Arya looked at Essa. Another pulse of sharp frustration passed through the bond between them, though Essa kept her expression clear. Arya tried sending calm and reassurance back, but didn't quite manage it, if Essa's wince was anything to go by.

"We will do our part," Niallin said. "When it is our turn."

Remien chose that moment to amble in, steaming cup in his hand. He sat next to Essa, took a sip of his tea, then waved for them to continue. His high-handed manner didn't improve Arya's growing temper.

She cleared her throat. "Niallin, who exactly is going to help farm and take care of the livestock if your people don't do it?"

"Bring some arwein here. That's what they're for."

"That's what they're *for?*" Arya barely stopped herself from snapping the words. "The arwein aren't the ones hiding here expecting my protection, and, apparently, all the hard work to be done for them. You and your people will pull their weight, just like everyone else, or you can find your own food. *And* protection. Is that clear enough for you, Niallin?"

His face flushed red, shoulders rigid, all traces of the amiable man she'd known gone. "That isn't what ..."

"What? What you signed up for?" She held his gaze. "What *did* you sign up for?"

"You are the Stormrider, the rightful heir, and we are your people. We supported you, we bled for you, and we never faltered in that support, even when it risked our lives."

Arya leaned over the table, palms pressed against the cool stone. "Let me be *very* clear. I value and appreciate your support, and in return for it, I offer you my loyalty and protection. I will fight for you and your freedom. But I am not the ruler of the riverfolk, I am to be the queen of *Andahar*. Your support does not entitle you to special treatment above any other Andahari."

His jaw tightened, but he gave a terse nod, then stood so suddenly his chair screeched back. "I will circulate the work rosters that Lord Inkweaver has drawn up amongst my people."

"Thank you," she said, then, as he reached the door. "Niallin?"

"My lord?" he asked stiffly.

"Next time Lord Inkweaver asks you to do something, you do it. She speaks with my authority in my absence. Am I clear?"

"Lord Stormrider." He left.

Once he was gone, footsteps receding, Essa said quietly. "Arya, you need to be careful."

Arya looked at her Inkweaver, then swore. Niallin had set off her temper, and even though she'd meant every word she said, he had been in her corner from the start. The riverfolk were the core of her support and she couldn't afford to lose them. Guilt squirmed in her chest. "I should have been gentler about it, but Niallin's attitudes are a problem I've been putting off dealing with for far too long."

"I agree. That was fun." Chiarn chuckled.

"They're not all like him," Tiya said. "Some of the riverfolk have been happy to help, but a lot feel the same way he does."

"Their warriors are willing and determined, but they think they're a cut above everyone else," Desomer added. "I've been working on beating that out of them, with limited success so far."

Arya winced. "Which is symptomatic of our bigger problem. I can't just have a riverfolk army. If I'm to reunite Andahar, I must do it with all its people."

"Isn't that something to worry about after you kill the Nightstalker?" Chiarn asked. "I don't know why we're farming and raising cattle when you have a war to fight."

"I used to think so," Arya said thoughtfully. "But now…"

"Now what?"

Arya stood. "I need you all to take care of things here for a while. Essa is my second. Agreed?"

A series of muttered agreements, and a warm smile from Essa.

"I'll be back in a few weeks. Contact me through the bond if you need me."

She felt Remien's sharp gaze on her back as she left.

Chapter 27

Arya lifted a hand, instructing her shield to halt. She listened, hearing nothing but silence echoing through the surrounding mist. For the hundredth time, she gave herself a little shake, trying in vain to clear the numbing fog that shrouded her magic in this place. Its absence was making her far more cautious than usual. When she was as confident as she could be that no ambush lurked ahead, she continued on, boots sinking into the muddy ground.

They'd ridden hard and fast from the Storm Spire, steering clear of towns and villages, a small, elite strike force; Arya's old Icecliff shield, now her personal protection, headed by Esdee. Still, it had taken almost two weeks to make the distance, and on reaching the Marshlands, they'd had to leave their horses behind, the terrain inhospitable to a mounted force.

Now, almost a full day's hike inside the marshy territory, they closed in on the location Darmanin had flagged where the Nightstalker planned to launch his first attack. The mist eddied and swirled around them, stunted trees pressing from both sides. The pungent scent of sulphur tainted what breeze there was. It burned the little hairs inside Arya's nose. As the trees around them began to thin, Arya paused again. *"Elendryl?"*

"Nothing." He was as tense as she was, not liking his lack of visibility or her inability to use magic. Unlike cazaix, her magic wasn't entirely gone, but even the effort of talking to Elendryl caused a throbbing headache to start in her temples.

"Then go and stay high. You know you can't afford to be spotted, especially since Xaphistryl is probably in the region."

More reluctance, but he did as she bade.

Arya continued, hand resting on the hilt of her sword, all senses strain-ing. A little further along the path, the trees opened into a massive, cleared area. It was Arya's first sighting of a marshfolk town, or at least … what remained of one.

She swore under her breath. They were too late.

Nothing moved in the twilight. There were no dogs barking at the ap-proach of intruders, no children playing or smoke rising from the chimneys. Arya glanced over her shoulder, searched out Esdee. "Take a third of the shield and circle around to approach from the north. Etan, do the same from the east. I want to make sure there are no surprises waiting for us. Once you're in position, I'll move in from here," she murmured.

"It looks like we're too late," Charlin said grimly.

"Let's be sure of that," Arya said. "Go. If there's an ambush waiting, we want to spring it before they catch wind of us."

"Aye, Lord Stormrider." Esdee called a soft series of orders, splitting the shield into three.

Arya waited, the remaining Raiders standing ready behind her as Esdee and Etan peeled off, their shadows disappearing into mist and darkness. Her gaze roved the town. Each building was constructed of wood and sat on short stilts sinking into the boggy ground. There was no stone or brick or marble in sight. It was too large for her to see the whole town from where she stood, but she guessed several hundred buildings, linked by wooden walkways or paths across more solid pieces of ground. There was a certain fairy beauty to it, if not for the smoke still drifting into the sky and the charred remnants of destroyed homes.

Judging her moment, Ayra started moving, Kait and Allicen falling in behind her. Their boots on a wooden walkway pressed it down into mud, making an unnerving squelching sound. They'd only covered a short dis-tance when a creaking broke the hushed silence that hung like an almost physical weight over the village.

All three drew blades, metal ringing, shifting into a fighting crouch. Arya's cazaix blade glimmered blue in the dim light as she looked towards the source of the sound; a door swinging in the breeze. It had been damaged—kicked in by the look of it—and now its splintered remains hung on only one hinge. "All clear, let's keep going," she said.

They'd made it into the centre of the town without encountering a single living thing when Esdee and Etan emerged from the mist ahead, Raiders behind them.

"All clear, Lord Stormrider," Esdee said. "We missed the attack."

"Survivors?"

"There's a pit of bodies just to the east of the village," Etan said grimly. "From the number in there…" He trailed off, head shaking.

Arya swore. She'd aimed to arrive before the Nightblade attack that Darmanin had been sent to oversee—hoping that her help in fighting them off would pre-dispose the marshfolk leaders to giving her an audience. Not to mention prevent more innocent deaths that Darmanin would torture himself over. But obviously he hadn't been able to delay the Nightstalker as he'd hoped.

She wondered if it might be best to turn and flee. If the Nightstalker was close, she didn't want to be caught here.

"*Stay high and distant,*" she reiterated to Elendryl, gritting her teeth with the effort it took to get that message through.

"I don't think there's much point going further, Arya," Wattin said, as if reading her thoughts. "The attacking force is long gone."

Esdee grimaced at him not using her title, but none in Arya's shield used it anymore. And she let it go. They were hers.

She nodded, glancing up at the sky. "We've lost light for the day, so let's make camp clear of the village and we'll move out first thing."

A defensible location for a campsite was quickly located, and Esdee set sentries while the others got a small fire going. Arya paced the edges, trying to figure out the best course of action. She didn't want to leave so quickly, not after coming all this way. But how best to approach the marshfolk leaders without leverage? That was if she could even find them. The Nightstalker's spies didn't have a firm grasp of who they were or where they were located, so Darmanin hadn't been able to tell her.

"Lord Stormrider?" Esdee approached, saluted.

"What is it?" Arya finally stopped pacing, and dropped onto the log one of the Raiders had dragged over by the fire.

"If you want us to be able to react to attacks like this in time, we'll need to consider forward-deploying shields to permanent encampments outside the Storm Spire," she said.

Arya eyed her, then waved her to sit down. "I get the sense this isn't a new idea of yours. Have you raised it with General Desomer?"

"I have. He says it's too risky, that there wouldn't be any backup for shields we deployed outside the Storm Spire, and that they're not experienced enough yet to survive on their own."

Arya stifled a smile. "Desomer is right. I'm loathe to risk good soldiers in what would be a highly vulnerable position. We'd have to expect the Nightstalker's spy network to learn about them quickly. Our army is too small to be able to weather constant losses."

"If we want to win a war against the Nightstalker, we can't stay within the walls of the Storm Spire. The distance is too far. You and your *cairdre* are the only ones who can travel *anywhere* quickly."

Arya gave the woman a sharp look, but then conceded her point with a sigh. "I'll think about it."

They sat in comfortable silence for a short time, watching the shield as they settled, and set a watch. The comfortably familiar movements of patrol life. Arya tried to breathe through her mouth; the pungent scent of the marshes seemed to taint whatever she ate or drank if she didn't.

Eventually, Esdee rose and stretched. "What are your orders for tomorrow, Lord Stormrider?"

Arya made her decision. "We move at dawn, deeper into the Marshlands. We're going to look for the next town, and from there find the marshfolk leaders."

***

Arya woke to a distant sound. She rubbed her eyes, sitting up in her blankets, scanning the darkness. The fire had burned down to embers. A short distance away, the sentries Esdee had posted stood watch.

Everything seemed normal.

Except—there. She heard it again. Faint, distant. The unmistakable sounds of fighting.

Nearby, Esdee's blankets rustled as she stirred. "What is it?"

Arya didn't answer. She was already rising, reaching for her sword, buckling it around her waist. "There's something happening nearby, a fight of some sort. At least, that's what it sounds like."

Esdee stood. "I'll rouse the shield."

"Get them ready, but stay here. I'll go and scout on my own first—less chance of being heard or seen. It might be nothing."

"Then I'll come with you," she insisted.

"Fine. Tell Allicen she's in charge until we return."

Arya slipped into the darkness, Esdee a shadow at her back. The faint sounds of fighting grew more distinct. A short time later, the sound of clashing swords carried clearly on a breeze that gusted through the spindly trees, and Arya slowed her pace. Her boots sunk deep into mud as they crept forward.

The first warning Arya had of a nearby presence was the faint but tell-tale prickling of instinct at the back of her neck. Her hand dropped instantly to the hilt of her sword, but it was already too late. Shadowy figures loomed out of the mist, surrounding them.

"Stand down." Arya snapped the command as she saw Esdee going for her sword. "If they wanted to kill us, they would have shot us through with arrows by now."

An amused chuckle.

"Who are you?" Arya spoke into the night.

"Who are *you* trespassing on land that isn't yours?" The same voice countered.

Arya hesitated only a moment. "I am Arya Stormrider, Sky Lord and rightful heir to the throne of Andahar. With me is one of my captains, Esdee Aurelian."

There was a long moment of weighted silence. Arya caught movement out of the corner of her eye and spun to face a man stepping out of the trees. He was tall, with a broad, muscular build and pale skin that made the tattoo on his neck stand out starkly, even in the darkness. "And why should we believe that?"

"I can prove it to you easily enough. I have the Stormrider mark on my arm, and no reason to lie to you."

He was silent a moment, then. "You'll come with us."

"I don't think so," Esdee said, her hand once again going to her sword.

"Riverfolk," a voice spat behind them, and steel rang as someone else drew a blade.

"Enough." Arya spoke before the tension could escalate. "We'll come with you. Will you at least tell me your name?"

"I am Baraal. My warriors will restrain your hands. If you do not resist, we will not take your weapons."

"I heard fighting nearby. Can we help?"

Another snort of contempt. "You cannot trust your senses here, Riverfolk. The fighting is long distant. Now, do we have terms?"

"Yes."

Two more men emerged from the trees, swift and practiced as they bound her hands. Everything in Arya recoiled at the feel of rope tightening around her wrists, but she forced herself to stay still. Beside her, Esdee stood rigid, jaw clenched in mutinous fury. "What are you doing?" she hissed as soon as they began walking. "We could have taken them easily."

"They weren't trying to hurt us. We came here to try and talk to the marshfolk, remember?"

"Yes, talk to them, not let them kidnap us."

"Let's just see how this plays out. If things turn ugly, I should be able to get us out."

"Should?" Esdee muttered.

Arya gave her a chiding glance, then almost stumbled on a tree root that loomed out of the darkness. She stayed silent as she concentrated on following the marshfolk warrior in front of her. *"Elendryl?"* she sent, giving him an image of what was happening.

A questioning image of the other wyverns came back.

"No, don't tell them," she said, wincing as pain throbbed in her temples at the effort of speaking to him at such a distance. *"If you do that, Chiarn and Essa will instantly rush down here, and that's the last thing this situation needs."*

Amusement. Followed by reluctant agreement.

It was a long walk through the dark night, the warriors leading them deeper into the marshes, further away from their camp. Eventually, the mud under Arya's feet turned to wooden boards. Lights appeared through the mist in the distance, and then dark shapes resolved themselves into small, low to the ground huts.

They'd arrived at another marshfolk town.

She and Esdee were taken to one of the structures and shoved unceremoniously inside. The door swung closed behind them and Arya heard chains rattling, presumably the warriors locking them in.

"I can't see a thing." Esdee's voice murmured in the darkness.

"Me either. It should be dawn soon, and then we'll have a better idea of our surroundings."

"I doubt this is more than a wooden hut. If we could get out of these ropes, our swords could cut through a wall easily enough."

"And we will, if that becomes necessary."

"I think it's necessary now. You're the Stormrider. How dare they—"

"That's right Esdee, I'm the Stormrider, which makes me their queen. I'm not going to kill any of them, or destroy their homes, unless I absolutely must."

Esdee hesitated. "Surely you already know that the marshfolk supported the Nightstalker when he took the throne by force, that they turned on him afterwards. Hence the civil war."

"Yes, I do know that much." Arya waved a hand. "Before I have to worry about the marshfolk betraying me, I actually need to have them *talk* to me. I'd prefer not to fight my way through the marshfolk to get to the Nightstalker, if I can help it, and that means not antagonising them more than necessary. So, we wait and see."

Esdee gave a sharp nod and turned to start pacing the edges of the room.

***

Morning brought dim grey light filtering through the cracks in the hut's doorway, and, as Arya had predicted, it wasn't long before two warriors arrived. One leaned inside to wave them out, warning, "Don't try anything, or we'll kill you."

"I don't plan to try anything," Arya told them as she emerged, eyes blinking as she adjusted to the light. "I would like to speak to your leader."

"You don't get to make requests. Come along."

They were led to a central area of the village. Arya looked around with interest as they walked. Mist still hovered close to the ground, but in the daylight she could easily see a myriad of huts in varying sizes connected by muddy paths, wooden walkways and even a bridge in one spot. Smoke curled from the chimneys, and children played happily, barely sparing a glance for the two prisoners as they were led past.

The centre of the village was a wide circle with a large communal fire pit in the centre. The older warrior from the night before, Baraal, stood with another man outside a larger building that faced the cleared area. The stranger wore a heavy pelt over his shoulders. Arya's eyes widened as she realised it was a large shadowhound. His tattoo matched Baraal's, though it had more intricate detail.

He crossed his arms as Arya and Esdee were brought to a halt before them. His mouth was a thin line, and he seemed unimpressed with what he saw. "I am Dorinaal, chief of the Inraki tribe, the largest in the Marshlands. Baraal is my war leader."

"I am honoured to meet you, Chief Dorinaal." Arya spoke formally. "I am Lord Arya Stormrider."

"I doubted Baraal's words, when he told me." Dorinaal scoffed. "But you look and speak like an arrogant riverfolk, and you have one of them at your side, so maybe you weren't lying."

Arya said nothing. Instead, she brought her right arm up, unbuckled her gauntlet, then rolled up her sleeve. The lightning scar was clearly visible, although Dorinaal's expression didn't change as he glanced at it. "I might ask why the Stormrider is travelling alone with only one escort."

So they hadn't stumbled across her shield yet. Good. Arya hoped Allicen was sensible enough to hold them back and stay hidden.

"*I* might ask why you've brought us here against our will," Arya said. "I have no fight with you or your tribe, Chief Dorinaal. In fact, I came to try and help. I know the Nightstalker's army is pressing you hard."

"You are trespassing on our lands," he said simply. "And now that I know who you are ... well ... the Nightstalker has placed a bounty on your head, and he holds many of our people prisoner. I have nothing personal against you, Stormrider, but my loyalty is with my own."

Esdee took a defiant step forward. "Lord Stormrider is your rightful queen. You owe her your loyalty."

Dorinaal flicked her a disdainful glance. "It doesn't surprise me to see the Stormrider heir surround herself with riverfolk loyalists. Your words carry no weight here."

"You do not recognise the Stormrider claim to the throne?" Arya asked carefully.

"Who are you to claim my allegiance?" Dorinaal stepped closer and forced her to look up at him. "Once we hand you over to the Nightstalker, he will kill you with ease." Anger flashed across the chief's face, and he stepped away from Arya. "Take her away."

Surprised by the extent of this marshfolk leader's disdain for her and her title, Arya struggled to come up with the best thing to say. She had been prepared for wariness from the marshfolk, but not extreme disinterest and contempt. It shook her confidence in her planning. Words weren't going to win them to her side.

Shouts of challenge echoed suddenly, and moments later two warriors emerged from the trees to the east, running straight to Baraal. The war leader stepped away to listen to their hushed report, his face tightening as he heard what they had to say.

"A battalion of Nightblades marching this way, Chief," Baraal reported. "And one of our scouts saw the smaller black wyvern in the skies this morning."

"Gather our warriors for an instant march. We'll meet the battalion before it can reach the town." Dorinaal said, sounding calm and well-practiced. "Detail two men to keep the prisoners secure until we return."

Arya and Esdee found themselves being taken by the arms and led back towards the hut they'd been held in the previous night. They were halfway there when the sounds of fighting broke out some distance away. Arya craned her head, trying to see, but was unable to make anything out in the mist beyond the huts.

The hut door was closed behind them.

Esdee settled a look on her. "Do you think this might be a good time to break out, Lord Stormrider?"

Arya considered. She could break out at any moment, but she wondered if it was worth staying, trying to talk to Dorinaal again when he returned.

If he returned.

"They won't treat with you." Esdee read her thoughts accurately. "He will do as he said and hand you over to the Nightstalker. Marshfolk care only about themselves."

Arya huffed a breath. "And you wouldn't, in his position?"

Before Esdee could reply, there was a sharp cracking sound, and one of the planks of wood in the back of the hut was ripped away.

"Get behind me!" Esdee said, shifting to stand in front of her, just as a second plank was stripped away, leaving a human-sized gap in the wall.

"Don't be ridiculous!" Arya stepped forward, drawing her sword.

"There's no need for swords, Lord Stormrider." A man stepped through the gap, hands spread wide to show he was unarmed.

Arya swore in surprise. "Arubon?!"

"Well met," the big man said tersely. "Now, if you'd like to get out of here, we need to go now. When Dorinaal returns victorious, he *will* hand you over to the Nightstalker. He has given orders to Baraal to make sure he takes captives today so he can send one back to his Nightblade camp with a message offering the trade."

Esdee shot her a pointed look.

Arya hesitated. She'd come to speak to the marshfolk leaders, and if Dorinaal's claim of being chief of the biggest tribe was true, then he was who she needed to negotiate with.

"He will not hear you," Arubon said, voice turning sharp with impatience. "We go now, Stormrider, or I leave you to it."

Raven's balls. Arya wavered. Arubon sounded so certain, and she'd seen no give in Dorinaal when they'd spoken earlier. "My shield. They—"

"Have been escorted *out* of our territory." Arubon's eyes glittered. "They are all alive. As long as they *stay* out."

She hissed a breath. "Fine. We're coming."

"You know that man?" Esdee demanded as she and Arya pushed through the gap in the wall after Arubon. The area behind the hut was empty for now, the thick mist still hugging the ground.

"We've met before. He has reason to help me, so I think we can trust him for now."

"I don't think you can ever trust the marshfolk," she said sourly.

They ran for what felt like several hours, only stopping briefly at a small stream to drink. Arubon said nothing, and Arya didn't attempt conversation. Gradually the mist around them began to lighten and the ground under their feet grew firmer. Soon after, Arya spotted the clear space beyond the trees ahead and they emerged from the marshes. Her shield waited a short distance off where they'd left the horses two days ago, having set up camp, all watching warily.

"Lord Stormrider!" Allicen said, looking an amusing mix of astonished and relieved. "You're alright?"

"Good job holding them back," Arya murmured.

"I knew you'd want me to, but those louts..." Allicen's jaw tightened, then she let out a breath. "What are your orders?"

Arya threw a regretful look back at the Marshlands border. "Back to the Storm Spire. Tell the shield to mount up."

A shiver from Elendryl, then an image of Arubon slipping back into the trees.

Arya spun. "Arubon, wait!"

He stopped, reluctance in every line of his body. "I owed you a debt. It is now repaid."

"We need to talk, Arubon." Maybe if she couldn't treat with Dorinaal, Arubon would be the next best thing. "Will you come with me?"

He looked her up and down. "I hear rumours you're building an army in the west."

"That is true. An army to bring down the Nightstalker."

"An army of riverfolk?"

She hesitated. "We need warriors like you."

He spat. "I've no desire to join an army of golden-haired, weak-kneed, pretty boys. This is where we part ways, Stormrider. Our debt is settled."

He was gone before Arya could respond, vanishing into the marsh as quickly as he had appeared. She swore under her breath. All this way and she'd made absolutely no progress. How was she ever going to reach the marshfolk?

"Lord Stormrider?" Esdee and her shield were already astride. Her captain offered a reassuring smile. "You tried."

"I did." Even so, Arya lingered, not mounting her waiting horse.

Darmanin's words came back to her. If she was going to win this, it would be because of her creative tactical thinking, her willingness to take what appeared to be big risks. And instinct told her that giving up on the marshfolk was the wrong move.

"Lord Stormrider?" Esdee pushed.

"We have your back, if you want to go back in there," Kait called out.

Arya stepped back from her horse. "I want you all to stay here. Stick to the camp and don't enter their territory. We're going to let them think on my presence for a time. Esdee, you'll return to the Storm Spire, let them know my return is delayed, and help General Desomer in training the army. You're of more use there."

Esdee lifted an eyebrow. "And what will you be doing?"

Elendryl plunged from the sky, his massive wings churning the air, sending dust swirling and horses skittering with nervous snorts. Arya strode toward him without hesitation, the wind tugging at her cloak. She tossed a grin over her shoulder. "I'm going to make a few visits."

Chapter 28

Arya and Elendryl flew southwest from the Marshlands. They landed at dawn a short hike from Ripley, the main port on the south coast that saw almost all shipping traffic that went to or from Andahar. She stripped off her mail and cloak, dressing in plain clothing that would hopefully render her anonymous. By mid-morning, Arya walked amidst a mix of traders, farmers, and travellers along one of the roads into Ripley. Nobody gave her a second look as she wandered through the streets, stopping at a market stall to buy herself a hot buttered roll that she ate as she walked.

The Hammer and Nail was already filling with the lunchtime crowd when Arya pushed through the doors. She took a moment to allow her eyes to adjust to the dimness before making her way to an empty table by the wall. A girl came over to take her order— cold cider and a slice of the chef's pie—and as soon as she was gone, Leanir slid into the chair opposite.

Despite herself, she was pleased to see him. "How are you, Leanir?"

He lifted a shoulder.

"Do you have any news for me?" she said.

He scowled. "This is where I need to point out that the spy network you've got me building will take time."

"Understood. What *can* you tell me?"

He glanced around, lowered his voice. "The Nightstalker continues to hunt for you and the rebels, but judging from the places he's looking, I don't think he's realised yet that they've all re-located to the Storm Spire. Your boy Darmanin is doing a remarkably good job."

"That can't last for much longer. He'll figure it out."

"Even if he doesn't, he knows at some point you have to come out of hiding to attack."

"True," she conceded. "I'm thinking of establishing forward encampments east of the Storm Spire. They would allow us to react more quickly to events. Any shields I send would be incredibly vulnerable though, so I'm hesitant."

A flash of a smile. "Are you asking for my advice, Stormrider?"

She glared at him.

"Set up a base near Tralana, it's three days ride north of here."

She lifted an eyebrow.

"The spies in that town all report to me now."

She grinned in delight. "You're good."

He scowled before looking around. "I've been here too long. Anything else before I go?"

"One more thing. I need information on something specific." She explained what she was after.

His gaze narrowed as he thought on that. "That should be easy enough to get."

"Can you make it your priority?"

A pause, then, "Will you tell me why?"

Another test, Arya wondered? After a moment, she explained part of what she was trying to do.

Leanir listened, and once she was done, he gave a single nod. "Consider it done."

With that, he rose, pulled his hood down and walked away.

***

A week after she'd been kicked out by Arubon, Arya found herself hiking back into the Marshlands, boots sinking into thick mud, senses drowning in the stink of sulphur. The sunny day above barely penetrated the gloomy canopy. Boots squelched as her shield trailed her. Elendryl circled high above, watchful. Charlin started swearing under his breath as another powerful waft of sulphur came to them on the stiff breeze, and she smiled to herself, but her smile faded quickly as that numbing sensation sank over her magic and she swore, trying and failing to shake it off.

"Such a pleasant place," Wattin remarked.

Kait made a face. "Pleasant isn't the word I'd choose."

"It's incredible," Etan enthused. "I've never seen anything like it. Can't wait to see one of their towns *before* it's destroyed."

"We approach cautiously," Arya repeated her instructions. "Be alert for attack, but don't initiate any fighting unless your life is in danger."

"All due respect, Arya, but they make a move towards you and swords are going to get drawn," Allicen said.

"Perhaps just avoid actually using them unless I'm bleeding—can we agree on that?"

"Suppose so," Charlin said.

She led them on, the light fading as they followed a faint path towards where she was confident the Inraki had brought her last time. Her Raiders had fallen into the old behaviour of patrolling the Diamondfang, gazes constantly flickering around and their hands hovering over their blades.

She felt so much safer with them at her back.

A drizzling rain started up. It soaked through their clothing as they trudged onwards. Arya saw no signs of life through the curtain of falling rain. The land around them was unchanging, boggy marshes, thick mud, and stunted bushes and trees. She wondered what it would be like to live in a place like this, where it was always damp, and the smell of sulphur permeated everything. There was a certain beauty about it, though, in its stillness and the mist that hovered over the ground. It still wasn't somewhere she'd ever want to stay for a long period of time.

Night fell with no sign of any living creature, let alone a member of the marshfolk. They made camp on a narrow strip of dry land between two bubbling bogs and Arya set a guard. They lit a fire only long enough to heat tea, and then doused it, knowing that such a light would be visible for miles around in the darkness.

Arya slept poorly before giving up at dawn. The air was damp and cold, and a thick mist obscured everything beyond their small camp. She sat up, pushing off her blanket. Kait stood nearby, staring out into the mist, watchful. "Anything?"

"Nothing," her Raider responded. "It's been quiet all night."

"All right, let's strike camp and get moving."

The Raiders were all too eager to move and packed up the camp swiftly. Soon after, Arya's instincts began to prickle. She narrowed her gaze, but the mist around them remained impenetrable. She reached up to check the quiver of arrows was firmly in place down her back, and that her bow was in easy reaching distance. "Be alert," she murmured. "I think we have company."

Despite her warning, nothing materialised out of the mist. It was roughly an hour or two later that they rounded a corner to be faced with several marshfolk standing on the path ahead of them. All were tall and muscular and held long spears resting against the ground.

Arya halted, keeping her hands clear of her weapons, and hoping her shield were doing the same. Rustling sounded to their left and right, resolving into more marshfolk warriors emerging from the mist to surround the shield. Most of these held spears too, but some were pointing drawn bows.

"Are you Inraki?" Arya asked. "I'm here to speak with your chief."

There was a long moment of silence in which the line of warriors ahead merely stared impassively at Arya. She waited them out. After a while, one of the men looked backwards, towards another approaching. This one pushed past the warriors to come and stand in front of Arya's horse.

"Baraal." She smiled. "It's nice to see you again."

"Why have you come back?" he demanded.

"I want to talk to Chief Dorinaal," she said.

"And what if we decide to kill you right here?"

Arya shrugged. "You can try. I *am* a Sky Lord though, with a full-grown wyvern nearby. Not to mention the warriors at my back are very good at what they do. We'll kill many of yours before we go down, and I don't think anyone wants that."

Baraal's face tightened. "Why do you want to speak with the chief?"

"That's my business."

They stared at each other until Baraal gave in. "My warriors will keep close and should any one of you reach for a weapon, we will attack."

"Understood. We mean no harm; you have my word."

***

Some hours later, Arya found herself sitting across a firepit from the Inraki chief. He had a healing cut on his cheek, and a clean bandage wrapped around his left wrist. The results of the previous week's battle, she assumed. Her shield were nearby, having been divested of their weapons and herded into a large hut which was now heavily guarded. None of them had been happy about it, but their discipline had held and none of them had made any threatening moves.

"You are lucky I haven't killed you already, Sky Lord, merely for trespassing on our territory without permission, *again,*" Dorinaal said, his eyes flat as they regarded her.

"I apologise. I am not aware of your rules. But I would be willing to negotiate a method by which I can request that permission before I cross your borders in the future."

Was that surprise that flickered over his face? Or menace? She wasn't sure.

He bared his teeth. "I don't *want* you here. You're a fledgling Sky Lord who foolishly thinks she can muster some sort of challenge against the Nightstalker, and I want nothing to do with it."

"I am the rightful heir to the throne of this country. Your people once swore allegiance to my grandfather."

Now he laughed. "That was a *very* long time ago. You haven't seriously come here expecting me to swear allegiance to you?"

"No. I've come to ask two specific things."

Dorinaal shifted back. As did Baraal, standing behind him and to his left. "Now I'm curious, so I'll hear you out before my warriors escort you to a hut to await the Nightstalker's response to my offer of a prisoner trade."

"My first request." Arya leaned forward. "Tell me what your people dislike most about the riverfolk and the horselords?"

"Ha! There are too many things to count." He spat on the ground near her feet. "What is your real question?"

"You tell me you are chief of the biggest tribe amongst the marshfolk. If that is true, then you must understand your peoples' concerns. What is your issue with the other folk of Andahar?"

Dorinaal studied her for a long moment, then true anger flashed in his eyes. "The riverfolk have controlled the trade in Andahar for generations because they own the riverways and the craft to move everything more efficiently than anyone else. And they use their control to exploit us with ridiculously high transport and storage costs. They choke the life out of the marshfolk by making it too expensive for us to buy the things we need to survive. Not only that, but they look down on us as inferior people."

"And the horselords?"

"They are no different. We need the wood from the trees that grow in Navaria; it is impervious to the acidic marsh mud and doesn't rot in the damp. We use that wood to build our homes and the pathways in our villages. In return for the wood, they extract everything they can from us because they know we cannot get it anywhere else."

"I see." Arya had paid minimal attention to Rorin's tutor when he'd been teaching how economies worked, but she did understand the basic concept of supply and demand. "But the Nightstalker presumably hasn't made things any better for you, or you wouldn't be fighting him?"

Dorinaal showed teeth. "The marshfolk bow to none, especially one who dishonoured his word to us. He expected instant obedience after his coup, but did nothing to address our concerns as he'd promised. Now he seeks to subjugate us as he has the other Andahari tribes."

Arya knew she should stick to what she'd come for, but his words made her curious, and she didn't like having Remien as her only source of information. "My understanding is that Lucius fought with my grandfather over how to manage the warring factions in Andahar. That Lucius wanted to solve the division, while my grandfather wanted to give you the freedom to do as you please."

"My grandfather stood at the Nightstalker's side as he waged war on House Stormrider. He believed that too." Dorinaal's eyes glittered. "Only, it turns out that the Nightstalker's solution for healing division was to control us all with fear and *more* authority."

"So now you fight for your freedom," Arya said softly, then met his gaze. "He'll win eventually, you *do* know that? It's a game of attrition, and he has more soldiers and magic to throw at your war than you do. You've already lost, Chief."

"Enough of this *talking*." Baraal roused, stabbing his spear into the ground. "My chief has already done you a great favour by answering your first request. What else do you want?"

Dorinaal glanced up at his war leader, then back to Arya, and lifted an eyebrow.

"I want you to lend me one hundred marshfolk warriors, one of your best battle leaders, and your heir."

Arya ignored Dorinaal's mocking laughter, and simply stared at him, expressionless. Eventually his laughter faded, and he seemed to realise she was serious. Baraal snarled and he lifted his spear.

Dorinaal stopped him with a gesture. "For what purpose?"

"My fight against the Nightstalker. I ask you to give them to me for six months only, and then I will return them to you. My word on it."

"You're crazy."

"I'm anything but, Dorinaal, and you're going to give me what I ask for."

He bared teeth. "Or what?"

She leaned forward, infusing her voice with a thread of steel. "Or I'm going to summon all four of my Sky Lords here and our wyverns are going to destroy your entire village and every single one of your warriors. You think I can't defeat the Nightstalker, Dorinaal? Maybe you're right, but I'm still a Sky Lord, and I command a *cairdre*. The Inraki will no longer be the most powerful tribe in the Marshlands after I'm through with you."

Affronted fury rippled across his face. Baraal swung the point of his spear towards her. In the two men's response, Arya saw the solution to winning a war in the Marshlands, and she wondered at the Nightstalker not having seen it. Possibly he'd never sat down to speak with those he wanted to subdue.

"Everyone hold!" Arya bellowed, gaze firmly on the Inraki chief. "Don't test me, Chief Dorinaal, because I am more than willing to make an example of you and your tribe. After I do that, I'm betting the next chief I speak to will do as I ask."

"The Nightstalker has not been able to defeat us in a decades-long war," Baraal hissed. "What makes you think you could even make a dent in our strength?"

"I'm not looking to win a war, just defeat your one tribe," Arya murmured. "Very achievable with wyverns and a skilled army. I wonder what would happen if the Nightstalker tried that approach ... taking you out one at a time?"

The Inraki chief had turned bright red, visible even against his dark skin. "You're bluffing."

Her voice was cold. "Am I?"

Into the silence after her words, Elendryl swooped low over the clearing, golden wings spread wide, letting out his wyvern's cry. It roared through the area, eliciting cries of fear and shuddering the ground on which they sat. Baraal cowered and Dorinaal reached for his blade, gaze wide on the sky.

"That's my wyvern, Chief, and I've got three others to call on. You've held out against Xaphistryl because the Nightstalker hasn't used her here. I have no such compunctions." She held his gaze. "I fight just fine without access to my magic."

Dorinaal turned to look back at her, voice thick with fury. "Fine. You'll have what you want."

"I want warriors from every marshfolk tribe included in the hundred you send," she said, rising to her feet. "Have them, along with one of your best commanders and your heir come to my camp at the western edge of the Marshlands within a week. I'll be waiting."

Something seemed to occur to Dorinaal, and he gave a bitter laugh. "Do what you want with my heir, Stormrider, I have little interest in him returning."

Arya nodded. "It's been good doing business with you, Chief. I'll see you in six months."

Arya left the camp, her shield falling in behind her, weapons returned to them. Elendryl flew low overhead, insurance in case Dorinaal tried to double cross her.

She was confident he wouldn't.

A smile tugged at her mouth. Would her next visit go this well?

Chapter 29

Leaving her shield encamped at the Marshlands border, Arya flew northwest on Elendryl. As they approached their destination, a stormfront gathered on the northern horizon, dark clouds boiling high into the sky.

The horselords who lived at Lightbringer's Tor seemed to have little regard for the approaching storm. Horses and people thronged the plains below the hillside castle. A group of riders raced horses around the perimeter of the tent city while some distance away others tended to a large herd of cattle. Arya looked upon the thick woodland running east over the hills behind the castle with new eyes—these must be the trees that the marshfolk relied upon for their homes and cities.

As Elendryl landed at the southern edge of the city, the racing riders turned almost as one, their horses quickly surrounding them in a dizzying loop. Arya made no threatening moves, but Elendryl let out a low warning growl, snapping at a rider who came too close. The woman laughed and turned her horse on a touch, avoiding the sharp teeth. Again, she was impressed by the level of control and trust these riders had with their horses. Even a trained Raider's mount would be backing away at Elendryl's presence.

"I'm Lord Arya Stormrider," she called out. "I'd like to speak with your king."

"We'll let him know you're coming and escort you in," a woman called back. "The wyvern stays here, *away* from all our horses and cattle."

"Understood."

Several riders peeled off to race for the castle, while the rest waited for Arya to dismount, and then followed as she walked down the long, cleared avenue of grassland leading to the castle. A small group of horselords emerged from the open front doors as Arya approached. Rylea, Miell's sister, walked at their head.

"Lord Stormrider, you've come back," she said, not bowing. Her entire stance screamed wariness.

"Greetings, Rylea. I was hoping to speak to your father."

She got a sharp nod in return. "We owe you that after what you did for Miell. Please be welcome to our home. My father has extended you guest rights."

"Thank you." Arya climbed the steps to join her. "How is Miell?"

"He's well." Raylea gestured. "Come with me. My father awaits you."

The king's daughter led her inside, straight through an entry foyer into a great hall with a high, arching roof. Two tall warriors with bows and quivers slung over their shoulders and long knives strapped to their waists stood at the open entrance. Arya followed behind Rylea, her eyes taking a moment to adjust to the dimmer light, and so it took her a moment to recognise Miell standing just inside.

"Arya, welcome to my home." He was taller than the last time she'd seen him, his sandy curls hanging down past his neck now. He fell into step with her as Rylea led them deeper into the hall.

"Miell! Aren't you supposed to be in hiding?"

Resentment flashed over his face. "I make brief, unannounced visits home. I closet myself in this hall so that none bar my sister and my father's most trusted bodyguards know I'm here."

Dangerous, but in this case, it was a fortunate stroke of luck for Arya and her plans. They reached a raised area at the end of the hall, where a man sat at a table finishing off a meal. Rylea moved aside to let Arya step forward. "Lord Stormrider, this is our father, Prince Rafel Lightbringer."

The king swallowed his food, and regarded Arya for a long moment before bowing his head slightly in greeting. Unlike Miell, he was big and burly, with a long beard and hair to match. Only their colouring was similar, tawny and gold. "Lord Stormrider. Welcome to my home."

"Thank you, Prince Rafel. It is an honour to be here." She kept her voice polite, confident. Arya focused on analysing every aspect of him, hoping to use that knowledge to get what she came for.

"What brings you to horselord territory?" he asked.

Right, so he wasn't one to beat about the bush. She could work with that. "Your Grace, I came here to ask you two things."

Rafel waved her to a chair opposite him. "Miell, Rylea, leave us."

Arya accepted a mug from a hovering servant. Its contents were cold and bright green. Not wanting to cause offence, she drank without hesitation. The taste of slightly honeyed grass filled her mouth. Rafel watched her, clearly waiting for her to spit it out in disgust, but she swallowed and took another sip. "Delicious and refreshing. What is it?"

"Tagar. We horselords live on it." Rafel sat back in his chair and reached up to pick a piece of rice from his beard before putting it neatly on his plate. "Ask your questions, Lord Stormrider."

"Tell me what grievances your people have with the marshfolk and the riverfolk."

Rafel looked as confused as Dorinaal had been at Arya's question. "An odd question, but easy enough to answer," he said. "The marshfolk are violent and unstable. They raid our rufaa forests, trying to steal the wood they want instead of paying honestly for it. My people die in those raids—we are invincible on horseback, but on foot, we are no match for the battle-hardened skill of marshfolk warriors." His mouth twisted as he said this. He clearly didn't like admitting to any shortcomings in his warriors.

"I see," Arya said. "Is that all?"

"No. Marshfolk don't understand honour, and they have no respect for our way of life. If they can't get what they want, they resort to violence to take it. You can see that for yourself in how they war with the Nightstalker even though it's a losing battle." Anger and resentment filled the prince's voice.

"And the riverfolk?"

"They control trade in Andahar, and because they have the monopoly, they charge extortionate prices for moving trade goods. It costs us so much to ship the rufaa wood north that we must charge ridiculous prices to sell it, reducing the numbers of those willing or able to buy. They refuse to institute fair trade practices. They're the richest folk in Andahari society, and they think that makes them better than the rest of us."

Rafel's answer matched almost word for word what Dorinaal had said. "What about the rest of the Andahari?"

"What do you mean?" he asked, looking mystified.

"I'm talking about those that aren't marshfolk, horselords, or riverfolk. The arwein. Farmers, mostly, as I understand it, the ones who farm the highly fertile Andahari land, both in the north and south."

"What do they matter?" Rafel's mystification deepened.

"Not much at all, it seems," Arya murmured. "Thank you, Your Grace, for answering my question."

He waved a hand in a dismissive gesture. "What is your second request?"

Arya smiled, braced herself for a reaction similar to Dorinaal's. "I'd like one hundred of your warriors, one of your best commanders, and Miell, for a period of six months."

His gaze narrowed. "No. It shows your staggering ignorance that you would even think to ask for that."

"I am your liege, am I not? Unless you've already sworn allegiance to the Nightstalker."

"I haven't, and I never will, but I haven't sworn to you, either." Rafel gestured to the servant, who brought a fresh mug of tagar. He took a long draw. "If that's all you wanted, then our business is done. You have guest rights and may—"

"You can be assured that I will treat your people well, and that I will protect Miell with my life. They will be returned to you in six months. You have my word on it."

Rafel's golden eyes flashed, and he put his mug down before leaning forward. Arya fought not to lean back. He was a big man and wore an intimidating aura of authority. Instead, she stayed where she was and drank another sip of her tagar. "I have made my answer clear, Lord Stormrider."

"I don't want to threaten you, Your Grace. And I don't need to. I saved the life of your son and heir, and now I'm calling in that debt. Give me what I'm asking for, and there will be no further debt between us."

"You ask a high price."

"Is your son not worth a high price?"

She had him. He made a face as he sat back. "For six months only?"

"I will personally bring them back after that time."

Rafel took two long swallows of his tagar before thumping the mug down and wiping a hand over his mouth. Then he sighed. "I am a man of honour, and the debt I owe you is large. However, should something happen to my son while he is under your protection, Lord Stormrider, it will be war between us."

"I will keep him safe, Prince Rafel."

"All right," he said. "You will have what you ask for."

Arya rose, keeping her triumph hidden and simply smiling in gratitude. "Can your hundred warriors, commander, and Miell be gathered here in four days' time?"

"My riders are swift. It can be done."

"Thank you, Prince Rafel, it was a pleasure doing business with you."

"A storm comes. You have been offered guest rights." Rafel ground out the words as if he wished he'd never given them. "Shelter here for the night, Lord Stormrider."

Arya cocked her head. "No doubt your father told you of the magic of House Stormrider, Your Grace? I thank you for your offer, but the storm is my home."

***

From Lightbringer's Tor, Arya and Elendryl headed south. They flew over large swathes of farming country, not unlike southern Ravenstrike or most of Hawkesdale. From her time as Desomer's apprentice, then as general to the warlord of Ravenstrike, Arya knew that these farms were the lifeblood of the country. While leaders and warriors fought over territory, trading rights, and who held and wielded power, these famers, and the blacksmiths, tanners and other trade workers who supported them were what kept the population fed, clothed, and housed. Yet in Andahar they were considered nothing.

Stopping briefly in Tralana, she went to the inn Leanir described and picked up the message he'd promised would be waiting for her. It gave her another location—the city of Alensk—a name, and a few brief lines of reasoning. Smiling to herself, she tore the note into pieces and left.

She was probably mad. But she liked where this was going.

The following day, Arya brought Elendryl down outside the city of Alensk, one of the largest towns in the southwest of Andahar. Situated on the lakeshore fed by a swift-flowing river running direct from the Horn, it was a bustling trading town easy enough for her to enter without notice. She made her way through the busy streets, taking the time to look around and study her surroundings. While the visible presence of Nightblades dotted around the place clearly made folk nervous, it was otherwise not unlike Gateport, or Murton in the Riverlands.

After asking one of the locals, Arya found her way to a large stone building where the offices of the farming guild headquarters were located. Inside, she requested permission to speak with the head of the guild, claiming to have recently inherited a farm from a distant uncle and wanting to learn more about what she needed to do. The clerk took her through to a corner office looking down over a busy intersection which hosted a bustling market. Arya could hear the calls of the stall owners even several stories up.

"Welcome to Alensk." An older man with short-cropped grey hair and a neat beard rose from behind his desk to greet her. "I am Tasker Ravin."

"Thank you for seeing me, sir." She shook his hand. "I know you must be a very busy man."

He smiled. "I enjoy any opportunity to speak with those my guild represents, not to mention the escape from paperwork. Please take a seat. My clerk tells me you've newly inherited a sizeable farm. May I ask your name?"

Arya sat down in the chair and looked him right in the eye. "My name is Arya Stormrider."

The blood drained from his face.

Arya rolled up the right sleeve of her tunic and showed Tasker the lightning scar on her inner forearm. "I am a Sky Lord and rightful heir to the throne of Andahar."

He swallowed. Sweat had begun to bead on his brow. "What do you want?"

"I'm not here to scare you or harm you, Tasker, I swear it." She kept her voice brisk but gentle.

"If King Nightstalker knew you were in my office right now, I'd be a dead man, as would all my family."

Arya squashed the guilt before it could rise. "He won't know. *Nobody* knows I'm here. You and your family are safe."

"I heard rumours that a Stormrider ... we all have. The Nightstalker has increased conscription, and ... there are so many rumours talking about Sky Lords coming back." His eyes widened in dread. "Your wyvern, it isn't—"

"He's well away from Alensk and nobody here will see him," she assured him. "I won't be here long." The guilt came back, this time harder to push away. This man was deeply afraid, and she was the cause of it.

He swallowed. "Why *are* you here?"

"I'll be honest with you, Tasker. I want my throne, and I want the Nightstalker destroyed."

"And you want *my* help?" The sweat beading on his forehead began sliding down his temple. "I can't help you. My family would suffer for it, my friends, everyone in this city. He'd raze us to the ground."

She hated the fear in his voice, hated that *she* was the cause of it, and spoke as calmingly as she knew how. "I'm not asking you to stand against him, not now, at least."

"Then what?"

Arya leaned forward in her chair and began speaking. By the time she'd finished, Tasker was unconsciously leaning forward in his own chair, eyes wide. "That's a grand vision, Lord Stormrider, but I don't know you. How can I be sure that you won't get us all killed?"

"You don't know much about me," Arya admitted. "But I learned about you before I came here. You're a good man, and an excellent administrator. You treat people well at the same time as being a strong and decisive leader. That's not an easy thing to master."

"I'm an *administrator*." He squeaked. "And I'm far too old to do what you're saying."

She smiled. "You mentioned family ... you have children?"

"A daughter and a son."

"What do they do?"

"My son works for the guild; he wants to take my place one day. My daughter is a blacksmith, but she's active at guild meetings." He smiled a little. "She has more passion than sense sometimes, but she fights hard for what she believes is right."

Arya smiled. "I'd like to speak with her, if you'll permit me."

"You didn't come here for me, did you?" he asked in sudden realisation. "You came for my heir."

"Yes."

"Losing either of my children would destroy me, and their mother."

"I know how you feel, Tasker, more than you know. I promise this will be your daughter's choice; I won't force her into anything."

"She will go with you," he said, sounding certain.

"If you are right about her character, then yes, I believe she will." Arya stood. "Shall we go now? I think the sooner I finish my business here and leave, the safer Alensk will be."

***

The next morning, Sefani Ravin sat behind Arya on Elendryl's back as they flew towards Navaria. They were spotted approaching Lightbringer's Tor, and by the time her wyvern landed, a large group of riders were mounting up in the clear space before the castle, as if they'd been waiting. Arya glanced over her shoulder to the blond-haired woman sitting behind her. She'd flown the entire distance without a single sound of complaint ... or retching. "You all right?"

Sefani's blue eyes lit up. "Are you kidding? That's the most exhilarating thing I've done in my entire life."

"Good. Stay here. I won't be long."

The king himself waited outside the open doors to his castle, long hair and beard lifting in the faint breeze. Miell and Rylea stood with him, as did two hulking bodyguards.

"Your Grace," Arya said formally as she came to a stop. "Thank you for doing as I asked."

"The debt between us is cleared, Lord Stormrider," he said. "You cannot use it to draw me into your fight against the Nightstalker."

"I never planned to," she said, looking to his left. "Ready, Miell?"

He stepped forward, waving to another man to join him. He was tall and rangy, with flowing chestnut hair and handsome features. "This is Herel, the commander my father chose to send with me."

Arya nodded. "Have your warriors follow my wyvern, Herel, we'll fly low and slow enough for your horses to keep up."

He huffed in disgust at her assumption. "We won't have any problem keeping up, Sky Lord."

"I'm glad to hear it."

He left, and Arya bowed her head to the prince. "Farewell, Your Grace. I'll see you in six months."

"I'd better," he said, stony-faced, brawny arms crossed over his chest.

Arya stepped up to Rylea, offering her hand in farewell, and taking the opportunity to lean in close and murmur. "Some advice? Use the opportunity of Miell's absence to show your father that capable leadership doesn't require being a man."

Rylea considered that with a little smile, then nodded, shook and stepped back.

Arya turned and began walking, "Come on Miell, there's no time to waste."

She brought the young horselord prince back to Elendryl. His gaze went curiously to the woman astride him. "Who are you?" he asked with interest.

"Sefani Ravin."

Puzzlement flashed over his face. "You're arwein."

"That's right."

"Sefani's father is the head of the farming guild, Miell," Arya said.

His confusion only deepened. "What's that?"

"Is the boy serious?" Sefani demanded of Arya.

Miell gasped, more surprised than upset. "I'm no boy, I'm the heir to the horselords."

"Good for you. Clearly a noble horselord education doesn't include learning anything of value." Sefani snorted and looked away, gaze roving the plains around them with interest.

He stared in astonishment, open-mouthed, and Arya clapped a hand on his shoulder. "Think you can climb up on your own?"

"With an arwein?"

"Yes, Miell. I suggest you make nice. It's going to be a long flight."

***

Arya returned to the Marshlands border, a hundred horselords trailing, to find her shield waiting in their neat camp, alone. Frustration built as Elendryl landed and she scrambled down from his back—planning to march right back into the marshes to demand Dorinaal follow through on his promise—only to stop as a hundred marshfolk warriors materialised as if from thin air, flowing out of the mist at a quick run, and startling her sentries. They came to a halt before her, ten neat rows of ten spear-toting warriors. Standing at their head were two other men. One she recognised instantly.

"Arubon," she greeted him, surprise filling her voice. "Are you the heir or the commander?"

He smiled without warmth. "I am Chief Dorinaal's younger brother and only living relative."

"I see. And you?" She looked at the other one.

"I am Carador, war leader of the Ebor tribe."

"Let me guess," she said. "The Ebor are the Inraki's biggest rival?"

His tight expression was all the answer she needed.

"Welcome, both of you. Please have your warriors fall in behind us. I'd like to leave immediately."

"Where are we going, Stormrider?" Arubon asked.

"Northwest. To your home for the next six months."

Chapter 30

A month and a half after leaving the Storm Spire, Arya led a much larger group towards its towering walls. It hadn't been an easy trip from the Marshlands and her patience was frayed. She'd been forced to keep the marshfolk and horselords completely separated after a few early incidents of fights breaking out. Miell and Arubon had stayed secluded with their warriors, and whenever Arya had brought them together with Sefani for a shared dinner at her fire, they'd treated each other with chilly disdain.

Still, some of her frustration faded at the sight of the plains surrounding her new home. A lot had changed in her absence. Several tilled fields now stretched out from the southern walls, breaking up the wild grasses, where workers were busy planting. A small herd of cattle and sheep grazed in a fenced area adjacent to the fields. Things couldn't have gone badly in her absence if they'd made such progress.

She'd already reached out through her bonds, finding all of her *cairdre* present, and letting them know she was on her way. The gates opened to let them in, the blue-uniformed soldiers on guard staring in puzzlement—and dismay—at Arya riding at the head of two hundred horselords and marsh-folk. She sent one of the guards running ahead to let Desomer know they were coming, and her general emerged from the barracks, Esdee trailing him, as Arya and her two hundred entered the main drill yard.

The horselords and marshfolk milled around, the two groups keeping a wide distance apart, while at a word from Arya, her personal shield headed for the stables and their barracks. Only Wattin and Etan remained as her guard. She waved them both over. "Would you take a message to Niallin for me? Ask him to meet us at the council chamber. When you're done, wait for me there."

"Right away." Etan nodded, and he and Wattin turned their horses back the way they'd come.

Arya grinned at the scowl on Desomer's face. Beside him, Esdee's expression was a fascinating combination of horrified and curious. "You asked for an army, General, here it is," she said. "Find a barracks to stick them in, but keep the two groups separate until I say otherwise. I've got to speak with my *cairdre*, but I'll come and find you later to explain."

Esdee saluted and moved to do Arya's bidding, but Desomer stayed where he was, his experienced gaze looking over the rows of new arrivals. "Unlike the riverfolk you saddled me with, these look like they know how to hold a weapon and march in a straight line."

"They do."

"They also look like they're about to start a civil war in the drill yard."

Arya chuckled. "I promise I will explain everything soon."

"Fine, I'll get them settled. Then I'll wait for your explanation." He wheeled off.

"Sefani, Miell, Arubon, you're coming with me!" Arya called.

Arubon's expression was thunderous. "I'm not going anywhere until I know where you're taking my people."

"Relax, Arubon, I didn't bring them all this way just to do them harm. The same goes for your riders, Miell. They'll be given accommodations, food, and rest. I give you my word."

"Fine with me." Miell shrugged.

Arubon's glare deepened, but he eventually gave a nod.

"Why haven't you gathered any arwein warriors?" Sefani asked as they fell into step.

"I assumed there weren't any. Am I wrong?"

"Yes and no. What do you think most of the Nightblade army is made up of?"

Miell gave a contemptuous snort. "Fodder is what they are."

Sefani rounded on him. "And you think that's okay?"

"None of us can do anything about the Nightstalker's conscription laws."

"Yes, except he doesn't conscript anywhere near as many soldiers from the tribes as he does the arwein."

"Why is that?" Arya asked, as much to forestall a fight as from her own curiosity.

"The tribes push back because they have the strength to do so. He can't afford to lose their support entirely."

"Yet we are the only ones willing to fight him," Arubon said darkly.

Sefani gave him a sharp glance. "Not all of us have the benefit of sulfuric marshes that dampen Sky Lord magic."

Nobody had anything to say to that.

It was late afternoon, and the fading winter sunlight lit up the buildings with a warm orange glow. When she entered the massive open square before the central tower, Arya glanced back to see Miell, Arubon, and Sefani all staring around with wide eyes. Smiling inwardly, she headed for the building where Essa had set up their meeting chamber. The two guards posted at the entrance looked as horrified as the soldiers on the front gates at the sight of Miell and Arubon, but saluted Arya anyway.

"Where have you *been*?" Chiarn shot to his feet when Arya entered, but he was smiling, clearly relieved to see her.

"I'll explain everything, I promise," Arya said, accepting a quick hug of welcome from Essa. "It's good to see you both. Is everything well here? I assume I would have heard through Elendryl if it wasn't."

"We've been fine," Essa assured her. "You've brought guests?"

Leanir spoke from the doorway before Arya could respond. "Well, well, if it isn't the prison enforcer. I never thought I'd see you again."

Arubon regarded him with disdain. "Me either. I can't say it's a welcome surprise."

"Everyone take a seat." Arya cut in before the bickering could escalate, waving a greeting as Niallin appeared, a frown crossing his face at the sight of the new arrivals. Behind him, Etan and Wattin took up guard positions across from the doorway.

She went to close the door, giving them a look. "Nobody gets within hearing distance of this room until I say so."

"Understood." Both nodded.

She closed the door firmly, then gave a little tug on her bond with Darmanin. She immediately got a little shiver back, making her smile, though she avoided looking directly at the closet in the far corner of the room as she returned to stand at the head of the table.

"I'm sorry I was away for so long, but I had reasons for it. Now, introductions first. Please make welcome Arubon Inraki of the marshfolk, Miell Lightbringer of the horselords, and Sefani Ravin of the arwein farmer's guild. Newcomers, this is my court; Niallin of the riverfolk, and my Sky Lord *cairdre*; the Flamewielder, Inkweaver, and Mindbreaker. General Desomer is busy settling your warriors in, but he's a member too."

Miell's mouth dropped open, golden eyes going wide as he stared at the Sky Lords. Even Sefani had a little smile of wonder curling at her mouth. But Arubon was unmoved. He sat with his arms crossed over his chest, expression unreadable. "You neatly left out mentioning the fifth member of your *cairdre*," he said. "The one that's been helping the Nightstalker wage war on my people."

This time Arya couldn't help her glance towards the closet. "Yes. He betrayed me. I have nothing further to say on that, other than that he is my enemy."

"You also didn't mention the two hundred warriors you brought back with you," Leanir said. "Mistryl almost ate them until Elendryl warned her off."

"Really?" Chiarn wriggled in his chair. "I'm all a tingle to know what is going on."

"First things first." Arya paused, bracing herself. "Look around you and get comfortable with each other, because I am naming this group the Conclave. Any further plans or decisions regarding the functioning of the community here at the Storm Spire must be agreed upon by the people in this room."

"Arya, that—"

"Please, Chiarn, patience, I haven't finished. Here are the rules. As rightful queen, I retain full authority to make some decisions autonomously, including how and when to fight the Nightstalker, making formal alliances, or declaring war. But for all matters relating to how the community here is managed, decisions will be made by a majority vote of this group."

"We can't—"

She raised a hand. "Still not finished, Niallin. I have one further stipulation. For *any* decision to be approved, I add one further condition; three of the four non-Sky Lords on the Conclave must vote in favour. If that cannot be achieved, then the decision does not pass." She met each of their gazes in turn, communicating with her stare how serious she was about this, then let out a breath. "Okay, I'm done. Questions?"

There was a long moment of silence as Arya's announcement was processed, and she waited patiently, trying to keep her façade of confidence, her shoulders straight, standing tall. It had been such a fight to even get them all here, but that was only the beginning. The next steps were going to be even harder. She hoped she was up to it.

Niallin spoke first. "You can't do this."

"Why not?"

"Why *not*?" Miell cut over the man's response. "You're a Sky Lord and future queen, and you're going to hand power over to a Conclave with an arwein on it?"

She gave him a look. "I still have power. I have a vote, as do all my Sky Lords."

"But we can be outvoted if three of them don't agree with us," Chiarn interjected.

"Exactly. Why does having magic give us the right to make decisions for the people here? How does it qualify us to make *better* decisions? As queen, I will be in ultimate charge, but everyone here has a right to their say."

"I couldn't agree more," Essa said, that determined glint in her eyes. "Our magic gives us the ability to protect Andahar and its people, but not to make unilateral decisions on its behalf."

Sefani, Miell, and Arubon all shot glances between Arya and Essa, as if they weren't sure what they were hearing was actually coming out of their mouths. Or that it wasn't a trick. Suspicion settled over Arubon's face, whereas Miell just looked out of his depth.

"The community here is a riverfolk one," Niallin said.

"Not anymore it isn't," Arya said. "A hundred marshfolk and a hundred horselords joined us today."

There was a beat of silence, then Niallin stood, furious. "Lord Stormrider, what you are proposing is unacceptable. You cannot give an equal vote to marshfolk and horselords, let alone *arwein*. We riverfolk have risked our lives to help win your throne back. We're the ones who built this community. If you insist on a Conclave, then we should have majority vote."

She tried not to show it as his words hit home. He and the riverfolk had been steadfast allies from the beginning, and she hated to imperil that trust and loyalty. But if she allowed them special treatment now, it would undermine everything she was trying to do. She had to set the example for how she intended to go forward. "Niallin, I am grateful to your people for what they have done for me, but you are getting dangerously close to insolence," Arya warned. "Andahar is not populated entirely by riverfolk, as much as you might like it to be."

"We are the lifeblood of this country!"

Arubon stirred, fury rippling over his face. Beside him, Miell sat up, an indignant flush staining his cheeks. Arya gave them both a hard look, warning them to keep quiet, before she continued. "Yes," she said. "But so are the horselords and the marshfolk *and* the arwein. Who grows the food that you eat? Who tends the trees that build your boats and marshfolk homes? Where do you find the mud that has properties that heal our illnesses? None of the answers to those questions are the riverfolk. *None*."

His mouth formed a thin line. "I won't be a part of this."

Arya sighed, sadness filling her. "You've stood at my side for a long time now, and you've earned the right to fill the riverfolk position on the Conclave, but if you refuse to take it, I will give it to someone else."

"Fine," he said. "Good luck finding anyone else, Lord Stormrider."

He strode from the room, slamming the door loudly behind him. Arya looked around the table. "Does anyone else have anything to say? This is your opportunity. I will listen."

Arubon's mouth curled. "I had similar thoughts to that oaf who just stormed from the room, but after his performance I have no desire to look so petty and stubborn. You said six months, and I will give you that, Storm-rider."

"I admire what you're trying to do," Sefani said. "It's never going to work, but I'm willing to do my part. I'll stay for six months."

"And you, Miell?"

The prince was staring at Sefani in confusion, as if he couldn't quite fathom that an arwein was being given a place on a ruling council. When the silence drew out, he gave himself a shake and looked back at her. "My father agreed to six months, so I will honour his agreement and participate in this ridiculousness until it fails."

"A ringing endorsement, thank you all," she said. "Miell, Arubon, find your folk and stay with them until I come and find you. I don't want anyone wandering around until I can be sure they won't start a fight. Sefani, speak to one of the guards outside and ask them to take you to the healing centre. There you'll find Tiya, our healer. She'll help you find quarters of your own and get you anything you need."

Arya waited until the three of them had filed out before dropping into a chair and rubbing her now throbbing temples. Guilt writhed in her for what she'd had to do to Niallin. She wanted to reward his loyalty, not make him feel discarded. She reminded herself that she'd always wanted this power, for these kinds of decisions to be hers, but it was small comfort.

None of her *cairdre* were startled when the closet in the far corner of the room opened and Darmanin stepped out. He strode to the table, confident and self-assured. Arya smiled, pleased beyond measure to see his face again. She'd missed him terribly. "You heard all of that, I hope?"

"I did." He took a seat.

"Do you have an opinion on this, Darkslayer, or are you just going to sit there and say nothing?" Leanir asked.

"Niallin's reaction was regrettable, and I hope it doesn't mean we lose riverfolk support, but I have faith in my wife, Mindbreaker, and I see no issue with what she's trying to do. In fact, I suspect I know where she's going with it, and if I'm right, well ... we'll see."

Arya shot him a grateful look.

"I'll say it again, I think it's a good idea," Essa said.

Leanir shot out of his chair. "I thought we were trying to destroy the Nightstalker. That's the only reason I'm willing to keep showing up when you call me. I don't understand why you're wasting time building a damned community that's only going to be destroyed when he figures out what you're doing and comes for you."

"He has a point," Chiarn said. "You rule as you think best, Arya, but as someone who is literally risking his life by agreeing to stand at your side, I'd much prefer if you were focusing your efforts on defeating the Nightstalker, especially since the odds of that are miniscule. You owe us that."

Arya's shoulders slumped. Were they right? Was she setting in place all these plans as a way of distracting herself from the real problem—facing the Nightstalker and winning? Was she failing them all once again?

Essa spoke quietly. "I have faith in you Arya, but can you at least tell us your plan?"

"When I have all the pieces of it together, I will, I promise you." She looked at them all, trying to convince herself as much as them. "This isn't just about building a community. It's about putting together a way to up-root the Nightstalker so fundamentally that he *can* be destroyed. I haven't seen my way through to the solution yet, but we're on the right track."

"*They* might trust you enough to wait for that, but I don't, Stormrider." Leanir said.

"I'm struggling too," Chiarn admitted.

"Stick with me for now, please," she asked.

"That assumes you even manage to come up with a plan." Leanir said. "That a plan exists that would actually succeed."

Arya had nothing to stay to that. All she could do was hope desperately that he was wrong.

Even though, deep down, she feared that he was right.

Chapter 31

It was late when Arya made it back to her quarters, weary to the bone. Night had fallen hours earlier. Darmanin emerged from the bathing room, hair wet and curling around his face. He kissed her forehead and drew her over by the window. A full moon made the sky outside clear and bright, lighting up the white-tipped waves as they rolled towards the cliffs.

She leaned into his side. "Thank you for supporting me earlier."

"Am I right, are you really trying what I think you're trying?"

"Do you remember when we all first arrived at Heathrock? There was so much trouble amongst the Raiders over my appointment as apprentice to Desomer."

Darmanin took her segue with equanimity. "Arken was the biggest problem, if I remember correctly. He thought he should be the apprentice."

"Arken was my biggest obstacle, yes," Arya said.

"And you solved him pretty handily, that morning when you thrashed him in the yard."

"I did ... but it wasn't about beating him in a fight."

"No, it wasn't." Darmanin's arm settled around her shoulders. "If you're doing what I think you're doing ... Arya, it's a much bigger challenge than winning over the Raiders at Heathrock."

"I know," she admitted. "Dar, if I'm going to pull this off ... it will be by force of will alone. I have to be better than just one person. I have to be great."

He turned her to face him, his face as serious as she'd ever seen it. "Arya, you already are."

She swallowed, the utter certainty in his face and voice sending all her self-doubt flying away as if it had never existed. "Thank you."

The following morning, Arya had all the new arrivals summoned to the yard outside the barracks Desomer had chosen for them. Before making her way to join them, Arya went looking for Essa, finding her eating breakfast in the communal space they shared in her tower. "Dare I ask where Remien is?" she said, taking a seat.

"You just missed him," Essa said dryly. "He's been spending a lot of time in the old library. It's a few blocks over. I've asked what's holding his interest so much, but he won't tell me."

Arya looked up from her food in surprise. "There are *books* still in it?"

"Old and dusty and some damaged with mould, but yes." Essa's eyes lit up. "I wish I had time to spend in there."

She made a note to go and visit it sometime, but for now she had weightier matters to deal with. "How did he react to the establishment of the Conclave?"

"He raised his eyebrows and gave a little chuckle." Essa sighed. "Then he looked constipated for a moment. Then he chuckled again and left."

Arya matched her sigh. "I'll find him later, try and figure out what he's up to. In the meantime, I came to ask for your help with the Conclave."

"How so?"

"I'm going to be busy for the next while, so I want you to manage it for me. It won't be easy, but I need you to get them working together. Schedule formal times for decisions to be made, and I'll make sure that I, and Chiarn and Leanir, are present."

Essa gave her a look. "I'm not sure this is such a great job you're giving me."

"It's not," Arya admitted. "But this needs to work, Essa, and we both know I don't have the patience for it. You're as tough as I am, which will be needed to wrangle their stubbornness, but you have better self-control, *and* you're smarter."

"Arya, I told you that I believed in what you're trying to create, and I meant it." The Inkweaver met her eyes. "If I do this, then I'm doing it properly. This can't be something you've set up just to keep people happy while you do whatever you want."

"I want it to work, truly." She spoke sincerely.

"All right. I'll get them together this morning and we'll start working through the petitions that built up while you were away. I'll make it formal; a Conclave meeting every morning, with provision to be called more frequently when needed."

Arya pushed back her chair. "Thank you."

"Arya, wait!" Essa stopped her at the door. "We need a replacement for Niallin on the Conclave."

"He hasn't backed down?" Arya asked, surprised. She had assumed that once Niallin's temper cooled, he would want to keep his position on the Conclave.

"No." She paused. "Quite the opposite in fact. There is a lot of discontent after yesterday. Many of the riverfolk are upset with your decision. I hope you don't think they're just going to accept it quietly."

Her temples ached. Arya pressed her fingers into them. "Which is why we need someone on the Conclave who will set a good example for the rest of them. Go and talk to Niallin this morning and see if you can convince him to reconsider. If he still refuses, then I want Rengalin to replace him."

"You can't unilaterally replace Niallin with Rengalin."

"Why not?"

"Because if you want this to work, then the riverfolk representative on the Conclave needs to be their choice, not yours."

Arya felt impatience flare, but Essa was right. "Fine. If Niallin refuses, then speak with Rengalin and ask for his recommendation. If his suggestion meets your requirements, then you have my blessing to bring them to Conclave."

"All right. Good luck with whatever you're doing."

Arya chuckled. "I suspect it will be as equally challenging as your job."

But more fun.

She opened the door to find Kait and Charlin had replaced her overnight guards. Kait called a cheerful greeting while Charlin gave a brusque grunt. Arya grinned at them both. "How were the barracks last night?"

"The tension was so thick you could have cut it with a knife," Charlin muttered. "There'll be a brawl within the week, I'd put gold on it."

"I told you!" Essa called from inside.

"It will be fine," Arya insisted, waving a farewell before heading towards the main doors, her two Raiders trailing.

***

Desomer had housed the new arrivals in a corner of the barracks just inside the outer wall, almost completely segregated from the main compound. There was only one entrance via a set of double gates into a spacious entry yard, which could also double as a drill yard. Expansive stables abutted the western side of the yard, where the horselords had been housed. Another barracks, for the marshfolk, stood on the opposite side of the yard, and joining them in the middle of the 'u' shape building was a mess hall. A little smile crossed Arya's face when she saw it.

Desomer had figured out what she was up to.

She walked through the gates to find three groups of equally sullen-looking individuals standing before her. The marshfolk stood to her left, in straight rows, spears pointed towards the sky. The horselords were in the centre, loosely gathered, looking distinctly uncomfortable without their horses. And one hundred of her own army, all riverfolk rebels, stood in neat formation to her right.

Desomer sat in his chair off to the side, and she went to join him. "I'm going to need to take the reins here," she told him.

He nodded. "I'm your general, Arya. I do as you command."

"I appreciate it." She stepped away, lifting her voice to a parade ground bellow. "Arubon, Miell, Sefani?"

She waited until they reached her. "You are Conclave members; you don't belong here. Go back to the palace and find Lord Inkweaver. The first Conclave meeting is to be held this morning."

"I am uncomfortable leaving my people here," Arubon said.

"Then get over it. All three of you will have quarters and offices near the council chamber. Your job is to participate in the running of this community. Go."

After a brief hesitation, they filed past her and left. The eyes of all three hundred warriors watched them go.

"Carador, Esdee, Herel." She addressed the three commanders. "Form up to my left."

Throwing glances at each other, they walked forward to stand just to her left. Again, three hundred pairs of eyes watched them. Arya felt the weight of those stares, but in this, at least, she was confident. She'd faced down rows of hostile warriors before and always come out of it successfully.

"Welcome to the Storm Spire," she told the assembled group. "For the next six months you are part of my army. I am your leader, and General Desomer is your commanding officer, and as such, you will obey all of our orders. I have a low tolerance for insubordination or laziness, and should any of you display either of those qualities, you'll be sent home as failures. You will work hard for me, and in return, I will make you the most effective fighting force in this country."

"You already have a riverfolk army, what do you want with us?" one of the horselords called out.

"You are going to be an irregular battalion under my direct command, divided into three units headed by Carador of the marshfolk, Herel of the horselords, and Esdee of the riverfolk. They will hold the rank of commander, and each unit will contain five shields. I will leave it to each commander to choose who captains those shields."

"For what purpose?" This from a marshfolk warrior. His voice dripped with scorn.

She smiled. "You'll find that out when you prove yourselves worthy. Are there any more questions before we get started?"

There was some muttering but nobody else spoke up. Arya gave them a moment to settle before issuing her first order. "The first three rows of every group, please step forward." When there was hesitation, she roared the words again. "The first three rows, step forward. Now!"

Boots sounded as they took a step forward with varying speed and willingness. Arya turned to Herel. "Commander Herel, please march your unit over to the side."

He frowned, looking puzzled.

"March your new shield over to the side. Now." An edge to her voice.

Herel gestured sharply for the three rows of horselords to follow him. Boots clattered on the stone as they moved over to the clear space to the left. Both front lines of marshfolk and riverfolk remained where they were. Arya and Desomer shared a glance. The old man looked deeply amused. She scowled at him.

"Commander Herel!" Arya called out.

"Yes, Lord Stormrider?"

"I think you left something behind."

Herel glanced between his horselords, and the two other front lines, looking confused. "You want me to...?"

"Did I not make myself clear?"

Herel straightened his shoulders and walked over to the riverfolk. With a gesture, he ordered them to move over and join the horselords. They were clearly reluctant, but by now they were soldiers who'd been under Desomer's command for weeks, and so they shuffled over to join the horselords. The marshfolk flat out ignored Herel's command, and Arya was forced to intervene.

"Do your warriors have a problem with their hearing, Carador?"

"You're asking them to fight under a horselord." He looked at her as if she'd suddenly sprouted feathers.

"Carador, if those men don't move within the next ten seconds, I'm sending you all home."

Fury flashed on his face, but something—marshfolk honour?—held him in check, and he barked a terse command. The marshfolk immediately moved across to join Herel's unit.

Arya noted that. It was good to know they would obey Carador without question.

"Next three rows, step forward please," Arya barked out. "Let's see if you can do it faster than the first lot."

They obeyed, knowing what was coming this time, and Arya looked at Carador. "Line your new unit up beside Herel's. Quickly."

Once the second group had moved, that left the final rows of each group remaining. This would be Esdee's unit. The woman was the youngest and least experienced of the three commanders, but Arya was banking on her creative mind and willingness to follow Arya's lead to help her make this work.

"That really wasn't so painful, was it?" she asked once the three new groups had formed. "Any questions?"

Deeply reluctant silence greeted her words.

"Good. Before we start any fighting drills, I want to make sure everyone is at a high level of physical fitness. So today we're going to run. I'll lead the way. Commanders, the unit that gets all its members back here first will avoid the hundred push ups that the rest of you will have to do as soon as we get back." She looked around. "When we return, General Desomer will take over."

Arya broke into a jog towards the other side of the drill yard, where a gate led to a path inside the outer wall of the palace. A short distance along that brought her to another gate leading outside the wall. From there, another narrow path led down the steep cliffs to the ocean.

When she reached the top of the cliff path, she glanced back to see her new battalion still straggling out of the gates. The riverfolk were doing well enough, accustomed to such runs under Desomer's training, but some of the horselords already looked like they were struggling. And the moment they'd been released from formation, all three tribal groups had gravitated back together.

This better work, she thought.

Chapter 32

A month passed during which time Arya fell into a routine.

She ran with her battalion every morning before leaving them in Desomer's capable hands. In the afternoons she and Essa and Chiarn—along with Leanir in the handful of times he visited—worked with Remien in learning to share their magic and fight together. At least there, they were making progress.

Her army had grown to thousands strong, and Desomer was shaping them into a force that looked like something resembling a disciplined group of soldiers. The community at the Storm Spire continued to grow, still mostly riverfolk who looked sideways at any of the marshfolk or horselords they passed in the streets. Rengalin had taken the riverfolk seat on the Conclave after a half-hearted vote by the few riverfolk willing to participate. Their obvious discontent was noticeable each time she stepped outside to walk through the streets. Still, so far it was all holding together.

But it was all far too slow.

With every hour, every day that passed, Arya grew more anxious that the Nightstalker would learn of their growing army at the Storm Spire and arrive on Xaphistryl to raze them to the ground. It was inevitable. Only Darmanin's presence at his side kept him occupied, focused on the Marshlands. But their time *would* run out. Arya didn't kid herself on that.

And even if she did have a mighty army that could march now ... that meant war. Death. Bloodshed. Grief.

But, most of all, she worried endlessly for her son. The nazal had been tracking him for a frighteningly long time, and Darmanin could tell her nothing of its progress. It was possible the monster had found her son already and … each time her thoughts went there she pulled herself away, distracted herself with something physical until the panic calmed again.

And Arya wasn't the only one who knew they were on borrowed time. The Conclave raised it one morning at their scheduled meeting.

"Lord Stormrider, you have us for six months, but judging from General Desomer's reports, we won't have an army strong enough to win a conventional war in that time." Sefani said. "Yet you can't afford to spend years building an army. The Nightstalker will find us before that."

Miell shot Sefani a surprised look, as if he didn't consider an arwein capable of such considered analysis.

"The arwein is right." Arubon said. Arya was sure he delighted in challenging her at every turn in these meetings, despite his fierce mien and the fact she'd yet to see a single smile.

"You have hit upon my conundrum nicely," Arya conceded, ignoring pointed looks from Chiarn and Essa. Remien too, who often sat in the back of the room as an observer, gave her a knowing look.

Rengalin caught it. "Perhaps Remien has information that could help you."

"I do. I have already passed it on." Remien said. "Lord Stormrider refuses to do what is necessary."

"What is he talking about?" Arubon demanded.

Shooting Remien a filthy look, Arya explained what he'd told her about Sky Lord magic. "I refuse to murder my Sky Lords, so that is not an option."

Several looks went around the table, but Arya couldn't quite read what was behind them. She hoped it was support. She didn't want to have to fight the Conclave on this too.

"What *are* you going to do, then?" Miell leaned back in his chair, the picture of indolence.

Arya sighed. Decided to give up a piece of her plan. "I'm doing my best to chart a course between waiting too long and moving too soon. As far as our army goes, we have allies. The Etherean, for one, and the Icefolk. But I think the key won't be either of them … it will be the Khadini and the cazaix they have access to."

Chiarn frowned. "Emperor uq-Danresan is allied with the Nightstalker."

"But we have allies in Khadini too, the rebels. They can bring us fighters and cazaix. Don't forget cazaix can harm Sky Lords and wyverns both." She should have gone to speak with them already, but Kirin was what held her back. By drawing Kulan into her war, she risked Kirin too.

"You're undecided," Arubon said. "But if it's true you have potential allies in the Khadini rebels then we should be treating with them now, learning what their demands are and whether we can meet them."

Arya swore. Was he reading her mind? "I know. I'd just like a little more—"

A knock came at the door, and Charlin poked his head in. "A new group from the Riverlands just arrived. They're on the way to the square."

Rengalin rose. "I'll go to greet them, unless there's anything else you need from Conclave today, Lord Inkweaver?"

"Nothing that can't wait until tomorrow," she assured him.

Arya was surprised when Sefani and Miell followed Rengalin to the door. Arubon too, though he trailed reluctantly. "What's that about?"

"They decided that since the Conclave represents our community, they should all be there to greet any new arrivals, no matter which tribe they're from," Essa explained, drawing a sharp look from Remien.

"Well, well, well." Arya said, leaning back and putting her boots up on the table. A smile tugged at her mouth. "What a development."

"I have to do *something*," she said to Tiya in frustration two nights later. "But I still don't see the path forward clearly. I know I can't move too soon or it will all fall apart, but waiting is driving me mad." There were pieces, all in play, but she hadn't quite found the thread to draw them all together yet.

"If it makes you feel better, I've almost finished training two riverfolk healing assistants. And Sefani has been able to tell us where to buy the weapons we need without drawing attention." Tiya nudged her. "That's something."

"It is." But it wasn't anywhere near enough.

And it was all so fragile.

"Arubon was right. I should think about going to the Khadini soon." Arya mused. She didn't want to do anything to endanger Kirin, but she *would* need the access to cazaix that Kulan could give her. She was also toying with the idea of offering him a formal alliance, his fighters in return for her material assistance in overthrowing his brother—once Kirin was safe.

With the Khadini rebels, the Icefolk, the Etherean and their healers ... Arya thought she had a genuine shot at winning territory beyond the Storm Spire. And once she had that ...well, her tactical skills and those of her general and commanders would ensure a slow and steady expansion.

Until the Nightstalker and his wyvern came for her and Elendryl.

It always came back to that.

"Have another drink." Tiya advised, lifting the bottle they were sharing. "It will help."

Arya did as she bade. They sat in companionable silence at the top of the western wall, watching the sun set over the ocean. Soon after, her bond with Essa rippled and she turned to see the Inkweaver approaching.

"Mind if I join you?"

"Please." Tiya filled a cup and passed it to her with a ready smile.

Essa settled with a sigh on Arya's other side and took a long sip. "I bring news."

Arya winced. "It sounds bad."

"It's both. The good news is that another group of travellers arrived this afternoon. They weren't just riverfolk. There were arwein amongst them."

Arya's eyes widened while Tiya gasped. "That's wonderful news."

"They're known to Sefani, apparently. She swears they can be trusted."

"That might be true, but eventually one of his spies is going to get in here." Arya added another task to her mental list. They'd need to be prepared for that.

"So maudlin, Arya." Tiya nudged her. "Have another drink."

Essa took one too. "The other news is that Niallin left this morning with no intention of coming back. Remien told me. Apparently the two have been talking recently."

Arya swore. "He really hated the Conclave that much?"

"It's not just him. A few left with him, and others are talking about doing the same," Essa said.

"Let them go," Tiya advised. "They've made their choice. And it's not like riverfolk rebels who've been fighting on your side are going to go anywhere near the Nightstalker or his Nightblades to report you."

Arya sipped at her drink, knowing Tiya was right. Short of hunting Niallin down, there was nothing she could do. But something about it didn't feel right. Uneasiness sat heavy in her gut, along with the guilt. She felt like she'd betrayed Niallin, even though she knew she'd made the right decision. Maybe once it was all over she could find him and they could talk.

Darmanin returned a few days later, arriving after sunset and sneaking into her tower room. She'd missed him terribly, so instead of discussing plans or strategies, she went to get some food from the kitchen, and they sat before her fire and ate and talked about boring, silly things. It was a break they both needed.

By midnight, Arya was fast asleep, Darmanin curled up beside her, ensuring she slept better than usual. But they both moved at the same moment when a sudden frantic knocking came at the door.

Wattin, her guard for the night, stood there, looking grim. "I've just had word of a fight in the barracks. It's bad."

Arya didn't need to ask which one. Swearing under her breath, she hunted around in the dark for her shirt and breeches, then hopped around trying to yank her boots on as quickly as possible.

She looked at Darmanin. "I'll be back soon … hopefully."

"This isn't good, Arya."

"I realise that," she snapped, dread curling in the pit of her stomach.

"Go and deal with them." He leaned down to kiss her. "I'll keep the bed warm for you."

***

She could hear the sounds of fighting well before they reached the gates leading into where her battalion was barracked. Several soldiers from her regular army had gathered nearby, looking uncertain as to whether they should intervene.

Arya shouted at them as she went through the gates. "Stay out here unless I call for you."

Her gaze went straight to where several men brawled at the entrance to the horselord side of the barracks. Flamelight flickered inside, as if a fire had been lit. The dread that had been building inside her on the walk over settled like a dead weight in her stomach. She feared very much what this meant. Still, that was for worrying about later. Right now, they needed to see their leader.

"Hey!" Arya bellowed. There were seven or eight all up, a mix of marshfolk and horselords. They were too involved in the fight to hear her, so she resorted to magic. Raising an arm, she brought a bolt of blue lightning sizzling down into the stone inches away from where they fought. It lit up the night and made a tremendous bang, sending all participants scrambling backwards, many falling over in their attempts to do so quickly.

"What is going on?" she roared. "Get on your feet and in a line, now!"

Thoroughly intimidated by the fury in her voice and display of magic, they hurried to obey. Most were bloody and bruised, but none looked badly injured.

"I want you all to form up over by the east wall," she snapped. "If I come back to find any of you have moved from that position, you will bitterly regret it. Am I clear?"

They scrambled away, and Arya paused long enough to see them reach the wall and start forming a line before heading inside. Marshfolk, riverfolk, and horselords filled the corridor, fighting in pairs and small groups. Arya dealt with each fight using a combination of her fists, the flat of her blade and the occasional display of magic. She'd dispatched at least twenty warriors out to the yard by the time she reached the mess hall, where it was clear the fight had originally broken out. Several tables and chairs were in pieces, and a massive brawl was taking place in the centre of the room. She had no idea what had started the fight, but now all three tribes were throwing punches and kicks without distinction.

An explosive shock wave of her magic, roaring through the room above their heads, broke up the fighting handily enough, and they all turned, gape-mouthed, to face her. The sudden silence was shocking, In it, Arya heard her own heart pounding. She fed her temper, letting it stay in control to give her strength and command.

"Get yourselves out to the yard," she bellowed. "Now."

They obeyed instantly, falling over themselves to push through the doors and escape the furious Sky Lord. Outside, all those who'd been fighting—roughly a third of the battalion—gathered by the far wall in formation. Arya was relieved to see that none looked badly hurt enough that they couldn't stand. Herel, Carador, and Esdee stood slightly to one side, and all were expressionless as Arya approached them.

"What happened?" she demanded. They were a sorry sight, and some of the dread came leaking back. More than a month together, and they were *still* so far apart?

When neither of the men responded, Esdee cleared her throat. "I was asleep when I heard the sound of fighting. I went to check on my unit, but many weren't in their beds. I sent one of them to run and tell you what was happening. I then tried to break up the fight, but it was out of control by then."

Swift as a striking snake, Arya's gaze swung to the other two. "Carador? Herel? Which one of you is going to tell me what started this?"

"I don't know either," Carador said, a nerve in his jaw ticking angrily. "The fight broke out while I was in bed too, but when I saw my warriors being attacked, I had to help them."

"*Your* warriors?" Arya asked. "Are you talking about the men and women in your shields, or the marshfolk that came here with you?"

"I am responsible for my people and their protection," he spat out. "And if they're attacked here, then—"

She cut him off. "Herel?"

"We were relaxing in the mess, having a few drinks after a hard day," he said. "Some of us were just playing around, you know, having a joke or two, but his folk are overly sensitive and took offence."

"*His* folk?" Arya gestured to Carador.

"That's right."

"And how did the riverfolk get involved?"

Herel rolled his eyes. "A couple of them tried to break up the fight, shouting something about orders and discipline, but one of them took an accidental punch, and well, it escalated from there."

Arya stepped back, rubbing the bridge of her nose as her head began to ache. "Get them back to their beds. Tomorrow you'll all clean up the mess you made. I'll use the rest of tonight to think about how to deal with this. Get out of my sight."

They moved quickly, but Arya halted Esdee with a touch on her arm. "I want to see you once your unit is settled. I'll wait for you in the mess."

"Yes, Lord Stormrider."

***

Arya didn't have to wait too long, seated at one of the unbroken tables, before Esdee appeared. It was well into the early hours of the morning, and the young woman looked as tired as Arya felt. Doubts festered inside her. What if she failed at this?

"Lord Stormrider, I'm sorry I failed you."

"Take a seat," Arya waved her to a chair. "The fight was out of your control."

"Yes, but I should have enough authority over my shields that they never became involved in the first place," Esdee sounded furious with herself. "*You* would have."

"Do you know why I chose you to become apprentice to my general?"

"Because you saw yourself in me," she said.

Arya smiled. "You certainly have my arrogance."

"It might be arrogant, but it's true," Esdee said. "And because of the opportunity you gave me, I will do anything you ask."

"I pulled you out of the rebel army because I saw in you the type of confidence and creative thinking that is needed to lead an army to victory. Now I need you to live up to what I saw in you."

Her shoulders straightened. "Just tell me what you need, and I'll get it done."

"I need you to win over Herel and Carador. If they don't buy in to what we're trying to do, the warriors never will. Leadership comes from the top."

Reluctance flicked over her face.

"If *you* don't believe in what I'm trying to do, they won't either," Arya said softly. "They are humans too. Just like the arwein. We're *all* worth something, Esdee. I'm determined to succeed here, but I can't do it alone. You, me, Herel, and Carador, we have to be a team."

She let out a long breath, but there was resolve in her eyes as she looked up. "You can count on me, Lord Stormrider."

"Thank you." Arya rose and began walking away, pausing after a moment to look back. "You're right, you should have better control of your shields by now. Learn from this, Esdee, that's how you get better. And seek General Desomer's advice. He's dealt with this before."

"I will."

"Get some sleep. We're going to be running extra far tomorrow. If they've got the energy to brawl, I'm going to sweat it out of them."

***

"You were right," Arya said as she paced her tower room early the next morning. She'd tried sleeping after getting back to bed, but failed miserably. Not that the thinking time had helped any. "Something's not working." She stopped pacing and looked at Darmanin. "Do you really have to go so soon?"

"Unfortunately, yes. He's recalled me to Darkclaw, and I can't afford to take too long in getting there," Darmanin said, looking up from where he was lacing his boots. "I have an idea that might help your problem."

"Tell me."

He crossed the room to her. "One way to force them to bond as a unit is put their lives in danger. The Nightblade army has broken through the northern boundaries of the Marshlands, and Lucius has recalled me to Darkclaw to help plan the capture of Vespir, the biggest town in the north. Once the Nightstalker takes that, he's going to hold significant marshfolk territory for the first time in this war. From there there's probably no coming back."

Arya leaned up to capture his mouth with hers. For a long moment she forgot about everything else and allowed herself to get lost in his closeness.

"What was that for?" he said as they finally broke for air.

"For being my partner, in everything," she told him. "For being patient enough to wait until I was able to realise how good we are together."

"I would wait forever for you," he said. "For the joy we've found."

She placed her hand against his stubbled cheek as he brought his forehead to rest against hers. After a long moment, she kissed him again, hard, then stepped away. "We'll march tomorrow."

He nodded. "I'll stall the Nightblade advance as best I can, give you time to get there."

"Be careful, Dar," she warned him. "If I take my battalion to help in the Marshlands, he might start to suspect someone is feeding me information." She worried for him every moment he was away. "He's not a fool."

"I'll leave the second I think he's starting to suspect me, I promise." Darmanin drew her in for a warm hug before letting go. "And when I'm back, let's talk further about your plans. Maybe it's time to consider me leaving him."

"That's a good idea. I want you here with me for what comes next," she said. "I love you."

"And I you, Arya Stormrider."

Chapter 33

Heavy rain hissed down through the canopy around them, deepening the stark scent of sulphur on the night air. Amidst the rain came the crash of steel, the cries of battle. Arya stood at the top of a rise amongst the trees, watching as the fighting unfolded below. Her battalion were lined up in the darkness behind her, and she could sense their anticipation and impatience at being forced to wait.

Darmanin had informed them of the planned sequence of Nightblade offensives against the marshfolk, hitting them at three different points just inside their northern border. Less than a half day's ride further south was the marshfolk city of Vespir, controlled by the Inraki and one of marshfolk's biggest strongholds. Arya had pushed the battalion hard to travel the distance.

They'd arrived in time. Just.

A flyover by Elendryl had shown that the Nightblades had overwhelmed the marshfolk defensive position, and the surviving warriors had fallen back in full retreat, the invading force hot on their heels. Arya's battalion had arrived at a village where the marshfolk were making another stand, fighting desperately—if they lost here, the Nightblade force would have a straight shot through to Vespir. To the east, a small group of warriors were shepherding the children and non-fighters away to safety, but a unit of Nightblades was already circling to cut them off. Arya made sure she'd gotten a full grasp of the unfolding battle before snapping over her shoulder. "Carador. Esdee."

"Lord Stormrider?" Both commanders materialised at her side.

"You'll lead your shields down in support of the marshfolk; Carador, you take point to make sure your fellow marshfolk don't turn on us. Esdee, you and your shields will back him up."

Carador blinked, as if surprised, but gave a sharp nod. Esdee did the same.

"Good. Herel?"

The horselord commander's long hair and beard were soaked from the rain, making him a fearsome sight. "Aye?"

"Your shields will ensure the children and non-fighters make it out safely; help keep them safe until the battle is over and they can return. If the battle goes badly, make sure they get to Vespir." Arya's gaze sought out each of them. "A single one of your warriors does something they're not supposed to, and I'll hang you for it. *Lead* them. Am I clear? Elendryl and I can bring support if needed, but it should *not* be needed here." Three hundred fresh fighters should easily force the Nightblades back.

Esdee glanced at the other two. "We'll do as you order and no more."

"Good. Go!"

Arya's battalion streamed out of the trees, the horselords uttering blood-curdling war cries that made Arya's eyebrows shoot upwards and Elendryl send her a little shiver of appreciation. He soared the skies high above, ready to intervene if needed, but watchful in case Xaphistryl appeared.

For the first few moments, confusion reigned as Arya's force joined the hard-pressed marshfolk warriors. Her hand moved to her sword, ready to join in if they needed help. But Carador had formed up his shields with his marshfolk in the lead, and with a series of quick exchanges they assured the marshfolk they were there to help. He and Esdee spoke briefly, and they began snapping orders, deploying their warriors to fill the gaps the Nightblades had forced in the marshfolk defensive lines.

A glance to the east showed Herel's shields reaching the non-combatants and surrounding them, two detaching to attack the Nightblades attempting to cut them off. Herel was easily visible as he roared orders and swung his blade like a cleaver. Within minutes the group of non-combatants was moving deeper into the marshes, surrounded by three of Herel's shields.

Arya *hated* standing and watching while her battalion fought, but they needed to do this without her. And she needed to assess them.

Men and women fought bitterly in the mud and rain, blood soaking into the rivulets of water running like streams through the village. Carador and Esdee let the local marshfolk take the lead, sticking to directing their fighters in a support capacity. And even though they were fighting in the Marshlands, Arya's riverfolk and horselords fought just as hard as the marshfolk.

And then it was over.

While the horselords whooped and shouted their triumph to the sky, the marshfolk methodically went to every Nightblade fallen and stabbed them through the heart with their spears. The riverfolk watched both with distaste.

"Carador!" Arya bellowed. "Take a shield to scout the area, make sure there are no more Nightblades on the way. Esdee, your unit will secure the village. When Herel returns, we'll move out."

"And who the hell are you?" A big marshfolk warrior came striding up the rise towards her, bloodied spear in hand.

"Lord Arya Stormrider," she said. "Are you the chief?"

"Chief Raminaal Ebor. You're the one who stole Carador from me."

"Borrowed." She smiled. "Can we offer any more assistance before we leave, Chief?"

The man spat. "You've got our warriors fighting with riverfolk and horselords. It's a disgrace. An offence to our honour."

"Indeed. Riverfolk and horselords who just helped save your village and stopped the Nightblade advance."

"They will turn on us at a whim. They cannot be trusted to have our backs, which means they, *you*, are a liability."

She fought to keep her tone calm. "I'm here to prove to you that we *can* be trusted, Chief."

Raminaal grunted. "You are trespassing on our territory. Don't let it happen again."

He turned and stalked back down the rise, calling for his warriors. Arya gathered that meant he needed no further assistance. Slowly, the village was secured, and both Herel and Carador's shields returned; the first with the non-combatants and the second with assurances there were no further Nightblades in the area.

"Casualties?" she asked her three commanders.

"A few cuts and bruises. No deaths," Carador reported.

"Same here." Esdee and Herel spoke at once, then looked at each other in startlement.

"Well, well, General Desomer has done an excellent job drilling the fundamentals into you all, hasn't he? You fought together and you won, and you didn't lose any comrades. Was it really so bad?"

The three looked at each other, then back to her, the silence drawing out.

"It felt good," Herel said. "Striking a blow against the Nightstalker. As small as it was."

"It felt *excellent,*" Esdee said wolfishly.

"I thank you both." Carador's words were stiff and reluctant. "For fighting to help marshfolk tonight."

Herel grunted, looked away.

"You are welcome, Carador." Esdee reached out, settled a hand on his shoulder. "It was an honour to fight with you, and I would readily do it again. My shields feel the same way."

Carador stiffened further, but he did give Esdee a terse nod.

Pride in her second flared and Arya had to stifle a smile. *This* was what she needed. Not to have to wage this battle alone.

"I am pleased with how you performed," Arya said. "Make sure to tell your shields that. We'll march to the Marshlands border tonight. I don't want to linger long enough for the Nightstalker to get wind of our presence. There I'll wait for word of whether any further assistance is needed." Hopefully Darmanin would be able to let her know whether they'd stopped the advance entirely, or only blunted it.

The three saluted her sharply and turned to go and gather their shields. They were only a few paces away when Arya felt a shiver run down the back of her spine. Her hand dropped to the hilt of her sword. Another whisper of magic washed over her senses and then Elendryl's voice was sliding through her mind. "*Wrong!*"

"*What?*" Arya sent back instantly, at the same time snapping Esdee's name in a quiet hiss.

Elendryl sent her an image of Alletryl swooping over the walls of the Storm Spire. In the next heartbeat, she felt a tug on her bonds with Essa and Chiarn, both urgent. She sent a wave of magic back, telling them she acknowledged the urgency and was on her way. It was something she'd learned in their lessons with Remien. Both sent a clear acknowledgement, along with a '*hurry*'.

Esdee turned instantly, reading the look on her face. "What is it?"

"Something is happening back at the Storm Spire. I have to go."

"What do you want me to do?" Esdee was cool and calm, and it settled Arya.

Elendryl swooped down from the sky, glimmering a faint gold despite the darkness. His taloned wings and waving tail tore the stunted Marshland trees to shreds as he made himself space to land in the mud.

"Take command of the battalion, get them back to the Storm Spire as quickly as you possibly can. They might be needed."

"Yes, my Lord." Concern etched Esdee's face. "Be safe."

But Arya was already running, scrambling onto Elendryl's back as he spread his wings to lift back into the sky.

***

Arya circled the Storm Spire several hours later, just after dawn broke on the horizon, having used her magic to speed Elendryl's flight. Her eyes and her magic told her nothing was amiss, but that Chiarn was the only Sky Lord present. Her *cairdre* bonds told her Essa, Darmanin, and Leanir were well, but far distant, and in different directions.

Elendryl landed on the roof of the central tower, Arya dismounting before he'd fully settled. Alerted by her tug on the bond, Chiarn was climbing the steps of the tower at a run, and emerged onto the roof, breathless.

"I'm glad you're here," Chiarn panted. "I wasn't sure how long it would take you to fly back from—"

"What's going on?" Arya cut him off. "Where is Essa? Is she all right?"

Chiarn's expression was tight. "She went to Khadini."

"What? Why?"

"Leanir flew in last night; he'd received word from his spies in Ripley that three boats of refugees from Khadini arrived two days ago. It seems the Khadini emperor has launched an all-out attack on the Khadini rebels."

"Taskari?" Arya asked, fear clutching at her heart.

Chiarn nodded. "That's why Leanir brought the news himself. Taskari is the worst hit, according to the reports he's received, but he wanted me to say he hasn't heard anything about Kulan specifically."

Fear crashed through Arya so powerfully that she swayed on her feet.

Her son.

Chiarn reached out a worried hand to help steady her. "I don't understand. Essa had the same reaction, though she waited until Leanir left to completely panic. And then she just flew off with Alletryl. I know Kulan is your friend and there are riverfolk on Taskari, but—"

Arya took a deep, steadying breath. "Taskari is where Kirin is."

"Kirin..." Chiarn trailed off, eyes turning to flame as the import of that revelation hit him. "Kulan is his father."

A sharp nod. "Chiarn, go and tell Sefani she's in charge of the Conclave until Essa and I return."

"What about me? I should come with you. Your *cairdre* should—"

"I need your help elsewhere." She settled a hand on his shoulder. "Kulan's first thought would have been to get Kirin to safety, *if* there was time. I need you and Asandryl in Ripley, finding those refugees before the Nightblades do, and getting them here safely. Chiarn, I know that risks exposing you to him, but—"

"I'll do it. Of course I will. If Kirin is with them, I'll protect him with my life, Arya." Chiarn swore. A wyvern's cry sounded in the distance as Asandryl roused from his nest.

"Thank you." She thought for a second. "Find my battalion on the way. Tell Esdee to march towards Ripley and rendezvous with you once you have the refugees out safely. Tell her why, but only her. Once the refugees are safe with the battalion, take Asandryl and scout the south coast for any more refugee boats."

"Done. I'll fetch my armour and fly at once." He sprinted for the stairs. Across the Storm Spire, Asandryl let out another cry. Elendryl lifted his head and echoed the cry.

Arya followed him, sprinting down the single flight to her quarters. She already wore her chainmail and gauntlets, but from the chest at the foot of her bed she retrieved her old Raider bow and a quiver full of arrows. Then, she pulled out two long daggers and strapped them to her calves. The weapons were a welcome weight as she marched back to the roof.

She was going to rain hell down on any who thought to threaten her son.

Chapter 34

Flying almost non-stop, Arya and Elendryl soared across the short patch of ocean between the Riverlands and Khadini three days later. The turquoise bay on the eastern side of Taskari looked empty without the fishing boats bobbing on its surface. As they came closer, Arya's sharp vision picked out tendrils of smoke curling from several places along the peninsula's cliff face. Terror at the evidence of an attack clenched at her chest so hard it physically hurt, and for a long moment she couldn't suck any air in. Was Kirin okay? Was Kulan and his family? She didn't know what she'd do if—

"Nightblades." Elendryl sent, turning Arya's attention to the figures patrolling the grassy top of the peninsula. His mental voice was tinged with weariness—even with her magic, the effort it had taken for her wyvern to travel so quickly was enormous.

"Take me in closer so we can get a better look, but fast enough they won't have time to loose any arrows at us."

Her Valheran dived out of the sky, Arya balancing gracefully on his back. Several Nightblades were guarding the clifftop entrance to the peninsular city, presumably controlling who went in or out. Beyond them, where the peninsula met the jungle of mainland Khadini, a neatly ordered camp sat. In the glimpse she got as Elendryl soared over them, she estimated several hundred Khadini Rangers and a much smaller number of Nightblades. Those who glimpsed the wyvern in the sky shouted and reached for bows, but Elendryl was gone before they could draw arrows.

"The Nightstalker's alliance with Emperor uq-Danresan is alive and well, I see." Was the Nightstalker's limited alliance with Khadini expanding? If so,

she was in trouble. *"They've cut off all land access to Taskari,"* she noted as Elendryl took them back up high into the sky, out of the range of arrows.

"Alletryl!" He sent sharply.

Arya scanned the sky, settling on a faint dot in the distance that quickly resolved into Essa's green wyvern. A series of images from Elendryl explained that Essa had gone into Taskari. She was well, and Arya's bond to the Sky Lord confirmed it, but Alletryl struggled to convey more than that to Elendryl.

Arya reached out to let Essa know she'd arrived, and felt ripples of tension through the bond, followed by a pulse of relief that Arya had arrived. *Hurry* Essa seemed to say, and then *not long*. Whatever that meant. While their ability to share and communicate through their bonds had improved under Remien's tutoring, only Leanir could connect them with the ability to have a conversation.

Coming, Arya sent back, then didn't hesitate any longer. If Kirin wasn't down there, if Kulan had had time to get him away by boat with the other refugees, then she'd have to hope Chiarn reached them in time to keep them safe. But if Kirin was still here ... he was in extreme danger. And Essa too.

It no longer mattered that she was close to exhaustion after the heady flight here, or that her magic reserves were low and Elendryl needed rest. Arya took a deep breath as he banked sharply and launched into a dive towards the Taskari clifftop. She focused herself, gathering what was left of her magic.

And then she let it loose.

The soldiers on the ground were completely unprepared for the bolt of lightning that came out of a clear sky and exploded in their midst, destroying those guarding the ladder entrance into the city. Nightblades scrambled away, crying out in fear. A few arrows clattered uselessly off Elendryl's scales, but none stopped Arya as she let loose multiple bolts of lightning energy. She bombarded the soldiers in the vicinity until all that was left was a mist of blood and gore.

In perfect rhythm, Elendryl banked, swooping down towards the jetties and the sea entrance to Taskari. In his place came Alletryl, letting out her wyvern's cry as she dropped out of the sky towards the Ranger camp, teeth bared. Her cry ripped several tents from their moorings.

Elendryl landed, sending the jetty rocking, and Arya scrambled down. *"Go, help Alletryl. Take out every soldier up there. I want to make sure no reinforcements are sent down into Taskari. And then hunt and rest, Elendryl. Same for Alletryl. We may need to flee quickly."*

"Destroy." He assured her with a bloodthirsty growl, then leaped back into the air. Arya watched him go with satisfaction.

Let the famed Khadini Rangers see how they fared against two angry wyverns.

Ahead of her lay the sandy cavern entrance to Taskari. It looked deserted, nothing moving inside. The hilt of her cazaix sword was smooth and cool in her hand as she drew it slowly from its sheath and started running.

She heard nothing but the sound of the ocean crashing against the rock of the peninsula and the occasional call of a gull flying overhead, mixed with the distant screams of those in the Ranger camp. Once she stepped into the dim light of the cavern, the roar of the ocean faded, and she was met with an uncharacteristic silence. The few times Arya had been here before, the space had been busy with folk moving through, most of them to or from the fishing boats from which the Khadini and the Andahari community made their living.

Urgency tugged at her, and when nothing greeted her at the entrance to the cavern, she moved forward more swiftly. The first arrow came hissing through the air when she was halfway across the open space, with no shelter close by. Swearing, Arya raised her hand and sent a bolt of blue magic flying in the direction the arrow had come from, a rocky outcropping at the edge of the cavern. The burst was weak, using the last dregs of her remaining magic, but enough to cover her as she pushed into a sprint towards the outcropping. More arrows flew at her. One glanced off the chainmail on her shoulder, but otherwise she reached the outcrop unharmed. Leaping high into the air, she landed on the top of the rocks, her cazaix blade sweeping the head off the nearest archer before she jumped down and flew at the remining two. Seconds later they were dead on the ground and Arya's sword dripped blood. All three had been Nightblades.

Bootsteps sounded, approaching quickly, and Arya dropped the sword, reaching up to unsling her bow and knock an arrow. She fired as the first Ranger appeared around the corner, hitting him clean in the throat before killing the two behind him. Arya paused a long moment after they'd fallen to the ground, listening carefully, but all was quiet.

She picked up her sword and cleaned it on one of the dead Nightblade's uniforms before rising to her feet and sheathing it. Then, bow hanging loosely from her left hand, she ran. It would be hours before her magic reserves returned, longer if she didn't eat or rest, so from here on out she had physical weapons only.

Taskari was a sprawling community with hundreds of tunnels, pathways, bridges and homes all tangling together like a rabbit warren along a cliff face at least a mile long. Arya could sense Essa's presence pulsing through their bond, but had no idea if she was anywhere near Kulan or Kirin, and even if she did, Arya wasn't familiar enough with Taskari to be able to navigate her way to a specific location. Her best chance was to head in the general direction of Essa's presence until she found the Inkweaver.

As Arya emerged onto one of the open cliff face pathways, her sharp hearing caught the ring of clashing steel on the salty breeze. Glancing up, she saw a small group of Khadini fighters halfway across a swinging rope bridge—they were being pressed hard by a larger group of Nightblades. Two of the Khadini carried a box between them, the strain on their faces indicating it was heavy. Three others tried desperately to hold the Nightblades back so those with the box could get away. To Arya's trained eye, it was a losing battle—they weren't going to make it.

It took her several seconds to survey the cliff between where she stood and the swaying bridge at least three stories above, calculating a path. Then, Arya slung the bow over her shoulder and began climbing. The incline wasn't overly steep and there were plenty of footholds in the craggy rock, so she made quick time.

Halfway up, one of the Nightblades caught sight of her and shouted the alarm. Two broke off the fight and lifted bows. Arya ducked as an arrow whistled close to her head. Swearing, she pushed herself even harder, ignoring the burn in her muscles and the heavy weight of her armour and weapons. Two arrows scraped off her mail before she reached the rock just below the bridge. Bracing herself against the hard surface, she pushed hard from her legs and leaped upwards, her hands just managing to catch the rope of the bridge. Using her momentum, she swung herself over and landed on the wooden planks between the Khadini and the Nightblades, sending the whole thing rocking.

Her sword was out before she'd even landed, and with her superior balance Arya attacked while the bridge was still swinging, blue metal gleaming as she engaged the first Nightblade. He was good, but too slow for her, and she got under his guard and sliced her blade along his throat. Blood sprayed, but she ignored it as she pushed forward to attack the second. By then, she'd pushed them back off the end of the bridge.

Turning to the rebels behind her, she bellowed. "Get clear! Quickly!"

Obeying the iron thread of command in her voice, they scrambled backwards. As soon as they were off the bridge, Arya lashed out with her sword, slicing through the ropes holding the bridge to the opposite end. She left one rope in place, then turned and began sprinting towards the Khadini. Her weight was too much for the remaining rope and it frayed through rapidly, snapping just as she was almost on the other side. Arya leaped forwards, diving into the tunnel beyond as the bridge fell away completely, leaving the Nightblades trapped on the other side.

She panted, skin lathered in sweat. Arya forced herself back to her feet with an effort and found the Khadini watching her with stunned awe.

"Who are you?" one of them asked. He seemed the most competent of the group, sword held correctly in his hand, ready to fight.

"Arya Stormrider, Sky Lord of Andahar," she said between panting breaths. "I'm a friend of Dostari Kulan. Is he here?"

"He is, but we're sorely pressed. My name is Rashwan." The rebel lowered his sword and stepped forward, gestured to the box two of his companions carried. "We ventured out to get medical supplies to treat our wounded, but the Nightblades caught us as we were leaving. You saved our lives, and those who need those supplies. Thank you."

"You're welcome." She was still breathing hard, legs wobbly under her. "Ventured out from where?"

"Dostari Kulan holds a section of the city deep inside the cliff. There are others too, we think, but we lost contact with anyone else here several days ago." Rashwan looked grim. "We're effectively trapped."

"Have you seen another Sky Lord here?"

"Yes, my Lord. It was her idea to come and fetch the supplies."

Arya's shoulders almost sagged in relief at the news that Essa was alive and well, *and* with Kulan. Some of her strength returned and she gave them a crisp nod. "All right, take me there. I'll follow and protect your back."

They moved quickly—too quickly for Arya's fading strength—through the narrowest tunnels and pathways in the cliff city. Rashwan explained they were taking a longer route through isolated areas which the invading soldiers were unlikely to have discovered yet. She was almost at the point of having to ask to stop for a brief rest by the time they headed down a narrow tunnel that ended in a solid oak door.

Rashwan rapped out a code on the door, and it quickly swung open. An armed woman waved them through, and closed it behind them, settling a thick bar into brackets in the doorframe. A long set of steps led downwards, and impatient now, Arya sidestepped the rebels and headed down at a jog.

She emerged into a low-ceilinged but massive cavern that was crowded with people. To her left, rows of pallets were filled with wounded while others sat or slept in the free space. Arya's gaze was immediately drawn to Essa's short figure standing in the middle of the room speaking with Kulan.

Essa was already turning, picking up Arya's presence. She came straight over, gaze narrowing at the sight of the drying blood splattered on her mail. She had dark shadows of exhaustion under her eyes, no doubt a mirror of Arya's. "You're not hurt?"

"Not my blood," she replied. "You?"

"Same." She touched Arya's arm in reassurance.

Kulan, who had dark circles under his eyes and was clenching his jaw as if in pain, came over, giving her a weary smile of welcome. Rough bandaging seeped blood on his left side. "Essa told me you'd come."

Arya swallowed, forced herself to say the words. "Kulan, you must know why I'm here."

His expression turned sombre and fear-filled. "Arya, I'm sorry, I don't know where Kirin is. I sent him with my mother and Kader to join those escaping by boat while my warriors and I stayed to hold off the Rangers and give them time to get clear, but I don't know if they reached the boats safely or not. We were cut off, then pushed down here."

"I'm sorry I didn't get here in time, Arya." Essa's eyes were wide with guilt.

"This is not either of your faults." Arya expelled a breath, once again mastering her fear. "If Kirin did escape with the boats, then Chiarn will be with them shortly, and he'll be fine."

Kulan's shoulders sagged. "Thank you."

"You know I'll protect him with everything I have." Arya looked at her friend, not knowing what to say to the man whose entire home had been destroyed. "I'm so sorry."

"The raid was completely unexpected; we didn't have time to prepare. I have to assume they hit all the other rebel units across the country too." Grief darkened his eyes.

"And they've got Nightblade help," she added.

Kulan's shoulders sagged. "My brother's new alliance is working out well for him."

Arya felt a hand settle briefly on her back. Essa, silently giving her support. She leaned into the touch, thanking her, then turned her mind to more practical matters. "If Kirin is still here, then it's imperative we find him, *and* your brother and mother. What's the situation?"

"Bad and getting worse. I had a hundred fighters with me to start with, but now we're down to forty, and half that number are wounded. There were other pockets of fighters elsewhere in the city who stayed to help the non-combatants get free, but we lost contact with them days ago, and I don't know if they're even still alive."

"You can't remain down here," Arya said, gaze scanning their surrounds. "There's no exit, and you're basically just waiting to be killed once the Rangers find you."

"I know that, but we've nowhere to run *to*." Kulan's eyes were frantic, hands clenching and unclenching at his sides. He winced at the movement, fingers drifting to his bloody side.

"I've been trying to think of a way out, Arya, but I don't know Taskari well enough to help." Essa sounded frustrated. "I could draw us a tunnel out, but Alletryl has shown me that the clifftop is full of Rangers and Nightblades."

Arya turned to her. "Not anymore, so we *can* get out that way, at least until Ranger reinforcements arrive."

Essa straightened, swinging to Kulan, "If you could get your people into the jungle, would you—"

"We'd easily be able to evade the Rangers in the jungle, it's our home ground," he cut in, light returning to his eyes. "I have to assume many of our safe houses have been breached, but the emperor can't know about all of them, especially not in the remote jungle region here in the north."

"We'd need to find and gather any remaining fighters first," Arya said. "Then fight our way out. I like your tunnel idea, Ess, but it would require an enormous amount of magic, and I'm not sure you've got that left in you." Arya could sense through the bond that Essa's levels were as low as hers, having drained her magic helping Alletryl fly quickly to Taskari.

For Arya and her son. Arya's heart clenched, and she sent a shiver of *thank you* through their bond.

"You're right, I'd need a full day's rest and more food than is available here." Essa thought that over. "But I still have enough magic left that the two of us together might be able to fight a path through to the top."

"Might?" Arya raised an eyebrow at her Inkweaver.

A smile glimmered in Essa's eyes. "How silly of me. Those Rangers and Nightblades are already dead. But we'd have to move soon. We don't know how quickly the emperor will send reinforcements to the clifftop."

"First we make sure Kirin got away," Arya said. "But then that's what we'll do. Kulan, we'll need you to plot us the easiest route to the clifftop noting we'll be taking injured with us, as well as identify all the potential locations where your people might be holed up so we can gather them before we go."

"I can do that." He glanced between them in burgeoning hope. "If you can pull this off, I'll owe you everything."

"You'll owe us nothing," Essa said. "Arya is right. You are family, and we look after our own."

Arya turned to Essa as Kulan moved off. "I worry about the timing of this."

Essa knew exactly what she meant. "You think the attack has something to do with Kirin?"

"A nazal has been hunting him for months. What if he figured out that Kirin is with the Khadini rebels—it's not a secret I spent time here after running the Dreadwater Gate? The Nightstalker doesn't exactly have Nightblades to spare to help the emperor deal with an internal Khadini issue, he'd only be helping him destroy the rebels for a good reason."

"Whatever the truth of it, right now the only thing we have to worry about is ensuring Kirin is safe and getting Kulan and his warriors out of here."

***

It took over an hour for Arya, Essa, and Kulan to hammer out a strategy for getting everyone safely up to the clifftop, including bringing enough supplies to survive for a few days in the jungle, not to mention care for the injured. They would split into three groups with an equal mix of warriors and injured, taking three different routes to the clifftop that would search for survivors along the way: led by Arya, Essa, and Kulan respectively.

While Kulan started briefing those in the cavern about what was going to happen, Arya and Essa worked through a loaf of stale bread and cheese between them, then started on a parcel of dried fish. With every bite, Arya felt some of her magic return. While she wouldn't be capable of riding a storm without proper rest, she would have enough to fight their way out of here.

Kulan was only halfway through his briefing when the door at the top of the stairs opened, and two rebel warriors came stumbling down the steps. One had his arm wrapped around the waist of the other, who was sheet white and bleeding from a nasty sword wound in his side.

"Tanifa!" Both Kulan and Arya spoke at the same time.

More warriors rushed to help, but Tanifa waved them off, glazed eyes clearing when she saw Kulan, then recognised Arya. "Dostari ... Kirin. He's..."

"Steady." Kulan moved to help her stand, only the tremor in his hands betraying his reaction to the mention of his son. "Take your time. What do you need to tell us?"

"Kulan ... Yarmana ... both here." Tanifa managed, eyes flicking closed as she concentrated her fading energy on conveying her message. "Stumbled across them, got hurt holding Nightblades off so they could flee."

"They're supposed to be on the boats!" Kulan said, horror rippling across his face.

Tanifa shook her head. "Still here. Don't know why."

Arya stared at her. Kirin was *here?* The fear that rose made her mind utterly blank and stopped her breathing. It took her a moment to get enough of a handle on it to snap at Tanifa, "How long ago did you see them? And where?"

"A half hour, no more. Down near the jetties."

"Get her to the healers." Kulan snapped, then turned to Arya, who was still reeling, trying to fight through panic for a clear mind. "I'll go now to get them, and—"

"No. Trust me, I feel the same urge, but there's a better way." Essa interrupted "The plan is ready, let's just follow it. We were splitting up to search for others hiding before meeting up in the seventh level to make our push for the top, right?"

Her calm reciting of the plan served to take the edge off Arya's panic, and she nodded, though sweat beaded on her forehead and her heart was still racing too fast. "Right."

"So we'll tweak things slightly so that all three of us go with one group, and we'll take the route sweeping through the tunnels near the jetties to find Kirin and Yarmana. If we don't find them, we'll keep to the plan, help everyone break out and get to safety in the jungle, then you and I will come back to look for them. All right, Arya?" Essa's gaze held hers, steadying her.

Arya took a breath. "Good plan. Kulan?"

He swallowed, rubbed a hand over his face; he seemed as terrified as Arya felt. "Okay. I'll brief the cavern now. We can't afford to wait any longer."

Kulan strode off, voice calling for everyone to listen. He'd just finished laying out the details, and was dividing everyone into groups and assigning them a route when a sharp pain spiked through Arya's head at the same time as her bond with Leanir pulsed. At her side, Essa gasped and lifted a hand to her temples.

And then, just like when the Etherean elder had dream-walked her in the past, Arya blinked and found herself standing next to Essa and Chiarn in some *other* place. Leanir was there too, expression grim, strain around his eyes. While Arya could see them all clearly, their forms blurred around the edges, and their surroundings looked like grey mist without any further detail. They'd tried this in practice before and failed because Leanir had been unwilling to open himself up to all of them. If he was doing it now...

"*What's wrong?*" Arya asked, her barely-controlled panic flooding back to the surface.

"*The Etherean citadel is under attack.*" Leanir's mental voice was clear but strained.

Shock reverberated through her. "*How do you know?*"

"*I was dream-walking Elder Salyarin, a regular exchange as you requested. We were mid-conversation just now when the attack started.*"

Shit. Arya swallowed, her mind again blanking. So much disaster all at once, how could she—

"*What could he tell you about the attacking force?*" Essa cut in, giving Arya a moment to steady herself. Panic wasn't helping, even though it felt as if everything was suddenly spinning out of her control, and that it would all end in disaster.

"*His commander reported hundreds of Nightblades coming up through the bowels of the citadel, led by more than one nazal.*" Leanir reported. "*Then he dropped out abruptly and I haven't been able to reestablish contact. I can't hold this much longer.*"

"*No shadowhounds, wraiths, or firedrakes?*" she asked.

"*Not that he said.*"

Her tired thoughts processed that. It was good news for the Etherean defenders, but she wondered at it. Maybe, if her theory about the nazal controlling the creatures was correct, it was *that* nazal currently away searching for Kirin.

"*We have to go and help!*" Chiarn exclaimed. His stridency snapped her from her sinking thoughts.

The images of them all shivered, held, and Leanir sounded again. "*Arya, there's more, the High Warlord is there at the citadel. I saw him with the elder.*"

"*Rorin is there? Why?*" Essa sounded as panicked as Arya felt.

"*I didn't waste time asking.*" Again, the images of them all blurred before clearing. "*I can't hold this. If you have instructions, give them now.*"

Arya swore loudly. "*I can't go to the citadel.*"

"*Why not?*" Leanir snapped. "*I assume you're at Taskari, but using magic, you could be there in a few hours.*"

"*We can't leave Taskari, it's under attack.*" Essa hesitated, glanced at Arya.

She took a breath, but there was no need to hide from her *cairdre*. "*My son is here. I can't leave until I make sure he's safe.*"

"*Your what?*" Leanir looked utterly floored, an expression Arya would have enjoyed if not for the dire situation.

"*I'll go. Arya, the Etherean are our allies. We're sworn to aid them.*" Chiarn said. "*I found the refugees as you asked. They're safe, moving north for the Storm Spire, and your battalion has almost reached them.*"

"You can't go, Chiarn. You can't either, Leanir." She hated every word she spoke. *"With more than one nazal leading the attack..."* They'd need their full *caidre* to meet that threat.

"You may have noticed I wasn't volunteering," Leanir snarled, but it was half-hearted, and he was staring at her as if he'd never seen her before.

She swallowed. *"Will you at least tell Dar what's happening? He should know—the Nightstalker may not have told him about the attack."*

"If you want me to be able to reach him, I need to cut this off now, before I'm drained completely. I can't bring him into the group, our connection isn't strong enough for that."

Essa spoke quickly. *"As soon as Kirin is safe, we'll come to the citadel. Chiarn, if you start flying that way, we'll meet you there."*

Arya nodded, *"But wait for us before you do anything. Leanir, please do what you can to warn Darmanin."*

More pain stabbed through Arya's head and the dream vision vanished, dropping her back in the cavern in Taskari. She found Kulan standing in front of her and Essa, looking panicked. "What's *wrong?*" he demanded.

"We have to hurry," Arya whispered. Her terror for Kirin wasn't enough to eclipse her new fear, for Rorin, for Salyarin.

"Arya..." Essa was white-faced. "We haven't rested or eaten enough. We'll need the rest of our magic reserves to fight our way out of here, we won't be able—"

Arya laid a hand on her arm. "One step at a time."

"This is deliberate, isn't it?" Essa asked.

It had to be. The Nightstalker was taking out her allies, and doing it in one fell swoop, limiting her ability to help.

Arya was in trouble.

Chapter 35

Despite being weary and injured, Kulan's people moved with a new purpose now they had a solid plan ... and hope. The injured who couldn't walk were made as comfortable as possible on stretchers. Those that could gritted their teeth and promised to keep up.

Kulan reiterated the plan for a final time as everyone gathered. "Any more questions before we leave?"

His warriors shook their heads or muttered a negative; to Arya's eyes they looked focused. That was good. The worry for Kirin that gnawed at her was all-encompassing, and she shifted impatiently, needing to move.

"Good luck, all of you." Kulan managed a confident smile for them. "Now go."

***

Sometime later, Arya, Essa, Kulan and their group moved along a dim tunnel. They'd made steady progress along their route, sweeping through a convoluted series of tunnels and walkways in the levels near the jetties. They hadn't found any rebels hiding.

Pale light seeped through small holes in the rock, the full moon outside offering little against the pressing darkness. Occasionally, distant echoes of battle reached them, faint and fleeting, but mostly silence wrapped them like a heavy cloak. Kulan's injured warriors made a valiant effort to remain quiet despite the pain they had to be in from the movement of the stretchers.

The hush settled, lulling them into uneasy stillness. Then—shouting erupted ahead, sudden and sharp. Everyone flinched.

Arya raised a hand for the column to halt, then placed a finger at her lips for quiet. Once they'd followed her instruction, she pointed at Essa and Kulan before gesturing forward, leaving the warriors behind to protect the wounded. She led them along the dark tunnel towards the sounds, and as they approached, Arya heard metal rasping, and then a grunt of pain. Her sharp eyes strained to pierce the dimness ahead. Then, a moment later, a child's furious scream echoed through the night.

Arya ran before the sound faded from hearing, barely noticing Essa and Kulan keeping pace behind her. Ahead the light improved where a section of the tunnel wall was open to the sky and bright moonlight poured in. Two lit torches lay discarded on the ground, casting more light on the wide circular area that served as a junction of several pathways and tunnels.

Arya's initial sweep of the area marked a woman slumped against the tunnel wall to her right, her hand pressed against a bleeding wound on her upper chest. A Ranger lay dead on the ground near her, a massive pool of blood under his left leg, where it looked like a blade had stabbed through his femoral artery. Several Taskari residents clustered a short distance off, some whimpering with fear, one sobbing. The rebel warriors that had been with them were dead, scattered across the sandy floor.

But Arya's attention went straight to the boy standing between the injured woman and a second Ranger, holding a long knife out in front of him, unwavering. The Ranger had his sword drawn, his stance shifting forward as he lifted the weapon to lunge at the boy, who looked tiny in comparison. But even with a Ranger bearing down on him, the boy stood steady, teeth bared in a snarl of challenge.

Arya raised her bow and fired without thought. The arrow caught the Ranger in the throat, and he died instantly, falling backward and hitting the ground hard, sword dropping from lifeless fingers. The boy swung towards her, a snarl ripping from him, his knife pointed at the new threat.

"Kirin!"

Arya startled at the sound of Kulan's voice. The rebel leader pushed past her, but Essa moved more quickly, grabbing his arm and halting him mid-stride.

"What are you doing?" Kulan demanded "Let me go!"

Essa spoke calmly. "Kulan, look at him. He's enraged; he'll go at anything that comes near him. Remember what he is."

"I'll go," Arya said, gaze still firmly on her son.

Kulan glanced between them. "That's my mother over there bleeding. Hurry, please."

Arya's focus had been so firmly on Kirin she hadn't realised that the injured woman was Yarmana. Kirin's grandmother. No wonder he'd gone for the Rangers.

Arya slowly put down her bow before walking forward. Kirin watched her come, indigo eyes alight with fury. He held the knife steady. Arya halted a few paces away and kneeled. Then she lifted her open hands, showing him, she was unarmed. "I'm not going to hurt you, Kirin."

"They hurt grandmamma," he shouted, rage-filled words. "I'll kill them all."

"They're both dead, Kirin," Arya said. "You already protected her."

His grip on the knife didn't waver. Fury burned from him like a live flame.

Arya held his gaze. "I know exactly how you're feeling. I know how the anger is burning inside you, making you want to yell and scream and attack anything that moves," she spoke, watching his face as her words sunk in. "You have to let the anger go, Kirin. It helped you protect your grandmamma, but now you have to let it go."

He swallowed. "How?"

Arya shifted closer. "It takes practice. Start with some deep breaths. Slow down your heart, I know it must be racing right now."

"How do you know?" he asked as her words sank in.

"Because I've felt the anger too," she said. "I feel it all the time."

He shuddered, his grip on the knife clenching and then loosening. "How do you get rid of it?"

"Deep breaths, Kirin. That's all. Just take some nice, slow breaths. It gets easier with practice, I promise you."

Arya reached out, taking gentle hold of his arm until he let go of the knife. It clattered to the ground, and he immediately began shaking, the fire in his eyes subsiding as fear and exhaustion took over. "It's all right, Kirin," she murmured, drawing him into her arms. "You did well."

He clung to her, his small hands digging into her collar, his body trembling against hers. Her son. She held him fiercely, heart in her throat. Footsteps sounded and Kulan appeared, looking down at the fallen Ranger full of holes. "He did that?"

"He's a Stormrider," Essa answered from where she kneeled by Yarmana. "Arya, we should get moving. I think she'll be okay as long as we get her to a healer soon. But any Rangers or Nightblades nearby could have heard the fighting and be on their way."

Arya gently pulled away from her son and stood up. "Kirin, your papa is here."

Kirin looked up, eyes shining as he caught sight of Kulan. "Papa!"

Kulan leaned down and picked up his son, hugging him tightly to his chest. "What are you doing here, Kirin? I sent you with grandmamma and Uncle Kader to the boats."

"I couldn't let you stay behind unprotected," the boy replied. "I slipped away from the boats as soon as I could, but grandmamma saw me and followed. By the time she dragged me back, all the boats had gone. So we came looking for you. We've been running and hiding ever since."

"Ravens' help us all, he's just like his mother," Essa said as she came to her feet, ushering over two warriors to help lift Yarmana to a spare stretcher. Arya blinked, the words startling her. But after what she'd just witnessed ... a shiver went through her. Essa was right. But it made her uneasy.

Kirin frowned at Essa. "Who are you? What does she mean, Papa?"

"A story for another day, Kirin." Kulan put the boy down. "Can you walk? We need to hurry now."

"Of course I can." He straightened his weary shoulders and looked determinedly at his father. "I can go as long as you need."

Kulan smiled and touched the boy's cheek.

"Take the lead, Kulan," Arya told him. "I'll watch Kirin."

As they left, Arya felt her gaze drawn to the fallen Ranger with multiple holes in his chest. Her four-year-old son had taken down a trained warrior.

She didn't know whether to be proud or horrified.

***

They made it to the rendezvous without further incident, for which Arya was grateful. She could tell from the look on Essa's face that Yarmana wasn't doing well, and Kirin was stumbling from exhaustion, only managing to keep going out of sheer pride and stubbornness.

With the knowledge of what was happening at the Etherean citadel in the back of their minds, Arya and Essa didn't hesitate once they reached the meeting point. Kulan's group had taken the longest to get there, so the others were all waiting, doing their best to stay quiet and still. Arya left Kulan to organise them while she and Essa marched forward, magic ready.

And they were ruthless.

Nightblades and Rangers came at them, only to be pulverised by the blunt force of Sky Lord magic, blue or emerald energy bursts tearing them to shreds before they could draw steel or loose their bows.

Arya's energy drained, bit by bit, but still she and Essa pushed forward, the Inkweaver's face set in grim resignation—Arya's heart breaking for the part of her friend that would be hurting at this wanton violence and destruction—as she didn't falter for a second, launching magical burst after magical burst.

And then it was done.

The clifftop entrance waited, deserted thanks to the wyverns, and Essa scrambled up to ensure the way was clear while Arya moved to the back of the column of Kulan's people to protect it as they slowly filed up the ladder and out of the city. She chafed at how long it took, especially getting the wounded up, but she couldn't abandon them now. This was their most vulnerable moment.

Arya and Kulan were the last to climb the ladder onto the dark clifftop. As soon as Kulan appeared, two of his warriors materialised out of the darkness. "Dostari. We scouted as you requested. Ranger reinforcements are approaching. The first two of our groups are clear into the jungle, but we stayed to warn you. They're roughly an hour away, coming from the southwest."

Kulan whispered. "Thank you. That's enough time for us to get clear. Now go, get to safety."

"Yes, Dostari."

They vanished into the darkness, and Kulan turned to Arya and Essa. "Is this goodbye?" he asked.

Arya shook her head. "The Etherean are under attack, I have to go and help them. But as soon as that's done, I'll come back. I need to make sure you and Kirin are safe and Yarmana is okay."

Shock flashed over his face. "The Etherean? But ... Damnit it. You're both exhausted. I wish I could help—"

"All you need to do is keep our son safe." Arya hesitated. "The Nightstalker has a nazal hunting him, Kulan. You have to be extraordinarily careful. These attacks may have been an attempt to flush you out."

Even in the dim light, she saw his olive skin turn sheet white.

"I'm so sorry," she whispered. "I'm going to end this, somehow, I swear it. Just keep him safe until then. Please."

"You know I will." He gave her and Essa a quick hug, then slung the pack off his shoulders. "Food rations. Split it between you for the flight to the Etherean. I know you need food to replenish your magic."

Essa protested, "We can't take your supplies—"

"You can. Others have packs and once we're in the jungle we can forage." He pushed the pack on them. "You remember Armani's farmhouse?"

"I do." The place she'd been reunited with Rorin after becoming separated on their Dreadwater run. That felt like so long ago now.

"That's where you'll find us. Good luck, Arya, Essa."

They waved him off, watching until his group all disappeared into the safety of the jungle. Then, they quickly divvied the contents of Kulan's pack between them. By the time they were done, both wyverns were dropping out of the sky. Dawn light was breaking across the horizon, bringing with it a cool breeze off the ocean.

"Ready?" She looked over at Essa.

"Always."

Arya watched the ground drop away as Elendryl spread his magnificent wings and launched into the skies. The two wyverns banked and headed northwest.

For the Diamondfang.

Chapter 36

Elendryl and Alletryl hit dense cloud as they approached the Etherean citadel. Arya couldn't see a thing. *"Can you find the entrance in this fog?"* she asked Elendryl.

A shiver of assent.

And then a pulse from Chiarn. Copper flashed through the mist, and Asandryl swooped down from high above. Relief creased Chiarn's face when he saw them. Arya waved both him and Essa close enough to shout, "Stay close behind so you don't lose me."

"What's the plan?" Chiarn called.

"No time for a plan. We go in hard and fast."

It was an unsettling feeling, dropping blindly through thick fog; Arya could barely see her hand in front of her face let alone anything else nearby, yet she knew both mountains and the citadel were out there, and close. If they flew into a mountainside...

"Here." Elendryl warned her.

"Drop me down then take to the skies around the elder's tower. If anything looks like it's attacking, take it out." Arya readied her magic, her reserves still low despite the food she'd eaten on the way. Proper rest was what she needed now, but that wasn't going to happen anytime soon.

Seconds later the fog cleared to reveal snow-covered rocky mountainside looming, the cavern entrance immediately ahead. Her wyvern landed with a jolt, keeping his wings spread so that as soon as Arya was down, he could launch back into the air.

"Hunt!" he roared into her mind.

Boots sounded as the other wyverns dropped their riders and Essa and Chiarn came running to join her. Just as Arya was about lead them into the citadel, a shiver came through her bond with Leanir, and then Mistryl appeared suddenly from the mist, a silvery ghost, wings spread wide, taloned feet stretched for landing. Arya's eyes widened as two riders scrambled down from her back.

"You came," Arya said as Leanir strode towards them, bow out, arrow held loose in his free hand. "And you brought Tiya."

"Your observational skills are as sharp as always, Stormrider. The healer demanded to come, and I wasn't in the mood to argue. Are we moving or what?"

She hesitated. "Tiya, it's going to be dangerous, I'm not sure—"

"I'll be careful, but I'm not going to hide." Her expressed was set and pale. "These are my people, and they're going to need my healing magic."

"All right. Let's go."

Arya led them at a run for the steps leading up into the citadel. She stopped at the first landing; it was deserted in both directions. Her lungs strained for oxygen. Damned thin air. It wasn't just that. She was exhausted, body and mind, and pushing too hard. But what else could she do?

She looked at her *cairdre*. "We make straight for the elder's quarters, taking out anything that tries to stop us as we go. Leanir, you cover us with your bow. Chiarn, you take the rear in case we're attacked from behind. We'll have to pace ourselves. It won't do the Etherean any good if we can't fight because we've succumbed to altitude sickness. Any questions?"

"You're assuming there's any fighting to be done?" Leanir asked. "It's been two days since the attack started."

"The Etherean have warriors, and they know their home ground, not to mention the thin air will be affecting Nightblades even worse than us. I'm not counting them out yet." Even though the empty halls and deathly silence didn't bode well. And if multiple nazal had been leading the attack … Arya felt sick at the thought of the destruction they might have caused.

She led them along the familiar route through the citadel towards the elder's quarters. Their boots echoed on the marble floors, announcing their presence, but they encountered nobody. As they reached the top of the steps that turned into a wide walkway leading across to the elder's tower, Arya's gaze went straight to the three Etherean bodies strewn across the floor.

"Arrows!" Arya heard the faint swish just before two arrows came flying down the hall towards them. One flashed past her head as she threw herself to the side, and the other clattered into the wall. They scrambled back around the corner as more arrows came at them.

"Chiarn," Arya snapped an order.

The Sky Lord nodded and his eyes flared orange; a moment later a wall of flame roared to life in the corridor ahead of them.

"Go!" she shouted.

They broke cover and moved down the hall, protected by the wall of flame. Chiarn dissolved the flame as they reached the landing where wide steps led up to the entry foyer outside elder's quarters. Arya was through and slashing at the Nightblade archer before he could knock another arrow. Her sword opened his throat, and he dropped, gurgling. Leanir had killed the second before she straightened, and silence descended. The sounds of fighting drifted to them, but not from inside the tower before them.

"That way." Leanir pointed left.

Arya frowned, trying to position where the sounds were coming from in her mental map of the citadel. Her thoughts were growing sluggish from weariness. "It could be the big amphitheatre adjacent to the elder's tower," she said, thinking back to her last visit. "Maybe the Etherean are making a stand there; it's a defensible space."

Essa drew knives. "Let's hope we can make a difference."

"Chiarn, get ready to cover us with your fire. There could be more archers beyond the doors, not to mention nazal," Arya said. "Tiya, you stay at the rear. If fighting starts you take cover. Understood?"

Tiya gave a tight nod.

Arya did her best to lead them to where the main entrance to the amphitheatre was. The set of arched double doors that opened into the reception hall were in splinters, and at first glance, the stage below was a bloody killing ground.

Arya's first sweeping gaze counted at least a battalion of Nightblades massing to try and get through a door leading off the side of the stage. A dwindling number of Etherean warriors soared above them, loosing arrows and trying to hold them back. But almost as many Nightblades had bows too and were relentlessly firing back. Even as Arya watched, one Etherean was hit, letting out a cry before spiralling to the ground with a nauseating thump.

"I'm guessing that door leads into the elder's tower?" Essa said in dread. "We're going to—"

A sibilant hiss echoed, tearing through every nerve in Arya's body, and she spun to face the hooded creature closing in from behind them.

A nazal.

There was nothing human beneath that hood as the creature pushed it back. Its form grew larger, taller, skin papery white, red eyes with veins spidering outwards from his eye sockets. It screamed, teeth bared, and magical energy sparked from its hands as it readied to attack.

"Oh, hell no," Arya snarled, absolutely done with being hunted by these things. "Leanir, I believe it's your turn. *Cairdre,* on me. Chiarn, I'm going to be pulling from your reserves. Tiya, take cover!"

She reached out to connect them all with the practiced ease they'd developed over long hours of practice, Chiarn opening himself up to her without hesitation. Arya drew from his fresh pool of strength, took hold of the magic Essa sent her, then pooled it with her own.

As the nazal flung its attack towards them, with a strength and power that would once have sent each of them flying, Arya let loose with their combined magic. The blue ringed spread of concussive energy swallowed the nazal's attack and flew towards it. The nazal screamed again, this time from fear. The Sky Lord magic hit it hard, sending it flying backwards, arms spread helplessly, neck bared.

And in the same moment, Leanir loosed his cazaix-tipped arrow.

As always, his shot flew true, driving deep in the nazal's neck. Its dying scream had them covering their ears with the intensity of it, and a throbbing pain started up in Arya's temples. The dead monster crumpled to the ground and Chiarn's fire quickly turned it to ash after Leanir retrieved his arrow.

Arya turned back to the amphitheatre. More Etherean warriors had fallen, and those protecting the doorway were down to a handful. "Can we manage one more burst like that?" she asked her *cairdre.*

"Easy," Chiarn promised. "I've got plenty left."

"Good." She took a deep breath in, pooled their magic once again, and then let it explode towards the stage. The lightning-edged magic tore through the Nightblades, while a wall of flame roared to life in front of the remaining Etherean warriors, protecting them from the Sky Lord blast.

And then it was done.

Arya let go of her magic, savagely glad at the carnage she'd just wrought, her satisfaction drowning the tide of exhaustion that followed. Leanir took the lead, bow up and knocked, heading down the steps towards the stage, Arya and the others trailing. Tiya stumbled once, and Essa had to steady her. The healer's face was stricken with horror at the sight of so many fallen Etherean. A familiar warrior came across the stage to meet them. He was pale, skin and uniform flecked with blood. "Lord Stormrider, thank you. We were almost lost."

"Rithil. Is the elder through there?"

"Yes, Lord Stormrider. But Elder Salyarin's personal guard blockaded it from the inside. We can't get through from here."

"Do you know if he's all right?"

He shook his head. "I haven't communicated with him since I took my squad to defend this entrance."

"And the rest of the citadel?"

Despair flashed on his face. "There was no warning. They cut through the lower levels before we could send warriors to help, and the nazal, they just..." His voice shook, steadied. "The answer is, I don't know."

"Arya." Leanir spoke. His eyes were distant, hooded, as if he were—

"You're dream-walking the elder?" She spun at the note in his voice. "Is he okay?"

"No." He blinked, coming fully back to himself. "He's hurt, and his message was garbled. I think there's another front of attack. Or there was. It's not clear. I saw a nazal in his mind."

Arya rocked, tried to fight back panic, found her ability to do so compromised by weariness. "Is Rorin with him?"

Leanir shrugged. He didn't know.

"Elder Salyarin sent High Warlord Ravenstrike to safety," Rithil jumped in. "With the children and those who can't fight—in the warrior's barracks. It's the most defensible building in the citadel, but I don't know how it fares."

Arya wanted to run there instantly, but she fought down the urge. The elder was in trouble. "Flamewielder, you're in charge here. Rally the Etherean warriors behind you and secure the citadel, level by level if you need to. Stick together. Rithil, I need you to take the Inkweaver to the barracks and make sure Rorin and the non-combatants are secure. Leanir and I are going for the elder."

"I'm coming with you." Tiya's voice was clear and determined despite the horror in her eyes.

"Lady *Tiya*?" Rithil's eyes went wide, voice ringing with shock. He clearly hadn't noticed her with Arya until she'd spoken.

"That's me. You're a little taller than the last time I saw you, Rithil."

Rithil didn't seem to know what to say. "I—"

Arya cut in. "Tiya, you're with us." If he was hurt, the elder would need his daughter's magic. "Let's go."

She started up the steps at a run, Leanir and Tiya at her heels. At the top she turned to make her way back to the entry foyer outside Salyarin's tower, but Leanir slid to a halt along one of the open-aired walkways.

"Something isn't right," Leanir murmured. "I can't hear fighting, but he was still alive a few moments ago. It's so still. The kind of still that assassins learn to avoid."

Tiya blanched. Arya felt for her, her own fear rising. The quiet probably meant the fight was over. They might be too late. "There's nothing we can do but get up there as quickly as possible," Arya said. "Come on."

Moving quickly, they returned to the entry foyer outside the entrance to the elder's quarters. The dead warriors they'd seen earlier were still there. Otherwise, all was quiet. She hesitated.

"There's something wrong," Leanir insisted.

Arya swore. Leanir's instincts were keen. So, despite her fear-fuelled instinct to go running inside, she quietly turned the handle and cracked the door open before slipping inside, sword drawn and remnants of her magic at the ready.

The foyer was empty of anything but the furniture, so she crossed to the closed door leading beyond. Once there, she placed her hand on the knob and looked back at Leanir. "Cover me?"

He nodded and raised his bow. Tiya hovered in the background.

As quietly as possible, Arya turned the handle and then pushed the door open, staying low to give Leanir a clear line of sight. He stepped into the open space, bow raised and ready to fire. He stood still for a minute, arms tensed, then lowered the bow and stepped through.

Arya followed him inside, one hand gesturing for Tiya to stay back. What she saw made her stop dead. Bodies littered the floor of the elder's sitting room, the light through his massive windows illuminating everything in excruciating detail; lying nearby were several black-clad Nightblades. Beyond that were three dead Etherean warriors. One of the windows had been smashed and icy mountain air whistled through the room.

"Arya!" Leanir moved suddenly, stepping gracefully over bodies to reach the centre of the room.

Arya, scanning to make sure there were no living threats before waving Tiya in, turned to see where he was going, and froze. "Salyarin?"

Leanir dropped to his knees beside the fallen body, placing two fingers on Salyarin's neck. "He's still got a pulse, but it's weak."

"*Xaphistryl!*" Elendryl thundered into her mind.

For a moment she wasn't sure she'd read Elendryl right, then... "*What! Where?*"

"*Heading away from the citadel.*"

That made no sense. "*She was here? When?*"

A shiver of doubt. Elendryl didn't know.

"*Warn the wyverns! Let me know if she heads back this way,*" she told him, then immediately sent a pulse of warning through her bonds with Chiarn and Essa. Both acknowledged, a ripple of fear coming from Chiarn. *Steady* she sent back.

She blinked back to attention to find Tiya kneeling by her father, already using her magic, eyes closed in focus.

"Arya." Leanir's voice had her eyes snapping to him. He was pointing to another corpse across the room "That's a dead nazal."

"That doesn't make…" Salyarin had killed a nazal? How? "Leanir, Xaphistryl is here, or *was* here. I think you're right, something is wr—"

He stood in one fluid movement. "A trap," he said. "Arya if the Nightstalker launched the attack in Khadini to take out your rebel allies, and he did it concurrently with his attack here to force you to choose who to protect, then it also makes sense he would see this as an ambush opportunity. He knew you'd come. Knew *we'd* come."

"Except we're here, and his wyvern is *leaving*." She blinked, thoughts racing. "And how did he know about Kulan and my friendship with the rebels in the first place? This doesn't make any sense."

"Arya, I need help from more healers." Tiya spoke up, terse but calm. "He's in a bad way."

"Where are you going?" Leanir snapped as Arya turned for the door.

"To fetch more help for the elder. Please watch over Tiya. I'll be back soon, and we'll figure this out."

She was only halfway across the entry foyer outside when Essa appeared from the opposite direction, a bloodied Rorin in tow. Relief flooded Arya at the sight of him. He broke into a relieved smile, and they hugged fiercely. "*The elder had his warriors get me to safety when the attack started.*" Rorin signed with shaking hands. "*He risked himself to do it. Is he okay?*"

"Tiya and Leanir are with him, but Tiya needs help, so I've come to fetch the healers. You're all right?"

"*Fine. We were in a defensible position and when Essa arrived it was easy to fight our way out.*" He shot her a grateful look.

"Good. Good." Arya thought. "Ess, something's going on, something we're missing. There's a dead nazal in there, and now Xaphistryl in the area."

"That doesn't make sense." Even her Inkweaver seemed at a loss.

"Will you both go and bring the best healers up here, then help Chiarn clear the citadel? I fear another attack coming, or a hidden force somewhere, or something we're missing. I'll stay to ensure Salyarin and Tiya are protected until the healers arrive."

"We'll be careful," Essa promised, reading the worry on her face.

"See you soon."

Rorin hugged her tightly before following Essa, and Arya turned back into the elder's quarters. Leanir was pacing the floor, glancing occasionally at where Tiya worked on her father. As Arya walked towards him, he looked straight at her. "Good, you're back."

The look on his face made her come to a stop, heart dropping to her toes. "What is it? Did he..."

"He's alive." Terse words. "He just woke briefly. He said Darmanin was here, that he saved them, killed the nazal, but the Nightstalker arrived and caught him. Darmanin fled, the Nightstalker pursued." Leanir paused. "He said Darmanin was hurt. There were so many Nightblades for him to fight off, and then the nazal."

Arya froze, horror creeping through bone and muscle.

It couldn't...

"He was drawing Darmanin out," Leanir said. "He's figured out your Darkslayer is a spy."

Not Darmanin. Her Darkslayer. The man who'd been risking his life every minute of every day for months now, all so he could bring her information they desperately needed.

She couldn't let anything happen to him.

"I'll go after them." She was already running for the broken windows, Elendryl winging his way towards her. "Keep the elder safe, Leanir."

Chapter 37

Arya sprinted through the debris of the elder's room and dived out of the broken windows, freefalling for several dizzying moments until Elendryl came up under her and she dropped into position on his back. As soon as she had her balance, she focused on her bond with Darmanin—it pulsed with tension and focus, and *pain*—and used it to locate him. It didn't seem like he was moving, which meant he and Zaphirdryl weren't in the air anymore.

That wasn't a good sign.

Gripped by the same urgency as his rider, Elendryl flew swiftly, wings beating hard, using every updraft and downdraft he could find to increase his speed, a golden blur amongst the snowy white peaks. Arya, needing to keep what magic she had left in reserve, couldn't afford to help him. Her brave wyvern wasn't going to be capable of much when they caught up.

Darmanin's presence steadily grew stronger as they arrowed in on his location. When they reached him, it was to find that Xaphistryl and the Nightstalker had brought their quarry to ground in a narrow valley. Arya could just make out two tall figures facing off on the valley floor. The two wyverns circled in the sky above, screaming, the much smaller Zaphirdryl doing her best to evade Xaphistryl's relentless hunting of her.

Elendryl let loose his wyvern's cry as he swooped downward. Xaphistryl responded, her cry louder and deeper and more fierce than anything Arya had heard before. It sent shivers along her skin. Elendryl didn't waste time in landing. He simply got low enough for Arya to jump to the ground, rolling through the snow before rising gracefully to her feet.

"*Help Zaphirdryl,*" she sent as he soared back into the air, arrowing for the dark nightmare that was Xaphistryl. "*But don't engage, you're too tired.*"

She got a dismissive snort in return—her wyvern's fiercely protective instincts were firmly engaged—and she tore her gaze away from him to study the situation before her. Darmanin and the Nightstalker circled each other a short distance away, swords out. Deep gouges in the earth and melted patches of snow were evidence of the battle already fought. Darmanin was breathing hard, and his left side was soaked with blood that dripped to the snow. Through their bond, she could feel his energy ebbing.

While she was almost out of magic herself.

Arya swore repeatedly. This was bad. *Very* bad. It didn't stop her from drawing her sword with a ring and striding towards them. She thought about summoning her *cairdre*, but just as quickly dismissed the thought. They were in no condition for a showdown with the Nightstalker. The goal here had to be escape.

Lucius' laugh rang through the icy air. "How nice of you to join us, Stormrider."

Arya ignored him. Darmanin risked a glance towards her, his face filled with so much worry it broke her heart. "Rorin?"

"He's safe, Dar," she hurried to reassure him. "Safe and well. I promise."

"Thank everything." A long breath escaped him. "Arya, you need to run. Let me hold him off so you can get free."

"I've never left you behind, and I'm not starting now." She stepped up beside him. "That's not how it is between us." Even if she risked everything by doing it. It was who she was.

"We can't defeat him, you know it, it's why you didn't bring the rest of the *cairdre*. If you stay, he'll just kill both of us."

"That's why we're going to fight our way free." She glanced from Dar to the Nightstalker facing them. All the progress she'd made; her victory in Dunidaen, the beginnings of an army in the Storm Spire, the extra knowledge she'd learned ... none of it came close to what she needed most. A way to defeat a being so much more powerful than she was. "We do that, and the wyverns will get us away."

He hesitated. "Arya, I'm hurt."

"I can see that." She risked looking away from the Nightstalker to meet his gaze. "We're going to get out of this. Okay?"

Before he could reply, a loud scream came from above, at the same moment a thrill of pain ripped through Arya's chest.

Elendryl.

Xaphistryl had landed a blow, her taloned claws raking down her wyvern's side. His blood sprayed through the sky.

"*Are you okay?*" she asked.

"*Shallow,*" he dismissed her concern, already banking so that he could angle for another attack. Zaphirdryl matched him from Xaphistryl's other side, her angry scream reverberating through the sky.

"I can see you've already worked out this is a losing fight for you." Lucius' voice cracked across the space, amused. "If you think I'm going to wait patiently until you decide which one of you gets sacrificed, you're sorely mistaken."

Black lighting crackled, slamming into the snow at Arya's feet and sending her flying backwards. Darmanin's form blurred as he shifted into a shadowhound, and his snarl reverberated through her bones. In his animal form, the nasty gash along his side was starkly obvious. Not a mortal wound, not yet, but one that *would* kill if not treated.

Arya scrambled to her feet, summoning her magic to bring lightning arrowing down on the Nightstalker. He stepped aside with ease before waving a hand and summoning a gust of wind strong enough to pick her up and bring her careening towards him. She landed hard only a few paces away from his tall form, every bone in her body rattling. She winced and rolled over, scrambling to her feet just in time to dodge a second lighting strike that forced back an attacking Darmanin. He snarled in pain, and she smelled singed fur. Arya reeled, completely on the back foot from the speed and intensity of the Nightstalker's attacks.

He'd been holding back on their previous encounters.

That knowledge hammered into her with growing despair. This time Lucius intended to kill them. Whatever had been holding him back from killing her was gone. Arya knew how her grandfather had felt, the fear and panic that must have coursed through him when he faced a Sky Lord who was more powerful than he was and had no other intent but to see him dead. The desperation of knowing there was no escape.

She picked up her sword, determined to fight her way out somehow. Not wanting to give him the opportunity to attack with his magic again, she went at him, a blur of furious strikes. He hadn't been expecting it, and one of her blow sliced open his tunic before he could get his sword in position to deflect.

"A joint attack," she murmured, risking a glance at Darmanin's shadowhound. "We force him back with a relentless push, then run, have our wyverns drop down and pick us—"

A magical gust of wind yanked her away from him. Arya hit the ground hard, this time banging her head, causing her vision to blur. Lucius Nightstalker strode towards her, knife in his left hand, his face a mask of intense focus. With his free hand he sent another gust of wind at Darmanin, forcing the shadowhound back despite his furious snarls.

She struggled to get up, his furious wind forcing her back down. Knowing she would die if she didn't move, Arya gritted her teeth and summoned the remnants of her magic. It exploded from her in an energy burst strong enough to halt the wind and give her seconds to get back to her feet and grab her sword. But the Nightstalker simply weathered the blast and brought the wind back to bear on her, this time a controlled gust stopping her from lifting her sword to attack.

There was a blur of black in her peripheral vision, an angry snarl, and Darmanin was there. He landed on the Nightstalker's back, teeth snapping for his throat, claws digging into skin and muscle. With a roar, Lucius Nightstalker spun, knife driving for Darmanin's side. The shadowhound leaped to the snow, forcing Lucious to turn left, opening his entire front to Arya, who lunged forward, yanking her knife from her belt and driving for his chest.

Only for the Nightstalker to vanish, her blade sliding through thin air, and reappear in the snow a few metres away. It broke his hold on the wind, though, and Arya was able to lift her sword. Before he could summon it again, Darmanin leapt teeth bared. This time he scored a hit, talons raking down the Nightstalker's arm and drawing blood. Arya lunged, taking advantage of the distraction, her sword skimming his side as he spun away from the blow.

A roar of genuine agony exploded from Lucius; her cazaix blade had sliced deep into flesh. He stumbled, hand going to his side, and he looked as if the blow had damaged him. Above, Xaphistryl roared in fury and redoubled her attacks on Elendryl and Zaphirdryl. Arya's sense of her wyvern told her he was fully engaged in staying out of reach of Xaphistryl's fearsome talons and teeth.

Brief hope flared. Maybe if she could wound him again with the cazaix, they could get clear to run, then—

"Enough!" the Nightstalker roared. Sweat beaded his forehead, and a feverish gleam lit his silver eyes. The cazaix had really hurt him.

But he knew it, and he wasn't going to let this drag out any longer.

Even as Arya flew at him, determined to get another strike in, Darmanin moving from the side to try and herd the Nightstalker towards her, he summoned his wind again. It was a fearsome gale that called up a flurry of snow, forcing Arya and Darmanin back, blinded. Then he vanished from sight.

Arya had time for a single, inwards gasp of air.

Then the Nightstalker reappeared right in front of her, knife already driving towards her heart.

It was too close. Too fast.

She was going to die. Arya knew it then, in that final bitter moment.

Then the snarl of a shadowhound tore through her ears, followed by a desperate wyvern's cry, so loud and intense everything seemed to go black for a moment.

A heavy force hit her, so hard she fell back into the snow. A weight landed atop her. Stunned, Arya was slow to respond. She didn't feel any pain, even though the knife must have gone into her chest. Lucius was backing away, one hand on the wound in his side, which bled freely. Sweat slicked his skin, his cheeks were flushed, and his attention on the sky above, where all three wyverns had started screaming. Arya struggled to get free of the weight, not understanding what it was, not until she felt fur under her searching hands, and then it all became clear.

"Oh no…." She pushed at the weight, trying to sit up. As she did so, her vision blurred and the body of a shadowhound became Darmanin, lying still in the snow. The Nightstalker's knife was in his chest, blood pouring from the wound.

"Dar!" She shook him, trying to get him to move. His grey eyes blinked at her, cloudy and barely conscious. "Darmanin!" she screamed.

Her voice seemed to jar him to alertness and his hand scrabbled, searching for hers. It was cold and clammy in her grasp. "What did you do?" She couldn't believe this, couldn't understand what was happening. "*What did you do?*"

"Hurry…" he gasped. "My magic … take it."

"What … no! Dar, you're fine. You're going to be fine."

He swallowed, eyes slipping closed before he opened them again with an effort. "Not long … take my power … before he can. Please, Arya."

Zaphirdryl screamed, a sound of desperate, clawing, unnameable grief. Air whistled, close by, and then leathery wings and inky black scales soared overhead and Darmanin's wyvern was there, snarling and spitting as she attacked Lucius Nightstalker; Xaphistryl left flat-footed by Zaphirdryl's unexpected move. The brave wyvern forced the Nightstalker further and further away from her rider's dying body, teeth snapping, snarling her rage and grief and despair. In the brief glance Arya had, it looked as if Lucius was trying to summon magic to defend himself but failing to do more than summon enough wind to just barely hold Zaphirdryl at bay.

Elendryl let out a blinding roar that echoed her rage and helplessness. He, too, fought, deliberately engaging Xaphistryl, keeping her from killing Zaphirdryl as the bigger wyvern flew to defend her rider. More of his blood steamed into the sky.

The wyverns were buying them time.

"Dar ... no. Please ... no." She felt the tears streaming down her face. "Not this. Not you."

"Rorin ... he's okay? Elder?"

"Rorin's fine. He's unharmed. And the elder has help. They're going to be fine. You saved them."

He squeezed her hand in response, his little smile flicking over his face, and she felt his weakened spirt pulling at her, trying to get her to connect via their bond. Arya opened her magic to him, instantly feeling his life force slipping away...

And like it had before, she went after him, to stop him dying, to hold him to her.

But this time he stopped her.

"No," he whispered. "Not this time. I've already lost too much blood from the other wound. You need to be strong enough to escape, to flee, or we both die here."

"I can still—"

"Take my magic, Arya, before he can. Use it to destroy him one day."

And he threw it towards her, all the silvery threads of his courage, his honour, and his sheer stubbornness. His deep and abiding love for her. For Rorin and Essa and their family. Her magic took hold of all those threads, twining them together with itself, gold flaring with silver.

"*Love you.*" He whispered in her mind, and then he was gone. She gripped his hand like it was a lifeline, her eyes snapping open to see him lying completely still, no longer breathing, a red stain spreading across his chest. The bond between them withered like a fraying rope until it was gone.

A cry sounded as Elendryl broke off from his attack on Xaphistryl and *dived* towards Arya. Xaphistryl banked but flew to protect her rider instead of pursuing Elendryl. Zaphirdryl had forced the Nightstalker so far away Arya could barely see them anymore, but she was alone against Xaphistryl now and had to break away, screaming her grief and frustration into the sky.

Elendryl landed in a gust of air. His head snaked out, giving her a sharp nudge, his mental voice exhausted. "*Flee.*"

Arya swallowed. She knew she had to go. Knew Darmanin's sacrifice would be for nothing if she didn't. But moving, accepting there was nothing she could do, that he was gone ... it was the hardest thing she'd ever done in her life. Sobbing, tears streaking her face, she gathered his body into her arms, ignoring how heavy it was, and somehow she got them both onto her wyvern's back.

And then Elendryl was launching into the sky, fleeing into the mists of the Diamondfang.

Elendryl flew, wings beating hard. Arya had no conception of how much time had passed, or even what direction they were heading in. Her entire body trembled with shock and exhaustion; her arms wrapped around Darmanin turned numb. He slumped lifeless against her, his blood soaking through her tunic and slicking her hands.

This was her fault. She'd told Leanir to warn Darmanin. She should never have sent Darmanin to the Nightstalker in the first place. If she hadn't, he'd still be alive, he'd still ... her breath hitched. Why was it so hard to breathe?

"*Arya.*" She felt her wyvern's warm breath on her face.

She blinked as Elendryl butted her gently with his nose again. They were in the entry cavern at the citadel. He'd landed without her noticing. She stared down at Darmanin, her arms tightening around him, unable to believe he was gone. When she didn't move, Elendryl let out a long, mournful cry.

The sound echoed through the cavern, up into the citadel, carrying out into the surrounding skies. It summoned the other wyverns, who swooped inside within moments, snarling and snapping in agitation.

Essa was the first Sky Lord to arrive, emerging into the entry cavern at a run, her face filled with a blind panic Arya had never seen in it before. Chiarn wasn't far behind. "Arya, what happened!" he screamed across the hall, his musical voice filled with all the horror and pain the wyverns were wrestling with.

Because they'd felt it too. The breaking of their *cairdre* bond to Darmanin.

Arya forced herself to clamber down awkwardly, keeping hold of Darmanin, but he was too heavy for her now, and she fell to the ground. Essa let out a long, keening cry when she arrived, hand rising to her mouth, eyes glistening. She kneeled beside Arya. "Arya, are you all right? Are you hurt?"

She shook her head, holding Darmanin close, refusing to let go. "Elendryl needs a healer," she whispered.

"Arya, please just tell me, are *you* hurt?" Essa spoke through tears sheeting down her face. "There's blood all over you! I need you know you're okay. Please."

"It's not mine," she said.

Chiarn arrived then, whispering brokenly. "No, no, no."

"I..." Arya swallowed. "He jumped in front of a knife the Nightstalker was aiming at me."

Chiarn flinched, taking a step backwards. A sob wrenched itself out of Essa and she bit her lip so hard it drew blood.

"I'm sorry," she whispered, her throat choking up as grief threatened to overwhelm her again. "It happened so quickly, and I didn't ... I couldn't stop him. I'm so sorry."

Essa put a trembling hand on Arya's shoulder, then looked at Chiarn. "We need to help her inside, and then take care of Dar's body. And..." Her voice hitched when Elendryl lifted his wing, revealing the nasty gashes in his side that Xaphistryl's talons had gouged.

Before any of them could do anything, Alletryl was there, nosing at Elendryl's side, then her long tongue snaked out, *licking* Elendryl's wounds. Asandryl snapped at Alletryl, forcing her to move to the side so he could get closer too, joining in licking the wound. As they all watched, shell-shocked with grief, Elendryl's wounds slowly closed over until they were nothing more than an angry red scar on his side.

Alletryl snorted in satisfaction, then moved away, Asandryl following. Mistryl watched from a distance, tail waving. Elendryl lowered his wing and settled more comfortably against the ground.

"*You okay?*" Arya asked him.

"*Fly. Then rest,*" he assured her.

Essa drew in a shuddering breath. "We should—"

Her halting words were cut off by the sound of bootsteps entering the cavern. It was Rorin, coming towards them with quick strides. Arya looked at her brother's face, taut with concern and worry, and couldn't say a word. The High Warlord of Dunidaen broke into a run, tears forming in his blue eyes, signing. "*What happened?*"

But even before he finished signing, he came close enough to see what Arya was cradling in her arms. Rorin's face crumpled, his whole body sagging, the light going out of his bright blue eyes. Essa reached out with her free hand to take Rorin's, speaking so that Arya didn't have to. "The Nightstalker killed him."

"He was going to kill me." The words burst out of Arya unexpectedly. "Dar jumped in front of the knife, and he..."

Rorin turned away, taking only one step before his shoulders began shaking and he began sobbing, deep, silent, heart-rending sobs. Arya stared at him, unable to move or to think, frozen by the depth of her own shock and grief.

"Is he..." Essa swallowed, visibly took a hold of herself. "Will the Nightstalker follow you here, Arya?"

She shook her head. "I nicked him with my cazaix blade near the end. It really hurt him. I think he's going to need recovery time before his magic works properly again."

Chiarn's face twisted, and he rubbed it with both hands, breath hitching. "Okay. Okay. What do we ... Arya, come on, we'll get you inside, then—"

"No." Arya shook her head. She couldn't be here right now. She just couldn't. "I'm just ... I need to go. I need to make sure Kirin is okay. A nazal is still tracking him. I have to go."

Essa stepped towards her, voice gentle. "Arya, you're in shock and Elendryl needs rest—"

"*Fly*," Elendryl insisted.

She ignored Essa, instead gently releasing her hold on Darmanin and staggering to her feet before climbing back onto Elendryl. "Look after Dar, please. And be careful, just in case I was wrong about him being hurt and he does decide to come here chasing me."

Chiarn reached up and settled his hand on her ankle, squeezing gently. "We will, I promise. Go and see your son, then come back to us."

Chapter 38

Arya paused at the edge of the jungle, watching Kulan and Kirin play in the fields around the farmhouse. Her son's laughter rang through the humid air, light and free. He was big for his age, with his father's dark tousled hair and light brown Khadini skin. The last time she'd stood in this spot, Darmanin had been with her, and that memory tore through her like a knife. Tears welled and she had to stand there for a long time before she had her emotions under control again.

How was she going to do this? Even taking another step forward seemed hard.

Kulan caught sight of Arya as soon as she broke the cover of the trees, and a broad smile of relief filled his face. He lifted his hand in a wave, and man and boy waited for her to come to them. Kirin regarded her intently, but said nothing.

"What happened?" Kulan's smile died as soon as he got a good look at her. "Elder Salyarin, is he...?"

"Badly hurt, but still alive when I left," she managed.

His gaze searched her face, then he bent down to Kirin. "Why don't you go and check on your grandmamma? She's probably woken from her nap by now, and you know how your hugs make her feel better."

Kirin glanced between them, clearly sensing he was being left out of something, but nodded willingly enough before turning to Arya and holding out his hand. "Thank you for helping me and grandmamma," he said.

She kneeled, taking his hand. He shook with all the gravity of a grown up. But after he let go, he hesitated, then he stepped forward and threw his arms around her neck, whispering a heartfelt, "I love grandmamma very much."

Arya held her son close, breathing in his scent, feeling the tears stream down her face. He was alive and well. She'd managed that, despite her heavy losses. It was something. "I'm glad I could help, Kirin. Really glad."

He started to wriggle, so she let him go, and he smiled at his father before running off towards the farmhouse. Arya watched him go, taking a deep, shuddering breath. Emotion wanted to claw its way out of her, and she didn't know what to do with it all, or even how to name it. "Yarmana's okay?"

"On her way to a full recovery," Kulan promised, then asked quietly, "Was it one of your Sky Lords? Rorin?"

"Dar."

He flinched. "Oh, Arya…" He seemed to realise words were useless and instead drew her into a warm hug. Then, he took her by the hand and led her back through the trees to the streambed they'd crossed all those years ago. Water trickled over the rocks, making pretty music on a quiet, sunny afternoon. They sat together on the rocks, Kulan merely sitting silently by her side.

Eventually, Arya lifted her left hand, showing him the narrow silver band on her finger. "I married him."

"You did?" Kulan stared for a long moment, the astonishment on his face deepening, but then he suddenly slapped his leg and started laughing.

"What?" she demanded.

"Now I suddenly understand why he always disliked me so much."

Arya smiled despite herself; Kulan's laughter had always been infectious. "I suppose he did."

"I never expected you would marry."

"Neither did I. But eventually I would have had no choice. I plan to be queen of Andahar, Kulan. I have a responsibility to provide stability."

"And that's why you're here?" Kulan sighed, sadness creeping across his face. "You want to take Kirin."

"Kulan—"

"No, really, it's all right." Kulan raised a hand to forestall her. "A boy should be with his mother."

"I *want* to take him," Arya admitted. "I've missed his whole life, and I feel so guilty about that, and I miss him every day. I *want* him with me."

"I won't stop you," Kulan said quietly. "Losing Kirin from my life will be worse than losing an arm or a leg, but I want what's best for him too."

She hesitated. Letting Kirin go, *again*, it was almost more than she was capable of. "After what happened in Taskari when he killed that Ranger ... Kulan, I don't want that for him. I don't want him to have a childhood like mine, where he's forced to be strong and ruthless just to survive. I want him to know safety, and happiness and contentment. One day he'll have to learn to be the heir to the throne of Andahar, at least if I manage to win, and if I don't then it's best he's well away from me. Either way, I want him to have a childhood first."

"I can give him that," Kulan said.

She huffed a breath, swiping at the tears on her face. "Your life is no different to mine, Kulan, as evidenced by the past week."

Kulan was already shaking his head. "My brother may not have destroyed us completely, Arya, but it's going to take decades to rebuild, and I don't have the heart for it anymore. I love my son and my family more than anything, and now I just want them to be safe. I'm out, Arya."

He must have seen the disbelief on her face, because he chuckled. "I'm serious. I've been thinking a lot recently, and I'm certain of my choice. I'm going to settle somewhere safe, far from my brother's reach, and I'm going to look after my mother as she gets older, and Kader too. I'm going to marry, because I want more children. And if you're willing, I'll look after our son and make sure he has a happy childhood. He might break an arm climbing a tree, or hurt himself going on adventures with his friends, but he won't ever be attacked by men with swords again."

Arya looked at him for a long moment, reading the sincerity in his voice and the resolution in his eyes. "You know he'll have to come to me one day. He's my heir."

"If you defeat the Nightstalker and win the war in Andahar, I'll send him to you when he's older, I promise," Kulan said, steadfast. "And if you don't win, then he'll never have to be anything more than a Khadini farmer's son."

She searched his gaze, wanting to be sure. Even with everything that had happened to her, all the grief and pain and fear and guilt … she couldn't step aside from her birthright. It wasn't in her. She would never be content with the life Kulan was suggesting. "What of your people?"

"I tried to help," he whispered. "But now I fear that if I keep going, I only offer them false hope, and what they'll receive in return is fear and pain." He paused. "Maybe one day, once Kirin is grown and safe, I will see where things stand. But for now, I have made my decision, and I am at peace with it."

"All right, Kulan," Arya said. She swallowed, trying to hide the surge of pain that swamped through her, knowing she was walking away from Kirin again, while grief for Darmanin was still a live creature inside her.

Kulan read it all on her face. "I'll keep him safe and happy; I promise you."

"I know." She forced a smile and reached out to squeeze his arm. "I think we should say goodbye now. If things don't go my way in Andahar, it's better that you and I have no further contact and that I have no idea where you and Kirin are. What I don't know I can't tell anyone or have tortured out of me. I have to assume his nazal is still hunting you."

"Until I hear word of Andahar's fate, I will ensure nobody finds us, I swear it to you." He nodded solemnly, before smiling his warm smile. "Friends and family, Arya. Always."

Arya leaned over and hugged him, clinging tightly. "Always."

***

Guided by their bond, Essa found Arya soon after she arrived back at the Etherean citadel several days later, exhausted and filthy, and uncaring about all of it. When her Inkweaver came through the open door of her room, Arya was sitting in a chair staring out the window.

"How's the elder?" Arya asked.

"He woke up late last night, and the healers are growing increasingly confident that he'll make a full recovery. It might just take some time." Essa ventured closer. "Kirin?"

"Safe. And loved. He's going to be fine too."

Essa was quiet a moment, gaze following Arya's out the window. "How about we get you cleaned up and into some fresh clothes? Then a hot meal and some sleep."

"Okay." She didn't have the energy to fight, or do anything really, so she allowed herself to be led through into the bathing room. A warm bath was soon running, and Essa stripped Arya of her blood-encrusted clothes before gently urging her into the water.

Essa kneeled by the bath and took her hand. "Arya, you're in shock."

Arya held that hand with a death-like grip. "I feel very unsteady, Ess. There's so much inside me that hurts and I don't know what to do with it."

"For now, you take a breath, and then the next one," Essa said. "I can't heal your pain, but I am here for you. I sent a messenger for Rorin. He'll be here soon."

Arya felt a flash of grief through her despair. "He must be devastated."

"He is, just like I am," Essa said, and for a moment Arya glimpsed the depth of the Essa's grief in her green eyes. "But he's your brother, Arya, you can help each other."

"I don't know if anything can help," she whispered, curling in on herself, arms wrapping around her knees.

"We *will* get through this. I promise you."

Arya swallowed, shaking her head. "I don't want to get through it, Essa. I just want him back."

Essa squeezed her hand in silent sympathy, and whispered, "I'm here, always, Arya."

"*Me too.*" Elendryl roused, his weary but loving voice soothing her mind.

There was nothing more to say then, and Essa picked up a cloth, briskly cleaning Arya up before helping her out of the bath. Arya waved Essa off then and dressed herself in fresh clothes. The fresh clean feeling did help slightly, and she tried to summon her frozen thoughts into some kind of order. "I'll have to go back to the Storm Spire, tell the Conclave what happened," she said as she tugged boots on. "The sooner the better." But how was she going to summon the energy for that?

"Arya, you don't have to—"

"I do. I'm their leader." Arya glanced out the window. "You'll come with me. We should leave today after I've spoken with the elder."

Essa's hand settled on her back, a light touch. "If that's what you want."

The door opened and Rorin entered. He was gaunt, pale, eyes shadowed, but he was *there*. Tears welled in his eyes. "*He was my brother.*"

"I know. And I'm so sorry." Arya stepped closer to him. "But you're mine, and I need you right now."

"*Oh Arya, I'm so sorry.*" He pulled her tightly against him.

She cried then, for the first time, she sobbed openly into her brother's chest, allowing his warmth and his love to keep her safe while she grieved.

Essa left them to it.

***

She wasn't sure how long she and Rorin clung to each other, but eventually they parted. As exhausted as she still felt, the overwhelming pain had eased, at least for now. "I have to leave, but I want to see the elder first."

"*We need to talk, soon,*" he said. "*But I'll settle with coming with you for now.*"

Salyarin lay snugly under layers of blankets, his big wings hanging over each side of the bed, as Arya entered his room in the healing centre. At her arrival, his eyes opened. Relief melted some of the anxiousness that had been a knot in her stomach since seeing him lying there in a pool of blood. At least they hadn't lost him too.

"How are you feeling?" Arya pulled up a chair by the bed.

"I heard the news, Arya, and I don't know what to say. Darmanin saved my life, he saved my people. If not for him, the nazal and the Nightblades would have killed everyone here."

Arya took in a shuddering breath. "I know."

"He was never the Nightstalker's man." Sick realisation shone in the elder's eyes. "He was helping you, and I never even thought of it."

The weight of her grief was too heavy for anger, so she simply said, "What have I been trying to tell you all these years? Darmanin was true, Salyarin, always and forever."

The elder was silent for a long moment before speaking. "I'm truly sorry for doubting him, Arya."

"It was me that you doubted," Arya said. "I told you all along that he would never betray me. I asked you to have faith in me."

"Yes, that's true, and I am sorry for it."

Arya stood and forced a firm decisiveness to her voice. "You know that Tiya is here, that is was her who saved your life?"

Something flashed over his face, an emotion she couldn't name. "Yes. You just missed her in fact. She insists on checking on me every half hour."

"You're going to be in recovery for a while. You'll need her help." Arya sharpened her voice further. "Take it."

"Arya, you don't understand that—"

"Oh, I understand just fine. She is your heir, and she is more than up for the task." Her mouth thinned, temper breaking through her non-existent emotional control. "I expect strength in my allies, not uncertain leadership because you can't get over the fact she doesn't have wings. If that happens, don't expect my help next time the Nightstalker attacks."

"I hear you," he said, pain flashing over his face.

Abruptly she felt guilty but squashed the feeling. "Get better, Elder. I am glad to see you well."

Arya left the room to find Tiya hovering outside, eyebrows raised. "How much of that did you hear?"

Tiya winced. "Most of it."

She let out a breath, all the strength she'd summoned for speaking with Salyarin draining as rapidly as it had come. "My intention wasn't to force you into anything. Just give you the option so that it is your choice. I'm flying back to the Storm Spire today, and you are welcome to come with me if that's what you want."

Tiya's gaze flicked inside the room. "He *is* going to need help. His recovery is going to be a long one and for a while he's not going to have the strength for the day-to-day tasks of running a kingdom. And rebuilding after the attack is going to be a lot of work."

"I can't say I'd want the job of ruling the Etherean right now. Not with a decimated army and the world outside on the brink of war, one we have no chance of winning. And not when you're probably going to have to fight and claw for your authority." Arya paused. "But I could use you as an ally, my friend. I have few of those left."

Tiya was silent for a long time, gaze distant. Arya waited her out, until she looked back at Arya, a little smile curling at her mouth. "Remember that tiny room I had at the Ruined Arms? The squeaky cot?"

Arya felt an echo of her old grin come back. "And the honey wine? I remember it well."

"Imagine if someone had told us back than that we would one day be facing each other in a hallway, formally allying with each other as the heirs to our respective kingdoms?"

Arya took Tiya's outstretched hand, shook firmly. "I'd have believed it."

Chapter 39

Three days later, Arya and her remaining Sky Lords returned to the Storm Spire. Rorin, who'd insisted on coming along, rode with her on Elendryl. Neither spoke much, but they leaned into each other, taking comfort from the other's presence in a way nobody else could match.

As soon as they landed, Essa sent orders for the Conclave to gather. While none had heard the news yet, the Conclave members turned sombre as they filed in to find Arya and Chiarn waiting for them and read the expressions on their faces. Essa arrived last with Desomer, closing the door behind them.

"Something has happened?" Arubon said, glancing warily between them.

Arya stepped up to the head of the table, needing to reaching deep inside herself to scrape together what remnants of strength she had left. Even then, she had to take a steadying breath, make sure she was in control of her grief, before she started speaking. "There is something you all need to know. The fifth member of my *cairdre*, Darmanin Darkslayer, never betrayed us. In fact, he and I were married, and he would have been queen-consort. He has been working as a spy with the Nightstalker. He is the reason the Nightstalker has not come for me yet. He's the reason we were able to stymie the Nightblade advances in the Marshlands."

A silence fell. Arya struggled to keep her composure, but the Conclave members all seemed to understand there was more. In the end, it was Sefani who spoke up. "I can understand why such knowledge had to be closely held. So I can only assume you're telling us now because … has something happened to Lord Darkslayer?"

Arya swallowed. "The Etherean citadel was attacked, as were our allies in Khadini. Lord Darkslayer intervened before the Etherean could be wiped out, but it broke his cover with the Nightstalker." She took a deep breath. "Lord Darkslayer did not survive."

Shocked silence filled the room.

Of all people, it was General Desomer who spoke first, his face grim. "Lord Stormrider. I am deeply sorry."

His simple words threatened to undo Arya, and she bit her lip. "You all deserved to know straight away, of course. This will change things for us, and I ask for a short grace period to reconsider my plans. I will report back to you as soon as I have something ready."

Her heart quailed at the thought. What *was* she going to do?

"Thank you for telling us, Lord Stormrider, we…" Rengalin began, then fell silent as words failed him. Miell glanced at the floor, clearly at a similar loss for words.

"We can wait, of course," Sefani said. "I know it will probably be of little comfort to you, but be assured things have been managed well here in your absence and there is nothing that needs your urgent attention."

"The arwein is right," Miell added, clearing his throat. "And we'll carry on looking after things until you're ready."

"Thank you. I'll see you all soon."

Arya walked towards the door, just wanting to go back to her room and sit with Rorin, but Arubon followed her, and she paused to find out what he wanted.

"I now see where recent setbacks in the Nightstalker's advance on my people must have been due to your husband," he said. "You have my sincerest sympathy, Lord Stormrider, on his loss."

"Thank you."

"In marshfolk culture, we do not grieve our fallen warriors long. Instead, we avenge them."

She nodded. "Then we have something in common after all, Arubon."

Arya found Rorin in her tower room, as she'd hoped. He stood staring out the window, his thoughts far away. She doubted he took in anything of the stunning view over the ocean. At her entrance, he turned to greet her with a sad smile. Arya joined him by the window and they stood there for a while in comfortable silence.

"Not that I'm not glad you're here, that you were there after..." Arya swallowed. She wasn't sure how she would have coped if he hadn't been. She was barely holding on as it was. "But why *were* you at the citadel when it was attacked?"

"*As you know, I held a State Council after you left for Andahar. One of the things we decided was to forge a formal alliance with the Etherean. I wanted access to their healers for our healing centres, and in return I convinced the warlords to re-open trade for the food they need. We'd only just started negotiations when the attack happened. Hawkesdale was going to join me in a few days; lucky he wasn't there too.*"

Arya nodded, and another comfortable silence fell.

"*What are you going to do next?*" Rorin asked.

"I don't know."

"*How was it going, before...?*" His signing trailed off.

Arya let out a long sigh. "I don't know. I was trying to implement a plan I had, but it was difficult and now ... now I just don't know. He's taken out two strong allies and my most powerful *cairdre* member." It all felt rather hopeless.

"*I have to go back. Essa and Alletryl are going to take me tomorrow, but I would like to formally meet this Conclave of yours before I go.*"

"A good idea. We'll arrange it."

"*I'm going to send Anjurin and Peemla back with Essa. They'll be safer here in the Storm Spire.*"

Arya frowned. "What do you mean? Anji is safer outside of Andahar, in Dunidaen."

"*Not anymore.*"

"Why?"

He turned to face her. "*I'm going home, and I'm going to raise the Dunidae army.*"

"Rorin, no, you can't. You just got your country back. The warlords won't agree—"

"*You really think so?*" he interrupted. "*You think the warlord of Crowtalon won't come at my call when he hears what happened? You think Hawkesdale won't? You really think any warlord of Dunidaen will stand by when one of their own has been murdered?*"

Arya sighed. "You don't have to do this for Dar. He wouldn't want you to put your country at risk just to avenge him."

"*I'm not doing this for Dar.*" Rorin's jaw tensed, and when he spoke it was with all the power and authority of the High Warlord of Dunidaen. "*Our whole lives, you've stood up for me, Arya. You've saved my life more than once, and you've saved my country. From that first day when Jenka and Warn were bullying me in the yard, every single time I've been in trouble, you protected me. Now it's my turn. I have an army at my command, and I'm going to use it. I'm stepping up to protect* you *this time.*"

"Rorin..."

He raised a hand, cutting her off. "*Dunidaen just declared war on Andahar. Expect to see an army marching through the Diamondfang at the beginning of spring.*"

"I don't know if I can be ready in time to..."

"*Be ready,*" he told her, then his face gentled. "*We're going to do this together, you and I. You are not alone, sister-mine.*"

As he hugged her, she curled her fingers into his tunic, taking the strength he was offering her. "All right."

After a long moment he pulled back and kissed her on the forehead. "*I'll see you soon, Arya.*"

He was at the door when Arya called his name. He turned back, eyebrows raised. "You're just like her, Rorin. Our mother. You're just as strong and just as brave."

He smiled. "*So are you.*"

"Lucky us."

"*Stay strong, Arya. It's what he would have wanted.*"

He was gone then, the door closing softly behind him. Arya turned back to the window, slowing pulling together the strength she needed to keep going. The problem was, she wasn't sure she had enough left. So much had been destroyed.

***

Arya woke suddenly from a nightmare, sitting with a gasp, heart thundering. Feeling her magic surge, she glanced down to see light flickering along her palms. When she realised it wasn't just the usual blue light, but also flashes of silver, she froze. Focusing her will, she tried to settle the magic, but no matter how hard she tried, she couldn't do it. The light continued to flicker along the skin of her hands and forearms.

Pushing back the covers, Arya got out of bed and pulled her boots on before leaving the room. Kait was on her door, and offered a small, sad smile. It didn't take Arya long to climb the stairs to the roof, and cool night air swept over her feverish skin as she stepped out into open space.

Closing her eyes, she tried to focus again, to bring her magic back under control. Fear licked at her when it continued to surge despite her efforts.

"*Here,*" Elendryl sent.

She stumbled over to him, pressed her palms against his scales, and let him help her fight her wild magic until eventually it came fully under her control. Then, exhausted, skin slicked with sweat, heart pounding, she lowered herself to sit on the edge of the roof, allowing her legs to dangle over the side. Elendryl bumped his nose against her shoulder and snorted warm breath against her neck.

"Dare I ask?"

Leanir's snide voice, usually infallible in raising her ire, had little effect tonight. Arya turned, part of her noticing that Elendryl hadn't responded at all to his presence. "What are you doing up here?"

"Looking for you." When she didn't reply, he walked over to stand a short distance off. "What happened just now? I could feel something weird through our bond."

"I had a little trouble with my magic."

"Has that ever happened before?"

Arya rubbed her throbbing temples. "It's fine. You can go now."

He nodded. "I'll be outside your door with your Raider if you need me."

His words took a few moments to register, but by the time Arya turned after him in confusion, he'd already disappeared down the steps. She sighed and turned back to staring out into the night. Soon she was shivering, the air cooling her sweaty skin. She felt sick, despairing, *grieving*. She wanted Darmanin's presence so badly that her chest physically hurt.

She'd told the Conclave she needed time to adjust her plans, but she didn't have a clue how she was going to do that. She was wrung out, despairing, tired. All the threads she'd been weaving together ... she'd lost her grasp on them. And she didn't know how to get them back.

***

To Arya's surprise, Leanir was present in their private sitting room the following morning when she went to get a cup of tea and some peace and quiet. He was clean-shaven and had re-shorn his hair. He'd even somehow toned down his murderous vibe so that she didn't get the impression he was ready to leap at anyone in the room with a knife the moment they looked wrongly at him.

"How are you?" he asked as Arya came through the door.

She gave him an odd look. "I'm fine."

"Any more issues with your magic?"

"It's only been a few hours, but no," she said. She'd managed a few hours sleep, curled up on the roof under Elendryl's wing, and felt marginally better, though still no more hopeful.

Leanir looked over as Chiarn and Essa walked in. "Good, I'm glad you're both early. There's something we need to discuss."

Arya wasn't sure which of the three of them was more stunned by Leanir's almost friendly tone.

"What is it that exactly?" Chiarn asked curiously.

"It's kind of obvious, and I'm surprised none of you have raised it already," Leanir said. "Who is going to replace Darmanin?"

"What do you mean?" Essa bit her lip, eyes sheening with tears.

"Aren't there always five Sky Lords?" Leanir asked. "Four to serve under the Stormrider monarch. Presumably someone out there is emerging as a Sky Lord after Darmanin's death. We need to find them before the Nightstalker does; until we do, he or she is going to be vulnerable and in significant danger."

"He's right," Chiarn said, startled.

Essa let out a long breath. "He is. Finding this person has to be a priority. How do we do that?"

Arya ran a hand through her hair, reluctant to speak but knowing she had to. "It's probably Anji or Kirin."

"What?" Essa demanded. "*Anji?*"

"They're children!" Chiarn said at the same moment.

"Exactly, which means they can't be Sky Lords for several years," Arya said quickly. At least she hoped so. How was she going to project Anji as well as Kirin if it turned out to be him? The Nightstalker wouldn't hesitate in going after a defenceless child. "We keep them out of this."

"How do you know?" Essa asked.

Arya shook her head. "I don't, not for certain. But I have an instinct about potentials, probably something to do with the fact that I command the Sky Lords."

"If you're right, then there's an adult potential out there now that will be awakened following Darmanin's death?" Chiarn asked.

"Maybe. I don't know how it works," Arya said helplessly. Guilt rose up, so much closer to the surface now. Was she putting *another* innocent person in harm's way?

"I'll ask Remien about it today before I leave with Rorin," Essa said.

"I'll come with you to speak with the old man, Essa. Then I'll spread the word among my network, ask them to keep an eye out for any potentials breaking out." Leanir offered.

"Please." Arya nodded, more grateful than she could express for their help.

"We'll go now." He headed for the door, waited for Essa to follow, which she did after another surprised hesitation. "It won't take me more than a few days, and I'll be back. Summon me if you need me back sooner, Lord Stormrider."

***

A week later, Arya's irregular battalion returned to the palace, escorting the Khadini refugees. She was there to meet them as they rode into the main square in front of her tower; Esdee, Herel, and Carador breaking off to report in while the warriors turned towards their barracks. Members of the Conclave waited to escort the refugees to food and shelter. To Arya's great relief, she spotted numerous riverfolk amongst the Khadini refugees from Taskari. Holding up a hand to the commanders, she strode over to the group. Tomin spotted her before she saw him, and broke away to come towards her. "Lord Stormrider."

"Tomin, you made it." Relief crumpled her shoulders. "Thank everything. What about Raysa and the others?"

"She travelled with Daarin and Atarin on a different boat; they made me get on an earlier one." Worry lined his face, adding to the exhausted circles under his eyes.

"We'll find them if they made it to Andahar, I promise," she said. "I have to go, but we have a healing centre set up that could really use your skills. It's just down there." She pointed.

"I'll be glad of having something to do," he said, relieved. "And thank you, Lord Stormrider. For keeping your promise to us."

"Always," she said, then left him to it, returning to join her commanders. When she glanced over her shoulder, Tomin was heading purposefully in the direction of the healing centre. It surprised her, how glad she was to have him here with her.

"Lord Stormrider." Esdee saluted, then hesitated. "Lord Flamewielder told me ... that is, when he and Asandryl flew over to check on us a few days ago, he said..."

"That Darmanin was killed." Arya saved her. "You can say it, Esdee. I don't want his name forgotten."

"I understand. I took the liberty of informing your battalion of his sacrifice. I hope that's all right." Esdee glanced at her fellow commanders, who wore grim expressions. "We are all sorry for the loss of Lord Darkslayer."

"Thank you, Commander Aurelian. You did well." Arya was just glad *she* didn't have to tell the story again. "Now, give me your report."

Esdee straightened. "Multiple units of Nightblades pursued the refugees from Ripley, some angling to cut us off as we headed north, which means the Nightstalker's spy network must have gotten word out quickly." Esdee glanced at Herel. "Our horselord scouts were able to identify the units before they reached us, however, allowing us to prepare ambushes."

"They tried to flee," Carador's lip curled. "But we hunted them down like the mangy curs they are."

"There were *children* amongst the refugees. Elderly." Herel sounded disgusted. "And yet the Nightstalker's soldiers did not care."

"Casualties?" Arya asked.

Esdee met her gaze. "None."

"We will keep hunting them, Lord Stormrider, and killing them. For you," Carador said. "If you'll allow us."

She didn't smile, not quite, but they saw it anyway. "Well done, all of you. Get some well-deserved rest, and report back to General Desomer day after tomorrow."

Her heart sank as they marched off, confident and raring to fight again. It was the spirit she'd fought so hard to instil in them, but now ... the Nightstalker had just cut her off at the knees. Before, the odds of defeating him had been long.

But now ... could she still promise them even a small hope of victory? Or was it a betrayal of their hopes to pretend there was any chance at all.

Chapter 40

When Arya slept, she found herself in a snowy forest clearing, and as her dream vision grew clearer, she realised it was a memory she was experiencing. But not hers. Her magic stirred, ready to defend her, but then she realised the shape and texture of the memory dream were familiar.

This was Leanir's magic.

So, Arya stayed, and paid closer attention. She was on the snowy highway leading into the underground road, thick forest lining its edges. Two groups of people stood facing each other on the road; Raiders and Shadeweavers. Realisation struck immediately. This was a memory of when she'd first met Ranier and Darmanin, that day when Ranier had offered her the help of the Shadeweavers to fight back the invading force from Andahar.

Arya looked at her seventeen-year-old self with wonder; she'd been so scrawny and young, the fierce look on her face belying her youth and powerlessness. For the first time, she saw how protectively her Raiders had stood behind her, how even then they'd looked to her for leadership. There was Laskin, younger, but still grizzled, watching her back as always. And Taze ... her heart broke at the sight. He'd been so young, even younger than her, yet even then he'd stood with a steadfastness that would come to characterise his time as part of Rorin's family.

Darmanin looked even younger, but he'd never lost that air of wariness, of wildness, about him. As Arya's dreaming mind watched, drinking in the sight of the man she missed so badly, the group began to break up. Darmanin's slight form waited for Arya and the Raiders to mount up, and then he led them away down the road. Arya's dream mind tried to follow, to soak up more of Darmanin, even if it was only a memory, but something—Leanir's magic—held her, following as Ranier and Leanir left the road and entered the trees.

Grief spiked powerfully as Darmanin vanished from sight, and it was a long moment before she paid attention to the conversation between Leanir and Ranier. Even then, she tried to tug herself away, back to road to follow Darmanin. But Leanir gently held her where she was.

"You'll be lucky if those Raiders don't run a sword through Darmanin the moment they get the chance," Leanir's voice snarled. A shudder went through Arya. It had been a while since she'd heard that vicious note in his voice. *"I don't care what happens to the lad, but I thought you did."*

"Darmanin can look after himself." Ranier shook his head. *"Did you really have to kill that Raider of theirs?"*

"I'm a killer, Ranier. It's what I do. It's what I enjoy *doing."*

"Shadeweavers, even our assassins, kill for a purpose, not for the pleasure of it," Ranier said. *"I won't have you with us if I can't control you."*

Leanir shrugged. *"Your control over me is tenuous at best, but it holds for now."*

"Then no more random killing."

Leanir didn't reply, instead changing the subject. *"What's your game with the girl? I know there's more going on than what you said to her."*

Ranier didn't reply for a long moment, his gaze distant as he stared at the snowy ground at his feet. When he spoke, it was almost entirely to himself. *"The daughter of Thiara Ravenstrike and Torin Stormrider. She's exactly what they were hoping for."*

"Who?" Leanir snapped. *"What are you mumbling about?"*

Ranier shook himself and looked up. Something like smug pleasure lit his dark eyes. Even in a dream memory it sent shivers down Arya's spine. *"You're right when you say my control over you is tenuous, Leanir, but one day she's going to control you completely."*

"That slip of a girl? She's more bark than bite. Besides, nobody is ever going to wield absolute control over me."

"It certainly won't be easy."

"It won't be possible," Leanir said firmly. *"Ever."*

"We'll see," Ranier turned away. *"Leave me alone, Leanir. I've got a fight to plan for and you know what your job is."*

The dream faded, and Arya's last sight was of Ranier walking deeper in the forest with quick, determined strides. Arya woke before he'd faded entirely from view. Blinking the sleepiness from her eyes, she sat up. It was deep night, and the fire had burned to embers. Her heart ached anew at having seen Darmanin. She wished so badly she could have stayed in the dream. But he was gone. He and Taze both.

"You're safe, Arya," Leanir's voice spoke from the shadows by her bed. "Nothing is wrong."

She eyed him. "You're back. And you're in my room in the middle of the night."

"I wanted to show you that memory."

She'd gathered as much. Pushing back the covers, she turned to face him properly, sitting crosse-legged on the bed. "Why?"

"Ranier was right."

"About what?" Her mind was slowly waking up, but she couldn't quite understand what Leanir was talking about.

"About you controlling me."

She sat up straighter. "Is that why you've hated me and pushed back against me all this time? Because Ranier told you I would control you one day, and you wanted to prove I couldn't?"

He gave a slight shrug. "I thought he meant that you would control me with strength, that you would be stronger than me. And I decided at a very young age that I would never let anyone be stronger than I was."

"I made a very similar decision when I was young." She gave him a sad smile.

"Ranier *was* right. Your magic as *cairdre* leader can control me utterly."

"Only if I choose to use it," she said softly. "And I won't, not ever again. I won't break my promise to you, Leanir."

He nodded, gaze lifting from the floor to her face. "Not even to save the man you loved."

"Leanir, I—"

"I was there at the citadel with you. I'm the deadliest warrior in this *cairdre*. I have the only magical ability that the Nightstalker does not." Leanir paused. "As a general, you've worked those things out long ago. You could have compelled me to come with you to rescue Darmanin."

"I didn't even think of doing that," she said honestly. "I gave you my word."

"Then why didn't you think to *ask* me?" The words tore out of him, sounding bewildered and lost.

"Because you would have said no. You don't care about anything but winning free of the Nightstalker."

He expelled a breath and looked away, something in his expression twisting. "I have a question for you."

"Ask me anything."

"Your son, Kirin." At the look that must have flashed over her face, he waved a hand. "No, I understand why you never told me about him. I'm not angry about it. That's not what I'm asking."

"Okay. Then what?"

"He's why you gave me up to the Nightstalker, isn't he? Because he was compelling you, and you had to give him something."

"How did you—"

"Essa told me back when we were training, about the bond the Nightstalker had to us through you, before you broke it. How he used it to hunt us. Then, after I learned about Kirin, I put it together."

"The answer is yes, Leanir. I had to give up something, and I chose you, because I had to protect Kirin at all costs. And because..." She faltered, but she wanted to be completely honest. "And because I chose to protect Chiarn and Essa and Darmanin over you too."

A long silence fell, Leanir staring down at the floor, one hand tapping out a rhythm on his leg. He was clearly wrestling with something, so she let him take his time.

Then he looked up, and he was almost smiling. "I wish that *my* father had loved and protected me in the way you did your son, Arya Stormrider. I have wished it with every breath I've taken since I was eight years old."

"Oh." That wasn't what she'd expected to hear.

"That hope is lost to me," he said, hesitating. "But having a *friend* who will love and protect me fiercely? I've been wondering. Perhaps ... I still might have that hope?" As he spoke, Leanir slowly lifted his gaze, until those dark killer's eyes were looking straight into hers.

Arya didn't hesitate. "It's already yours, Leanir."

He took a deep breath, then smiled properly. "And I finally believe you. I can't change who I am, and I'm not suddenly going to be a good person, but I'm yours."

"And I am yours." She sent a shiver through their bond to reinforce it.

"The next time someone you love is in danger, Arya, all you need do is ask, and I will hunt down your enemy with all the ferocity I possess." He paused, held her gaze. "As I now know you would do for me."

Leanir rose and left then, the door clicking closed behind him. Arya swallowed, tears streaming down her face at the same time as a smile curled at her mouth.

Lucius Nightstalker had taken everything from her, just like Remien had promised he would. Her allies, her beloved husband. One by one. But she was still standing. And she had something the Nightstalker would never, *ever,* possess. Leanir had just proved it.

Arya stood and went to start pacing by her windows, her favourite thinking spot.

She was going to win this.

And she knew how.

Chapter 41

Arya stood at the head of the table, facing the Conclave.

Essa had returned from Gateport, where she'd left Rorin and picked up Anjurin and Peemla. For this session, Arya had included Esdee, Carador, and Herel. They stood, straight-backed, along the wall behind General Desomer's chair. Remien was there too. Now, she tried to keep her shoulders straight and her voice firm, despite the sleepless nights and the constant gnawing ache of grief in her chest.

"We're only halfway through the six months that we all have together, but recent events have moved the timetable up. Darmanin is no longer here to hold the Nightstalker back from coming for me. Dunidaen has declared war on Lucius Nightstalker, and their army is gathering to march under the Diamondfang. *Our* army is now several thousands' strong, but only half that number is sufficiently trained for war. But before we plan what comes next, I have something to say to you all."

"How intriguing," Miell said, lounging in his chair, a smile tugging at his mouth. Sefani shot him a scowl. He winked at her.

"Joining me in war was not part of the deal I made with your leaders, and it would not be right for me to expect you to remain the full six months I asked for. So, you are free to go." Arya paused. "But I also want to point out that none of *you* are bound to hold to the promise I made."

Sefani lifted a hand. "Meaning what exactly?"

"Meaning that you can all choose to stay here, with me." Arya made sure her glance included the three commanders lining the wall behind Desomer's chair.

Arubon bared teeth. "And why would we choose to do that? As you say, you're about to ride to war with a few thousand against an army hundreds of thousands strong, led by a man several times more powerful than you are. Icefolk and Dunidae warriors alone will not win this for you."

"A fair question." Arya smiled a little. "And the answer is—*if* you stay, then this Conclave will remain in place, both during and *after* the war. I give you my sworn word that *you* will rule Andahar under me."

"Under you?" Sefani asked. "As in, we'll do everything you say?"

"No, Sefani. The same rules we have now will continue to apply. I will have control over declaring war, deploying our military, or making formal alliances. I would also like to retain veto power over some other matters, but I am open to negotiation on what those are. Otherwise, the Conclave will run the country."

Miell grinned, leaning back in his chair. "You're going to hand power to *me*, someone who's only barely come of age."

"Yes, because of Blackstone," she said. "You know fear, Miell. You know what it's like to truly believe you're about to die. More than that, you know how to survive it. You have strength that you don't even know about, and Andahar is going to need that."

"Your words are pretty but pointless," Arubon said. "You can't beat the Nightstalker. The last time you faced him, you barely escaped with your life, and you lost one of your Sky Lords."

"I didn't claim that this would be an easy choice for you to make," Arya said. "It's dangerous, incredibly so. And it's *your* choice."

"You are truly giving us your word?" Rengalin said. "You must understand our doubt. Andahar has always been ruled by a Stormrider monarch."

"It will continue to be led by a Stormrider monarch, Rengalin," Arya said. "But your people will have a say in how your country is ruled, I promise you that. It's the only way I can think to start working towards healing the differences between us."

"You have not addressed Arubon's incredibly salient point," Remien said. "You won't do what is necessary to beat the Nightstalker. What has changed that you think you can beat him now?"

"I learn each time I lose, and you won't find a greater tactical mind on this side of the battle than me." To her left, Desomer snorted. "I ask for your faith and trust. Faith that I can and *will* learn how to defeat him." She leaned forward, placing her hands on the table and looking them each in the eye. "But trust me now, when all you have is faith, and I promise you a better future for *everyone* in Andahar. You have my word on it."

"We have to think on it," Sefani said.

"I understand. But you should also know that I will be moving soon. We won't be able to hide here much longer." She wanted to keep the advantage, which meant moving *before* the Nightstalker came for her. "Come to me when you have made your decision."

One by one they filed out, leaving her with Desomer and her *cairdre*. Arya finally allowed herself to sit, dropping into her chair at the head of the table.

Essa went first. "You just ceded a significant amount of your future power to a group of people that are wary of each other at best and outright detest each other at worst."

"I'm a soldier, a military strategist, Essa," Arya said. "I inspire warriors. If I have ten soldiers behind me, facing a wall of wraiths, I know I can lead them to victory. Leading ordinary people in peacetime is vastly different and it's not my skillset. I will need help to do it."

"*If* you win," Chiarn said. "Which is a huge assumption."

"I realise that," she said. "But don't you see, Chiarn, it's not enough to just defeat the Nightstalker. To save this country, I have to find a way to heal the rifts between its people."

Essa nodded. "You asked for faith, Arya, and you have mine. You always will."

"And mine," Chiarn bowed. "I know I've had my doubts about your approach, but when I think on it, I want more than just to survive. I want a good life after, even if the chances of that are small."

"You have my support also," Leanir said. "In whatever you choose to do." Everyone turned and stared at him. He ignored them.

"General?" Arya asked her old mentor, who'd been silent so far.

"It takes a good leader to see where they fall short, and plan appropriately," he barked. "You're a good leader."

She couldn't help it, she chuckled, her heart suddenly lighter. "I think that's the nicest thing you've ever said to me." Arya stood. "Remien, a word before you leave? The rest of you are dismissed."

***

That night, Arya woke with a gasp, her dream of using magic becoming reality. Her back arched off the bed with the force of the power roping through her, and the dark room turned bright from the blue lightning flashing sizzling across her palms. Throwing back the covers, Arya rolled from the bed and fell to the ground, gasping. Sweat beaded on her skin as the magic roped through her overheated her body.

With an effort, she managed to clamber to her feet and get to the door. Closing her eyes, Arya concentrated fiercely, trying to calm the magic raging through her. It was no use. Whatever was happening to her was beyond her control.

She had to get to Elendryl. He could help her.

"Arya?" Charlin's startled voice sounded. "Are you okay?"

"Fine..." She groaned, forcing herself to move forward, one hand on the wall for support. "Stand down."

Somehow, she made it up the steps and out onto the windswept rooftop. Groaning again, she dropped to her knees, her body beginning to convulse. Elendryl was there, helping her focus on trying not to explode outwards and destroy everything around her, but even his presence wasn't enough.

What was happening?

Her body convulsed again, and pain speared down both her legs as if they were stretching or contorting out of shape. The pain rapidly spread, making her cry out, her fingers curling against the marble floor.

Then, abruptly, more magic swept through her, but it wasn't her own. This was the essence of Darmanin, and it burned with the ice-cold anger that had always lived deep inside him. Arya's eyes slid shut as for the first time in weeks she felt his presence so strongly it was like he was right beside her. She sank into the sensation, allowing it to wrap around her.

Then, her magic surged again, and she screamed, only it came out of her mouth as a deep, angry snarl. The door to the roof burst open and her Sky Lords came running out. Arya faced them on four legs, her head coming up as she snarled a challenge at them.

"Darmanin?" Essa asked, looking shocked.

"No." Leanir pushed the other two back. "It's Arya."

"Arya?" Chiarn demanded. "How can that be?"

"He gave her his magic when he died," Leanir snapped. "Get back."

"I'm not afraid of Arya," Essa said, shoving him out of the way. "She won't hurt us."

Inside the shadowhound, Arya summoned enough emotional strength to let go of Darmanin's presence. Almost immediately she felt the odd stretching sensation in her limbs, although this time it didn't hurt. Moments later she was in human shape again, sprawled, gasping, on the ground.

"Just leave me alone," she told them. "I'm fine. Please, just go."

Both Chiarn and Essa hesitated, but Leanir urged them back through the tower door. It closed behind them, though Arya could feel Leanir's presence as he took up a watchful presence on the other side. She curled up, wrapping her arms around her knees, and stared out into the night, ignoring the chill as the sweat dried on her skin. A moment later, Elendryl's wing settled protectively over her.

***

Arya worked out every bit of energy she had left the following morning drilling with her personal shield. Afterwards, she headed to her usual daily meeting with her *cairdre* in their private sitting room. Exhaustion trembled through her, and as she sank into a chair, all she wanted was a hot tea and her bed. Instead, she faced them all, waiting for the inevitable questions.

None came.

"Really?" She managed a weak smile. "Nothing?"

"I can't imagine what it must be like," Essa said. "I'm sorry, Arya, for how difficult all this must be for you."

"We're your *cairdre*, and we'll do whatever you need." Chiarn said. "We spoke earlier, and we're confident that through our bonds we can help you contain your new magic until you learn it."

"We thought perhaps some practice, together, once a day," Leanir added. "We should be practicing anyway, if Remien will agree to resume teaching us."

"I fell off my chair when he suggested it," Chiarn remarked. "So, I blame him for the great big bruise on my elbow."

Arya's smile widened. "That sounds like a great plan. Thank you, all of you."

"In other news, I've had no reports of new magic-wielders popping up or baby wyverns being spotted," Leanir continued. "My network still has large gaps, though, and Remien was annoyingly vague about when or how the new potential will appear."

Arya sighed. The older Inkweaver brother had said the same to her when they'd spoken the previous day. "It will happen, I can guarantee that, but when I cannot say. In the past it has happened from days after the death of a Sky Lord to nine months later."

"Has it ever been a child?" she'd asked.

Remien had frowned in thought, pushing back the collar of his shirt to study one of the tattoos on his left bicep, a small wyvern curled around an egg. "No, not in recorded history."

That, at least, had caused some relief.

A knock came at the door, and Leanir moved swiftly to open it before Chiarn could, his hand falling to the knife sheathed at his side. Both Essa and Chiarn's eyebrows shot skywards at this behaviour, but they said nothing. Leanir saw who was outside and waved them through with a terse gesture.

Esdee, Carador, and Herel filed in and stood in a line, shoulder-to-shoulder, heads up.

"Is something wrong?" Arya asked, heart sinking at the thought there might have been another brawl.

The horselord and marshfolk commanders glanced at each other, then stepped forward together. Carador spoke first. "We've considered the offer you made at Conclave yesterday, Lord Stormrider, and we have decided to stay. We ask to enlist in your unified army of riverfolk, marshfolk, and horselords. Arwein too, one day, we hope."

For a moment she wasn't sure she'd actually heard those words. And then … hope flared. So powerfully that she shot to her feet, feeling strong for the first time in days. "And your warriors?"

"We've spoken to them all," Herel said. "They will all be staying too."

Carador muttered. "No marshfolk is going to back out of a fight."

"And no horselord will either." Herel shot him a scowl.

Arya stood before them. "It would be an honour to have you in my army. Thank you, both of you. Please pass my sentiments along to your warriors."

Both saluted.

"You're dismissed for now, but General Desomer and I will be needing you soon, so make sure your warriors stay sharp."

Herel nodded. "We look forward to it, Lord Stormrider."

As the two men saluted and left, Arya looked over at Esdee and uttered a heartfelt, "Thank you."

She bowed, fist over her heart. "I am yours, Lord Stormrider."

"This is good!" Arya turned to her *cairdre*. "That is one of the key pieces I needed."

"For what exactly?" Chiarn asked.

"Oh, you'll see," she said, her smile turning wolfish.

Chapter 42

A week later, Arya stood at the east-facing parapet of the Storm Spire's outer wall, hands resting lightly on the cool marble. A breeze blew, sending strands of her blonde hair waving around her face. She barely noticed, her attention focused below, where their fields stretched out from the walls.

Workers were out there, planting or watering or tilling new fields while the sound of hammering came from further to the south where others were building new fences to hold more cattle. Horses grazed to the south. River-folk were the majority of those working, but arwein were there too—hand-picked by Sefani to join the community at Storm Spire. Khadini refugees too.

The Conclave had managed the running of the Storm Spire better than Arya could have hoped. She knew from Essa that it was not always smooth sailing, but they were learning to work together.

And the Nightstalker would destroy it all with a single blast of his powerful magic. Everything Arya had fought and bled to build. All that those down below had fought and bled to build.

She shivered. Hope was a fragile thing.

Her gaze finally shifted from the fields below to the curled parchment in her hand, a note from Rorin. The warlords had agreed to his request and the Dunidae army was gathering. He expected to be marching through the underground road in six weeks, an army ten thousand strong. Word from Tiya had come soon after. Salyarin had agreed to deploy his Etherean warriors across the entry and exits to the underground road, ensuring no word travelled to warn the Nightstalker of the marching Dunidae. More,

Etherean healers would join the Dunidae army and fly west to Arya's army at the Storm Spire.

Ten thousand Longbows, Raiders, Knights, Lances, Aggressors, and Fireman. Etherean healers. Her own army. It was a formidable force.

And a fragile one when faced with the might of Xaphistryl and her rider.

Sighing, she tucked that parchment away and tugged a second piece from her pocket. This one was torn and stained, the writing on it small and spidery. She'd received it that morning.

A faint tug on her magic warned her of Essa's approach, and Arya quickly crumpled the note and tucked it up her sleeve before turning to her friend and forcing a smile.

"Are you all right?" Essa asked.

Arya eyed her warily. "Why do you ask?"

"The Arya I know would be completely energised planning a war march, yet you've barely spoken two words since your offer to the Conclave. And nobody seems to be going anywhere."

"We can't move too early. We must wait for the Dunidae."

Essa merely levelled a look on her.

Arya turned to face her. "Will you ask General Desomer, Carador, Herel, and Esdee to meet us in the Conclave room? Remien too. I need to give them this update from Rorin and Tiya and then we should begin planning our approach."

Essa hesitated. "Remien's gone. That's what I came to tell you. I went looking for him this morning, and when I couldn't find him, I asked around. Nobody has seen him since your meeting with the Conclave."

"I see." Arya let out a breath, ignored Essa's worried look. "Then please gather the others. I won't be long."

Arya followed her friend down the steps, but there they diverged, Essa towards the central tower, Arya heading to Leanir's tower, knocking on the door to the quarters he'd chosen, feeling a little strange. She'd never visited his personal space before. Curiosity took hold, and she wondered if he'd let her in.

The door swung open, and the Sky Lord lifted an eyebrow in surprise. "Arya. What brings you to my door?"

"I'd like to speak with you about something."

He stepped back without a word. Arya cast her eyes around the interior, seeing an extremely neat space. The covers on the bed were perfectly straight and a nearby pile of clothes sat neatly folded on a chair. The only interruption to all the order was an untidy pile of books on the floor by the window.

"You're a reader?"

"You're not?"

Arya shrugged. "I never had much time for books. I'm too impatient to sit down for long periods of time with nothing but words to entertain me."

"That stuns me, Stormrider," he said. "What brings you to my door? You know people have been muttering, wondering what the delay is, why we're not taking action after Darmanin's death and the formal alliance with Dunidaen. Some think you've lost your nerve. Others think the Darkslayer's death has rendered you mad."

"Well, I do need to wait for the Conclave's decision," she pointed out, then lifted her eyebrows. "Which theory do you subscribe to?"

"None of them," he said flatly. "You've never done anything according to other people's expectations of you. I imagine this situation is no different."

Arya took a seat in one of the chairs by the fire, waving Leanir over to take the other one. "I'm not going to defeat the Nightstalker in a battle of strength and magic, Leanir."

"I know," he said. "It's a hopeless cause. It always has been. Yet, we're all still here."

"I do have one advantage over the Nightstalker."

"And that is?"

She smiled her wolfish smile. "I'm smarter than he is. And I have a Mindbreaker."

Dawning realisation crossed Leanir's face. "You've thought of a way to beat him. Tell me."

Arya leaned forward and began talking, relating to Leanir all the pieces of her plan that had been coming together for months. Part of her wished this was Darmanin she was relaying it to, that she had his tactical mind and confidence to challenge her sitting across from her, listening and ready to provide counsel. But as she spoke, Leanir's gaze narrowed in focus, his assassin's mind clearly turning over every word, every implication, and some of her aching grief faded.

Her Mindbreaker was silent for a long moment after she finished speaking. Eventually, he sat back in his chair, one hand reaching up to rub over his shorn head. "I was wrong. You *have* gone mad."

She laughed.

His gaze narrowed. "There are about a thousand things that could go wrong. Success will require trust in so many places, from people that have not shown they even *like* you, let alone can be trusted."

"Even a small chance of victory is better than none."

"Small?" Leanir looked at her incredulously. "You mean infinitesimal. If I didn't know you better, I'd say that you actually wanted to die, Arya Stormrider."

"I have a son and a *cairdre*, Leanir," she said quietly. "The last thing I want is to leave them, despite how much I miss Dar and Taze and my mother." She held his gaze. "But I won't be able to do it without you."

"No, you won't," he said. "Count me in, Stormrider."

Those Arya had asked for were waiting in the Conclave chamber when she arrived, in addition to two others, both of whom brought a smile to her face. "Peemla, Anji!"

"Hello, Aunt Arya." Gone were the days when the toddler Anji had been unable to say Arya's name. Now a sturdy four-year-old stood before her. He had his father's blonde hair and twinkling eyes, though the older he grew, the more of his mother's warmth Arya could see in him. She also saw a startling resemblance to Kirin, despite their different colouring, and now understood it. Both boys shared Thiara Ravenstrike's head tilt and patrician nose.

"He wanted to join us, I hope that's okay?" Peemla asked.

"Of course it is." Arya hugged the boy. "It's good to see you, Anji. Now, this is a serious meeting, so you must treat it that way."

"I understand," he promised, shoulders straightening in pride.

"Then go and sit next to General Desomer."

At first the crusty old general looked horrified as a small child scrambled into the chair next to him, but when Anjurin beamed at him with Rorin's sweet smile and offered his hand in introduction, the stern façade crumpled.

"I thought..." Peemla hesitated. "Well, I thought if you're planning a war march, then perhaps I could help with logistics. I know I'm not a military leader, but I am good at—"

"Yes!" Arya said fervently. "Please, join us. We could definitely use you."

She settled into a seat at Arya's right hand just as the door opened to admit Sefani Ravin. "Lord Inkweaver sent me a message to let me know you were meeting." She paused. "And I'd like to join you, as the arwein representative on Andahar's ruling Conclave, now *and* after the war."

Arya tried to hold back on the grin that wanted to stretch across her face, and waved Sefani to a seat. "I'm glad you're here."

Sefani took her normal seat, and Arya dropped into hers at the head of the table. Desomer started without preamble. "We have two significant problems if you intend to march to war, Lord Stormrider."

Before she could reply, the door opened again and Miell entered, slouching, hands in pockets. His golden gaze went straight to Arya. "What you said about Blackstone," he told her. "You were right. I'm in."

"I'm glad to hear it. Take a seat, Miell."

He went to his normal chair beside Sefani, but before sitting, he held out his hand to her. "I look forward to working at your side to rule our country, Sefani Ravin, even if that is only for another few weeks before we're both killed."

For her part, Sefani snorted in amusement and shook his hand without hesitation. "I feel very much the same, Prince Miell."

"My friends call me Miell." He sniffed and dropped into his chair. "What have I missed?"

"General Desomer has two problems to face as regards marching to war." She looked at him. "Supply lines and the Dunidae army, am I right?"

"You are," he said. "The further we run supply lines from here, the more vulnerable they'll be. Also, the Dunidae army is approaching through the Diamondfang from the north—how are we going to get over the Horn to meet up with their forces?"

"Neither of those things are going to be a problem," Arya said.

"Why, exactly?" Desomer barked.

"I'm not going to tell you everything yet, only the pieces you need to know," Arya warned them. "Too much is riding on this to risk betrayal. For now, I need all the efforts of the community here turned in support of General Desomer. Our warriors need to be prepared to depart within six weeks, weaponed and provisioned for a week's long march." She turned to him. "General, I need your best, as many fighters trained up marching out of here as you can possibly deliver."

"You'll have it, but I'm not sending green men and women out to be slaughtered."

"Agreed. Peemla, can I put you in charge of working with the Conclave to organise provisions for those marching?"

"I can do it." Peemla glanced at her son. "Perhaps you'd like to be my assistant, Anjurin?"

The boy's eyes shone, and he straightened in his chair. "I won't let you down, Mama."

"Will you have our battalion marching with your main army, Lord Stormrider?" Esdee asked.

"Not quite. The four of us are going to spend the next six weeks training for a particular kind of assault." She nodded at Herel, Carador, and her second. "Lord Inkweaver. I ask for your help too, you and Alletryl. There are messages I need carried and a dangerous but critical mission carried out."

"Whatever you need." Essa promised.

Arya stood, smiled, tried to project as much confidence as she could. "Then let's get to it."

Chapter 43

A misty fog hung low over the Storm Spire, although the morning sun was already piercing through the wisps of cloud. In the central tower, Arya buckled her sword belt over her chainmail as she stood by the window, staring out over the ocean.

This would be her last stand against the Nightstalker. Some deep instinct told her there would be no more chances.

Could she do it? She'd barely slept the night before, anxiety over all the parts of her plan that could go wrong plaguing her. Was she a complete fool for thinking she could best the Nightstalker, when he'd so easily beaten her down each time they'd faced each other?

Probably.

But if she wanted Kirin to grow up safe and happy, if she wanted her family to be protected, if she wanted a life for herself—or at least the opportunity to try and rebuild one without Darmanin—then the Nightstalker had to die.

Arya reached for her mailed gloves and gauntlets and buckled them on. Finally, she slid her silken Stormrider cape over her shoulders and took a deep breath. No more time for fear or doubt. She'd made her plans.

She opened her room door to find Arubon hovering outside, being closely watched by Allicen and Wattin. She hadn't seen the man since offering the Conclave power, and had begun to assume his silence meant he'd decided against joining her.

"Walk with me," she said.

He fell into step with her, yet said nothing for a long time. They were halfway down the stairs before he spoke. "I spoke with Miell and Sefani last night," he said. "They told me your plans."

"They probably shouldn't have done that," she said dryly.

"I disagree," he said. "We will need to work as a team going forward, and that means not keeping secrets from each other."

Arya stopped in surprise. "Does that mean...?"

"I will remain here and be on your Conclave, Lord Stormrider." He grimaced. "Even if our longevity might not be longer than a couple more weeks."

"I ..." She was genuinely stunned. "Why?"

His face twisted, as if he were torn. "I want to believe in what you're offering, even though I think I am a fool for doing so."

"I won't let you down, Arubon."

"I hope that's true." He hesitated. "I am not like many of my kin. Even if you win against the Nightstalker, the marshfolk will never bend to your rule."

"A problem for us to tackle together, Arubon." She offered her hand.

He took it.

***

A hush hung over the square outside her tower as Arya walked out. Elendryl waited nearby, head held high. Her army of riverfolk rebels stood in perfect rows with the crisp perfection of a Desomer-trained army. Fifteen battalions. Alongside them stood her irregular battalion. And lined up at the base of the steps was Arya's personal shield. All members of her Conclave stood there too, along with Essa. The morning fog was lifting, sending sunlight glittering across the marble buildings.

The Storm Spire was putting on a show for its army. She felt it dance around her, excited, delighted, by how she'd brought the place alive again.

The entire community that now lived at the Storm Spire surrounded the square to wave them off. All broke out in cheers when Arya appeared. She lifted a hand to acknowledge them, trying to give them the appearance of strength and invulnerability, knowing they needed to believe she could win. Their hope both buoyed and terrified her.

Then, her gaze settled on the rider at the head of her army, a smile tugging at her mouth. He might be getting on in years, but Desomer still looked every inch the general.

"Are you ready to march, General Desomer?"

"We've been ready for half an hour, Lord Stormrider," he grumbled.

"And you're clear on your orders?"

"Since you've explained them six times, yes."

"Then go." She lifted her voice so that all her army could hear it. "Help deliver me a victory."

If there was any reluctance in her soldiers about what she was sending them to do, none of them showed it as Desomer wheeled his horse and barked a series of commands that had the battalions setting off at a crisp march down the wide avenue to the front gates. Their boots echoed crisply on the ground, and the Storm Spire sparkled brightly under their feet, sending them off.

A ringing cry sounded through the morning. It was Asandryl, copper wings flashing like fire as he dropped out of the sky into the space where the army had stood, so that his rider could scramble onto his back. Chiarn would guard Desomer and his soldiers as they marched to their destination.

"Be safe," she murmured as she sent a pulse of reassurance along the bond between her and her Flamewielder. Chiarn lifted his hand in a jaunty salute. Everyone watched as the wyvern took to the skies, letting out another cry as he crested the walls.

Arya headed down the steps, making for her battalion, Essa coming with her. The sight of three hundred battle-tested warriors kindled a flame of excitement in her, and she could see the same feeling matched in Herel's gaze, Carador and Esdee too. "Are you ready for this?"

All three saluted but it was Herel who spoke. "More than ready, Lord Stormrider."

"Then give the order to march, Commanders."

Herel turned, bellowed the order to move. The soldiers gave a unified shout of acknowledgement, and almost as one, they lurched into movement. The horselord cavalry moved smoothly ahead at a quick trot, the foot soldiers falling in behind them, marshfolk spears glinting in the sun. Arya's personal shield of ex-Raiders brought up the rear, riding straight-backed and proud. She would rendezvous with them later.

"No turning back now," Essa murmured at her side.

"Do you think we should?"

Essa didn't answer for a long time, her green eyes staring unseeing into the distance. "No. I think we've done the best we can."

"What if I get them all killed?"

A cry cut off any response Essa might have made as Alletryl, shining green, landed nearby. She and Essa would escort Arya's battalion to *their* destination.

Essa reached for her hand. "See you soon, Arya."

"Stay safe, Ess."

***

Arya and Elendryl flew east. Giving the Horn a wide berth, they soared over the picturesque Riverlands until the hazy outline of the Diamondfang became visible in the distance. Rorin's last message had indicated his army was about to emerge from the tunnels, and as Elendryl came in low over the foothills, she saw the rows and rows of tents that marked an army camp. They sprawled over the rolling grassland, in an isolated area of the country far from any main towns.

But still ... Arya worried. All it would take was one person seeing them and telling someone else. Eventually word would get to the Nightstalker's spies.

She stifled her worry. It was too late for that now.

Arya's sharp eyes picked out the maroon and black of Ravenstrike, the green and brown of Hawkesdale and the blue of Falconcrest. She couldn't help but smile at the evidence of Arken's command; he'd made sure the fastest and most mobile elements of the Dunidae force emerged from the tunnels to enable scouting of the countryside and a quick retreat if needed. The Longbows gave them the ability to cover that retreat and hold any unexpected force off long enough to muster a defence.

She brought Elendryl down at the far edge of camp, leaving him to nap in the sun. She blinked a few times to adjust to the sunlight reflecting off so many tents, and so it took a few seconds to recognise the stocky figure walking towards her.

Her heart leaped. "Laskin!"

A smile cracked his weathered face, and when he tried to stop and salute, she jumped forward and wrapped him in a hug instead. "I've missed you, old man."

He hugged her back, a little awkwardly, then cleared his throat and stepped away. "Missed you too, Lass."

"How are you?"

"Busy," he said. "It's not the easiest thing in the world trying to manage an army belonging to five different warlords, but General Rosenthal and the High Warlord are managing the hard heads well enough." He hesitated. "How are you doing?"

"I'm fine, Laskin."

"You're always fine."

"I have to be fine," she said. "I miss Dar every single day, and there's not a minute that passes where it doesn't physically hurt that he's gone, but I know he'd want me to carry on."

He squeezed her arm. "Let's go see who you need to see."

They walked through the camp in companionable silence, Laskin's mere presence a balm to her fear and growing anxiety. When they reached the command tent, Arya pushed through the flap to find two familiar figures standing there, deep in discussion.

"Warlord Hawkesdale," she greeted the big man, pleased to see him.

"Lord Stormrider," he bellowed. "Welcome to the Dunidae war camp. I don't think you've met Warlord Falconcrest?"

Arya turned to the tall, willowy, woman at his side. She had dark skin and long black hair barely contained by a single hair tie. "Warlord Falconcrest, a pleasure to meet you."

"I think we've met once before. You came to dinner at the Falconcrest townhouse in Gateport once when you were Ravenstrike general," Dahlia Falconcrest said, reserved but polite. "You weren't a Sky Lord back then, and I was only a fifteen-year-old girl."

"Things have certainly changed." Arya wasn't sure what the warlord truly thought of her; she'd murdered her uncle, after all, forcing Dahlia to become a warlord. She was closing in on twenty now though and seemed perfectly at ease in her environs.

Dahlia smiled slightly. "You can be assured I am here in good faith to lead my Aggressors in battle against this Nightstalker menace."

"I appreciate that," Arya said. "I noted flying in that almost half the army is already through the tunnels."

Hawkesdale grunted. "Indeed. Raiders are scouting nearby countryside for any sign of Nightblades, and the Longbows are in the process of setting up a defensive ring."

The tent flap lifted again, and Rorin and Arken strode in, both looking pleased to see Arya. With a nod of greeting, Arken unrolled a map of Andahar on the table and got straight to it. Rorin came to stand by her side, one arm wrapping around her waist. She leaned into him.

"The full army will be out of the tunnels by dawn tomorrow. We can prepare to defend ourselves against attack here, but my preference would be to march as soon as possible, rather than risk getting bogged down." Arken looked up. "But that depends on your plans, Lord Stormrider. The High Warlord has instructed us to act in a support capacity here."

"And you're all okay with that?" She scanned the room.

"It's your crown we're trying to win," Hawkesdale barked. "And this isn't our land. So, yes, I'm willing to follow your lead."

"Dunidaen would have been lost without your aid, Lord Stormrider. So, it is a matter of honour that my Aggressors provide whatever support you need," Dahliah said. "At which point the debt between us will be cleared."

"And I would send my Lances to your aid whenever you asked it of me," said a new voice.

Arya spun as Andrian Crowtalon entered, Amius SparrowWing close behind. His handsome face looked haggard, deep shadows under his eyes. He smiled at her though, drawing her into a quick hug. "I'm so sorry," he whispered in her ear.

"So am I," she whispered back, holding him tight before letting go.

"Arya." Amius gave her a friendly nod. "I too am fine with the High Warlord's direction."

"My thanks to you all," Arya said. "My army is also on the move, so we can expect the Nightstalker to soon be aware of what we're up to. So, you are right, General Rosenthal, we need to move quickly."

"But in which direction?" Arken swept a hand across the map.

Arya shifted closer to the map, running her finger along the river systems drawn on its surface. "By nightfall you'll have several riverfolk guides arriving here, so tell your Longbows not to shoot them. They'll help move your army west along the waterways quickly and safely. By doing that, you should stay ahead of whatever counterforce the Nightstalker sends to intercept. We'll rendezvous here at Darkclaw Deep, the Nightstalker's seat. It's a strong, defensive fortress, and if we can take it, we'll land a significant blow against him. From there we can consolidate our hold on the Riverlands before looking to push west into the rest of the country."

"By moving that fast, we risk getting too deep into Andahari territory where we can be encircled by his numerically superior army." Andrian frowned, several in the room nodding agreement. "In that scenario we'd be wiped out."

"I agree that it's a risk, but if we take Darkclaw quickly enough, it won't be an issue," she said.

"How many soldiers are you bringing to this, Lord Stormrider?" Dahlia asked.

Arya hesitated only a little before replying. "Approximately three and a half thousand. And four Sky Lords and their wyverns."

"What about the Icefolk?" Amius asked.

"They're in play too, but the less you know the better."

"Understood," Arken murmured, gaze on the map, mind clearly racing. "Warlords, I suggest yourselves and your generals ride with me as we move west. That way we can plan the best approach for taking Darkclaw when we arrive."

"It is critical that you reach the rendezvous ten days from now so that our forces are coordinated," Arya told them. "At dawn on the eleventh day we launch the attack on Darkclaw. You can't afford to linger once you arrive. Are we agreed?"

"Ten days? That's pushing it." Hawkesdale grunted.

"Not with the riverfolk taking you along the waterways it's not."

"What happens if the Nightstalker himself attacks one, or both, of our armies *before* we get into position to attack Darkclaw? It would be the tactically smart thing for him to do." Falconcrest wanted to know.

"I do have a plan for that eventuality." Arya glanced up, met Arken's gaze, gave him a little nod.

"*All right.*" Rorin signed. "*In eleven days, we strike Darkclaw Deep and take it for House Stormrider.*"

***

Rorin lingered with her in the command tent after they'd finished up and everyone else had filed out.

"*You're mulling something over in that brain of yours,*" he said.

"I'm mulling a number of things at the moment," she conceded. "Are you sure about this? I can't guarantee that any of us are going to make it out, and you and the warlords only just got your country back. If your army is destroyed here, the Nightstalker could take Dunidaen in a matter of weeks."

"*I've never been more certain about anything,*" he told her. "*If the Nightstalker isn't stopped, he'll come for Dunidaen again. I know our chances are slim, but the best chance we have is for all of us to do this together.*"

"Thank you," she said.

"Arya, do you remember when you first came to us at Heathrock? I watched you win that hard-bitten Raider army to you heart and soul." Rorin looked into her eyes. *"You can do this, I know it."*

She allowed him to pull her into a warm hug. Eventually, they parted, and Rorin gave her a sad look. *"Am I going to see you again before the big fight?"*

"Of course." She told him with false cheer. "There's a long way to go yet."

She left the tent and walked back towards Elendryl. Night had fallen, and she could only just make out Arken's figure as he waited for her nearby, casting wary glances in Elendryl's direction.

"We couldn't talk back in the command tent? Winter in Andahar might be milder than Ravenstrike, but it's still blasted cold," he grumbled at her.

"No. I needed to speak with you, but I don't want anyone else to know we're talking."

"Why not? Is there something wrong?"

"No, nothing like that." She hesitated.

His gaze narrowed. "What is it?"

"I didn't tell them everything back there, I couldn't risk it."

Arken let out a breath, one hand lifting to run through his short-cropped hair. "Oh dear. This is going to be like that time you thought a single shield could break through the siege on Icecliff, isn't it?"

"Indeed." She was startled into a grin. "Here's all of the plan."

Arya spoke quickly and quietly, outlining her strategy for Rorin's general. When she'd finished, she waited in silence while he thought it over.

"I can see why you don't want anyone else to know about this."

"Them knowing ahead of time ... there's nothing they can do but worry. But *you* need to be ready."

Arken rubbed his chin. "You're asking a lot of me, Arya Stormrider. If the timing falls apart, we'll all be lost."

"I'm aware."

Trust, Leanir had said. Required from so many. Arken being one of them.

A long silence ticked over and Arya did her best to wait patiently, to let him come to his decision.

"I'll do my part," he said, offering her his hand. "No matter which way things go; you can be assured I'll do everything I can. Good luck, Lord Stormrider."

"I know I can trust you." She shook his hand warmly. "Which helps more than you know."

His mouth turned up in a smile. "I'll see you on the other side."

Arya nodded. "On the other side."

Chapter 44

Eleven days later, Arya walked through the pre-dawn stillness. Her stomach was knotted so hard that she felt sick. Despair that she might fail weighed heavy on her shoulders.

"Arya?"

She looked up to see Chiarn already in the clearing where their wyverns slept. "You didn't sleep either?" "I don't think any of us did." Essa's voice sounded from where she sat curled up against Alletryl.

"I slept fine." Leanir came striding up from behind Arya. Mistryl's form roused through the mist. "This thing is either going to work or it's not. We'd best just get on with it."

Arya stilled in the middle of the clearing, let her head fall back, and took a deep breath of the chilled, damp air. She reached for their bonds, feeling Chiarn's fear, Essa's determination, and Leanir's single-minded focus. And in return, she let them feel her own fear, her own determination, and the underlying doubt.

"*Elendryl?*"

His low snarl rumbled through the clearing. "*Hunt.*"

A smile spread over her face. "Leanir's right. Thank you, all of you, for being here with me today. For better or worse, we do this together."

"*Together.*" All four sent the sentiment rippling back through the bonds.

Arya thought of Kirin, of the life he'd have if she didn't kill Lucius Nightstalker, running and hiding and afraid. And she let that focus her mind into a perfect clarity.

"Let's get this done."

***

It was almost dawn as the four wyverns crested a mountain peak and found the hulking shadow of Darkclaw Deep below. A thick fog hugged the hillside and the plains below the hulking fortress, limiting visibility. The Dunidae army should be out there, moving into position with the help of their riverfolk guides, preparing to launch their attack. Arya silently wished them luck before turning her attention to the fortress below.

The wyverns circled above the flat roof of the northern half of the fortress, where the Nightstalker had his seat. It was an open stone square, ringed by a waist-high battlement. And it was empty—Xaphistryl obviously nested somewhere else nearby. Arya's sharp gaze picked out the numerous Night-blade guards outside the fortress, posted at all the entries, and the bridge leading to the trading post on the southern side. Worry flickered in her, but she stifled it.

"You're up, my friend," she sent to Elendryl.

Without hesitation he lifted his head and let loose his wyvern's cry.

It shook the very foundations of the world.

And when Alletryl, Asandryl, and Mistryl echoed their leader with their own screaming cries of challenge, stone crumbled and fell from parts of Darkclaw Deep.

Elendryl dived, wind whistling through his wings at the sharp descent, taking Arya down to the roof, letting her jump down before soaring back into the sky. The other three wyverns followed suit. And the moment her boots touched stone, another wyvern's cry ripped through the pre-dawn. This one was old and powerful and *furious* at having her territory invaded.

Xaphistryl.

Arya steadied herself against the effects of that cry, gaze scanning the skies, waiting for her enemy. And come he did, flashing into existence by the northern parapet at the same moment Xaphistryl swooped up from the trees below, her outspread wings momentarily framing her rider in a dark crown. Her darkness blotted out any light in the sky.

The angry wyvern arrowed straight for where Elendryl's golden scales glimmered in the pre-drawn. But as Xaphistryl closed on him, Asandryl dropped down from above and Alletryl and Mistryl shot up from the forest. They swarmed the much bigger wyvern without closing completely.

"*Be safe for me, my heart,*" she whispered to her wyvern.

"*Safe. Hunt,*" he sent back.

With that, Arya let go and turned to her fight. The wyverns knew what they needed to do. She glanced over her shoulder at her *cairdre*. Each knew what Arya wanted of them too. Her last look was at Leanir, questioning as much as reassuring. He gave her a slight nod.

Arya walked forward as the line of blue light on the horizon signalled dawn's approach and drew her cazaix sword with a clear ring. Lucius Nightstalker watched her come, his own sword still sheathed. He seemed fully recovered from his wound, but she noted that today he wore light armour. He'd learned from their fight, then.

"Predictable," he said. "Delivering yourself to me on a platter once again. Have you learned nothing?"

The sound of his voice, rich with contempt, sent a rush of pure fury flooding through Arya. This was the man who'd killed her husband and her mother, whose attack on Gateport had led to Taze's death. She fed that fury, allowed it to burn away every other emotion she felt. No more fear or doubt or grief.

Only the conflagration of Stormrider anger.

"My death isn't as certain as you make it seem," she said. "But this is the last time we face each other, pretender. One of us will not walk away today."

He blinked, looking genuinely bewildered. "How could you possibly think it would be you?"

"Because I am *better* than you, Lucius Nightstalker." She said those words for herself as much as for him, willing herself to believe them. Darmanin had. Rorin did.

"Darmanin's death broke you, didn't it?" Realisation crept over his face. "Well, I *am* glad that this will soon be over. You've caused enough trouble for me, and I have bigger problems I need to focus on. I had hoped for your help with that. The addition of your power to mine should have—" He cut himself off with a snarl of impatience. "Stealing your magic will do just as well."

His first bolt of magic came swiftly, a black streak of lightning arrowing straight at Arya. Swift as thought, she stepped aside, and it ploughed into the stone at her feet. She raised her sword and let loose her own bolt of lightning. His magic easily deflected it, and then he responded instantly with a howl of wind that descended on Arya.

This was harder to fight against, and she struggled to stay on her feet, gritting her teeth with the effort it took. Eventually she summoned more lightning, forcing the Nightstalker to halt his attack to defend himself. This wasn't how she was going to win a fight with him, but she needed to—

"Is your *cairdre* planning to just stand there and watch?" he shouted across the intervening distance. "Are they nothing but pretty ornaments? You think to beat *me*, when you don't even have a functioning *cairdre*?"

"While you seem to think you're going to taunt me into defeat." Arya circled him, wary of the wind he could use. "Nice try."

As she spoke, a wall of flame appeared in the air behind the Nightstalker. Xaphistryl screamed a warning and banked towards her rider, but Elendryl and the other two Valheran dropped out of the sky, intercepting her before she could reach him. She lashed out with talons and wings, catching Alletryl in a glancing blow, but she was forced to bank and defend herself rather than protect her rider.

Arya took advantage of the distraction to go at the Nightstalker with her sword. She swung at his head, and he dodged aside, bringing his own blade up to clang loudly against hers. He gave another shout as he summoned his wind to rip Chiarn's fire to shreds and then throw Arya across the roof.

She hit the hard stone and rolled to break the fall, coming to her feet quickly, and then moving sideways with quick steps. She'd learned from how the Nightstalker had killed Darmanin—his ability to vanish and reappear at will was devastating in a fight, and the only way to counter was to be in constant motion so that he couldn't pin her down.

A quick glance showed her Essa edging sideways, staying out of the fight in the shadows along the opposite edge of the roof, out of the Nightstalker's attention. Chiarn's face was a mask of focus as he attacked again with his flame, but the Nightstalker blew it out with insulting ease. Leanir lingered in the corner, eyes hooded as he watched.

Returning her focus to the Nightstalker, Arya leaped at him again, attacking with sword and magic at the same time. He engaged her, and for a long time they were a flurry of clashing blades and bursting magic. Arya just managed to stay ahead of him, escaping a magical attack on several occasions by mere inches. It felt *good,* to throw everything of herself into a fight, to shake of the doubt and fear and just feel the burn in her muscles and the quick draw of her breath. Even if she knew he was still finding it easy to fend her off. She couldn't match him one-on-one.

Dimly, she heard the screaming of wyverns as they fought bitterly in the skies above. Her connection to Elendryl remained strong, telling her he was all right, but otherwise her attention was entirely focused on the Nightstalker.

Dawn was rising, now, burning off the fog, and as their latest flurry of blades broke off, Arya risked a glance over the parapet, down to the plains below Darkclaw, where the Dunidae army should be moving into position to launch their attack.

The Nightstalker chuckled, and he glanced over the wall too. "You look surprised, Stormrider. Is that because the plains down there are empty when you expected them to be full of an invading force of Dunidae soldiers?"

She visibly started, head snapping to look at him.

"They're not there, Stormrider. And they're not coming. I heard word of their invasion, and the details of their approach via the waterways, days ago. Thousands of Nightblades were dispatched to meet them. By now they've been destroyed."

Arya sucked in a steadying breath, but he didn't miss the shock that crossed her face. She gave a fatalistic nod. "Someone betrayed me. Let me guess. Remien?"

"You assumed he wanted freedom." Lucius laughed. "Because you're idealistic and naive. What he wanted was what I gave him; a comfortable residence in Blackstone and the power of ruling the prison population."

Arya said nothing, simply lifted her sword, ready to attack once again. Nothing was going to make her back down or give up. Not this time. Not ever again. She pictured Kirin in her mind's eye; his laugh, his fierceness, and she let that focus her for what came next.

"You should have allowed me to kill you when I killed Darmanin," he told her as they circled each other. "The fact you thought I'd fall for your feint here only confirms that you're no match for me, not in the end."

His attack came too quickly this time, and Arya was sent flying again. When she hit the stone wall, she banged her shoulder hard, and pain stabbed through her. Swearing, she stumbled to her feet, only just managing to step aside as the Nightstalker sent a blast of deadly lightning at her. Two knives, flashing across the roof in quick succession, forced the Nightstalker to dodge aside just as he was about to drive his sword through Arya. Both bounced off his armoured shoulder but gave Arya time to steady herself.

"*Thanks!*" she sent a quick burst to Essa.

At the edges of her hearing, she caught the sound of clashing swords, cries of battle. Somewhere below her feet. She looked at her adversary, but he didn't seem to have noticed over the screaming wyverns—he was too busy gloating, his sword hanging loosely as he watched her, breathing hard and cradling her left arm to her chest. He was *savouring* her pain. Her defeat. Arya bent down and picked up her sword, and as she did so, she turned to look at Leanir. Beads of sweat coalesced on the assassin's forehead, but his expression was focused, resolute. His dark eyes met hers and she gave him a slight nod.

Arya turned back to the Nightstalker. "Let me ask you a question. When you sent those thousands of Nightblades to crush the Dunidae army, where did you get them from? After all, you recently lost a lot of your soldiers when you abandoned them in Dunidaen. My guess is you had to draw upon your forces fighting in the Marshlands."

The Nightstalker frowned, confused.

"I hope my guess is right, because right now my army is launching an attack on your Nightblade positions in the Marshlands. And I know *exactly* where those positions are, *and* how strong they are, thanks to my Darkslayer. And if I'm right, well then..." Arya let a smile spread over her face. "As of now, or very soon, the Marshlands are free and your army there is destroyed."

"You couldn't have." The Nightstalker laughed in contempt. "You're bluffing in a pitiful attempt to distract me."

She cocked her head. "Am I?"

"Yes, you are." He was confident as he stalked towards her. "You consider Dunidaen your true home. You would *never* have sacrificed their army just to take the Marshlands from me. And I know that your army is entirely made up of riverfolk. They'd *never* agree to help free marshfolk."

A brief silence fell as the wyverns momentarily broke off their battle, and now Lucius heard the sounds of fighting from below. His gaze narrowed and he cocked his head, as if trying to place where the fighting was coming from.

A smile tugged at her mouth. "You're wrong on both counts, Lucius." She gestured at the battlements. "Take another look."

"Now, Elendryl!"

Scoffing, the Nightstalker looked over the walls.

And this time he saw reality as Leanir let go of the illusion he'd woven in the Nightstalker's perception. Thousands upon thousands of Dunidae soldiers marching towards Darkclaw Deep; the mist clearing as a bright sun rose above the horizon.

A cry sounded from above. The wyverns re-engaging in battle.

Only now, the four Stormrider wyverns were harrying Xaphistryl with a focused intensity, swarming her, snapping and slashing and *pushing*. They took damage from it, torn wings and gashes in their scales, and Arya's heart broke with every wound sustained.

But Xaphistryl finally lost patience and broke clear, breaking east out over the Dunidae army and swooping to attack, presumably at her rider's direction.

And as soon as she did, the Lances blew their horns, the mournful howls echoing through the morning. And with each blast of their horns, the Hawkesdale Longbows let loose a hail of arrows at the Nightstalker's wyvern.

Xaphistryl screamed when the first arrow hit her, and the second.

"NO!" the Nightstalker screamed too, pure fury and pain opening his face, exploding out of him.

"Cazaix-tipped arrows, Lucius," Arya said. "Thanks to a little trip my Inkweaver made to the cazaix forge in Khadini recently."

Xaphistryl banked, screaming, flapping desperately to get clear of the cloud of arrows that were slicing into her wings and scales. Her blood streamed into the sky, and the Nightstalker roared his pain and anguish as he watched.

She did get clear eventually, still aloft, but clearly hurt. She might even have survived.

But then Zaphirdryl dropped out of the sky above her, hidden until now by the angle of the sun. Darmanin's wyvern was quick and merciless, landing on Xaphistryl's back, her jaw opening to close around the other wyvern's neck and *rip*.

The howl the Nightstalker let loose was otherworldly, and in it Arya heard pain and grief and madness. His fingers dug into the stone battlement, gouging stone, tearing skin and muscle.

And as Arya watched him, the first stirrings of triumph lit in her chest.

He turned on her before Xaphistryl's lifeless body had hit the ground, teeth bared in a rictus of rage and grief. He countered her first two strikes, and she got inside his guard on the third, the blade screeching along his mail. Grunting in anger, he shoved her backwards and came at her with renewed vigour. She countered the first slash, and the second, then saw the third coming before he'd even moved.

Instead of countering, Arya stumbled slightly, sliding out of position to be able to launch a counter to his thrust. She tried anyway, bringing her blade up too late to stop the Nightstalker's from driving deep into her shoulder. She cried out at the hot flare of agony, then she staggered backwards and fell. There was nothing to break her fall onto the hard stone and for a moment she saw stars as her head cracked against the surface.

Arya heard Elendryl's scream through her mind, and then Essa's physical scream, but all that was pushed from her thoughts as she watched the Nightstalker lean over her, triumph mixed with maddened grief gleaming in his eyes.

"Go on!" she hissed, taunting him, blood running down her side. "Do it, if you think you're strong enough to kill me and steal my magic."

The Nightstalker kneeled and clamped his hand ruthlessly around Arya's neck. As he did, she felt Leanir work with sublime skill as he slid through their bond before brushing up against the Nightstalker's magic. Slowly but surely, he took over the Nightstalker's perceptions, reinforcing his belief that Arya was dying.

At a subtle pulse from Leanir, Arya allowed her eyes to slide close and her body to sag lifelessly against the stone. The pain in her shoulder made that hard, but she gritted her teeth and fought to hold still, pretend to be dying. The Nightstalker dived deeper into Arya's mind and magic, reaching out to steal it from her as she died.

Instead, he dived into the trap that Leanir had fashioned.

"*Cairdre, to me!*" the Mindbreaker screamed through their bonds.

Then Chiarn and Essa were there, and all four Sky Lords threw everything they had at the Nightstalker, Arya's magical strength doubled now with Darmanin's magic added to hers. Leanir relentlessly attacked the Night-stalker's mind and magic while Essa and Chiarn and Arya used their power to hold him in place and stop him escaping.

Arya's Mindbreaker slowly but surely ripped the Nightstalker's mind apart. She sensed his cold glee as he did it, felt the steel of Essa's inner strength as she brought everything she had to bear on stopping the Nightstalker from escaping Leanir's hold, Chiarn's bravery as he fought as bitterly as the other two.

And Arya *rejoiced* in the blunt use of every bit of raw power she had, slapping down every effort of the Nightstalker's to escape. In a physical battle of magic, he was their superior, but trapped in his mind, in *their* minds, Leanir held all the advantages. And they were *cairdre*—Darmanin with them in spirt as Arya used his magic without respite.

The Nightstalker screamed, trapped outside his body, all his magic being sucked away by Leanir's power, unable to escape no matter how desperately he tried.

Then everything was a bright, agonising flash of light as together, Arya's Sky Lords combined behind Leanir to finally destroy the essence of Lucius Nightstalker.

The cataclysm of their enemy's magic imploding sent everyone flying from her mind and magic, and Arya was left splayed out on the cold stone, watching as the sun rising over Andahar lit the roof in a golden glow.

Chapter 45

When Arya opened her eyes again, it felt like a long time had passed, but the early morning sunlight was still only creeping over her boots and lower legs. Essa, Chiarn, and Leanir all kneeled around her, hands clasped, sending her their strength under Leanir's careful guidance.

"That's enough." She pushed them away gently. "You're exhausted too. I'm okay."

"You're bleeding everywhere." Chiarn pointed out.

Arya barked out a laugh, then sat up and threw her arms around her Flamewielder, ignoring the pain stabbing through her shoulder. Essa was next. "You wonderful, wonderful, wonderful, *cairdre.*"

"I don't get a hug?" Leanir asked.

"Do you want one?"

"No, but I would like to bandage that wound before you bleed to death."

Arya nodded. Looking down, she saw the amount of blood seeping over the tear in her mail and blanched. She sat, hand in Essa's, as Leanir roughly bandaged her up. Arya looked at the Inkweaver, seeing how pale she was, and the dark rings under her eyes. Chiarn and Leanir didn't look any better. "Are you all okay?"

Essa smiled, highlighting her stunning beauty. "Oh Arya, of course we're all right. Do you know what we just did?"

Arya looked over at the prone body of the Nightstalker. Wincing, she staggered to her feet and limped over. He lay on his back, arms spread at his sides, the face that had once been alive with dark magic now utterly lifeless. It was almost impossible to believe, that the larger than life figure that had plagued her for so long, that had brought her so much pain, was gone.

"He's definitely dead!" Chiarn kicked the body.

"I'd make sure of it if I were you," Leanir said.

Chiarn nodded and clicked his fingers. Instantly the Nightstalker's body was wreathed with red-hot flames.

"*Xaphistryl is gone too,*" Elendryl's tired voice spoke into her mind. "*Zaphirdryl made sure of it.*"

"*Elendryl.*" She closed her eyes and soaked in his presence. "*You're all right?*"

"*Hurting,*" he said. "*Alive.*"

"I can't believe it," Arya said.

Essa chuckled. "Neither can I, to be honest."

"You outsmarted him," Leanir said.

"It was you that did it," Arya said, turning to him. "It was your magic that allowed me to bring him down."

"No." Leanir disagreed. "It was all of us. Had the Flamewielder and Inkweaver not come to join me the instant I called ... had they not been willing to open their magic completely to me, we would have been lost."

"I suppose we are a *cairdre* after all," Chiarn sounded rueful.

"We shouldn't linger," Essa said. "The Nightstalker is dead, but his army is still out there, and presumably at some point the guards here are going to come running. I'm surprised they haven't already. There's still one nazal alive too."

Arya smiled, leaning down to pick up her sword and sheathe it at her waist. But before she could answer, the door to the roof slammed open.

Esdee was in the lead, Carador and Herel hot on her heels, the warriors of their battalion streaming behind them to spread out over the rooftop. All were bloodied and torn, teeth bared, weapons out, ready to fight if needed.

"Is the fortress ours?" Arya asked, her voice whipping across the rooftop.

"Aye, Lord Stormrider." Herel reached her first. His long hair was matted with blood, and a makeshift bandage wrapped the entirety of his right forearm. "Your battalion swept through and killed every Nightblade we found."

Esdee glowed. "Both sides of Darkclaw Deep are back in the hands of its rightful owners, House Stormrider."

"Look, Lord Stormrider." Carador pointed.

She glanced over to the southern half of the fortress, the trading post, where the black flags showing the Nightstalker sigil had vanished. Rising in their place, as she watched, were new flags.

Blue background. Lightning and raven sigil in silver emblazoned in the centre.

"Not Lord Stormrider." Leanir said, voice cold and commanding. "The Nightstalker is dead. Kneel before your queen."

Her Mindbreaker was the first to kneel, but the others all followed. And below, as they caught sight of the new flags flying over the keep, the horns of the Dunidae army blew in triumph.

***

The Dunidae army looked magnificent as Arya and her *cairdre* and commanders walked out to greet them. Only Leanir wasn't there, having left with Mistryl at a request from his new queen. The warlords came to meet her, Arken too, but Rorin broke into a run as soon as he saw her. The worried look he wore faded as he stopped and got a good look at them. Then, a genuinely joyful grin lit up his face. "*You did it, didn't you?*"

Essa nodded, eyes shining. "We did."

Rorin let out a silent whoop and caught Essa up in his arms, swinging her around before letting her down and throwing his arms around Arya. "*I knew you could do it,*" he signed. "*I knew it.*"

"What's going on?" a deep voice bellowed. "Why are we celebrating before the war is won?"

Arya let go of Rorin and turned to Warlord Hawkesdale. "Warlord. The war most certainly *is* won. The Nightstalker is dead."

"What about the battle?" Hawkesdale stared around. "The fight. Where are his Nightblades?"

"They were all sent to intercept you on your way here, to foil my plans." Arya shrugged. "They might have gone looking for you in the wrong place, though."

Something happened then that Arya had never thought she'd see. The irascible Hawkesdale's mouth dropped open in astonishment. "Explain yourself!"

"I never wanted another full-blown war, Warlords, not for Dunidaen, and not for my people," she said. "So, I used you as a decoy, and to help me kill Xaphistryl, but the battle was won before you arrived. My warriors have taken Darkclaw, and I'm awaiting news that will hopefully confirm we've won the Marshlands too."

Eyes wide, Hawkesdale turned and bellowed loudly enough for anyone nearby to hear. "The Nightstalker is dead." His cry was taken up by those who heard it and soon the news was spreading across the waiting army, followed by loud cheers.

"What of the Nightblades he sent to intercept us?" Andrian asked, sharing a look of astonishment with Amius.

A cry from the Dunidae sentries interrupted before she could respond, and all turned in the direction they were pointing; the woods to the east that Arya had once walked through with Niallin, where she'd rescued Esdee and the other conscripts.

One moment all they could see was trees, gently swaying in the morning's breeze, and then ... hundreds of Icefolk warriors emerging at a sprint, forming into neat lines, and then slowing to a halt as they reached the edge of the Dunidae lines. A small group kept running, making for where Arya and her *cairdre* stood with the warlords.

"Greetings all." At'eir arrived, flushed, eyes bright, snowy braids swinging. His normally pristine furs were spatted with dried blood and gore. "Lord Stormrider, I can proudly report victory. We ambushed and destroyed the Nightblade force. They were right where you said they'd be."

"You have my eternal thanks, Er'fin At'eir." Arya bowed her head, relief shuddering through her.

"All is not yet won." Essa stepped forward. "We hold Darkclaw, the Marshlands, and the Storm Spire. But the Nightstalker had many barracks spread across Andahar, including here in the Riverlands. Thousands of Nightblades are still out there, not to mention a remaining nazal. Not all will surrender to us."

Rorin turned, looked at his warlords one by one, then turned back to Arya. *"If you will grant us your riverfolk guides for a little longer, Your Grace, I offer to attack and destroy any barracks that will not surrender to us on our march back to Dunidaen."*

Your Grace.

Her brother had addressed her as queen.

"As much as I appreciate your offer, High Warlord, those Nightblades are my people, even if they did fight for my enemy. As such, I must deal with them."

He smiled his beautiful smile. *"I understand."*

Falconcrest didn't. "They might be your people, but they're an enemy force. You're best not leaving them alive to pose a threat."

"I agree," At'eir said.

"Even so," Arya said. There had been enough destruction in Andahar. She'd deal with the Nightblades her own way. Her gaze took in all the warlords. "Go home with my deep gratitude and thanks. Lord Flamewielder will escort your army to the Diamondfang to ensure you reach it safely."

"A whole lot of fuss for nothing," Hawkesdale grumbled as he ambled off.

"I *am* a little disappointed, if I'm honest." Eaglesoar agreed with him.

"I'm not." Amius said, sharing a look with Andrian. "Arya was right. There's been enough bloodshed."

***

Back inside Darkclaw, Arya asked around the staff—currently rounded up and under the watchful eye of members of Carador's shield—for directions to the library. By the time she found it, her shoulder throbbed and exhaustion was a heavy tide tugging at every part of her body. She cracked open the door and stepped inside, gaze sweeping the rows of shelves, the books lining the walls, before landing on the man sitting at a table by the fire, frowning over a large map unrolled on the surface before him.

"I was hoping it would be you coming through that door, not him." Remien observed. "Though I admit to a small amount of anxiety about it."

"You came through for me." Arya dropped into the chair next to him with a sigh of relief.

"It wasn't hard. After Niallin, he was expecting more betrayals."

"So, it *was* Niallin who told him about my plans to ally with the Khadini rebels and the Etherean?" Her heart broke at that. So many deaths, and if she'd treated Niallin a little more gently, he might never have ... she swallowed and tried to keep the guilt from overtaking her.

"I'm afraid so." Remien shrugged. "But in the end that served us too. Lucius ate up everything I told him. He sent his soldiers right where I told them your Dunidae army would be."

"And where At'eir and his Icefolk waited to ambush them instead." They shared a fierce smile, but then Arya sobered. "What you did was incredibly dangerous. Why choose to be loyal to House Stormrider this time, Remien?"

"It's simple, really." Remien pointed to the map. "You earned it."

"It *was* power you wanted, all this time," she murmured. "But not power for yourself. For the people of Andahar. It was the Conclave that won you over." Arya did her best to conceal the inward burst of triumph she felt. "What has the map got to do with it?"

"Lucious was studying this, see his notations all over it?"

She let out a sigh and humoured him, leaning forward to see. It looked incredibly similar to the one Remien had hung in his room in Blackstone. A grouping of four islands a large distance east, and more to the north. Most of the scrawled notes were clustered in the north of the map, though she couldn't make out the Nightstalker's handwriting.

"You have won a throne, Arya Stormrider, but that does not mean this kingdom is safe forever."

She huffed a laugh. "In that case, will you come back with me? I still need the knowledge of the Inkweaver archive if I'm going to succeed in bringing this country together."

He pushed the map aside, smiled to himself. "First, I think I'm going to go and visit my brother. I abandoned him once, and I'd like the chance to try and make up for that."

Arya winced inwardly at the thought of unleashing both Inkweaver brothers running the Shadeweaver network on Rorin, but another part of her was glad for Ranier. Maybe he could start to learn that loss wasn't always the outcome of risking everything.

The door cracked open, and a wide smile spread over Arya's face as she saw Tiya walk in. "Did you just arrive? Did they tell you we won?"

"Yes, and yes." Tiya's blue eyes gleamed. "And my healers are already helping those of your battalion who were injured."

"Good. You're a sight for sore eyes, Tiya."

"And you're bleeding all over that nice chair." Tiya sniffed. "I'm here to fix you up."

***

Leanir and Mistryl returned later that night, bringing word that General Desomer and her army had won a sweeping victory in the Marshlands. Tiya had worked on Arya's shoulder, closing the wound over and restoring some of her energy. Esdee and Essa had brought food, lots of it, and now they sat by the fire, eating hungrily.

"Tell me." Arya waved Leanir to a chair and some food.

"General Desomer carried your message to Chief Dorinaal of the Inraki," he explained. "That the marshfolk lands were now free and that their chiefs are invited to meet with you and Arubon at the Storm Spire to talk about the best path forward together."

"And their response?"

Leanir's mouth twitched. "They told him he and his army were trespassing on marshfolk territory, and they should leave before they found themselves under attack."

Arya groaned, lifting a hand to rub at her aching temples. The triumph of defeating the Nightstalker still glowed inside her, but she'd known all along that defeating him wasn't going to solve everything. Something told her she had some tough days ahead.

She pushed herself out of the comfortable chair. "Esdee, you have command of Darkclaw for now. My *cairdre* and I need to return to the Storm Spire and let our Conclave know the news. While we're gone, I want you and Carador and Herel to work together to figure out a plan to deal with the remaining Nightblade barracks."

Esdee's mouth tightened disapprovingly. "You should just—"

"I'm not murdering them all. Come up with a plan. We'll discuss it when I'm back."

***

They arrived at the Storm Spire not long after dawn, all three wyverns circling low over the walls to warn everyone of their arrival. As Elendryl landed in the square outside her central tower, hundreds were arriving, all gathering behind the members of the Conclave. As if it already knew of their victory, the walls glowed brightly, sparks of blue lighting shimmering across the marble.

Arya climbed down, stroked her wyvern's nose affectionately, then walked to greet them, Essa and Leanir falling in behind her. With every step she felt confidence and power fill her, the realisation that she'd defeated her enemy finally sinking in.

She came to a stop before the Conclave, saying simply. "He's dead. The Marshlands are freed. We hold Darkclaw and the Riverlands."

For a moment all those in the square stared at Arya, unsure if she could be believed.

She smiled, lifted her gaze to include them all. "It's true, my friends. Three days ago, we faced the Nightstalker, and we emerged victorious. The war is over."

Rengalin's mouth dropped open as burgeoning hope spread over his face; Sefani lifted a shaking hand to her mouth, tears welling. Arubon swallowed, his brown eyes turning suspiciously dark.

"We did it, my friends. Together." Then Arya lifted her head to the sky and roared, "The Nightstalker is dead!"

It took a moment for them to realise what she was saying, and to realise she meant it. The first cheers were ragged, but they quickly turned into full blooded roars of victory.

And then as one, they all kneeled before her.

Arya sucked in a breath, momentarily overcome. *The power to make things right*. It was what she'd always wanted.

And now she'd won it for herself.

Epilogue

It took almost a year, but Arya and her court gradually stabilised Anda-har. She still only ruled half the country—negotiations with the marsh-folk and horselords were ongoing, but neither tribe wanted war with Arya, and Miell and Arubon were committed to figuring out a way forward. It was a fragile peace, and she wasn't certain it would hold, but she didn't intend to stop trying.

Her insistence of giving all the Nightblades the option of surrender, of joining her army, was a major impairment to forward progress. When one barracks had rioted and attacked a shield of Arya's army, the Conclave had almost quit as a group when she refused to change her policy. Still, those Nightblades that did surrender and agree to join her army she'd placed under Desomer's command. She could only hope they would prove worthy of her risky decision.

The other major lingering problem was that they hadn't yet managed to track down the Nightstalker's fifth nazal. No matter how far and wide they looked, she hadn't been able to find it.

A week before her coronation, Arya and Elendryl flew southeast over the ocean. They took their time, both still tired from days and weeks and months of fighting and wrangling and working desperately to hold her fledging country together. Eventually, they circled a small farmhouse on a humid, sunny afternoon. Not wanting to alarm anyone, Arya asked Elendryl to land a short distance away. She dismounted gently, making sure the precious cargo she carried in a sling was secure, before walking towards the house.

The sound of wood clacking on wood made her change direction, towards a grassy area on the banks of a swiftly flowing stream. There Kulan and his son were playing with a set of wooden swords. The boy's laughter rang through the afternoon as Kulan caught him and swung him high into the air.

Both spotted Arya at the same time. Kulan dropped his sword and came striding over, worry creasing his handsome face. Kirin remained behind, watching them warily.

"I got your message, finally," Arya spoke quickly. "I've been waiting and waiting for it."

"I'm sorry it took so long. News takes a while to reach us because we're so isolated, and my brother keeps a tight grip on what is circulated..." He trailed off. "It's really true? The Nightstalker is dead?"

She couldn't help the grin that crossed her face. "He is. We won, Kulan. Andahar is mine. I am to be crowned in a week."

His shoulders sagged in relief. "Congratulations, Arya. That is good news indeed."

For a long moment they simply smiled at each other, Kulan understanding exactly what Arya had been through, what good news this was for *his* country. Eventually, his eyes flickered downwards, and his smile softened to one of bittersweet sadness. She nodded, swallowing, and his hand reached out to squeeze her shoulder. By then, Kirin had decided she wasn't a threat and wandered over, pretending indifference.

"Hello, Kirin," Arya greeted her son, forcing herself to sound casual, to not leap the distance between them and gather him into her arms.

He watched her, indigo eyes bright. "You're my Mama, aren't you?"

She didn't look away. "Yes, I am."

"I'm going to leave you alone for a little while," Kulan said, leaning forward to kiss her cheek. "Take as long as you need."

Kirin was silent as they walked over to the stream and then sat down on the edge, Arya adjusting the bundle she carried carefully. "You must have a lot of questions. I promise I'll answer as best I can."

"I asked Papa about you, after you left last time. I wanted to know why you'd helped us, why you looked at me so strangely." Kirin was five years old, but he sounded grown. "He told me that a lot of bad people were hunting you, and so you left me with him, so I'd be safe."

"That's true." She yearned to reach out, to take his hand, but he still seemed so wary. "If I'd had any choice, I would *never* have left you, Kirin. Never."

He nodded. "Have you come to take me away now?"

"No," she said. "At least, not yet. Have you heard of Andahar?"

"I started attending lessons in the village this year," he said proudly. "The master tells us about the other countries in the world. He said a monster rules Andahar."

"Not anymore, Kirin. I killed the monster." She couldn't help the pride that filled her voice. "Now *I'm* queen of Andahar. Maybe you can tell your master that at your next lesson."

"I will," he said, then eyed her. "Does that mean I will be king of Andahar after you die?"

"Yes. You are my eldest child."

He considered that for a moment. "I won't be able to stay here forever then, will I?"

"No, but when you do come to me, know that I will love you and protect you as much as your father has."

"All right." He seemed to accept that, and his gaze drifted to the sleeping bundle nestled against her chest. "Who's that?"

Arya smiled. "This is your sister, Nyasa."

Delight flashed on the boy's serious face. "I have a sister?"

"Yes, you do. I've been telling her all about you."

"Hello, Nyasa." Kirin smiled at the sleeping baby, reaching out a gentle hand towards her. Nyasa woke, startled, but beamed toothlessly at Kirin and curled the fingers of her tiny hand around his thumb. Kirin's eyes widened in awe.

"When I come to you, I'll be coming to her too?" Kirin asked.

"Yes. Even if we're apart for now, we're still a family, the three of us." Arya smiled at his excitement. "You have cousin too, Anji. He's very excited to meet you."

A joyful smile spread across Kirin's face as he played with Nyasa's hand, making her giggle. "All right, Mama. Will I see you again soon? Nyasa too? And I'd really like to meet my cousin."

"I'd like to visit as often as I can, if you don't mind? I'll bring Anji and Nyasa with me next time."

"No," he said, very serious. "I don't mind at all."

***

Arya was formally crowned as queen of Andahar on the roof of her tower at the Storm Spire, with Elendryl watching protectively. It was the Conclave who spoke the formalities and placed the golden circlet on her head. Rorin Ravenstrike, High Warlord of Dunidaen, witnessed the crowning, as did Queen Is'heim and Er'fin At'eir of the Icefolk and Elder Salyarin of the Etherean. At Salyarin's side stood Tiya. She hadn't yet been acknowledged as her father's heir, but Arya was confident that would come in time.

Emperor uq-Danresan had declined the invitation, but that was okay. Arya had plans where he was concerned. Already a niggle of anticipation roused in her at the thought.

She felt more than just the physical weight of the circlet as it was placed on her head, and then the Conclave stepped away and bowed to their queen.

"Are you ready to address your people, Your Grace?" Rengalin asked.

Thousands had travelled to the Storm Spire for the coronation, even more than Arya could have hoped for. Her goal of complete unification was still a long way off—it would be a lifetime's work, maybe beyond—but there was a lot of hope already building.

"I'll be with you all in a moment."

They bowed and filed down the steps to await her below. Arya took a deep breath, reaching up to settle the circlet more firmly on her head. It was cool to the touch, but smooth under her fingers. Then she turned to where her brother waited a short distance off.

He smiled, sadness lurking in his blue eyes. *"I suppose this is it."*

They had thought it best he leave after the coronation. Rorin had a country to rebuild, and so did Arya, and she suspected both feared if they didn't part now, they never would.

"I suppose it is." Arya bit her lip. She wished with every fibre of her being that Rorin could stay. Victory hadn't erased her grief over Darmanin, or made it any easier to live with all the losses that had built up. And ruling was often a lonely place to be.

His hands moved as he began signing, but stopped as a lonely cry echoed through the sky. Zaphirdryl soared out over the ocean, alone, as was her want these days.

"Remien told me wyverns often die if their riders are killed," Rorin signed. *"I wonder why she held on?"*

"She awaits Nyasa," Arya said. "Darmanin's daughter."

Understanding flashed over Rorin's face, and it crumpled as grief rose. *"Visit when you can, Arya. I will miss you."*

She nodded. "I will try."

He hugged her then, wrapping his arms around her and pulling her close. Arya returned the embrace, holding him as tightly as she knew how. Tears welled in her eyes, and she turned her face into his neck, her tears soaking his shirt. Her fingers curled in his tunic, as if holding on for dear life.

Then, slowly, she mastered her sadness. She took a deep breath and buried the emotion down as deeply as she could, pushing it further and further away until it was barely there anymore. Uncurling her fingers, she straightened her shoulders and stepped backwards.

"Good luck, High Warlord."

"And you, queen of Andahar."

Rorin turned and headed over to where Essa and Alletryl waited. Essa helped Rorin scramble onto Alletryl's back, her gaze holding Arya's. "I'll be back soon."

Arya tried for a smile, failed. "And then your cottage. You must be so excited."

A little smile crept over Essa's face. "Maybe someday. For now, well … I find I'm quite enjoying running the Conclave."

Arya sucked a breath in, hope creeping in. "Really? You're going to stay?"

Essa nodded, eyes full. "I'm going to stay."

"Okay." Arya swallowed. "Okay. That's good."

Essa's smile widened. "And I'm sure you've noticed that Chiarn hasn't moved out yet?"

She'd noticed. But hadn't dared hope. Maybe now she'd let herself.

Essa turned, climbing up behind Rorin. Both waved as the wyvern launched into flight. Arya watched until they were out of sight.

Then, she started down the steps, boots echoing as she took each step one by one, finally reaching the bottom, where her Conclave waited by the great double doors. She crossed towards them, boots echoing through the cavernous space, alone, until a second pair joined her, a half-step behind. "Laskin, you're late."

"I'm never late," he said. "I'm always here, watching your back."

More bootsteps, and her old Icecliff shield; Etan and Kait and Allicen and Charlin and Wattin, all of them, crisp in their uniforms, forming a neat line behind her.

And Arya felt safe.

Ahead of them, Esdee stepped forward to push open the doors. Bright sunlight spilled through into the chamber, but Arya didn't blink as she continued moving. Laskin stopped at the doorway and Arya stepped out into the sunshine, walking forward to the top of the steps as the Conclave lined up in a row behind her.

As soon as they saw Arya, the crowds gathered below broke out into cheers that rocked the very stone on which she stood.

House Stormrider had returned.

Here ends The Inkweaver Archive

***

Want to read another epic fantasy by Lisa Cassidy? Why not try A Tale of Stars and Shadow

The Dock City Chronicle

·

Want to delve deeper into the Archive?
Buried in the depths of the Inkweaver Archive is a prequel novella: *The Stolen Throne: a hidden Record from the Archive.*
Set decades before *The Nameless Throne*, this story follows a dangerous escape involving the fearsome Nightstalker — and it's yours free when you sign up for my monthly newsletter, **The Dock City Chronicle**.

·

Each edition *of The Chronicle* is filled with:
Insider updates on my books
Fantasy world news and hot takes
Hilarious book memes
My book recommendations
Exclusive sneak peeks

·

Sign up for *the Chronicle* at my website: lisacassidyauthor.com

~

Become an Inkweaver?

This is your invitation.

I'd love to welcome you into my **Inkweaver Community**—a private space for readers who love epic fantasy, found family, and all the feels.

.

Whether you've read *The Inkweaver Archive*, *A Tale of Stars and Shadow*, *The Mage Chronicles*, or *Heir to the Darkmage*, you'll find fellow readers who are just as invested as you are.

Inside my Inkweaver community, you can:

Discuss characters, moments, and theories

Chat with me directly

Access behind-the-scenes insights, sneak peeks, and the occasional spoiler

.

It's also a place to talk fantasy more broadly — to share recommendations, discover new favourites, and connect with readers who speak your language.

The adventure doesn't end on the last page.

Join me in the Inkweaver Community:

(https://inkweavers.mn.co)

About me

I'm a self-published fantasy author by day and book nerd in every other spare moment I have. I'm also self-confessed coffee snob (don't try coming near her with any of that instant coffee rubbish) but I am willing to accept all other hot drink aficionados, even tea drinkers. I live in Australia's capital city, Canberra, and like all Australians, I'm in pretty much constant danger from highly poisonous spiders, crocodiles, sharks, and drop bears, to name a few. As you can see, I am also pro-Oxford comma.

A 2019 SPFBO finalist, and finalist for the 2020 ACT Writers Fiction award, I'm the author of young adult fantasy series *The Mage Chronicles* and *Heir to the Darkmage*, and epic fantasy series *A Tale of Stars and Shadow* and *The Inkweaver Archive*. I'm currently working on a sequel to *A Tale of Stars and Shadow*.

As part of my writing journey, I've partnered up with One Girl, a charity working to build a world where all girls have access to quality education. A world where all girls — no matter where they are born or how much money they have — enjoy the same rights and opportunities as boys. A percentage of all my royalties go to One Girl.

You can follow me on Facebook and Instagram. I also have a fantasy reading community – The Inkweavers - where you can jump in and talk about anything and everything relating to books and reading.

I also have an author street team. I call them the *Wolves*, after Prince Cuinn's fierce personal guard in *A Tale of Stars and Shadow*. If you'd be interested in becoming a Wolf, you can email me at wolves@tatehousebooks.com. Everyone is welcome, and I'd be more than happy to answer any questions you have.

If you want to learn more about me and my books, head on over to my website at lisacassidyauthor.com

BORROWED FROM
The Inkweaver Archive